THE KISS OF A VISCOUNT

LINDA RAE SANDE

Twisted Teacup
PUBLISHING

For Mom

ALSO BY LINDA RAE SANDE

The Daughters of the Aristocracy

The Kiss of a Viscount

The Grace of a Duke

The Seduction of an Earl

The Sons of the Aristocracy

Tuesday Nights

The Widowed Countess

My Fair Groom

The Sisters of the Aristocracy

The Story of a Baron

The Passion of a Marquess

The Desire of a Lady

The Brothers of the Aristocracy

The Love of a Rake

The Caress of a Commander

The Epiphany of an Explorer

The Widows of the Aristocracy

The Gossip of an Earl

The Enigma of a Widow

The Secrets of a Viscount

The Widowers of the Aristocracy

The Dream of a Duchess

The Vision of a Viscountess

The Conundrum of a Clerk

The Charity of a Viscount

CHAPTER 1
AN EARL TAKES A TUMBLE

*D*ecember 1814

Gabriel Wellingham, Earl of Trenton, pulled on his blue satin breeches as he regarded his reflection in a mirror. Despite having just tumbled the tavern's bar maid, his blond curls were still presentable, although a bit tousled from the wench having run her fingers through them. He glanced at the reflection of the young woman who had been the object of his attention for the past hour. She was watching him from the room's only bed, where she lay on her stomach, one leg bent so her foot circled in the air. Propped up on her elbows so her breasts mounded a bit where they touched the mattress, she gave him a look that suggested he should return to the bed.

"I am tempted, Sarah," Gabriel admitted to the reflection, "But I really must take my leave." He pulled his linen shirt over his head, taking care to straighten it as his valet would do before shoving the tails into his breeches.

The bar maid cocked her head to one side. "Must you?" she countered, giving him her very best come-hither look. She didn't really *want* him to stay—he was terrible at kissing and seemed to enjoy licking too much, and not in the right places—but the man was handsome. And he had given her a sovereign for her time and attention, far more than she could get for the same services from any of the other patrons of the Spread Eagle, given its rural location in Staffordshire.

Sarah wondered if the man had a mistress. If not, she thought of asking if he wanted one. Perhaps he would put her up in a cottage, or, if he was really as rich as his purse seemed to indicate, a townhouse in Wolverhampton. Before she had a chance to offer herself, though, the dandy turned in her direction. "You have such a round..." He motioned with his hands to indicate her hips. "Rump," he finally added, a teasing smile displaying his perfect white teeth. "I do believe you're a better lay than the mistresses I keep in London," he commented before donning his gold embroidered waistcoat.

Mistresses? As in, *more than one?* It took all the acting skill Sarah had to continue smiling. "Isn't London an awfully long way to go for... a tumble?" she asked, drawing one of the bed linens over her backside. Round rump or not, she suddenly felt very exposed, given the man was nearly dressed.

Gabriel sat down on the edge of the mattress, lifting one bare foot to rest on his other knee so he could pull on a stocking. "It is, indeed," Gabriel answered, his brows furrowing when the stocking didn't go onto his foot as easily as when his valet did it. "But that is why I sought you out," he said, his attention still on this foot. "Damn it, how does this work?" he complained *sotto voce*.

The tavern wench reached over and positioned the stocking so it would slide on easier. "Does that mean you will seek me out again?" she asked hopefully, one finger moving from his foot to the mound that was silhouetted in the satin breeches.

Jerking reflexively, Gabriel gave her a huge smile. "I would, but I will be leaving for London soon," he said, careful not to tell her it was to search for a wife. He had a few young debutantes in mind, but he still wasn't quite sure what he should be looking for in a wife. *Beauty? A dowry?* He was as rich as Croesus, so money wasn't an issue. *A good tumble?* And how would he discover a girl's ability between the sheets if he couldn't try her out in advance of the betrothal?

"Ah, headed to the Marriage Mart, no doubt," the bar maid guessed, rolling her eyes.

Gabriel struggled to maintain an impassive expression. *Was it that obvious?* "That and... well, let's just say I have some reconnaissance to do before I settle in Mayfair."

The wench sat up, pulling the bed linens to cover her generous bosom. "Reconnaissance?" Sarah repeated, her interest piqued. "Are you a *spy?*" She asked this with such excitement in her eyes that Gabriel nearly admitted to being one. He shook his head instead.

"More like, a political researcher, I suppose," he countered. "I am of the opinion that certain *older* members of Parliament should be stripped of their powers."

Leaning her head away from Gabriel as he moved to pull on his other stocking, the tavern maid eyed him with suspicion. "If you are successful in stripping them of their powers, who would then have the power?" she asked, returning her hand to the bulge beneath the satin breeches.

Gabriel mirrored her posture, leaning away so her finger could no longer reach his hardening cock. *Was she a spy?* The very last thing he expected from a tavern wench was this level of perception. "Better educated lords. Younger lords." *Me,* he almost added. "I just have to figure out how."

A slow smile spread over the tavern maid's face. *He's a lord.* No wonder he had tossed a sovereign on the bed when he had first followed her into the room. He could probably afford a crown or more. His mistresses were no doubt set up with their own townhouses and modistes and private boxes at the theatre.

"What are you thinking?" Gabriel asked as he watched her expression change.

Sarah straightened as she considered how to respond. Who could undermine a respected member of the House of Lords? Who wielded the most power? Who controlled the lives of the aristocrats? Who hosted the balls and musicales and every event where political decisions were discussed and debated and decided outside of chambers?

Why, the *women* behind those lords, of course. The mothers, the wives, the... "Marry the daughter of the most powerful lord," the wench blurted suddenly. "The daughter of your most influential political opponent."

Gabriel Wellingham stared at the woman, stunned at her perfect solution. He swallowed. He blinked. He shook his head. "That's genius," he breathed, his appreciative gaze making the tavern maid sit up a bit straighter. The bed linen didn't follow, however, and the tops of Sarah's breasts were suddenly on display. "As are those," he added with an arched brow. Reaching into his topcoat pocket, Gabriel withdrew his purse. "And worth at least another sovereign," he added as he fished a coin out of the velvet pouch and tossed it in her direction.

Sarah caught it and gave the earl a gracious nod, deciding not to explain just then that the plan might not work. Probably *wouldn't* work.

The daughters of the aristocracy were powerful in their own right, after all.

CHAPTER 2
A VISCOUNT AND HIS MISTRESS

*J*anuary 1815

Josephine Wentworth was reading the latest treatise on the failures of the monarchy in France when her butler cleared his throat. She looked up to find him standing in the doorway of her parlor, his hands clasped behind his back. "Yes, Frederick?" she said, a bit startled at his sudden appearance and wondering just how long he had stood there attempting to get her attention. The treatise was interesting and well-written, after all.

"Mr. Bennett-Jones is calling. Should I tell him you are not receiving visitors today?" he asked, knowing full well she would tell him to admit the caller. She always accepted George Bennett-Jones' visits.

As the man's mistress, she was expected to do so.

"He seems... *distraught*," the butler added, his hesitance apparent. He knew it wasn't his place to comment on the state of mind of Josephine's visitor, but for reasons not yet apparent to her, Frederick thought it was best to do so in this instance.

Josephine set aside the booklet and stood up quickly, smoothing her skirts and trying hard to mask her alarm. George was rarely emotional about anything; if Frederick thought he was *distraught*, then something was wrong. "I'll see to this. Could you bring tea, please? And maybe the brandy, too," she added, just in case something was *really* wrong. George wasn't one who allowed himself to get upset over anything. He lived a rather calm life. A boring life, one might say. Like clockwork, his twice-weekly visits were always on the same days at the same time. Any changes to that schedule were due to his very occasional trips to his family's estate in the country or a fencing match at Angelo's Academy.

Perhaps he had come to end their relationship, Josephine considered. Or he had met someone he wanted to court. He had always said he wouldn't keep a mistress if he married.

Hurrying to the elegant townhouse's small vestibule, Josephine found George, hat in hand, his back against the front door, his dark blue eyes closed. He appeared haggard, as if his cheeks were about to slide off and take the outer edges of his eyes with them. He was not a particularly handsome man, and now that his face was a picture of pain, he appeared even less so. But when he smiled, Josephine thought George was one of the most handsome men in London. He wore his sable hair cut short and sometimes combed forward; otherwise, the top would be tousled from having run his fingers through it, as he did when he removed his hat. His six-foot frame was that of a fencer, lean but sculpted with muscle, his broad shoulders and chest tapering down to a somewhat narrower waist and hips. The buckskin breeches he favored fit as if Weston himself had sewn them, and his navy-blue topcoat was made of the highest quality superfine. Bronzed from having spent too much time out of doors, George did not look like a typical aristocrat.

But then, until that morning, he wasn't one.

As Josephine rushed to meet him, he pushed himself away from the door. He wrapped his arms around his mistress at the very moment she lifted her arms to his shoulders. "Oh, George, what has happened?" she whispered, putting as much sympathy into her voice as she could manage. She felt his face press against her hair, felt his arms tighten around her so she could hardly breathe. And when she felt his heart beat against her bosom, she knew its rhythm was much faster than usual.

He held her like that for several seconds before he could say anything. "Uncle has died," he croaked, his voice so husky Josephine didn't recognize it. He leaned against the door, a solid surface that seemed necessary to hold him up.

Never in her eight years as George's mistress had Josephine ever seen him so... *distraught*, just as Frederick had said. She allowed him to continue holding her, the fronts of their bodies pressed against one another. It was not unlike the nights they spent in her bed, holding one another close after frenzied love-making, as if they had to hang on to each other for dear life or risk losing themselves in the splintered aftermath.

And then she comprehended the larger implication of his simple statement. *Uncle has died.* Joseph Bennett-Jones, Viscount Bostwick. A viscount who was briefly married and left a widower upon his wife's death during childbirth. Although the son she bore him survived his birth, a fever took the child's life during his fourth year. The viscount never remarried. For a few Seasons after that, quiet gossip suggested he preferred the company of men. As his only nephew and an orphan since his twelfth year, George had been his uncle's heir apparent for nearly twenty years.

George was now Viscount Bostwick.

Lifting her head so that she could look at George's face, Josephine pushed his shoulders gently and then cupped one cheek with a hand. "I am so very sorry for your loss... *my lord*," she whispered, remembering to add his new title at the last moment.

George sucked his next breath through clenched teeth, bristling at her use of the title. "Josie, *please*, do not call me that," he murmured, his voice indicating his revulsion. It was one thing to wake up to find you were a viscount. It was quite another to deal with the everyday consequences. He was not yet ready to deal with those, even if one of them was as trivial as the addition of a title to his name.

"Come. Let's have some tea," she urged, moving her body away from his and grabbing his hand. She kissed the palm as he wrapped an arm around her shoulders and allowed himself to be led to the parlor. A list of things to do in the event of a peer's death filled her head. "Do you need assistance with the arrangements?" she asked quietly, as she took a seat on a chaise. She expected George to take an adjacent chair; instead he sat between her and the arm of the chaise, clutching her close. Josephine considered protesting, but thought better of it when she determined she was holding his body upright. If she moved away, he would simply topple over.

"Peters is seeing to most of it," George replied, referring to his uncle's manager. "I've asked him to stay on until I can learn whatever it is I need to know. Even then, I may need to keep him on to manage the Sussex properties whilst I'm in town. Given Uncle's tight-fisted ways, I am sure they are all in need of repair. In the meantime, the townhouse here in Mayfair needs a good deal of work. I'll hire someone to oversee the remodel as soon as possible."

Josephine wondered what the "learning" would involve in the case of the Bostwick viscountcy. Estate management, no doubt—George's uncle held lands in Sussex, in which there were several coal mines and a country manor house near Chichester. The townhouse George mentioned was in Park Lane and, indeed, required a remodel.

But what about the politics? George was a viscount now, which meant he needed to apply for a writ of summons and take his place in Parliament. He would need to be briefed on the current issues. "So, you'll be leaving for Sussex then?" she asked, allowing her head to lean against his shoulder.

"Not for a few months. I... I'll spend the summer there and be back in London in the fall. For Parliament. The townhouse should be ready to occupy by then." He paused a moment to kiss the top of her head. "You'll come with me, of course," he stated, not making it an invitation.

Josephine inhaled sharply, a bit surprised by the overture. There had been only one other time when he had *expected* her to join him on a trip. That had been very early in their relationship. They had been the only "family" in residence at the country estate for an entire fortnight, spending their days riding and walking the lands around the manor house, and their nights sharing a bedchamber. She wondered for a long time why he had felt it necessary to take that trip, supposing at the time it was merely a whim. His uncle had been quite strict with him back then, forbidding him to frequent gaming hells or brothels, and limiting his allowance to ensure he complied. He encouraged George instead to learn how to fence and shoot guns, pursuits that didn't cost a great deal of money.

After a few years, Josephine realized why.

Joseph Bennett-Jones was a miser.

His one expenditure with respect to George, beyond the costs of sending his nephew to Eton and then to Cambridge for his education, had been to pay for a mistress.

"Are you... certain?" Josephine asked, her voice barely a whisper. Besides the time she had been there with George for a fortnight, there were other shorter stays when he had extended the invitation and left it up to her to decide if she wanted to join him. On those occasions, she was free to roam the estate when his uncle wasn't hosting visitors. She rather enjoyed long walks or a ride on horseback over the rolling hills and next to the forests that surrounded the home. Otherwise, she would be sequestered in a suite of rooms she shared with George in a wing on the second floor, her presence unknown to anyone but George, his uncle and a few members of the household staff.

"I'll die of boredom if you are not there. Although—" he paused for a moment as if an idea had just formed—"now that I have access to a good deal of money, I suppose I can finally see to it some things are changed down there. Better housing for the miners, more money for the orphanage, replacing the roof on the church. That sort of thing." He took a deep breath, nodding as he did so. Then his eyebrows cocked up. "And besides, I have to have someone bring me up to snuff on what's been going on with the government," he declared, his lips curving a bit to indicate the worst of his mournful thoughts had passed.

Josephine smiled. She followed all the news from Parliament, subscribed to three newspapers, and was always aware of current events and applicable gossip where she could find it. If anyone could educate George on the current situation in Parliament, it was she.

George quickly sobered again, though. "Marry me, Josie," he said as he squeezed one of her hands between both of his. "Please."

Her back straightening with the familiar request, Josephine turned to look him in the eyes. "George. You know I cannot. I am your *mistress*. And five years your senior. You must marry a woman who can give you an heir," she explained patiently.

She had given him the same excuses the other four times he had asked her to marry him over the years. There had been only one of those times when she was tempted to accept his offer, and then only because she thought she carried his child. Although she was merely late with her monthly courses, the situation had made her realize many things. George's insistence on keeping her for so many years made her believe she was his first and only lover. But her life as a mistress had convinced her she did not want to give up the freedom she enjoyed while being his mistress, and she did not want a child with him. She had other plans for her future, a future that involved a different man. If that man from her past still wanted her as his wife, as he claimed in every missive she received from him over the years, then she would agree to a marriage once she was sure the man had made his way in the world.

"Must I?" George countered, his hang-dog expression returning.

Josephine gave him a wan smile as she nodded. "When we get to the country, we have some work to do," she murmured, her smoky green eyes turning quite serious. At his cocked eyebrow and quizzical expression, she added, "to get you ready for the Little Season, and for courting a lady of the *ton*." She did not immediately clarify what her intentions were, but his altered status meant many things, including a change to the way he interacted with the eligible females of the *ton*. Given his age and his need to start his nursery soon, he would need to find a wife —the sooner, the better. After so many years with the same mistress, George had become somewhat lax in his attitude toward women, not taking the time to learn much about the few already in his life—their lives, their families, their hopes, their dreams. He needed to learn a bit more about members of the opposite sex if he had any hope of landing a wife suitable to his new station in life.

And it meant Josephine needed to teach him how to please a woman in bed—and out of it—to ensure he wasn't cuckolded by his new wife. He was adequate in bed, she had to admit, but there were subtleties he lacked in the way he used his eyes, the way he used his voice to flirt. He was sometimes impatient with his foreplay. And the pressure of his touch against feminine skin was perhaps a bit too bold when he was aroused.

Swallowing hard, George finally nodded. "Promise me something, then, Josie," he whispered, moving one hand to rest on the back of her waist. At her wary nod, he said, "You'll remain my best friend until the day I die."

Josephine Wentworth regarded her lover for several moments before leaning over to kiss his cheek. *Such a simple request, and so easy to grant.* "Until the day I die," she agreed, a grin appearing before she kissed him again.

CHAPTER 3
AN EARL MEETS A LADY

arly June 1815

Lady Elizabeth Carlington met the Earl of Trenton at the last ball of the Season. Upon seeing her descend the stairs into the elegant ballroom, Gabriel Wellingham, Earl of Trenton, walked very quickly to stand directly in her path, bowed over her hand—which he had to retrieve from her side because she was caught by surprise and hadn't yet offered it— and kissed it. Before Elizabeth could curtsy in return, a maneuver made almost impossible given she was still standing on the last step and there was no room to do so, Gabriel asked if he might reserve a dance.

Her dance card wasn't even secured about her wrist!

Lady Elizabeth almost agreed. How could she refuse the unmarried earl, whose blond curly hair, sky blue eyes and handsome features made so many of the debutantes in attendance flutter their lashes and nearly swoon in his presence? But she had watched him execute the same maneuver with another young lady only moments before from her vantage point at the top of the stairs, so she decided it would be better to learn a bit more about the earl before she allowed him a dance.

After the more formal introductions were made by one of her young, married friends, Gabriel seemed quite attentive. Once he heard she was the daughter of the Marquess of

Morganfield, his face lit up with what might have been recognition.

A more cynical sort would have recognized the look for what it was.

Predatory.

"Lady Elizabeth, it is truly an honor to make your acquaintance," he said, bowing over her gloved hand and once again brushing his lips over the back of her knuckles.

"And yours, my lord," she replied, a bit cool in her response. The fan she held in her left hand fluttered twice before she snapped it shut, all the while holding his gaze with her own. "Have you just arrived in town?" She hadn't seen him at any of the balls or soirées held during the spring. Perhaps he was new to his title.

"Only last week, my lady," he confirmed with a nod. "I inherited the Trenton earldom last year upon my father's death." At Elizabeth's appropriate look of sadness, he added, "I have been in mourning, of course. I held off visiting London until my solicitor required my presence here." The words were delivered without inflection, suggesting his mourning period was truly over, if indeed he had ever really mourned the passing of his father at all.

"I am so sorry for your loss," Elizabeth replied with a solemn nod. She had heard of the Trenton earldom—knew it to be one of the wealthier titles in Great Britain. And then she remembered how he had hurried to the base of the stairs when she was making her way to the ballroom floor. He had sought *her* out. Or found her appearance pleasing enough that he would make a spectacle of himself in front of Lord Esterly's guests—not just once, but several times. Thinking he spoke with good diction, knew his manners and was quite possibly the most beautiful man she had ever met, Elizabeth decided she could bestow her best smile on him. "I do hope you find your stay here satisfactory."

The earl allowed his gaze to sweep boldly over her from head to toe. "I already have, my lady," he answered, his brow cocking in such a manner as to suggest he had found *her* to be the reason for his satisfaction. "The sight of so many beautiful women in one room is almost too much to bear, but then my own beauty requires a woman with at least as much to match my own."

A bit shocked that Gabriel Wellingham would be so bold, both with his words and his rakish manner, Elizabeth held her face as impassive as possible. He was too handsome and might be a bounder, she decided, her own head leaning to one side as she considered whether or not to introduce him to her friends. "Are there other traits you find too much to bear in a woman, my lord?" she teased, wondering if her comment would cause him to blush or if he would list his proclivities.

Gabriel straightened and placed the palm of one hand against his chest, as if he had suffered the cut direct. His face brightened. "Why, Lady Elizabeth, your boldness is not one of them," he answered with a huge grin. "Either you are testing me or you are teasing me, but I find I am not the least bit offended by either."

Her mouth forming a perfect 'o,' Elizabeth realized too late the earl was not the stuffy, overbearing sort she expected.

He had a sense of humor.

"I was teasing, of course," she answered with a tap of her fan against his arm. "But my question remains unanswered."

The earl regarded her with a calculating grin and finally sighed. "I do not care for dishonesty, gossip or cleverness in women, but then, I do not tolerate them from those of my sex either," he said, his face taking on a more serious expression.

Elizabeth sensed the change in him even before she heard his words. She found herself wondering if this was the man she would marry before Christmastime. "Well said, my lord," she agreed, giving Gabriel a nod.

"Said well enough that you might now grant me a dance this evening?" he countered, his expression remaining serious.

Apparently, her earlier refusal had bruised his ego.

For a moment, Elizabeth wondered at the change in his mood. She hadn't meant for her teasing to leave him in ill humor. She lifted the wrist from which her dance card dangled.

"I believe I have an unclaimed quadrille here," she suggested, taking her eyes off his in order to search for the blank on the pasteboard. She found a line on which there was no name scribbled. "Here 'tis," she offered, holding the card out to him. He gave her a nod and took up the small pencil attached to the card. He wrote 'Gabriel' on the one blank line. "Thank you, Lady Elizabeth," he said, in a voice that indicated he was dismissing her. "I shall find you when it is my turn," he added, bowing deeply.

Elizabeth curtsied in return and watched the earl take his leave.

There was definitely an attraction there, she was sure, enough so she decided not to search for Lady Hannah and offer an introduction to her. Although Hannah was a beauty in her own right, her porcelain complexion, dark eyes, rosebud lips and platinum blonde hair making her look like a delicate doll or a fairy princess, the younger woman had a rather odd attitude when it came to considering potential husbands. She believed men only ever loved their mistresses, and only married to have a mother for their children. It had been that way for her father, after all.

As for Lady Charlotte, she was already betrothed to the Earl of Grinstead and so wasn't in need of a suitor.

The earl's mood was considerably lighter when he came to claim her for the quadrille. They danced, but due to the intricacies of the quadrille, they were unable to exchange more than a few snippets of conversation. Once they parted company, Elizabeth rather hoped the earl would decide to spend part of the summer in town; perhaps they would see one another whilst shopping or in Hyde Park.

Later that week, she learned from Lady Charlotte that the earl had returned to Staffordshire the day after the ball. Disappointed but determined they would renew their acquaintance during the Little Season, Elizabeth put thoughts of marriage and the Earl of Trenton on hold for the summer. Instead, she concentrated her attention on a far worthier pursuit.

Charity.

CHAPTER 4
A LADY ATTEMPTS TO MEET
A COMMONER

Two nights later

Charity was on Elizabeth's mind because a rather disturbing situation had her wondering what she could do to alleviate a particularly vexing problem.

Arm-in-arm with Lady Charlotte, she attended Lady Worthington's annual *musicale* in the company of her parents. Their hostess, Adele Slater Worthington, was the widow of a man who had made his fortune from the early steamships. Not having produced an heir for Samuel Worthington, his fortune —as well as his house—was now hers, and Lady Worthington hosted the fête in an effort to raise money for her favorite charity.

Elizabeth gave up her shawl to a footman as Lady Morganfield and Charlotte did the same, their gazes surveying the guests that had already arrived and were milling about in the great hall. "Lady Worthington always has such an interesting crowd," Elizabeth murmured so only Charlotte could hear.

"Oh, I don't mind," Charlotte whispered. "I rather like that she includes some who are not of the peerage." Possessed of a pleasant manner and the ability to remember the names of everyone to whom she was introduced, Charlotte made friends easily. "Makes for more interesting conversation."

Elizabeth knew her friend spoke the truth when she recognized her father's banker, an official from the East India Company, and a chemist from Floris even before they reached the large parlor where rows of chairs had been assembled. "I don't suppose you know who that is?" she asked as she pretended not to stare at a man engaged in conversation with the Duke of Westhaven. "He looks familiar, but I'm quite sure we've never been introduced."

Charlotte frowned as she attempted to make out the identity of the gentleman in question. She guessed he was about thirty, on the tall side, but definitely not lanky. His posture, perfectly erect, suggested he was a military man. A small scar from what might have been a knife wound marred his otherwise handsome face. His most interesting feature, though, was his lack of a right arm. The bottom half of his topcoat sleeve had been pinned up to his elbow. "I've no idea," she finally admitted, but when she noticed Lady Pettigrew approach the man and touch his sleeve with a gloved finger, she blinked. "But Lady Pettigrew does." When another guest stepped aside, she was about to lead Elizabeth toward the gentleman when Elizabeth pulled her back.

"Lady Chichester is waving at you," Elizabeth said, referring to Charlotte's future mother-in-law. "You go on. I'll find you when it's time to be seated."

Nodding, Charlotte hurried off to greet the Duchess of Chichester as Elizabeth surreptitiously watched the gentleman. She managed to move close enough to overhear part of his conversation with the duke.

"When I returned to London last week, I expected to be back at the bank in my old position," the man said as Westhaven arched a brow. "But they seem to believe I cannot be a clerk with only one arm, despite the fact that I never used this arm when I was employed there before the war," he complained.

"Surely you can land a position somewhere else," Westhaven replied. "I would hire you to do the books for my estate, but I know you have no intention of moving to the country, and I have no intention of living here in London again. Two years was enough when my daughter was introduced to Society."

The man gave a nod. "I appreciate you saying so. Something will turn up, I'm sure." The words didn't sound very hopeful, though. "Now that Napoleon has been defeated, all the old fogies will be returning from France and Belgium. I'm afraid there will be far more men in the same position as me. Able to work but with no hope of being hired."

Old fogies? Elizabeth thought, wondering at the term. She spied Lady Pettigrew in conversation with Lady Worthington and waited until their hostess hurried into the parlor before approaching the old woman.

The viscountess didn't even allow her a greeting. "Elizabeth. That's a gown we've seen before, is it not?" Eunice Pettigrew queried, a bit of spite sounding in her voice.

"Why, Lady Pettigrew, you have an excellent memory," Elizabeth acknowledged, ignoring the woman's insult. "I wore this to a ball just last year, in fact." She paused, attempting to keep a happy expression. "I wondered if you might introduce me to one of the guests here this evening?" she asked, angling her head in the direction of the man who was just then ending his conversation with the Duke of Westhaven.

"Mr. Streater?" Lady Pettigrew clarified, her face displaying a grimace as she followed Elizabeth's line of sight. "Why ever would you wish an introduction to *him?* He is Baron Streater's younger brother, but he's a *commoner,*" she complained. "He's back from fighting in one of the wars. An officer, I think. Heaven only knows why Adele invited him."

Elizabeth jerked back as if she'd been slapped. "I simply wish to learn more about him," she replied with a shrug. Even if he was a commoner—a clerk, given his words to that effect—he seemed to be an acquaintance of the Duke of Westhaven. Her curiosity had been piqued not just because he was missing his right arm, but because of his comments to the duke about his inability to secure his old position at the bank.

Perhaps if a member of the peerage could make an appeal on the behalf of the man, he could be reinstated.

The sound of a gong reverberated through the great hall, and both women turned to stare into the crowded parlor.

Lady Pettigrew let out a huff. "That's the first warning. The music is about to begin. Time to find your seat, young lady," she ordered. "Or you'll be forced to stand with the men. Do forget about Mr. Streater, won't you? It isn't proper for you to be seen in his company."

And with that, the old woman rushed into the parlor.

Stunned, Elizabeth stared after Lady Pettigrew, shaking her head in disbelief. That is, until she spotted her husband's banker finishing his drink. She hurried up to him, giving a quick curtsy. "Good evening, Mr. Whittaker."

Avery Whittaker stared at her a moment, blinking at her sudden appearance. "Why, Lady Elizabeth," he replied, giving her a bow. He was about to say a pleasantry when Elizabeth spoke.

"What must a man do to gain a position as a clerk at your bank? If he's qualified? If he suits the position?" she asked in a hushed voice.

Whitaker blinked. "Apply for the position, of course," he replied with a shrug.

"And if he already has?" she countered.

The banker furrowed a brow just as the gong sounded again. "Offer me a bribe, I suppose," he said with a grin. He gave a bow. "Pardon me, but Mrs. Whitaker will be furious if I'm not seated next to her this very minute."

Just as Lady Pettigrew had done, the banker hurried into the parlor at the same moment Charlotte approached from the other direction. "Hurry, or we'll be left standing against the walls," she warned.

Once they were seated, Elizabeth was oblivious to the musical performances, her mind on Mr. Whittaker's parting words.

Offer me a bribe.

Well, there were more honorable reasons for a charity to exist, she supposed. But if a bribe helped in putting old fogies back to work, it seemed it might be worth the effort.

CHAPTER 5
LESSONS OF A MISTRESS

ate June 1815

"Now, there are some rules I think you should learn, George," Josephine said just before she nodded to the footman who was filling her breakfast plate with coddled eggs and a rasher of bacon.

George cocked an eyebrow in response, wondering what she had in mind for his next lesson. For the past few months, Josephine had hinted they would be spending their time in Horsham on matters related to finding him a wife.

Finding and keeping a wife.

Having successfully avoided her hints that they should start his education while he was still in London, George claimed he needed to concentrate on matters of politics and his viscountcy. Josephine spent those months briefing him on everything she knew of Parliament and its members, but warned him summer was coming. He would have to prepare for courting.

Josephine had already seen to it he had a stack of reading material ready for his perusal as well as a dance instructor to teach him the cotillion, quadrille and waltz. He had grown up performing the contradances, the dances done longways, and announced with some derision that he had no intention of doing them in order to court a lady of the *ton*. "How am I supposed to carry on a conversation with a lady if I'm constantly changing partners?" he argued. "Better I escort her to the supper or converse with her in a quiet corner."

Josephine rolled her eyes but didn't argue the point. "How will you introduce yourself to the lady?" she asked as she helped herself to a piece of toast from his plate.

"My lady, I am George Bennett-Jones, at your service," he replied as he mimed lifting one of the woman's hands to his lips and kissing the back of it.

"Oh, that would be good," Josephine commented, patting his knuckles. "Except you really should have someone else introduce you to the lady. Her chaperone or a relative. No one need know you have a title until it becomes necessary for them to know. Use it as a last resort."

George raised an eyebrow. "Really?" he replied, not quite believing her comment. "My uncle seemed to think it would provide respectability."

"It will come in handy when you need assistance from the hired help, of course. Butlers may not allow you into a lord's home unless you give your title." She took a sip of coffee. "On that note, have you ordered new calling cards?"

Screwing up his face in dismay, George shook his head. "I still have so many of the old ones," he complained.

"Order them. Or have your man of business see to them," Josephine ordered. "Now, when you're in conversation with a lady, you must make her feel as if she is the only woman in the room."

Pausing before putting a forkful of eggs into his mouth, George considered her words. "And if I am in conversation with more than one woman?"

His mistress regarded him with a bit of surprise. "Oh, my," she replied, her face displaying her amusement. "Then you must make them feel as if they are the only *women* in the world. Hold her gaze. Appear as interested as you possibly can. Even if you're bored to tears and want nothing more than to make haste to the card room."

George frowned. "I wouldn't necessarily make haste to the card room even if I was bored," he countered. Cards sometimes bored him more than standing next to a potted palm at a *ton* ball. At least he could watch those in attendance from the relative safety of the plant. That was far more entertaining than looking at a handful of cards and making bets on their worth.

Josephine ignored the comment, not having been in public with George to know how he really behaved. "So, what do you say to a lady when you first meet her? After the introductions, of course?"

Opening his mouth to respond, George suddenly closed it and thought for a moment. He recalled and then repeated conversations he overheard at the few Society events he had attended.

"You appear in fine health."

"Is that a new bonnet, perhaps?"

"Your gown is stunning. Is that silk de Naples? Or Indian silk?

"And from where did you purchase that lovely corset I see when I peek down your bodice?"

Covering her mouth with a hand, Josephine let out a giggle. "George!" she admonished him. "Really, there's no need to comment on the fabric of a lady's gown." When George's eyebrows lifted, she added, "Or on the corset. And never let a lady know you've looked down her bodice." She thought a moment. "Unless she's a widow, in which case she may welcome your glance in that direction."

"Josie!" It was George's turn to admonish his mistress, surprised she would make such a claim. "If I'm not to make mention of her gown or her cleavage, what can I say?"

The older woman regarded him for a moment and angled her head to one side. "Keep your compliments light, and be self-deprecating when it makes sense to do so."

George sighed. "I can do that," he replied with a nod, his attention on the sideboard. "So, once I have complimented her on the color of her gown, and I've made a fool of myself by being self-deprecating, then I suppose I need to ensure the conversation continues."

Straightening in her chair, Josephine smiled. "Oh. You're doing very well, George!"

He gave her a look of uncertainty. When was the last time he had carried on a conversation with a member of the fairer sex? Other than with Josephine, of course? "And how should I proceed?" he asked, his face screwing up into an expression of pain.

Sighing, Josephine replied, "Ask questions that show you are truly interested. And then listen to their replies."

George considered her words. "Did you finish reading the pamphlet on the Corn Laws?" he asked suddenly, his brow furrowing. "I should like to know your opinion."

His mistress raised her eyebrows at the apparent change in topic. "They are... extremely unfair and quite costly for the general population of England," she responded carefully, repositioning herself in her chair so she faced him more squarely.

"And how do you propose the situation be changed?"

Josephine regarded George with surprise. She sat very still for a moment, seeming to collect her thoughts. "The laws must be repealed. The inflated price of English-grown corn is forcing those who are already poor into talk of an uprising. This country cannot survive what happened to the French monarchy," she replied, leaning toward him as she did so.

"I will ask the Lord Chancellor to add the topic to our agenda when our session resumes in September. I will do what I can," George promised with a nod. After a pause, one in which he kept his attention on Josephine, he asked, "How did I do?"

Her mouth dropping open in astonishment, Josephine realized George had merely been practicing his conversational skills with a topic he knew she would find interesting. "Oh, George. I do believe you can converse with the best of them. Just remember, most chits aren't going to know a Corn Law from a cob of corn. Better you keep the topic on something like... the theatre or the latest fashions from Paris."

Shrugging, George finished the slice of toast Josephine had abandoned on his plate and took another sip of coffee. "What else?" He knew his mistress had other suggestions, other recommendations for how he could increase his chances with a lady of the *ton*. Better to get them all out of her today so he had the summer to practice.

Josephine angled her head to one side. "My poor little dog has disappeared, George, and I am simply inconsolable. Boohoo," she said in a whiny voice that could have belonged to just about any debutante in the *ton*.

George blinked once. Twice. He shook his head.

Sighing loudly, Josephine took a deep breath. "Offer condolences when appropriate, help when needed, and be a knight in shining armor whenever given the opportunity."

Holding up a hand to indicate he understood, George nodded once and then gave her his most sympathetic expression. "My dear Josie, you must be beside yourself with worry. I know how much you love that little... Brutus," he said, supplying a name, and noting with amusement that Josie rolled her eyes. "Whatever can I do to help? I can take you in my curricle and we can search for Brutus together. I shan't give up until he is safely back... in your arms, my lady. And when he is, we shall see to it he has another to keep him company so he will not run off again," he intoned, placing his hand on Josephine's arm and giving it a reassuring nudge.

Josephine grinned. Then her smile broadened. "Bravo, George. Always promise her more. I do believe you'll be ready for the Little Season."

George sat back in his chair and sighed as if the lesson had taken every bit of energy he had in him. "God, help me," he whispered. "This had better be worth it."

A footman entered the breakfast room, a newly ironed copy of *The Times* in his hands. "Ah, a newspaper," he said, hoping Josephine's interest would be redirected to it. He held out his hand and the footman gave it to him, bowing as he did so. George nodded in his direction and turned his attention to the headlines.

Upon reading the headline, he hid his initial astonishment from his mistress, thinking that, for once, he had actually learned something of political import that she wouldn't yet know. Napoleon Bonaparte had just lost a battle at Waterloo to a coalition of forces led by Wellington and von Bluecher. The tyrant had finally been defeated. Perhaps this time they would see to his death so that he couldn't escape and continue his war on England.

When George glanced back at Josephine, he noted that his mistress looked a bit crestfallen, but at the moment he couldn't give her his full attention. The war against France was over, which meant his best friend would be returning soon—if he had survived. He barely heard Josephine's words. "Of course, it will be worth it, George. Especially since I intend for you to marry a woman perfectly suited to you," she said rather carefully. "Most young ladies are not going to be acceptable to you. I realize that. Which means you need to have your sights on a woman who can challenge you a bit."

He looked up from his copy of the week-old paper and regarded his mistress with a cocked eyebrow. "Does one actually exist that meets with your approval?" he asked, deciding he would allow her to read the paper and learn of the news herself.

"Yes, actually. I do have a woman in mind whom I think you should marry," Josephine replied as she watched George's reaction.

Damn! She's already vetted someone! "Playing matchmaker now, are you?" he asked, with more than a hint of accusation in his voice. *Why is she bringing this up now?* he wondered. They wouldn't be back in London for a few months, and then it would be another two weeks or more before the Little Season started. His gaze settled back down onto the article he had been reading.

Josephine shrugged as if his comment held little merit. "Lady Elizabeth Carlington."

George looked up from the paper again, his face taking on a look of concentration, as if he was trying to recall a mental image of the woman Josephine named, but all he could really think of was his friend, Teddy Streater. *Did he survive? Would he be returning to England's shores soon?*

Perhaps he was already back in London. *I can only hope.*

When Teddy had last been in London, George was still just

a nephew to a viscount. He rather hoped his title wouldn't preclude Teddy from renewing their friendship. As the younger brother of a baron, Teddy had opted to serve as an officer in the British Army in the latest battles against Napoleon, leaving his lucrative position as a clerk at a bank in order to do so. The man was a perfect fencing partner, and he shared George's dislike of the gaming tables.

"I don't think I have had the pleasure," George finally responded with a shake of his head, after realizing Josephine was waiting for a response. He had to admit to a bit of curiosity about the chit, though. Josephine wouldn't have suggested Elizabeth Carlington if she hadn't done her research on the young lady.

Sighing, Josephine leaned forward. "If you would have attended at least one *ton* ball during the past three Seasons, you would not be able to make that claim," she stated firmly.

George leaned back in his chair and regarded his mistress. "Carlington? As in the Marquess of Morganfield?" he asked, trying to imagine if he had ever seen David Carlington in the company of a daughter. He had only ever seen the marquess in White's and once or twice at Angelo's Academy. The marquess was decent on the piste and could be an exceptional fencer if he practiced more.

"The very one," Josephine replied, rather happy George was giving her suggestion some thought.

"Was this his idea or yours?"

Josephine huffed. "Mine, of course. Morganfield doesn't know yet."

"But you're going to tell him." It wasn't a question. George knew of Josephine's occasional visits to Carlington House to apprise the marquess of her latest deductions on the political and social happenings in England. She had been doing it since before George knew her, and she had been forthright about her intention to continue doing so even after Joseph Bennett-Jones arranged for her exclusive services on George's behalf.

"I will... *discover* if arrangements for his daughter have been made. And, if not, I will make the suggestion. Unless you'd rather me not," she added, suddenly acting as a submissive wife might.

George frowned. This wasn't like Josephine. Not at all. "Not having met the chit, I cannot yet find fault with your plan. However, Josie," he added, his voice taking on a tone of warning. "Should Miss Carlington—"

"Lady Elizabeth," Josephine corrected him.

"Should Lady Elizabeth turn out to be some spineless milk-and-water milkmaid who faints at every turn and frequently suffers from vapours, then I shall demand your hand in marriage as recompense."

His mistress stared at him for a full second, rather stunned that George Bennett-Jones could be so persuasive when he needed to be. "I assure you, George, Lady Elizabeth will never be mistaken for a milk-and-water milkmaid, she probably hasn't fainted a single time in her entire life and, as for vapours, none of us seems to know what that even *means*, so I rather doubt she has succumbed to them, either."

Grinning at her insistent tone, George nodded. "Then I suppose I must look forward to the day Lady Elizabeth and I are introduced." Seeing Josephine's look of satisfaction and concilia-tory nod, George reopened *The Times* and returned to his reading.

CHAPTER 6
WHAT MEN WILL DO FOR
MONEY

J uly 1815

Andrew S. Barton, Esquire, regarded the young lady who had breezed into his shabby office as if she owned the place. She probably could, he considered, his gaze taking in the quality of her clothing and the elaborate bonnet covering part of her auburn hair. A lady's maid had followed her into the office in Oxford Street, although that young woman had taken up residence in the corner near the door and displayed an expression suggesting she had been following her mistress about all day and was foot sore and bored.

"Good morning. Mr…" His visitor paused to review a clipping from a newsheet. "Mr. Barton?"

"I am Mr. Barton. What can I do for you, Miss…?"

"Carlington." She held out her gloved right hand. Barton reluctantly shook it, half-wondering if she expected him to kiss the back of it. "I have your advertisement for the space next door. I should like to let it for use as my charity's office. *Finding Work for the Wounded.* That is, if we can come to an agreeable sum."

Resisting the urge to roll his eyes, Barton sighed. "Finding work for the wounded?" he repeated.

The young lady nodded. "I arrange employment for soldiers

returning from the wars. I've only just begun but find I am in need of a larger space from which to operate the venture."

Not having heard of the charity, Barton was about to ask for more details but decided her interest in the next-door office might dissipate when she learned how much it would cost. "Twenty pounds per annum includes the desks and chairs. If anything else is required, you'll have to make the arrangements on your own," he replied. He had been prepared to quote two-and-twenty pounds, but her comment about using the office for a charity had him reconsidering.

Lifting her reticule to her lap, the young woman opened the gathered fabric and was about to reach in for some coins when the solicitor said, "What are you doing?"

"Why, getting the money to pay you, of course," she replied. "I should like to get started as soon as possible. Do you suppose I could move in this afternoon?"

Barton suddenly frowned. "You'll need to sign a contract, Miss Carlington, and I rather doubt you're old enough." She couldn't be five-and-twenty! She probably hadn't yet reached her majority! "Where is your husband?"

The young lady stared at him for a moment. "I don't have one of those," she replied, as if a husband might be something she would acquire from a shop in New Bond Street.

Barton blinked. "A... a father, then?" He couldn't help but notice how her shoulders slumped, nor how her one hand was suddenly filled with a variety of coinage. She obviously had enough blunt to cover the yearly rent and then some.

"Oh, must we involve him?" she countered in a voice filled with disappointment. "He's a marquess, so busy with estate matters and such, you see. Oh, I suppose I can arrange an appointment—"

"A marquess?" he interrupted. *Carlington?* Barton struggled to remember which aristocrat was associated with the Carlington family name. *Morganfield!* Eying the young woman's fist full of money, Andrew S. Barton did something he never thought he would do as a solicitor—forgo a contract in favor of a simple verbal agreement until such time as she could arrange a signature from her father. "Do you swear you'll see to it your father's seal is affixed to this contract?" he asked as he pulled a half-sheet of parchment from a drawer.

His visitor's eyes widened in shock. "Swear?" she repeated, as if she were horrified. "But… I never curse," she claimed.

Barton cleared his throat, once again resisting the urge to roll his eyes. "Can you assure me you'll see to it this contract is signed by Lord Morganfield? I'll see to it my clerk has a copy ready tomorrow."

Giving him a nod, Lady Elizabeth replied, "Of course, Mr. Barton. And if you can give me a receipt and the key to the premises, I shall give you the money now."

Five minutes later, Lady Elizabeth left Barton's office, walked a few steps down Oxford Street to the next door, and entered the home of 'Lady E's Finding Work for the Wounded.'

CHAPTER 7

A CHARITY IS BORN WITH A BRIBE

September 5, 1815

"I must admit, Lady Elizabeth, I am quite curious as to why you would wish to see me," the portly banker said as he motioned for her to take a seat in front of his rather large, ornate mahogany desk. Avery Whittaker took care in seating himself in the leather chair on the other side of the desk. When he was comfortably ensconced, the light glinting off his bald pate, he leaned forward, resting his elbows on the edge of the gleaming surface, and gave his visitor an expectant look. "I thought your father's solicitor did all the banking for the Carlington family," he ventured, wondering if she had come without her father's knowledge to request an advance on her allowance.

"Thank you again for agreeing to see me on such short notice," Elizabeth said with a curt nod. She'd had a footman deliver a note that morning with instructions to wait for a reply. The footman wasn't gone long, and her requested appointment time of two o'clock was confirmed in the return note from Whittaker. "It's about a position you have open. For a clerk," she added quickly.

Mr. Whittaker regarded her for a long moment before one bushy eyebrow cocked up. "Indeed?" was all he could manage to say, suddenly afraid Lady Elizabeth had come to apply for the position.

Elizabeth saw his sudden fright and gave the man one of her brilliant smiles. "Oh, Mr. Whittaker," she admonished him with a wave of her gloved hand. "I ask not for myself, of course, but for one who has served King and Country and has held such a position here at the Bank of England prior to his service with the army," she explained, her voice light as she leaned forward to place a character on the banker's desk. "Mr. Streater is quite qualified and looks forward to the opportunity to continue his work in the banking field."

Picking up the character by the edges of the paper, as if the document might explode in his hands, the banker glanced quickly at the perfectly penned resume, taking in the name, Theodore M. Streater, and the qualifications of the man in question. He noted the fact that Streater had worked as a bank clerk for many years at the Bank of England prior to serving nearly three years as an officer in the British Army. His time with the army had ended nearly three months ago, however, and Mr. Whittaker raised his eyebrow in query. "And why hasn't Mr. Streater come to apply for this position of his own accord?" he asked, impressed by what he was reading about the man and his experience.

"He has. Twice," Elizabeth replied lightly, keeping a pleasant expression on her face despite the nervousness she felt.

She had never done this before.

Never used her relationship to a marquess to secure an appointment.

Never come to an employer and basically begged him for a position on behalf of someone else.

Never carried a purse stuffed with thirty guineas in the event a bribe was necessary to secure the position.

But when a person of good character couldn't gain employment on his own, she had decided she could use her name and influence to help him secure a position. If she could succeed on behalf of Theodore Streater, she was prepared to continue finding positions for others like him. An unusual charity, to be sure, but one of her own creation and, at the moment, a bit thrilling.

"I don't understand, Lady Elizabeth. I would have hired Mr. Streater directly based on this character," Mr. Whittaker claimed, confusion quite evident on his face. "When may I meet the man?"

Elizabeth felt a jolt of excitement at the banker's claim, but tamped it down. The next few minutes would be most telling. "Why, this very moment, if you would like. Are you prepared to make him an offer?"

Mr. Whittaker sat up straight, his eyebrows now forming a single caterpillar of gray hairs. "I... I would like to meet him first, milady," he hedged, wondering why Lady Elizabeth hadn't brought the applicant into the meeting with her.

"Before I ask him to join us, please tell me, Mr. Whittaker. How much would you require to give Mr. Streater the position for a one-month trial period?" she asked as she struggled to keep her face impassive. *We're almost there.*

"How much?" the banker repeated, his expression turning to one of puzzlement. "Do you mean…?"

"How much does one pay to secure a clerking position at your firm, Mr. Whittaker? Will twenty pounds be sufficient? Or do you require more?" *Almost. Almost.* Her heart was pounding so hard she thought perhaps Mr. Whittaker could hear it from across the desk.

The banker stilled himself as he regarded the young woman who sat across from him. He had to admit to a certain attraction to the auburn-haired beauty. Who could resist such pretty eyes, fair skin, and pink lips? But he was old enough to be her father. *Grandfather, even*, he thought with a bit of dismay. And an alarm bell was going off in his head that would give him a headache if he didn't address it that very moment. "I insist on meeting Mr. Streater," he announced as he stood up, or tried to as the movement seemed to take a great deal of effort on his part.

Startled, Elizabeth had to suppress the urge to counter with a protest. "Very well," she sighed, moving to the door to open it.

"Mr. Streater, please do join us," she said in as calm a voice as she could muster. When the nattily dressed man moved through the doorway, he bowed in a most formal fashion and nodded to the banker. Besides wearing clothes that could have been tailored by Weston for a lean body obviously well exercised, Streater's hair was trimmed short, and he carried himself as if he were still a soldier of the British Army.

"I am Theodore Streater. Thank you for agreeing to see me," he said by way of a greeting.

The banker stepped forward and held out his right hand. Streater regarded it and held out his left hand, clasping the back of Mr. Whittaker's hand and shaking it, the motion quite awkward for both the banker and the applicant. It was then Whittaker noticed Mr. Streater was missing his right hand, perhaps most of his arm. "Avery Whittaker, at your service," the banker said, suddenly nervous.

"It was blown off in a battle in France," Streater said before Whittaker could ask. "But since I write with my left hand, I am able to work quite effectively. All I ask for is the chance to prove myself."

The banker's frown worried Elizabeth; she had seen his immediate reaction and was momentarily angered that Whittaker would change his good opinion of Theodore Streater based on his lacking a right arm. "How much, Mr. Whittaker?"

His eyes widening, Avery Whittaker swallowed and regarded Streater with a quick glance. "Twenty guinea," he announced with a nod. "And you have three weeks to prove your worth," he said tersely. The banker was obviously a bit miffed at being put in the awkward position of having to hire Streater, but there was a hint of anger in Streater, as well. The man had tried twice before for the position; nothing had been said about a bribe making it possible to secure the position those two times.

But a bribe required blunt, and he didn't exactly have it to spend in that way.

Elizabeth, who had been holding her breath, let it out slowly. *Over twenty-one pounds!* Just to guarantee the position. "Agreed," she stated, not allowing Streater to voice the objection he was about to make—the look on his face made it quite clear he was about to do so. She placed a hand on his left arm. "Congratulations, Mr. Streater. I will leave you two to work out your schedule. Please let me know how it goes." Turning to the banker, she quickly fished several notes and a few coins out of her reticule. Holding them out to him, she said, "Here you are, Mr. Whittaker. I do hope you'll keep up your end of the bargain. My father will be so pleased to know you have given Mr. Streater this opportunity," she said brightly, couching the warning as nicely as she dared. Curtsying to the two gentlemen, she bid them *adieu* and left the office.

Once the door was shut behind her, she leaned back against it and closed her eyes. *Yes!* She *could* help crippled soldiers find gainful employment. The *bribe* was the key. She could simply use her allowance to bribe employers into hiring wounded soldiers. A few more weeks, and she would have enough money to help another.

Elizabeth waited until Mr. Streater joined her in the hall outside the banker's office. "Well?" she asked, a bit worried at how long he had been in there with Whittaker.

"Well, I have a position," he responded with a tentative smile. There was a kind of relief that had settled over him. "Thanks to you, of course. I will be forever in your debt, Lady Elizabeth. However... however can I thank you properly?" he asked then, his eyebrows taking on a worried expression. He was quite aware of the monetary cost to the marquess' daughter, and he still found it hard to believe a charity existed that did what Lady Elizabeth had just managed to accomplish.

"Perform well enough in the position so he cannot let you go," she answered with a smile, pulling on a glove. "When do you start?"

Mr. Streater shrugged, the motion made awkward by the missing arm. "Now, it seems. I must go to the clerk's office to get my assignment and will continue working until as late as seven this evening."

Startled by the news, Elizabeth gave him a brilliant smile. "Very good then. Do you have money for a hackney to get you home?" They had traveled to the bank from her office in Oxford Street using her father's town coach.

She hadn't explained to anyone that her father knew nothing of it.

"Oh, I can see my way home, my lady," the clerk replied with a nod.

Feeling as if she had embarrassed the man, Elizabeth held out her left hand, and Mr. Streater regarded it before returning her smile and shaking it. Then she pulled a pasteboard calling card from her reticule. "Should you know of someone else in your situation who is in need of a position, please give them my calling card and have them contact me, won't you?" With that, she took her leave of Theodore Streater and left the Bank of England.

CHAPTER 8
WHO IS LADY E?

*T*eddy Streater regarded the bright white pasteboard with the black script for a moment. *Lady E's Finding Work for the Wounded.* At the very bottom of the card was the address of Lady Elizabeth's office in Oxford Street—the office to which he had been summoned a few days ago with a note claiming a position could be arranged on his behalf. Not necessarily believing the claim, curiosity had him paying a visit to the spare office where he found Lady E reading a newspaper she held in one hand while she held a pair of scissors in the other. A servant, no doubt her lady's maid, sat at the other desk whilst she sewed.

Although he recognized her, Teddy knew they had never been formally introduced. He knew she had sought an introduction, though, for he had overheard her asking Viscountess Pettigrew if she might do the honors during Lady Worthington's *musicale.*

If only she had asked someone else besides the old biddy! Lady Pettigrew would never deign to introduce a lady to a man who was on the fringes of the *ton.* The younger son of a baronet didn't warrant a second thought. Had she made the request of their hostess, Lady Worthington, he might have made Lady E's acquaintance that very evening and secured the clerking position last month!

Teddy slid the calling card into his coat pocket and hurried off to the clerk's office.

When his work was complete at six-thirty—he had finished every assignment and was told to return at eight in the morning—Teddy hired a hackney coach. "Angelo's," he instructed the driver as he tossed him a coin. Once at the fencing academy in Bond Street, Teddy disembarked from the coach and glanced around, hoping he wasn't too late to secure a match with an old friend. "Have you seen George?" he asked of the attendant on duty. The man nodded in the direction of a piste on which two men were sparring. Nodding his acknowledgement, Teddy moved quickly to stand amongst the three other men watching the match.

George Bennett-Jones, his rapier held nearly vertical as he regarded his shorter opponent, straightened his entire body and pulled his legs together. His opponent, a rather portly man who was sweating profusely, seemed confused by the move and let down his guard. With that mistake came George's attack, and soon the man was stumbling backward as he was forced to parry and retreat from George's swift advance. His retreat ended when he landed on his backside, cursing loudly enough for the entire audience to hear. A smattering of applause ensued as George offered his hand to his opponent and pulled him to his feet. After exchanging bows, George left the piste and headed toward the changing room.

"George!" Teddy called out, his head lifting a bit as he nodded toward his friend.

The taller man halted in mid-step and grinned when he caught sight of Teddy. "They really do let in anybody," George said with a teasing grin, indicating with a wave that Teddy should join him. Friends since their days at school—they had both been born on the fringes of the *ton* but were educated with boys who would one day inherit titles—the two had excelled at fencing.

"As I recall, they used to welcome me with open arms," Teddy replied with a wry grin, his left arm spreading wide. The empty sleeve of his right arm, folded and pinned against the side of his top coat, was made more apparent by the action.

"That's because you had two and the blunt to pay your dues," George countered playfully.

There was a time when George would never have been so callous in the comments he directed to his friend.

Less than a week ago, in fact.

But the few hours they had spent together since George's return to London proved Teddy Streater wanted things to be as much like the old times as possible. And that meant a good deal of teasing and a few drinks at White's.

"I'll be paying those dues at the end of the month," Teddy said proudly.

George paused before continuing into the changing room, his friend on his heels. "What's that you say? Did you rob a bank?" he asked as he set down his rapier and stripped off his gloves.

"Something like that," Teddy countered, his lips curving.

George stopped unbuttoning his uniform jacket to regard his friend, saw the hint of a smile, and continued changing into his suit of clothes. "Indeed?" was his only reply. Curiosity was apparent in his expression, though, but he waited for Teddy to explain himself rather than ask outright.

"I got my old position back. At the bank," Teddy explained, barely able to maintain his composure.

George stared at his friend with a mixture of surprise and horror. "I am happy for you, Teddy, of course, but... at what cost?" Teddy Streater hadn't had a pence to his name for months now. If it wasn't for the kindness of his friends and his older brother who gave him a pittance of an allowance and allowed him the use of a townhouse in Piccadilly, Teddy would be living in the streets. Where had he come up with the blunt to ensure his employment?

Teddy shrugged. "Twenty guineas," he said, his face sobering. At George's stunned expression, he pulled out the pasteboard card the woman from the charity had given him. "I will pay it back eventually, of course," he said as he held out the card, "But it was this lady who spoke with Mr. Whittaker at the bank. And she came up with the blunt. You'd like her," he added with a glint in his eye. "Not your typical *demoiselle*."

Reaching for the calling card, George gave his friend a wary glance. "*Demoiselle?* Do you know her?" At Teddy's quick shake of his head, he added, "Then how ..?" He looked down and read the card, his brows furrowing at the information. "How did you find out about this 'Lady E'?" he asked. Instead of handing the card back to his friend, George slipped it into his waistcoat pocket and continued dressing.

Teddy shrugged, a movement made awkward by the lack of a right arm. "She found *me*. I've seen her before, though. In fact, I think I know who she is. But she sought me out. Sent a note requesting I pay a visit to her office. So, I met her at that address—" he indicated the calling card—"and a day later, I have my position. And, I'll be getting a wooden arm next week. Some carpenter is carving one for me now. She saw to that, too."

George realized he had been staring and tore his gaze away from Teddy's empty sleeve. "She's paying for that as well, I take it?" The comment wasn't meant to sound judgmental, but somehow it came out that way.

Teddy stiffened at the tone in George's voice. "As I said, I will pay it back. The charity exists to help us cripples get our old jobs back." He paused when George seemed surprised at the comment, wondering then if his friend had misunderstood the name of the organization on the calling card.

"And did you ask whose blunt is behind the venture?" George asked, his expression softening a bit. He knew at once he should be happy for Teddy, but he couldn't help but be a bit suspicious at the same time. There were dozens of charities in London that could claim they helped war widows and their children, but none he knew of that existed to help find employment for wounded soldiers.

"I think the only funding available right now is this woman's own pin money," Teddy replied.

Pin money? Twenty guineas wasn't exactly pin money!

As he buttoned his breeches, George considered his friend's explanation. So a woman had founded a charity with the sole purpose of helping wounded war veterans gain employment. *What was in it for her?* He couldn't say why he felt so suspicious of the woman's motives just then, but when had anyone done something so generous without the expectation of something in return? "You say you know who she is?"

Shrugging again in that way that seemed just a bit awkward, Teddy replied, "Yes. I'm fairly sure she is Lady Elizabeth Carlington."

George's head snapped up. "Lord Morganfield's daughter?" Not too long ago, Josie had talked about the young woman— thought he should marry her! He had never met Lady Elizabeth, but overheard comments made at White's led him to believe the young lady was unmarried, quite spoiled and very beautiful.

The money to fund her little venture was probably coming from her father.

"Yes. In fact, I am quite sure of it," Teddy went on. "I once saw her at the theatre before I left for France. I wouldn't have given her a second glance except that my brother was quite taken with her and thought to court her. Then, a few months ago, she was at Lady Worthington's *musicale*. She seemed to want an introduction, but some old biddy refused to allow it."

Frowning, George considered Teddy's words. "Your brother, a *baronet*, thought to court the daughter of a *marquess*? Aiming a bit above his station, wasn't he?" he asked as he folded his uniform. An attendant would see to its storage on his behalf.

"I suppose, but why not? Her dowry is probably in the thousands. Who's to say her father wouldn't allow her a love match if that's what she wanted?"

Daddy's only daughter would not be allowed to marry for love, George thought to himself. Not if David Carlington was the father. Despite a scandal that had nearly knocked him out of power many years ago, Morganfield was quite resilient, well-respected by his peers, and one of the most powerful lords in Parliament. He would no doubt be the architect of an arranged marriage for political gain. "Because you're speaking of David

Carlington," George countered, his grin returning. "And unless your brother had some way to become a member of the *ton*, it's rather doubtful he would have a chance in hell at becoming Morganfield's son-in-law."

Teddy was forced to agree. And then his grin widened. "*You're* a member of the *ton* now, George," he commented with an arched eyebrow. "Perhaps you should consider courting Lady Elizabeth. You'd like her," he added as his elbow found its way into George's ribs.

"Ouch," the viscount replied as he stepped to the side. Trying hard to hide his sudden grimace, he regarded his friend. "And why would I be interested in a woman who runs a charity that is no doubt funded by her father? A *spoiled demoiselle*, no less."

As they took their leave of the changing room and headed toward the academy's front doors, Teddy said something that stayed with George for the rest of the night. "I do not believe the marquess is funding Lady E's venture. At least, not directly."

A footman held open the doors for the two gentlemen as they left Angelo's. "What makes you say that?" George asked as he led Teddy down the street toward White's.

"I could be mistaken, but I am almost positive she used her allowance to pay the bribe at the bank," Teddy answered. "And when I looked at Lady E, I did not get the impression she was spoiled in the least."

George cocked an eyebrow. "When you *looked* at her, were you looking at her... face? Or some other parts of her?" he asked in feigned disgust. "And was she looking down her nose at you? With her chin somewhere in the next layer of atmosphere?"

It was Teddy's turn to huff. "I appreciate a pretty face when I see one, George, and hers is more than pretty. As to her other parts, I can't say for certain since she was wearing one of those..." He waved his arm in the air as he tried to find the correct word. "Pelisses, that's it," he announced proudly. "She was wearing it over her gown. But I can imagine she's a good figure. And she never treated me like a commoner, George. She's got pluck, I tell you. And she is *beautiful*."

Suitably dressed down, George considered his friend's words. And he was surprised at the reverence he heard in them. Obviously, this "Lady E" had made quite an impression on Teddy. Perhaps she didn't expect anything in return for her charitable endeavor. "It sounds as if you were saved by an angel, my friend."

Teddy grinned. "I do think of her as an angel. But I have a feeling she will be unable to share the good news of her charity with any of her own titled people."

George gave his friend a sharp glance. *Titled people* now included him. And why shouldn't he look kindly upon Lady E's charity? He voiced the question and heard Teddy snort in reply.

"I would think it's not seemly for an unmarried lady of the *ton* to be involved with cripples," he replied in a matter-of-fact manner. "At least, not directly. Could be quite scandalous, in fact. She didn't even have a chaperone with her when she met with the banker today. Well, other than me," he added.

George stifled the surprise he nearly displayed at hearing the comment. Considering his friend's words for the rest of the night as they played whist at White's, George wondered how Lady E was funding her charity. Did she have to keep it secret from her family as he had kept secret the funding of the Chichester orphanage from his uncle all those years? Or had her father allowed her the privilege? Perhaps he would ask Lord Morganfield about his daughter's charity in such a way as to discover if the marquess was providing funds for it. And, if it became clear the marquess knew nothing of the charity, then George decided Lady E should have some help with her charity.

Monetary help.

She would need a good deal of blunt if the enterprise wasn't being funded by her family's money. There were far too many wounded soldiers looking for employment these days, and once news of the charity spread, there would be a number of men lining up in Oxford Street seeking Lady E's help.

An army of them, in fact.

CHAPTER 9
CHARITABLE THOUGHTS

*L*ater that night, Elizabeth Carlington climbed into bed feeling an immense sense of satisfaction. Despite having given a banker twenty guineas that afternoon, money she would have otherwise used to buy gowns, bonnets, ribbons or perhaps gifts for her dearest friends, she knew it had been far better to use it for a man's welfare.

She thought back to that week after the last ball of the Season. With most of the *ton* summering at their estates outside of London and very few social occasions at which to spend time with eligible bachelors, it was the need for diversion during those summer months that had led to her notion of starting her own charity. The memory of *almost* meeting Theodore Streater at Lady Worthington's *musicale* had stayed with her, haunted her for all those weeks before she determined she should offer some kind of assistance to the man.

After arranging to let the office, Elizabeth had visited a print shop for calling cards and stationery. The following day, she had returned to the solicitor's office and collected the lease contract for her office space. Once she was home and sure her father wouldn't be returning until it was time for dinner, she had surreptitiously entered his study, borrowed his seal, and signed the contract. She returned the document to Andrew Barton's office the next day—the same day she arranged for a shingle to be hung above the charity's door.

For the past several days, Elizabeth claimed she was going shopping with her maid and took her leave of Carlington House in her father's town coach. Instead of going to Jermyn Street, though, she had the driver take her to Horse Guards and watched as hundreds of soldiers went in and out of the War Office. She discreetly distributed the cards to those she recognized as needing assistance—men who were missing limbs or who limped or appeared hopeless.

Now, she took great pride in the fact that Theodore Streater was gainfully employed. He would one day be able to pay back some of the money it had cost for his bribe.

Then she would have those funds, as well as her next allowance, to help another.

And once more men were gainfully employed, they might help fund the charity, too. With a steady stream of money, she could afford to send applicants to tailors for suits of clothes, to pay bribes, and to hire help in the office. She would need assistance in searching the newspapers for job openings and in interviewing soldiers to determine what positions they might be best suited to work.

Yes, there was a good deal of work to be done if this charity was going to be successful. But in the end, funding from those who had already been helped would be the key to its success.

CHAPTER 10

A MISTRESS PAYS A CALL ON
A MARQUESS

*S*eptember 6, 1815

The butler opened one of the double front doors of Carlington House, not a bit surprised by the identity of the visitor—once he sorted it was she beneath the black veil, black bombazine gown and black mantle she wore. "Miss Wentworth," he acknowledged with a nod. He stepped aside as Josephine entered the vestibule and held out her calling card.

"Alfred," she said brightly. "If his lordship is in residence, would you be so kind as to ask him if I might have a few minutes of his time? It's about politics, of course," she added, wanting to be sure the butler didn't get the wrong idea about her frequent visits. The last thing she wanted was for the household staff of Carlington House to think she was there in any other capacity than as a visitor. Wearing widow's weeds was merely a way of hiding her identity from nosy neighbors. Although it was unlikely, should someone recognize her as a mistress, the gossip would last at least a week and put David Carlington in a very precarious position with his wife. The very last thing Josephine Wentworth wanted was to be the *on-dit* in London. She had spent more than eight years ensuring she was unknown among the *ton*.

Alfred hurried off to the Marquess of Morganfield's study and was back before Josephine could complete her perusal of the vestibule. A few things had changed since her last visit. The color of the satin on the walls was a dark forest green, and the addition of an oil painting on the west wall seemed to warm up the room considerably. Adeline Carlington, Marchioness of Morganfield, was obviously having a positive effect on the household, even if it was several years past due.

"Lord Morganfield will see you in his study," Alfred said with a nod as he turned to lead her there. Josephine followed at a respectful distance, allowing the butler to set the speed at which they walked down the wide hall. It gave her time to study the slight changes in décor that had been made in the hallway as well. A new painting here and there, a dais displaying a suit of armor from what looked liked the age of the Crusades, a marble bust of a Greek god—Apollo, she thought from her quick glance—and myriad *objets d'art* atop pedestals. No matter how many new things might be added, she decided that Carlington House would always seem *old*, somehow, as if the place were a museum.

Even before they reached the door to David Carlington's study, Josephine detected the scent of an expensive cheroot recently extinguished. Alfred stepped to one side and motioned for her to enter. "Thank you, Alfred," she said with a nod as she crossed the threshold.

Once inside the marquess' study, Josephine curtsied before reaching up to push back the black veil off the front of her hat. "How do you do, Morganfield?" she said with a nod in his direction. "Thank you for seeing me."

David Carlington stood up from behind his massive desk, the surface of which was covered in papers and a few books. The remains of his cheroot were still giving off tendrils of smoke from the crystal ashtray in the center of the desk blotter. "As if I would not," he replied warily. "Should I ask who died?" he asked, with a nod toward her gown.

Josephine gave him a wan smile. The expression helped to soften the effect of the severe coloring of her gown against her pale skin and light auburn hair. "I would hope you have heard about the Wainwrights," she answered, her smile suddenly gone.

The marquess sobered, motioning her to a chair. She took the seat that was offered, carefully arranging her skirts as she did so. "The *on-dit* has it that the entire family was lost to a fire," he finally offered, wondering why Josephine would see fit to wear widow's weeds for a ducal family based in Sussex.

Josephine shook her head. "Then you have not heard of Lady Charlotte's involvement."

David straightened in his chair, leaning his elbows on his desk as he did so. "What has my daughter's best friend done now?" he asked, his brows becoming one.

"Joshua Wainwright survived. But he was badly burned and is in hospital. St. Bart's. Lady Charlotte saw to it he was transported from Kirdford yesterday. Apparently, the village doctor who was seeing to his care used all of his stock of morphine in the first few days following the fire."

Sucking air through his teeth, the marquess eyed Josephine with a bit of suspicion. He was having a hard time believing Lady Charlotte would have enough pluck to get herself down to Kirdford and arrange for a badly wounded man to be brought back to London. But her father would have been useless, and her mother suffered from vapours when anyone looked the least bit askance at her. Someone had to have helped. Since Charlotte Bingham's charity was to assist in the children's ward at St. Bartholomew's, it didn't surprise him that she would have Joshua placed there for his medical care. "Will he live?"

Josephine shrugged. "He must. He is the sole heir to the Chichester dukedom," she replied. "Lady Charlotte was betrothed to his older brother, the Earl of Grinstead. Since he perished in the fire, as did the duke, it seems she will become a duchess should she choose to marry Joshua." She paused a moment before adding, "A far better fit for Lady Charlotte than John the younger was, to be sure."

David couldn't argue there. John Wainwright II was a rake of the worst kind. He wouldn't be missed by anyone but those whose clubs and brothels he frequented when he was in town. "Let's hope Joshua agrees and marries her then," he replied. The marquess realized then his attention had been deliberately misled by the woman who sat across from him. "But the Wain-wrights' deaths aren't the reason you wore black today," he stated finally, realizing there was more to Josephine's visit than news he could get from *The Times*.

"Indeed. I had word from the Continent that my sister died." She said the words without the least bit of sadness to her voice.

David blinked and then furrowed his brows, unaware Josephine had any siblings. She had never spoken of a sister before. "I take it you two were not close," he ventured. He wondered if he should extend sympathies but thought better of it when Josephine shook her head.

Josephine had to breathe very carefully in order to stave off the warring emotions she was experiencing. Relief, at hearing her sister had finally died of the French pox she had contracted while a mistress to a French army general, and hatred that her sister had been a traitor to the Crown. "At one time, we were. Before she broke one of the cardinal rules of being a mistress," Josephine remarked, wondering if she could now tell David Carlington the true identity of the woman who had sold his pillow talk to the French and nearly forced him to give up his marquessate and his seat in Parliament.

"There are *rules*?" he teased, trying to lighten the mood in the study. He thought of asking if he might light another cheroot. Even if it was still morning, this type of conversation warranted a smoke. Or perhaps a brandy. "I wasn't aware."

There were rules, of course, and Josephine knew the man was aware of at least a few of them. Or perhaps he wasn't, and that's why he had been so unguarded back then.

Shame on him.

Josephine regarded David Carlington for a long minute, deciding she should tell him what she knew. "My mother taught my sister and me that we were to take only one client at a time," she commented lightly, as if she were reciting a rule of business. "You see, if a mistress takes money to warm a man's bed, then she cannot in good conscious take money from another in exchange for the knowledge she has gained at the expense of the first." She sat very still for a moment, wondering if the marquess would make the connection. Apparently, he did not. At least, not right away.

It had been ten years, after all.

David stiffened, his gaze on her suddenly wary. "Does this have anything to do with the note you sent me about my mistress sharing information with the enemy?" he asked, remembering the day he received the damning parchment. The beautifully written but startling missive described how everything he had shared with his mistress was being passed on to the French. He hadn't known Josephine back then, so the signature on the note meant nothing. And he chose to ignore the warning, thinking a jealous peer was trying to stir up trouble. He was sure Genevieve could be trusted. "How did you... *know?*" he asked, his face suddenly hardening.

Back then, when they had finally met in person, he didn't ask Josephine how she *knew* about Genevieve and her arrangement; his only query regarding the note, asked of her during one of their late morning meetings, had to do with *why* she would send a note to a man she had not yet met telling him his mistress was selling his secrets to the enemy. And she was quick to explain that she was loyal to Crown and country, having already gained an appreciation for politics from her second protector.

Josephine knew from David's face that he was making the connection. "Genevieve's real name was Jennifer Wentworth. She was my sister."

The marquess held very still for a long time, his expression not giving away the tumultuous feelings he was experiencing at that moment. There was relief, to be sure, in finally knowing the true identity of the woman who had betrayed him, but the addition of grief and anger made for a heady mix. He shook himself from his reverie. "I am sorry for your loss," he said quietly, realizing he meant what he said. Despite her traitorous turn, the woman was Josephine's sister. A woman he at one time had happily bedded and perhaps even loved. A woman with whom he had shared far too much and, as a result, had been forced to pay dearly for the mistake.

"Thank you," Josephine replied, knowing the sentiment only applied to her and not to the dead relative.

"A drink?" he asked, reaching for the brandy decanter on the counter behind his desk.

"It's not even half past ten, Morganfield," she countered, although the sound of her voice indicated she would welcome the drink. Even before she finished her comment, the marquess had poured a finger's worth into a small rummer. He held it out to her. She took it with a black kid-gloved hand and waited as he poured one for himself.

"And isn't it a bit early for *you* to be making calls?" he countered as he leaned back in his seat behind the burnished mahogany desk. Mistresses were usually abed until after noon. By asking the question, the marquess was reminding her that he was aware it was still her profession.

Josephine smiled at that. "I haven't kept late hours in a very long time," she answered lightly, deciding the few moments she had mourned Jenny were quite enough for the time being. "One has to be up early to read an entire copy of *The Times* and half the *Observer* before noon."

Remembering what Alfred had given as the reason for her call, David regarded Josephine for a moment. Their rather odd association had begun many years ago, quite by accident and because of the man to whom Josephine was contracted at the time. With Genevieve's betrayal of him to the French came scandal, loss of power, and a stain on his political career. At home, the fallout from the scandal caused his world to collapse. His wife, Adeline, barely acknowledged him, but was able to continue her movement in Society by immersing herself in charity work.

Josephine's protector, an earl, had mentioned Josephine's political acumen over a game of cards. During the course of several months, the earl relayed her recommendations to David—recommendations based on her analysis of news from around the world as well as political happenings in England—as a means of helping the marquess restore his name and good standing in Parliament. Besides being instrumental in restoring his credibility in the House of Lords following the scandal—she knew how to steer reporters to her cause and knew how to start and stop gossip—she continued to be a valuable resource when she would warn him of impending power plays, describe the maneuverings of political opponents, and recommend society events to attend for political gain.

And her loyalty to him was unquestioned.

When he had asked many years ago why she would provide him with such information, apparently with no strings attached and for no recompense, she responded with a shrug. "I merely wish to see our government act in the best interest of the country," she had said. "And one day, I expect I shall be married to a man of industry. Anything I can do now to make it possible for his business to thrive in the future makes it worth the effort."

Odd, he thought, that a mistress would expect to marry a cit. *Unless she is already betrothed.*

"I appreciate your keeping up on current events, Josie," he finally acknowledged, as he leaned forward, his elbows resting against the front of the desk. "What have you discovered since our last meeting?"

The mistress took a sip from her brandy and leaned back in her chair. She should not have been surprised that he would serve her his best, so she held the liquid in her mouth and savored the smoky flavor before swallowing. "Although he did not make an appearance in chambers before the summer, the new Earl of Trenton will do so when the sessions begin in the fall," she stated in a matter-of-fact tone. "You will find his attitude a bit... uncouth. He is young, rather brash, quite rich, and..." She held her breath for effect. "Very spoiled."

Josephine paused again, remembering the letter she had received from Staffordshire a few months ago. How fortuitous that her friend Sarah had been the one to service the newly minted earl whilst he spent an evening at the *Spread Eagle*. "The earl's views are diametrically opposed to yours. He will attempt to embarrass you if you appear to hold fast to old ideals. He is hungry for power. He will be very determined to make his mark. Every unmarried young lady in the *ton* will want him as a husband.

"And he is looking to marry." This last comment was delivered with an arched eyebrow, suggesting she knew just the debutante that might appeal to the new earl. Then she said something so incongruent, it actually surprised the marquess.

"Lord Bostwick is also looking to marry."

David swallowed the rest of his brandy in a single gulp and regarded Josephine, trying to figure out for himself how the young upstart earl might upset the House of Lords. If the man was as young and brash as she suggested, he wouldn't be taken seriously by his peers. *And what did it matter that both an earl and a viscount were in the market for a wife?* "So, what am I to do about this new Earl of Trenton?"

Josephine placed her rummer on the small table next to her chair and sighed. "Oh, Morganfield." She took a deep breath. "I know, despite what you have done in the past, you have *said* you do not wish to influence your daughter as to whom she will marry. But the Earl of Trenton will probably ask for her hand. He knows that once his views become apparent to the peers, and that your views are opposite, a marriage to Lady Elizabeth will be seen as an embarrassment of sorts. He'll be *family*. How can you be seen opposing your own son-in-law?"

David Carlington's face displayed a look of shock. "And how can *he* be seen opposing *me?*" he countered defensively, his ire suddenly up.

Josephine leaned forward. "He is young and brash. Eton- and Cambridge-educated. You will not wish to get into a war of words with an upstart earl. Especially now that John Wainwright won't be there to help you."

Reeling at the comment, David sat back in his chair. *So, that's why she brought up the Wainwrights,* he suddenly realized. Shaking his head, the marquess regarded Josephine for a long minute. There was a hint of anger in his eyes—that last bit had stung—but he finally forced it under control. After this many years, he knew not to kill the messenger. Especially not this messenger. "So, what do you suggest I do?" he asked, leaning over the desk.

A smile widening on her face, Josephine paused a moment before answering. "Consider George Bennett-Jones, Viscount Bostwick, as a son-in-law." She watched with a great deal of satisfaction as David Carlington sat back in his chair and seemed to give her suggestion its due.

Then she saw his brow furrow and his head shake from side to side. "Why ever not?" she asked, a bit exasperated and trying desperately to keep a calm façade. She clasped her hands together in her lap in an effort to keep them from drumming against her lap.

She had thought this out quite thoroughly. It was a good plan. It made good political sense. Lady Elizabeth was determined to marry before Christmas. And George needed a wife. The sooner Josephine got him married off, the sooner she could make plans for her own marriage—for her own future.

"Elizabeth would never give George any consideration as a possible husband," the marquess finally answered with another shake of his head.

"And why not?"

David sighed, and his shoulders actually sagged a bit. "While I am not opposed to her marrying beneath her station, I doubt Elizabeth will consider anyone less than an earl. And I rather doubt her mother would agree to such a match," he added quickly. "She wants to see Elizabeth suitably settled, preferably as a duchess." He said this last with a hint of humor, as if there wasn't a chance his daughter could marry a duke. It wasn't as if there were a number of them needing wives just then. "But she'll accept her as a countess. Probably not as a viscountess."

Despite the reasons he had just given for his daughter and wife to oppose the marriage, Josephine could tell from his expression that David Carlington at least found merit in the suggestion that George Bennett-Jones would make a suitable match.

And more importantly, he wasn't *opposed* to the suggestion.

"I see," she said with a slight nod, pretending she was giving up on the idea. "I have taken too much of your time already, my lord. Please let Lady Morganfield know I was here in the event a neighbor asks about the widow who paid a visit, won't you?" she said as she stood. She gave an elegant curtsy to David's perfunctory bow.

"I will be sure to do so," he acknowledged, always impressed with how Josephine was able to keep secret her visits to his home. "And, thank you, Josie. You always bring me such interesting information," he added.

George Bennett-Jones' mistress left the study and hurried to the vestibule, pausing to hand the butler a small note. The words *ostrich feather* were written in a perfect script. "See to it her ladyship gets this, won't you, Alfred?" she asked. "They're all the rage in fashion now," she added, hoping her comment would deflect the butler from guessing the real reason for the note. "Oh," she said as she held up a finger and fished a charcoal pencil from her reticule. "Let me add something on the back." She took the card from the butler and wrote in the same perfect script,

Do not discount a viscount.

Handing the card back to Alfred, Josephine gave him a nod. She then hurried to her waiting coach, remembering at the last moment before leaving the house to pull down the somber veil to cover her face.

CHAPTER 11
DAUGHTERS CONSIDER MATRIMONY AND BONNETS

*S*eptember 7, 1815

"So, will you accept the earl's suit? You must know there is talk that he will ask for your hand," Lady Charlotte spoke softly, leaning sideways a bit so that she wouldn't be overheard by a passing shopper. Arm in arm, she and Lady Elizabeth strolled along New Bond Street, stopping at nearly every window to marvel at the colorful displays. Their maids trailed behind, both bored by the tedium of following their mistresses on their day of shopping for the first ball of the Little Season.

Elizabeth paused in mid-step, surprised by her best friend's comment. "What have you heard?" she gasped, glancing about to be sure no one had overheard Charlotte's comment. "And from whom?"

The honey-haired beauty pulled Elizabeth into the closest shop, where bonnets were artfully perched on a series of shelves. "I was at hospital today..."

"You're *always* at hospital," Elizabeth countered, with a teasing roll of her aquamarine eyes. "I am beginning to believe Joshua was never in a fire, and that you and he are simply using the place to meet for secret assignations."

Charlotte's eyes widened in shock. "Elizabeth! How dare you?" she exclaimed, her gloved hand immediately covering her mouth as she realized she could be overheard by anyone in the shop. The fact that they were the only two people in the shop, besides the bespectacled owner, who stood at the counter reading a copy of that morning's *The Times*, didn't seem to register.

Elizabeth didn't mean what she said, of course. Her friend had been a volunteer at St. Bartholomew's Hospital for several years, spending most of her time there tending to ill children. Lately, though, Charlotte had been spending several hours a day at Joshua Wainwright's bedside whilst he lay in St. Bart's. Even if the man was unconscious all of the time, Elizabeth worried that the impropriety would start tongues wagging among the town gossips.

Charlotte sighed. "I assure you, I merely... when I am not seeing to patients, I sit by his bed. He is completely unaware of my presence!" she hissed. She wasn't about to admit she held Joshua's undamaged hand when no one was about, or that she spoke in low tones to him about the happenings in London. The poor fellow was rarely conscious, and when he was, he was in so much pain it brought tears to her eyes.

"I apologize," Elizabeth said suddenly. "It was wrong of me to make light of his situation." Her expression took on a look of appropriate guilt. "Lottie, he will be right as rain, you must know. And when you turn one-and twenty, you shall go to him and become his bride."

Charlotte gasped, surprised by her friend's insistent tone. "You really believe I will just... go to him and *offer* myself as his betrothed?"

It was Elizabeth's turn to show surprise. "Well, isn't that what you want? To marry him? You went off and rescued him from certain death in that backwater village!" she countered, as if that kind of bold action was something Charlotte Bingham did on a daily basis. What did it matter that the Earl of Torrington had provided assistance in the form of his traveling coach-and-four? "You do... feel *affection* for Joshua, do you not? You always have. We always knew he was better suited to you than his brother, John. And given what has happened, he will need a strong wife who has been training to be a duchess for her entire life. That's *you*, Lottie," she stated firmly. "There can be no other wife for Joshua Wainwright."

Charlotte stared at Elizabeth for several seconds, struck by her words. For a long time, she hadn't been certain her friend was aware of her desire to wed Joshua, even in his current state. And the comment about Joshua needing a strong wife only served to reinforce her desire to see herself wed to the duke.

Because Charlotte had been betrothed to Joshua's older brother since she was three, there had been a kind of security in knowing whom she would marry, and she had felt a bit of relief in not having to participate in the annual Marriage Mart. But now that John Wainwright was dead and his younger brother had the title of Duke of Chichester, Charlotte was no longer so sure of her own future. Elizabeth's words had helped to reassure her, though. "Thank you," she whispered, her head nodding as if she had been doubting her fate.

"Of course," Elizabeth replied with a lift of one shoulder. "Now that we have your future worked out, please, Lottie, tell me what you have heard regarding Gabriel," Elizabeth pleaded, her voice a near whisper.

Charlotte did her best to suppress a gasp at hearing her friend refer to the Earl of Trenton by his given name. Elizabeth Carlington could be the most frustrating of friends. As the daughter of a marquess, she had been raised to expect a life of luxury and marriage to a member of the *ton*. Those who knew her as well as Charlotte did were well aware that Elizabeth was not nearly as spoiled as her behavior would sometimes suggest. She was dedicated to her mother's charities, some of which could be construed as inappropriate for a woman of her station, and she was kind to the household staff at Carlington House. Everyone thought her beautiful, if for no other reason than her captivating, almond-shaped eyes and auburn hair. Last spring, she had begun her third Season in Society and had decided that this was the year she would accept an offer of marriage.

With the Little Season about to begin, it left her with just a few months to land a man. But referring to the Earl of Trenton as "Gabriel" seemed a bit too familiar to Charlotte Bingham.

"Gabriel?" Charlotte repeated in surprise. "Has he given you permission to address him that way?" she asked aloud, moving down one aisle of the hat shop to look at the bonnets.

Elizabeth shrugged. "He took me for a ride in Hyde Park last week and requested I save the first waltz for him at Lord Weatherstone's ball," she said quietly, her eyes dancing in delight at sharing the news. "I said I would, of course," she added, as she glanced about the shop, apparently just then realizing it offered hats for sale.

"Did you, indeed? Charlotte said. "Well, I did hear from Penelope Winstead Seward, who said she spoke with Lady Asheford, who apparently heard from Lady Worthington that Gabriel Wellingham's *mother* was especially happy that her *son* had decided this was the year he would marry, and that he had decided to pursue the daughter of a certain *marquess* that wielded a good deal of power in Parliament." At Elizabeth's amused expression and quick wave, she followed her friend through to the back of the shop. "And then Hannah Slater's father mentioned it last night during dinner," Charlotte added, almost as an afterthought, her voice returning to its normal rhythm and pitch.

Lady Elizabeth paused before trying on a jaunty bonnet of deep green velvet adorned with peacock feathers. "Good heavens," she replied, her eyes wide. "The Marquess of Devonville mentioned it?" she asked in disbelief, the bonnet falling to one side of her head. She caught it in her gloved hands before it fell off completely. "Oh, dear. This is happening much faster than I thought it might," she added, when she saw Charlotte's raised eyebrow.

"Oh, taradiddle! You've known for the past *week* he would ask for your hand," Charlotte scolded, suddenly wondering at which social engagement the two had originally met.

"I did not," Elizabeth protested, her voice carrying a bit

more than she intended. The man at the counter—Elizabeth was fairly certain his name was Mr. Peabody—glanced up from his reading to give them a curious look. "I merely... suspected," Elizabeth added, holding the feathered bonnet as if it were a weapon. "And if I must marry someone, why not Gabriel Wellingham? I rather adore his blond curls, and those blue eyes, and the ten thousand a year I hear he's worth," she said, in a voice that clearly mocked the way young ladies talked. "And being a countess seems like a perfectly acceptable way to spend married life, don't you suppose?"

Charlotte smiled at her friend's description of the earl. She might have agreed, but having listened to Lady Hannah's father complain about the man through two courses of last night's dinner party, she was having doubts.

After the gentlemen had enjoyed their cheroots and port following dinner, she and Lady Hannah had left their parents to play cards. It was during their card game that Hannah mentioned how her father, the Marquess of Devonville, had voiced similar complaints about the Earl of Trenton nearly every night for the past week. Apparently, Gabriel Wellingham's youth and lack of decorum in the House of Lords was a distraction, and his political views were at odds with her father as well as Lady Elizabeth's father, the Marquess of Morganfield. "Why, Lady Elizabeth, I cannot believe you would settle for something less than a duke," Charlotte teased then, her grin betraying her mock seriousness.

Elizabeth's eyes widened. "Unlike you, Lady Charlotte, we can't all be *duchesses*," she countered happily, a flush turning her face a soft pink as she considered Charlotte's news.

So the earl may offer for my hand!

The gossip was merely confirmation of what she already suspected. Gabriel Wellingham had been quite attentive these past two weeks, ever since he had returned to London from summering in Staffordshire. During their drive in Hyde Park, after the earl's request that she reserve a waltz with him at Lord Weatherstone's ball, the rest of their conversation had been the usual banter about weather and fashion before he started extolling the virtues of his new horse and a phaeton he had on order, the renovation work he was having done to Wellingham Manor in Staffordshire, and his good fortune in securing an appointment with Hoby for a new pair of boots. It was only when he seemed to run out of safe topics to discuss that he asked about what she had done over the summer. As she briefly described her three weeks at the Morganfield estate and the week in Bath, she was sure she saw genuine interest on the part of the earl.

Never mind that most of it seemed aimed at her bosom.

Gabriel Wellingham was a man, after all, and she had been told by her mother that most men were attracted to women with ample breasts. Her mother seemed to know such things with a degree of certainty that sometimes made Elizabeth wonder *how* she knew.

"Will your father even *allow* you to marry the earl?" Charlotte asked in a quiet voice. "If I understand what Father said, and hearing the Marquess of Devonville say it, too, the Earl of Trenton does not share your father's political views." She spotted a dark blue riding bonnet and was admiring the decoration attached to it when she noticed Elizabeth was suddenly uncomfortable. "What is it?"

Sighing, Elizabeth pursed her lips. "I do not believe Father would begrudge me the groom of my choice," she said very carefully. "But I do wish he would at least... take an *interest* in whom I might marry," she added, her attention going back to the bonnet she held. Unlike for Charlotte, a marriage had not been arranged for her, nor had her father made suggestions regarding possible matches. If it was up to her to choose, she would do so based on the suitor's title, his annual income, and whether or not she found him to have a pleasant countenance. There was the hope he could please her in other ways, as well, but she rather doubted she could expect so much in just one man.

"Be careful what you wish for," Charlotte whispered as she

leaned toward Elizabeth's ear. "My father is suddenly showing entirely *too* much interest in my situation. Despite the arrangement he made with the Wainwrights, I do not believe he wants me to marry the Duke of Chichester." She straightened, her worried look completely at odds with her earlier joy at sharing her news about the Earl of Trenton.

"Why ever not?" Elizabeth asked, her eyes as wide as they could be. "You would be a duchess, for goodness sake!"

"Father has heard the *on-dit*. He believes Joshua will never recover enough to assume his duties," Charlotte explained, her voice rising enough so that the man at the counter looked their way again.

Elizabeth forced her face to remain impassive. She had heard the very same gossip. "But, he will. Won't he?" Elizabeth stammered, suddenly not so sure. *What if the gossip was true?* She had been wondering if Charlotte's expectations for Joshua Wainwright's recovery weren't just a bit too high. What if Joshua didn't recover? Charlotte was due to marry when she reached one-and-twenty, just six months from now. If Joshua could not fulfill his duties as a duke, perhaps it was better that Charlotte be married to someone else. Another year or two and she would be too old to be considered biddable for most titled gentlemen.

The crestfallen look on Charlotte's face made Elizabeth want to take back her query, though. "I apologize, Charlotte. Please forgive me," Elizabeth whispered quickly. "I hear such terrible things, but you *see* him every day—"

"He *will* recover," Charlotte assured her, her head nodding quickly. "I have seen to it he has the very best doctor, and there is a nurse—a nun, actually—who sits with him when I cannot. The physician said that since Joshua has survived this long, he will live. Another week, and he'll be past the worst of the pain."

Elizabeth gasped at the suggestion that Joshua Wainwright was still suffering. It had been several weeks since the fire. "I am relieved to hear you say so. You... you haven't said as much, at least to those who ask after him. Perhaps you must be more forthcoming with what you know," she suggested, realizing Charlotte's information was more hopeful than most had heard.

"And you must be more forthcoming about his improving state. In fact, you must *start* your own gossip!"

A pink flush spread over Charlotte's face, the young woman feeling obviously uncomfortable with her friend's suggestion. Gossip could be a hurtful, damaging tool when used by those out to destroy someone. But perhaps it could also be used to good effect.

"I .. I suppose I must," she agreed finally. "Yes, in fact, I think I shall have to, if for no other reason than to be sure my father hears the good news of Joshua's recovery from someone other than me."

Elizabeth regarded the peacock feathered bonnet she still held, admiring the workmanship and deciding it would be a good match for her teal carriage gown. "I think I will buy this," she commented, nodding her head in the direction of the man at the counter.

Charlotte seemed surprised by the choice. "A bit... daring, don't you suppose?" she commented.

Smiling, Elizabeth nodded and strolled up to the counter. "Yes. And it's about time I was," she answered in a whisper. She directed her attention to the shop owner. "Put this on my father's account, won't you, Mr. Peabody?" She thought of paying for the bonnet out of the bit of pin money she had with her, but thought to keep it for her charity.

The shopkeeper set aside his newspaper and nodded at Elizabeth Carlington. "Of course, Lady Elizabeth," he said with a hesitant smile. "Should I deliver it, or will you want to take it with you?"

Charlotte stepped up to the counter. "Oh, let's do take it with us. And this one, too," she said as she placed the dark blue riding bonnet on the counter. "If our mothers are to believe we went shopping this afternoon, we'll need to come home with *something*."

Mr. Peabody nodded. "As you wish, Lady Charlotte."

As the shopkeeper wrapped the bonnets in tissue and placed them in pasteboard boxes, Charlotte wandered toward the front of the store. Glancing out the window nearest the door, she noticed their maids flirting with a groom and tiger who were standing ready next to a rather new town coach. She was reminded of the day before yesterday, when she and her mother, Lady Ellsworth, had called at Carlington House. Although Lady Morganfield had invited them to have tea with her in the parlor, Elizabeth wasn't in residence at the time.

Elizabeth retrieved the two boxes from Mr. Peabody and moved to join Charlotte. A nattily dressed gentlemen held the door for them as they made their way out. "Thank you, sir," Elizabeth said with a nod as she passed the man, his face hidden by the brim of his beaver as he bowed.

"Where *were* you the day before yesterday?" Charlotte asked as she stepped past the man, nodding her thanks as she did so and moving to stand in front of the window of the shop next door. Her attention was drawn to a reticule in the women's accessory shop window. "Mother and I called on your mother, and even she seemed surprised you weren't yet home from morning calls." The shorter woman had wandered onto the next shop window, admiring a row of brightly colored silk fabrics displayed much like a rainbow.

Charlotte was asking about the period of time when she would have been at the Bank of England, bribing Mr. Whittaker to offer Mr. Streater the clerking position. She wondered how much to tell her friend. Her first foray into arranging a position for a wounded soldier had been successful, but the *how* of it wasn't something she felt comfortable sharing, even with her best friend. If Charlotte somehow found out about her charity, though, she would be hurt to discover Elizabeth hadn't trusted her enough to tell her about it from its start.

Elizabeth pulled a pasteboard card from her reticule and held it out to Charlotte. "I have started my new charity, 'Finding Work for the Wounded.' I placed my first client the day before yesterday," she explained in a lowered voice. "And I just interviewed two more gentlemen this morning. I am thinking of hiring them to help me with my venture."

One of Charlotte's eyebrows arched up as she regarded the large script 'Lady E and Associates' in the middle of the card.

"Finding Work for the Wounded" was centered below the "Lady E", and below that, an address was listed. "You started your own *charity?*" Charlotte asked in surprise, rereading the text and the address on the calling card. "Elizabeth! This is... this is very *worthy*," she got out before biting her lower lip with a tooth. "Is Lord Morganfield your associate? Did he provide assistance in arranging this... 30 Oxford Street location?" she asked, glancing between the card and Elizabeth.

Her friend sighed, suddenly afraid that most would jump to the same conclusion. "My father knows *nothing* of this. At least, I have not told him of it." At Charlotte's soft gasp, Elizabeth added, "I want to prove I can do this before I tell him," she explained quickly. "And before I ask for an increase in my allowance." It would be some time before Theodore Streater would be able reimburse the charity. She would need more funds before she could hope to place any more men into positions.

Charlotte gasped again. "You're using your own *pin* money? Whatever for?" she asked, a bit alarmed. A lady of the *ton* could align herself with a multitude of charities, but their patrons generally held soirées to generate operating funds.

"Rent," Elizabeth responded with a nod. "I've let a street-level office from a solicitor in Oxford Street. I intend to keep regular hours, perhaps ten to one. But there are so many expenses, Lottie. Writing paper, ink, postal costs." She paused a moment, deciding not to add *bribes* to the list. "I never knew it would be so difficult to convince employers to hire our wounded soldiers."

Charlotte shook her head. "Now that the war is over, there are a large number of soldiers looking for work. It must be hard for all of them. I hear some must *pay* to gain a position." Her attention was once again drawn to where their maids hovered a few feet away, the girls' attentions still on the groom and tiger who were posted near their master's very new town coach and four matched Cleveland Bays next to the sidewalk.

Elizabeth considered the reasons an employer might charge a new employee—it guaranteed the new hire would report to work and perform the task in a manner satisfactory to the employer.

She recognized it wasn't such a preposterous idea after all.

However, the wounded men she had been helping didn't have any funds from which to pay to gain employment. Most were quite poor. And those who sought positions as clerks needed a good suit of clothes, boots or shoes, and a haircut in order to appear professional enough for their interviews. "So, when I placed my first client at the Bank of England two days ago, it cost me twenty guineas," she finally admitted, needing to tell *someone* of her success, although at the moment, success felt as if it came with too high a cost. She didn't need to look at Charlotte to know her friend was stunned by the news.

"Oh, Elizabeth," Charlotte breathed, her gloved hand moving to the top of her bosom and pressing hard against the dark blue pelisse she wore. Charlotte took another breath, the look of shock on her face so apparent Elizabeth thought she might faint. "Why so *much?*"

Elizabeth felt tears prick the corners of her eyes. "My client... he... he is missing an arm," she finally got out. "But he writes with his left hand and was a clerk with the bank *before* he joined the army to fight the French." After pausing to blink a couple of times and gather herself, she added, "I have a wood-worker making him an arm..."

Charlotte's eyes widened again. "An *arm?*" she repeated, sounding as astonished as she looked.

"So there will be something to put in his *sleeve,*" Elizabeth clarified in a hoarse whisper. "With a hand of sorts attached at the end. It will be covered with a glove, of course, so it should not be so... noticeable," she added, hoping she was making sense. "The thing of it is, *all* of my clients have some sort of evident wound or impairment that makes it impossible for them to land jobs which they were perfectly suited to do before the war."

Charlotte shook her head. "This is going to cost you a fortune!"

Elizabeth nodded in a way that indicated she had come to

the same conclusion. "I expect it will at first. But I have decided on a way to help pay for some of it. As these men make their wages, they are to give some back. To reimburse the kitty, so to speak, and provide the funds necessary for the next man in line to land a position."

Her friend regarded her for a very long time. "You've given this a lot of thought, haven't you?" she asked rhetorically, a bit surprised that a woman such as Elizabeth Carlington could have come up with such a novel idea for funding a charity. "If Joshua wasn't a duke, he might have need of your charity, I expect," she said solemnly, her gaze on something far away.

Frowning, Elizabeth considered her friend's comment. "He was not wounded in the war," she replied, realizing there were others out there like Joshua Wainwright who had wounds that prevented them from being able to easily reenter society. "But I think I could see my way to make an exception for situations such as his," she added thoughtfully.

"Oh, Elizabeth," Charlotte sighed, "I do hope this works for you. For your... clients."

Shrugging, Elizabeth sighed. "Me, too."

At least Theodore Streater was employed. He had sent a note saying he had finished his first day at the bank, and it was as if he had never left his position to join the army. This morning, when she had met with the two ex-soldiers she planned to hire as her assistants, she had been assured there were more wounded who wanted an audience with her. And given the nature of her charity, news would spread amongst those who had served together. Soon there would be several in the office every day.

Elizabeth wondered how long it would be before the Earl of Trenton learned of her charity. And would he feel obliged to help her continue her work should they marry, perhaps even agreeing to fund the enterprise?

He could certainly afford to do so.

Or would Gabriel require that she turn her venture over to someone else to manage? Perhaps assuring her that she could continue her participation in a less active role? Or, worst of all, would he require she stop the charity altogether, claiming that it didn't suit a lady of the *ton* to be associated with crippled men?

Given she hardly knew the man, she could not begin to guess how Gabriel Wellingham would react to the news.

So, until she knew otherwise, she decided it would be better if she didn't tell him.

CHAPTER 12

A THANK YOU GIFT

"Good afternoon, Peabody," George Bennett-Jones said in greeting as he made his way to the back of his late mother's favorite millinery shop.

"Ah, George," the shopkeeper said as he looked up from the counter. He held a quill in one hand. "Fine day, no?"

George grinned as his gaze swept the store to find no other shoppers inside. "Yes, very. And it was made even finer by those two young ladies who just departed. It looks as if they made some purchases," he said in a conversational manner, hoping the man would share some information. He removed several coins from his pocket.

"Those were the ladies Charlotte Bingham and Elizabeth Carlington. Real beauties, both of them. Both got bonnets," Neville Peabody commented as he waved to the papers he was filling out.

A quick glance at the counter showed two bills of sale. George saw the top one and noticed the name "Lady Elizabeth." "And charged them to their daddies, I suppose," George said with a grin.

Neville shrugged. "Yeah. A bit odd in the case of Lady Elizabeth, though," he said as he indicated the bill he was completing. "She usually pays in cash."

Interesting, George thought to himself. A lady of the *ton* who used her own pin money to pay for her purchases? Except she had probably spent all she had to secure the clerking position for Teddy Streater. "How much for the bonnet Lady Elizabeth purchased?" he asked suddenly, surprising himself with the query. *You cannot buy gifts for young ladies,* he remembered Josie saying, when she was teaching him about proper manners. Well, this wasn't a *gift,* he decided. This was... well, he didn't know what it was, but it wasn't a *gift.*

After all, Lady Elizabeth wouldn't even know he had paid for the bonnet.

The shopkeeper gave him a glance before reading the amount on the bill of sale. "Half a crown," he stated. "It was green velvet and had peacock feathers," he added, as if he needed to justify the cost of the bonnet.

George tossed a coin onto the counter, wondering if he would ever see the bonnet perched on Lady Elizabeth's head. "I'd like to pay for it," he said as he motioned toward the bill of sale. "As a... thank you... for something she did... for a friend," he added, when he noticed the shopkeeper's arched eyebrow. At first, he hadn't considered the implication of his comment, and now he hoped Neville Peabody wouldn't spread gossip about his having paid for the bonnet.

Neville smiled and handed him the paper. "That's an awful nice thank you," he commented lightly.

Nodding, George agreed. "Well-deserved, though. Good day, Peabody."

He pocketed the receipt and left the shop, a bit relieved to see that Lady Elizabeth and Lady Charlotte and their respective maids were no longer nearby. His tiger opened the town coach door. Quickly stepping up and inside, George gave instructions to the groom to head for Bostwick Place.

CHAPTER 13
A BONNET BECOMES A
MYSTERY

*L*ady Elizabeth bid farewell to Lady Charlotte as her friend and maid took their leave of the Carlington town coach. Once the women were safely inside the Ellsworth townhouse, Elizabeth knocked on the trap door in the ceiling of the coach. The groom opened the door and peered down. "Where to next, milady?" he asked.

"Back to New Bond Street, Jackson. I'm afraid I've forgotten to buy a gift for a dear friend," she lied. Having reconsidered what she had told the shopkeeper about sending the bill for her bonnet to her father, she needed to get back to the hat shop and pay Mr. Peabody.

Although she wanted to keep the money for her charity, her father had been giving her a monthly allowance for the very purpose of paying for frippery such as bonnets. And he had done so to prevent—how had be put it?—"being inundated with bills from merchants all over town."

Unlike most members of the *ton*, David Carlington did not like credit, which meant he did not like having purchases put onto bills of sales for payment at a later date. It also meant he had to carry some blunt and provide his wife and daughter with pin money to pay for their purchases.

Elizabeth's intention was to return to the shop and offer cash payment immediately in return for the receipt. When she reached the shop, however, Mr. Peabody was quite surprised to see her.

"I haven't got the receipt, Lady Elizabeth," he said, with a shake of his head, when she asked to pay the bill.

Confused by the shopkeeper's reply, Elizabeth took a small step back. "You've already sent it to my father?" she asked in disbelief. *Oh, dear!* If she hurried home, she might arrive before the postman. Perhaps she could intercept the bill at the house before her father saw it.

"No, milady," Mr. Peabody replied, shaking his head. At her expression of confusion, he leaned over the counter. "The bill has already been paid," he said *sotto voce*, as if he was afraid of being overheard, despite the fact that there were no other customers in the store at that moment.

"Paid?" she repeated in disbelief. "Paid by *whom?*" She was sure Charlotte hadn't done so; her friend rarely carried money. And her maid had been outside during the purchase and otherwise with her the entire time she wasn't in the shop.

Mr. Peabody straightened and gave her a shrug. "I couldn't say." Although George hadn't exactly said he needed to keep his involvement a secret, Peabody had the distinct impression he should.

Elizabeth stared at the shopkeeper for several moments, her eyes becoming slits when she realized Mr. Peabody knew *exactly* who had paid the bill. "Couldn't say? Or *won't* say?" she queried, suddenly suspicious of the shopkeeper and his motive for not telling her what she wanted to know. What she *needed* to know. Someone had paid for her peacock feather bonnet!

The man took a deep breath and rolled his eyes. "Won't say *who.* But I will tell you that he said it was a *thank you* gift. For helping his friend."

Her mouth forming a perfect "o", Elizabeth struggled to maintain her composure. *Someone who was a friend of someone paid for my bonnet as a thank you gift?* Then she remembered that the only person she had helped in any way recently was Theodore Streater. *So a friend of Mr. Streater paid for my bonnet.*

But who? She hadn't been gone from the shop more than forty-five minutes. They would have had to…

She remembered the well-dressed man who held the door for her and Lady Charlotte as they took their leave of the shop. He had been tall, well-built, with manicured hands, his tapered fingers on the long side. His face had been hidden by the brim of his hat, though. Perhaps he had been the owner of the new town coach parked in front, the employer of the groom and tiger who waited curbside while flirting with the maids. *Perhaps Anna knows the groom.*

"Did you help someone recently?" Mr. Peabody asked, his tone suggesting he didn't necessarily believe the comment made by George Bennett-Jones, which meant he had likely jumped to an incorrect conclusion.

Elizabeth nodded her head in response, deciding to admit to what she had done in order to prevent the man from imagining something salacious. "I did, indeed. I was able to convince a banker to rehire a man for his old position."

The shopkeeper's eyes widened. "Well, the gentleman seemed to think it was worth a half a crown, milady," he said with a shrug, apparently disappointed there wasn't a bit of scandal attached to the gift.

Half a crown?! It was just velvet and peacock feathers! "Was he… a gentleman?" Elizabeth asked then, hoping to narrow down the prospects from among the half-million men of London.

"Yes, my lady," Mr. Peabody replied as he crossed his arms. "But I am sworn to secrecy. I won't be telling you his name."

Elizabeth regarded the shopkeeper with surprise. "Well, I suppose I shall never know," she said at last, her shoulders slumping as she headed for the door. Despite the shopkeeper's refusal to divulge the identity of the man who had paid for her bonnet, Elizabeth couldn't help but smile to herself.

She had never been given a thank you gift before.

Once she was back in the carriage, her skirts spread out on the leather seat, Elizabeth leveled her gaze on her maid, Anna. "Tell me, Anna. Do you remember the groom and tiger you were speaking with in front of the hat shop earlier?" She kept her voice light.

Anna stiffened in her seat, her posture suddenly erect and her face pinking up. "Yes, milady," she answered nervously.

Damnation! Elizabeth cocked her head to one side, not intending the query to make her maid uncomfortable. "Oh, it's quite all right, Anna. Do you know who *owns* the town coach, by chance?"

Her maid seemed surprised by the question. "No, milady. But it was very new. So new, it didn't yet have a crest painted on the door! Groom was a bit proud, if you ask me, though. Like he was something special, he being able to drive a coach-and-four like that." She relaxed a bit into her seat. "I think he said his name was Forsham. The tiger was very... right proper, though," she added, her face taking on that pink blush again. "James, his name is. Said they live in a carriage house behind a townhouse in Park Lane."

Elizabeth nodded and settled into her seat, just a bit disappointed. "Park Lane?" she repeated with a nod. *My bonnet was paid for by a gentleman living in Park Lane.*

Well, that narrowed it down a bit.

CHAPTER 14

A STOLEN KISS AT LORD
WEATHERSTONE'S BALL

September 14, 1815

Given Lady Charlotte's assurances that the Earl of Trenton would offer for her hand, Lady Elizabeth wasn't too surprised when Gabriel Wellingham sought her out so quickly at Lord Weatherstone's ball. Just as he had done at the last ball of the Season, he met her before she had even stepped onto the ballroom floor, reminding her of her promise to grant him the first waltz.

His mood was one of merriment. While they danced, his conversation included compliments for her gown as well as her dancing skills. And he asked about taking her on another ride in the park. "I was thinking we could go riding at eleven o'clock tomorrow morning," he said as a way to introduce the topic. "But seeing as how I must meet with my solicitors in the morning, I am wondering if my lady would accompany me for a ride later in the day? I have heard it's only fashionable to ride in Hyde Park in the late afternoon. Say at five o'clock?" he proposed, his blond brow arched up so his expression appeared especially quizzical.

Elizabeth found his expression a delight as it made her think he was waiting with bated breath for her to give him an answer. If he intended to take her in his new phaeton, there would likely not be room for a third person on the bench seat, though. "I will have to bring my maid, of course," she finally responded, with an intonation that suggested she was daring him to withdraw the invitation. She caught the slight change in his countenance before it was quickly restored and wondered if he was disappointed in her response.

"Of course," he replied quickly, acting as if the condition of her company was expected. "I was considering taking out the curricle. I have a new grey Thoroughbred I'd like to try in the harness."

Elizabeth widened her eyes to make it seem as if she was impressed. "You've been to Tattersall's, then?"

His expression faltered again, but was soon back to its pleasant state when he replied, "I was there just yesterday, in fact," he confirmed with a nod, the dance just about to end. "You know of it?" he asked then. He seemed surprised that she would know of London's premier source of horseflesh.

The music ended and Elizabeth stepped backward to curtsy. "Of course, my lord. I believe all the horses in our stables came from there."

Gabriel finished his bow but did not let go of her hand. "Your stables must be the envy of all," he responded, a hint of a grin appearing.

Not believing his comment warranted a response, Elizabeth shrugged one satin-clad shoulder. She followed his lead as he pulled her toward him and then turned to head them to the French doors on one side of the ballroom. Beyond the stone-covered patio were the extensive gardens of the Weatherstone estate.

Placing her hand on his arm, Elizabeth walked alongside Gabriel as he escorted her outdoors and along the flagstone path. *Never once did he ask me if I would accompany him!* A sense of excitement gripped her as she sorted why he might be taking her to the gardens.

He intended to kiss her, of course.

As to whether or not she would allow the impropriety, Elizabeth was still contemplating what she would do when they passed behind an especially tall hedgerow. Gabriel gave no warning as he suddenly turned around, moved his body in front of hers and lowered his face to hers. Pausing just a moment to alter the angle of his head, his lips came down over hers so quickly, Elizabeth was unable to prepare herself. Startled by the hard pressure and the sudden wetness of his mouth on her lips, she recoiled a bit. Gabriel was quick to reposition himself and the kiss softened, but the wetness seemed to get worse.

Just as Elizabeth thought she might get used to the sensation, she felt his tongue attempting to separate her lips and she stepped back in surprise, nearly colliding with the branches of the hedge. Gabriel's hand moved to the back of her waist to provide support and then pulled her body toward him. "I apologize, I... I was overcome by your beauty," he breathed, his eyelids so heavy they nearly covered his eyes. He leaned down and slid his tongue along her cheek, finally pulling away when the sound of something moving in the bushes behind them caught his attention.

Elizabeth swallowed hard and dared to meet his gaze. "Apology accepted, of course, my lord," she replied, surprised she could get the words out so they made any kind of sense. She was glad for the darkness as she felt a flush creep up her chest and face.

The earl had just kissed her.

And he had attempted to slide his tongue into her mouth!

And then he had licked her!

Revolting!

The rustling in the bushes behind Elizabeth gave them both a start, and Elizabeth gasped softly. The beginning strains of music for the next dance made their way to her ears.

The next dance!

"Forgive me, my lord, but I have promised this dance to Lord Nesbitt," she said, still breathless and feeling a bit panicked. If she did not appear in the ballroom for the dance, the baron might attempt to find her in the gardens. Her exit from the ballroom on the arm of the earl was no doubt seen by *someone*. And if that *someone* should say *something*... scandal was not something she could abide. Not this Season.

Even if it was due to the Earl of Trenton.

Stunned she was about to take her leave of him, Gabriel straightened, his stance a bit awkward. "Oh. Um. Of course. Tomorrow at five, then," he said, his voice making it sound as if he was experiencing some discomfort.

Elizabeth murmured her assent and curtsied before hurrying off to the ballroom, dabbing at her mouth with her handkerchief as she did so. Coming up to the French doors, she slowed her steps and entered the brightly lit room. She glanced to the left and right, appearing to look for her next dance partner. When she did not immediately see Lord Nesbitt, she strode quite purposely to where her friends stood in wait to be claimed for the dance.

George Bennett-Jones kept very still where he stood on the other side of the hedgerow. Secretly pleased his intervention had prevented the Earl of Trenton from getting more than a stolen kiss with the daughter of the Marquess of Morganfield, he emitted a sigh of relief. He watched Lady Elizabeth Carlington hurry past. Did her manner suggest that she was as relieved as he was that she had escaped the clutches of the Earl of Trenton? Or was it just her need to be present in the ballroom for the next dance?

Perhaps there is hope for me, he thought with a smile.

CHAPTER 15
A VISCOUNT MAKES
HIS MOVE

The early autumn Weatherstone ball was the first of the Little Season, a diversion for the members of the *ton* who had returned to town for the beginning of Parliament. And, although it wasn't supposed to be a Marriage Mart, there were plenty in attendance who were either looking or being looked at for the purposes of matrimony. Those *demoiselles* who hadn't snared a husband during the spring Season were paraded in front of the likes of George Bennett-Jones. So, although he wouldn't admit to being in the market for a wife, could at least look and not feel like a rake ogling them from the bow window at White's.

But Elizabeth Carlington hadn't been paraded in front of him. At least not by a desperate mother looking to get her dear daughter betrothed to a nobleman. No, he realized with a sudden sourness, she had been put on display by the man with whom she was dancing the first waltz of the evening.

Gabriel Wellingham, damn him. The Earl of Trenton, *double damn him.*

Every Season seemed to feature a few like Wellingham. Men who were impossibly handsome, impossibly rich, and impossibly perfect. Men like Wellingham, who drew the young ladies to their countenance like bees to honey, their colorful satin evening clothes surrounded by the bright white gowns of young ladies of quality.

George considered his own choice of garments for the ball. He had worn black satin breeches that fit him quite well, snug around thighs well-developed from fencing and horseback riding. His silver embroidered waistcoat was almost too conservative—he had considered wearing the red one with the gold embroidery but thought it better suited to an evening at a gaming hell. The tailcoat, in black satin, was tailored by Weston to fit his athletic body and yet allow him to dance. His valet, Elkins, had tied a perfect mail coach knot in his snowy white cravat before adding a diamond-tipped pin that matched the diamond cuff links at the end of his sleeves. Buckled dancing shoes over silver knit stockings completed his ensemble. He had dressed correctly, he knew, but without Wellingham's handsome features, he was sure he would not be given a second look by the likes of Elizabeth Carlington.

But, because of a duke with two supposed left feet, he was.

For it was during the second waltz of the evening, the supper dance, when Lady Elizabeth was deposited—there could be no other word to describe how her dance partner spun her— directly into George's arms.

The man had apparently tripped.

Watching the spectacle as it happened, George was quite sure it all occurred in slow motion, a kind of whirling dream where dance partners spun in their own orbits and rotated about the center of the ballroom in perfect measure.

Except one orbit was about to change quite drastically.

Having the foreknowledge that such an event was about to occur, George knew if he positioned himself just so, he would gain his own moon if he just held out his one arm at waist level and prepared to begin moving in the same direction as Lady Elizabeth. The Duke of Somerset's misstep caused the man to lose his grip on Elizabeth's waist. With her momentum still sending her in a circle, her spinning skirts adding to the effect, she was unable to stop without stumbling and had to let go of the duke's hand. George managed to capture her waist against one palm while raising his hand to gently grasp hers in mid-air.

Anyone watching might have figured out the entire maneuver was carefully planned and executed, except that the duke was left breathless and apparently embarrassed at the edge of the dance floor, and George was suddenly enjoying himself. The duke hurried away, telling a nearby associate that his shoe's heel had come loose, and he left the ballroom, presumably to see about getting it repaired.

"Oh!" Elizabeth let out suddenly, her gorgeous eyes so wide George was sure he could climb in and drown in their aquamarine depths. She dared a glance over his shoulder as they spun away from those who stood near the edge of the dance floor and the scene of the hand-off.

"Are you quite all right, my lady?" George asked, giving voice to his first concern, after being sure he had them waltzing in a safe direction and to the actual rhythm of the music and not to the staccato beating of his heart.

Elizabeth stared at him and then blinked, as if she did not believe him to exist. "Why, I was quite sure I was going to end up on the *floor*," she said in astonishment. She took a breath and looked about, realizing her new dance partner was doing all the work in keeping them moving.

Had she been unfamiliar with the waltz, she might have stumbled several times just since her new partner's arrival. But this was her third Season, and he was a strong lead. "I must be unharmed as it appears I am dancing, although I must thank you for making all the effort. I have been of absolutely no help," she replied finally, her eyes still wide as they took in the amused expression of her rescuer. Sable hair, cut rather short and combed forward in the latest style framed a face that was not particularly handsome. The bronzed skin suggested a man who spent a great deal of time out of doors—horseback riding, she thought as she considered his developed physique. Tiny lines at the edges of his brown eyes made her guess his age at somewhere near thirty. The straight, sloping brows were full at the base of his high forehead. His eyelids tucked under a stretch of skin that followed the line of his brows, making him appear just a bit sleepy. There was a hint of a hook at the end of his arced and somewhat crooked nose, making her think it might have once been broken. And he had an easy smile that displayed even, white teeth and laugh lines on either side of his mouth.

It was his mouth that had Elizabeth mesmerized.

He had perfect lips. A lower lip that wasn't too full and an upper lip with rounded triangles on either side. Some might call them chiseled. *Kissable lips*, she thought, her face coloring up as she made the assessment. She was suddenly reminded of the kiss the Earl of Trenton had bestowed on her in the garden and quickly put it out of her mind.

"I say, that was rather an abrupt departure on His Grace's part," George began, his eye brows furrowed in feigned disgust. "Are you sure you are unharmed?" he asked as he regarded the young woman, her cream tulle and satin skirts swaying against his legs as the waltz ended.

Elizabeth Carlington smiled as she gazed up at him, the hand she had placed on his shoulder during the dance now lying against her beautiful bosom, just above the edge of her low-cut bodice and the swath of ruched cream tulle decorating the top of her gown. She struggled to catch her breath.

George was awestruck as her eyes again met his, their long lashes framing the wide almond shapes topped by eyebrows that were arched into an expression of delight. Her brilliant smile, outlined by lips that he thought would be delicious to kiss, the straight nose, not too long and not too flared at the bottom, and high cheekbones were encompassed in a perfect oval with a hint of a widow's peak at the very top. And that led to that gorgeous auburn hair, dressed into a mass of curls and adorned with baby's breath and tiny cream rosebuds.

She was a luscious-looking woman, George decided right then.

"I am," she replied, as she took another quick breath and gave him a nod of assurance. "His Grace may not be, I fear," she added, her happy countenance belying her words. "He quite suddenly grew another left foot..." She stopped in mid-sentence, her face coloring to a pink that was quite fetching. "Oh, please forgive me," she breathed, the smile suddenly disappearing from her face.

Realizing what she was about to say, George allowed his own smile to broaden. "There is nothing to forgive, my lady. You made His Grace look a far sight better than he has in years," he declared as he regarded her, suddenly wondering if he should be so bold as to suggest he escort her to supper. Several couples were already leaving the dance floor and moving in that direction. "Forgive me. I am George Bennett-Jones, your servant," he said as he hesitantly reached for her gloved hand, an eyebrow cocking as if to ask permission to kiss the back of it. He wasn't yet used to introducing himself by his title. When he thought to add it at the last minute, he remembered Josephine's instructions and did not offer it.

Her smile slowly returning, Elizabeth removed the hand from between her breasts and held it out to him. With it no longer covering the most beautiful cleavage George had seen the entire night, he was able to sneak a glance at the gentle swell of the tops of her rising moons as he brushed his lips over the back of the cream kid glove. He felt his loins tighten and had to swallow in an effort to regain control of himself.

"Lady Elizabeth... Carlington," she responded as she curt-sied, not taking back her hand with any kind of haste.

"May I escort you to the supper? I realize the Duke of Somerset was probably expecting to do so," George said, *before he grew his additional left foot.*

"I would like that very much, Mr. Bennett-Jones," Elizabeth replied with a shy smile, her gaze never once leaving his to look for the Butter Blond that probably expected to dine with her if she wasn't with the duke.

George offered his arm, and Elizabeth placed her gloved hand on it. A frisson passed through his arm as he felt her light touch. He noticed the contrast of her cream kid gloves on the sleeve of his black satin tailcoat. This was a woman he wanted on his arm at every event, he thought suddenly.

What the hell am I thinking?

They made their way to the supper room. Set up with a dozen round tables dressed in white linens, with crystal and chargers, the room's main feature was its long, well-stocked buffet table. An ice sculpture of a swan bobbed in its own pond atop the table, its neck towering over the roast pig below. Footmen served a variety of foods from several locations and also carried trays with glasses of champagne.

George searched for a table set away from the growing crowd, noticing one in front of a wall of windows that looked out onto a terrace and garden. Paper lanterns lit the gardens beyond the windows, giving the area an ethereal feel, unlike the rest of the supper room. "Will this do for my lady?" he asked as he moved to pull out a chair.

"Of course," she replied without hesitation. She took the chair that George held for her and glanced up at him with an appreciative nod.

George still expected someone to come claim her.

"Might I fill a plate for you? Or would you prefer to join me at the buffet table?" he asked. He noted there were very few woman in the line, and those who were in line were dowagers; most men seemed to see to their lady's meals.

Lady Elizabeth blushed. *She blushed!* "Oh, I do not need an entire supper," she answered, turning to take a glass of champagne from a passing footman. "Perhaps I can just help myself to some nibbles from your plate?" she suggested, her teeth suddenly catching her lower lip and her eyes widening, as if she had caught herself saying something not quite acceptable.

Nibbles!

It was nearly his undoing. Besides the sudden humor George felt at her comment, his cock was responding as if it wanted to *be* one of those nibbles. George tried hard to suppress the grin that tugged at the corner of his mouth and found he could not. "You can help yourself to nibbles from my plate any time, my lady," he said with as much humor as he felt, deciding a bit of flirtation and his easy smile could only help his cause.

Giggling so that a dimple showed in one of her cheeks, Lady

Elizabeth took a sip of champagne and watched as George made his way to the buffet. He felt her eyes on him while he chose foods most easily eaten with fingers, including an array of sweets. When those that recognized him nodded or made comments, he acknowledged in kind but did not initiate any conversation that might keep him from Lady Elizabeth's side any longer than was necessary.

When he returned to their table, he was almost surprised to find her still there, although Lady Charlotte was leaning over Elizabeth's shoulder, speaking in hushed tones. He heard only a snippet of their conversation as he moved to his seat on the other side of Elizabeth, but the snippet included the name of a man who had recently inherited a dukedom.

Joshua Wainwright.

He grimaced as he watched the Earl of Bingham's daughter. A good friend of Lady Elizabeth's, Charlotte had been betrothed to the Earl of Grinstead.

Poor thing.

Having been in Sussex when the Earl of Grinstead and his father died in a horrible house fire—the entire wing of Wisborough Oaks was said to have been destroyed—George could only hope Charlotte was now betrothed to Grinstead's younger brother. The new Duke of Chichester, Joshua Wainwright, had survived the fire, but lay nearly comatose in a London hospital. If one believed the *on-dit* spoken in parlors throughout Mayfair, the young man's body was entirely covered in burns that would leave him disfigured for the rest of his life. *His Grace with half a face,* he had heard someone say at the ball the night before. To hear Lady Charlotte speak of him, though, one was led to believe he would be fully recovered in a few months and ready to take on the duties of his new title.

George decided the truth was somewhere in-between.

And he also knew why Lady Charlotte might welcome the change in future husbands. Grinstead had a penchant for bedding whores even while employing a string of mistresses while Joshua Wainwright's only vice seemed to be gaming hells.

He favored faro but was known to limit his bets to those he could cover with his own allowance.

Given the amount of work the new duke had in front of him, George hoped Lady Charlotte would be at his side as his duchess.

CHAPTER 16
LESSONS OF A MISTRESS PUT INTO PLAY

*J*osephine's advice proved invaluable during the ball's supper, for after Lady Charlotte finished her comment to Lady Elizabeth about the health of Joshua Wainwright, the new Duke of Chichester, Lady Elizabeth introduced George to Lady Charlotte.

"Mr. Bennett-Jones," she started to say, as she indicated him with a wave of her hand.

No one need know you have a title until it becomes necessary for them to know. Use it as a last resort, Josephine had instructed. "Please, call me George," he insisted as he nodded to both ladies. "Everyone else does."

The eyes of both widened, indicating he had shocked them with his plea. "George," Lady Elizabeth said, as if she were saying it for the very first time in her life, drawing out the name so that it was two syllables rather than just the one boring syllable he'd heard hundreds of times in his life. "I would like you to meet Lady Charlotte Bingham, daughter of Lord Ellsworth."

George, who was hearing her say his name in his mind for at least the third time, as if he stood on the edge of a canyon, and it was echoing to him in that marvelous voice of hers, nearly missed the introduction. He knew who Lady Charlotte was, though, since he had been in Sussex during the Wainwright fire. News had reached him that the daughter of Edward Bingham had made a hasty trip to Kirdford to retrieve Joshua Wainwright and arrange his transport to a hospital in London.

George bowed and then took Lady Charlotte's gloved hand to kiss the back of it. "My lady, it is so good to make your acquaintance. I must admit to a hope you will be the next Duchess of Chichester," he said with a solemn nod. "And I look forward to the day Wainwright can assume his duties as duke." He pulled out the chair next to Elizabeth's. "I do hope his recovery is going as well as I have heard. Will you join us?" he added as he held out an arm to indicate the chair next to Elizabeth's.

Lady Charlotte angled her head to one side, the look on her face indicating she was very surprised by his comments. Pleasantly surprised, if one read her reaction correctly.

Charlotte wasn't aware anyone in Sussex even *knew* she was betrothed to the new duke.

At least, she *hoped* she was betrothed to the duke.

And everyone in London seemed to think her betrothed was on his deathbed. Badly burned, yes. Disfigured on one side of his face and along one side of his body, yes. About to die? No.

Not if she could help it.

"Why, thank you... George," she replied, her eyes quickly glancing in Elizabeth's direction before she took the proffered chair and gave George a tentative smile.

Make them feel as if they are the only women in the room, he remembered Josephine telling him. "May I fill a plate for you?" George asked then, noticing Lady Charlotte had neither food nor drink. He motioned for a footman and a glass of champagne was placed in front of Charlotte.

Charlotte exchanged a quick look with Elizabeth, noticing the filled plate George had deposited in front of her. "That's very kind of you, George, but a footman can see to my meal." She nodded to the servant nearest their table and pointed at the plate that rested in front of Elizabeth. The servant took note, nodded, and was off to the buffet table. "I feel as if I have interrupted," she spoke quietly, as George took the chair on the other side of Elizabeth.

Lady Elizabeth shook her head. "Not at all. George escorted me to supper since he so elegantly rescued me from a fate worse than death." She reached out with a gloved hand to pat his sleeve. Warmth crept through his arm at her light touch.

Lady Charlotte's eyes widened at the implication of Elizabeth's statement.

Keep your compliments light and be self-deprecating when it makes sense to do so.

George leaned forward a bit to catch Lady Charlotte's eye. "She means the Duke of Somerset, of course," he said in a teasing voice. "I just happened to be in the right spot when he grew another left foot. Although if I had not been, Lady Elizabeth would have managed to finish the supper dance even more beautifully without me." He finished his comment by winking at Elizabeth, the wink witnessed by her and her friend but by no one else in the room.

Elizabeth's sudden inhalation of breath was quickly covered by her hand while it was Charlotte's turn to giggle. "George," she whispered in astonishment. "Everyone *knows* the Duke of Somerset already *has* two left feet!" The three of them broke out into laughter that drew the attention of several nearby diners, who, when they determined the joke was private, merely smiled and returned to their suppers.

Ask questions that show you are truly interested. And then listen *to their replies.*

"So, tell me Lady Elizabeth. What is your favorite entertainment?" he asked, noting the footman was setting down a plate full of a little bit of everything in front of Lady Charlotte. Her eyes were once again wide as she took in the sight. George took the opportunity to eat a sweetmeat from the plate he and Elizabeth were sharing, although Elizabeth had so far only helped herself to a strawberry. He'd watched in agony—as her lips surrounded the red fruit, as her fingertips pulled out the stem and leaves, as she swallowed the ripe berry—before she turned to answer his question.

He found himself wondering if she would ever allow him to feed her.

"I rather enjoy the theatre, but I find that those in the audience seem far more interested in the rest of the audience rather than in what is happening on the stage," she responded before helping herself to something else on the plate.

"And isn't that because you *are* more interesting?" he countered playfully. *Dare I say what I really want to say?* The words were out of his mouth before he could censor them. "You're certainly more lovely than any of the actresses in Drury Lane. But I digress. Opera or plays?"

The two ladies exchanged quick glances, as if they couldn't believe their supper companion's banter. "You are too kind, George," Elizabeth said in response to the compliment as she blushed. "I prefer plays," she added, attempting to keep her lips in a tight line but failing. A brilliant smile appeared.

"Forgive us, George," Charlotte said as she leaned forward to better see him. "Lady Elizabeth and I just saw *A Midsummer's Night Dream* last night, and we were most amused by the story."

"And by a certain actor," Elizabeth interrupted before rolling her eyes. "He made a spectacle of himself, and he had the entire audience laughing so hard, the other actors could not speak their lines."

George grinned. Although he hadn't been to the theatre in months, he was at least familiar with some of Shakespeare's works. "A fan of the Bard, are you?" he asked then, hoping he wasn't getting into the wrong territory. He knew immediately after he asked the question that he was, but it was too late to steer the conversation to a different topic.

Elizabeth sobered quickly, considering his question. "The comedies, yes. The tragedies, not especially."

Charlotte placed a hand on Elizabeth's arm. "We've had a bit too much tragedy in real life," she said, and dropped her eyes to their dinner plates. Between the two women, they had managed to eat most of the finger foods from both plates.

George thought at first the tragedy to which they referred was the quick consumption of their food, but he gave up on that idea when Elizabeth reached out and helped herself to the last of the rolls of roast beef and cheese.

Offer condolences when appropriate, help when needed, and be a knight in shining armor whenever given the opportunity.

Taking on a look of concern, George said, "I am, of course, familiar with your tragedy, Lady Charlotte, but Lady Elizabeth, whatever has happened?"

The woman dared a glance in his direction, her solemn face suddenly turning a bright pink. Her eyes glanced at the chandeliers above before she returned her attention to George. Lady Charlotte's face took on a look of curiosity, as if she wasn't already privy to the tragedy that had beset Lady Elizabeth.

"Oh, my dear Lady Elizabeth, whatever has happened?" George asked, his voice full of concern as he reached over to take her hand in his. He placed his other hand atop hers, stroking it gently.

Suddenly embarrassed and a bit surprised he would take her hand in his, Elizabeth took a deep breath, her glance dropping to his hands. *I have to tell someone!* "This is not nearly so tragic as what Lady Charlotte has had to endure, I assure you. In fact, you both will likely find it... humorous. Even so, you must promise you won't... please say you won't laugh at me." This edict was directed at both George and Charlotte. "And you cannot think ill of me, for I was not a willing participant," she added with a quick shake of her head.

"Of course, I will not," George promised, his hands tightening over one of hers. He felt her pulse quicken. Was he holding her hand too tightly and cutting off her circulation? He didn't sense she wanted him to let go, so he simply held on.

"*I* certainly will not," Charlotte agreed, now hanging onto Elizabeth's other hand.

Elizabeth closed her eyes, causing the tears that had welled up to spill out the corners. "I experienced my first kiss earlier this evening," she announced quietly, her eyes opening and still bright with tears. "I did not initiate it, of course. It happened quite by surprise," she said in her own defense. There were those who thought a kiss before marriage scandalous, after all. "And it was *horrible!*" She could hardly believe she was telling a stranger she'd been kissed! And badly. *What must this man think of me?*

Glancing at Elizabeth's empty champagne glass, Charlotte knew why her friend's tongue was so loose.

George's first thought had him believing he had somehow become the brunt of a joke the two girls were playing. Perhaps Elizabeth had seen him behind the hedgerow and knew he had paid witness to at least the sound of her kiss with Butter Blond. But Charlotte's mouth had dropped open. She closed it, although she was obviously stunned by Elizabeth's announcement. George wondered if her shock was due to Elizabeth's admission about being kissed or because the kiss had been horrible.

He fished his handkerchief out of his waistcoat pocket, silently praising Elkins for having insisted he take one with his initials embroidered in one corner. Handing it to Lady Elizabeth, he said quietly. "I wish to offer my sincerest condolences, Lady Elizabeth, and assure you that whoever kissed you probably lacked any... proper instruction... in the art of kissing," he managed to get out, his voice sounding appropriately solemn.

"Proper instruction?" Charlotte repeated, her eyes once again wide with surprise.

"The art of kissing?" Elizabeth repeated, her attention entirely on George. "It's an *art?*"

George's eyes flicked between the two ladies. "Well, of course," he replied hesitantly, rather enjoying the attention the women showered on him at that moment. A brilliant idea formed in his head, almost too fast for him to fully consider before he blurted, "Should you wish me to, I would be happy to help erase the memory of that horrible kiss with one far more suited to you, Lady Elizabeth."

Lady Elizabeth batted her eyelashes at least three times, her expression of surprise matched by Lady Charlotte.

George's eyes were so captivated by the aquamarine of Elizabeth's, he couldn't look away. Indeed, he decided he could drown in them quite happily. The impertinence of his offer suddenly struck him, though, and he finally closed his own eyes, breaking the spell she had cast over him. "Forgive me," he begged then, swallowing in disgust at himself. *What have I done?* He was convinced he had ruined his chances with the beautiful woman.

Apologize! He could hear Josephine's voice in his head even as he realized he must make amends.

"Lady Elizabeth, it was most... inappropriate of me to make you such an offer. Can you ever forgive me?" He dared to look into her eyes again and was surprised by what he found there. For he discovered her gaze was not one of disgust or offense, but rather one of... interest... intrigue, perhaps, as if his suggestion held some merit for her.

"Are you claiming, George Bennett-Jones, that you are a better kisser than Lord Trenton?" Elizabeth asked, her voice so low he barely heard it above the din of nearby diners. Her lips were entirely too close to his jaw, so close he could feel her warm breath wash over his skin. If he turned his face just so, he could capture those lips with his own and prove his point that very instant. But the words she had just spoken were finally percolating into his addled brain.

Are you a better kisser than Lord Trenton?

George had to use every bit of control he possessed to keep his face impassive and to prevent his impulse to shout out in pure, unadulterated joy. "Yes, I suppose I am," he agreed with a careful nod, allowing his face to take on the expression that Josephine assured him made him look most handsome.

He dared a glance at Charlotte, wondering if she was privy to Elizabeth's words. Would he need to prove himself to her, too? Because, as he gave *that* thought some consideration, he knew he had no intention of kissing the woman Joshua Wainwright should be marrying.

But he suddenly had *every* intention of kissing Lady Elizabeth Carlington.

"I must think on this," Elizabeth replied quietly, swallowing nervously and taking a deep breath as she continued to regard him with those gorgeous eyes.

"Of course," George stated, nodding with what he hoped

looked like reassurance. Thinking fast, he determined his moment of opportunity was about to pass. The musicians would begin to play shortly, and those in the supper room would soon be making their way back to the ballroom. "May I inquire, Lady Elizabeth, do you plan to attend Lady Worthington's ball?" The widow always hosted an early autumn ball, an event considered a requirement for unmarried ladies to attend, as Lady Worthington saw to it that every eligible bachelor worth any kind of fortune was invited.

At one point, George thought Adele Slater Worthington hosted the event so she might find a suitable groom for herself.

Lady Worthington had been married to Samuel Worthington, a self-made man who had earned his fortune building the early steamships. When he died quite suddenly, the glamorous woman was left with a vast fortune—a fortune entirely available for her to spend as she saw fit. Her charities included help for war orphans and war widows, but many suitors hoped she could be persuaded to marry so that she might use it to pay off their gambling debts.

William Weston—a distant cousin to John Weston, the tailor—had almost managed to get Lady Worthington to the altar. Her discovery of his excessive debts prompted the widow to call off the wedding, however. She had later explained to a friend that the damning information had been delivered in the form of a letter from Lady Ellsworth, who claimed to have learned of Weston's debts when she overheard her husband talking with Milton Grandby, Earl of Torrington. George thought it rather fortuitous timing for the earl, for no sooner had the wedding been called off than Lord Torrington started paying calls on the widow. The two had spent the entire Season attending every event as a couple and most of the summer together at his estate. Now Torrington would be standing alongside Lady Worthington, playing host for the ball that would take place two night's hence.

"Oh, yes. I am very much looking forward to Lady Worthington's ball," Elizabeth replied as she turned to her friend. "You are coming, too, Lottie?" she asked. "Lady Worthington's balls are always the very best."

Charlotte smiled demurely. "I will be there, of course," she agreed, and then leaned around Elizabeth to ask George, "And are you planning to attend, George?" She seemed to struggle with using his first name, as if she thought she was committing some kind of *faux pax* by being so familiar.

"Indeed. In fact, I asked in the hopes that I might secure an early reservation on your dance cards. I expect you'll both be rather in demand, and if I should be a bit late in arriving, I would be bereft at finding your cards already full," he explained, one open hand landing on his chest as he made the claim.

Elizabeth giggled, a charming sound that forced him to regard her for a moment, his gaze once again mesmerized by her eyes. "I shall leave *two* dances for you, George," she said then, her smile slowly disappearing until she added, "But that does not mean we have to spend the time dancing." This last line was delivered in a near whisper, her face turned toward him completely, so Charlotte couldn't overhear nor see her lips move.

The connotation of her statement was perfectly clear to George. His heart leapt in his chest, and he suddenly had trouble breathing.

"And I shall leave you one," Charlotte promised, unaware that George was about to expire from the sheer excitement Elizabeth's hint had caused in him.

The sounds of instruments being tuned filtered into the supper room, and the murmur of conversation halted as those around them began to take their leave. George nodded to Charlotte, "Thank you, my lady," he acknowledged as he stood up and offered his hand to Elizabeth. "May I escort you two back to the ballroom?" he asked then, hoping his voice was louder than the pounding of his heart.

He was sure everyone in the room could hear it.

"I believe I have that honor," David Carlington said as he stepped up behind the ladies. The Marquess of Morganfield, his green eyes especially bright from having drunk a few too many glasses of champagne, nodded at George. "Thank you for escorting my daughter," he added. Although the statement might have seemed perfunctory to anyone listening, George didn't take offense.

"It was my pleasure," George responded, ducking his chin in return. "Ladies, I shall take my leave. I look forward to dancing with you both at Lady Worthington's ball," he finished graciously. "My lord," he added as he bowed. Once Morganfield acknowledged his bow with a slight nod, George took his leave of the supper room and headed straight for the card room.

CHAPTER 17
AN ODD NIGHT REVIEWED

*L*ady Elizabeth placed her hand on her father's arm while Lady Charlotte did the same on the other side of the marquess. Elizabeth was tempted to watch George as he took his leave of the supper room, but she forced herself to look instead to her father.

"Was it acceptable for me to allow him to escort me to supper?" Elizabeth asked as she followed her father's lead. "The Duke of Somerset suffered a mishap of some sort," she added, noticing that her father was frowning.

"The heel of His Grace's shoe came loose," the marquess explained as he paused to allow Charlotte to precede him through the ballroom doors. Charlotte stepped aside to allow him and Elizabeth to come alongside once they were through the crowded opening. "It was most fortuitous that you had someone come to your rescue," he added as he grinned, his smile a bit crooked. "Better George than some rake."

Elizabeth stepped back near a potted palm and turned to regard her father. "You know him then?" she asked, her lips left parted by her question.

David Carlington paused in mid-step, as if pondering the question. "Of course. An honorable man. I would trust him with you," he commented as his gaze swept the room, his eyes finally finding his prey. "I will leave you ladies to your dancing.

My next dance partner has just come out of the retiring room, and she looks quite lovely, wouldn't you agree?"

Elizabeth turned to look in the direction her father indicated. Seeing her red satin-clad mother making her way in their direction, she smiled broadly. "Oh, Father. You are such a romantic," she whispered.

She was secretly pleased her father seemed to be so in love with her mother.

It hadn't always been that way. When Elizabeth was younger, her parents carried on as if their arranged marriage would never be anything more than a marriage of convenience. Once her younger brother was born, her father renewed his contract with his long-time mistress, and her mother busied herself with affairs of the marquessate and various charities. If the marchioness cuckolded her husband, she did so most discreetly, for there was never any scandal associated with the Morganfields. But Elizabeth lived with the estrangement long enough to realize something wasn't quite right in her parents' relationship. They loved one another, she was sure, but didn't seem to know how to go about being a husband and wife. When scandal erupted, it did so on the political front. Her father was forced to give up his power and influence in Parliament. There had been several weeks when neither of her parents were in residence at Carlington House. And then... things slowly changed.

Now, Adeline and David Carlington behaved like happily married newlyweds.

Elizabeth grinned as she watched them meet on the dance floor, finally turning to her friend when she noticed Charlotte trying to get her attention.

She followed Charlotte as her older friend led her to the retiring room. Once inside, they rushed to take a place on one of the chaise lounges.

"What was *that* all about?" Lady Charlotte asked as she watched Elizabeth shake her skirts out before taking a seat next to her. Charlotte's gloved hand clutched Elizabeth's wrist and shook it, a testament to her building curiosity.

Realizing Charlotte referred to the supper they had shared with George Bennett-Jones, Elizabeth finally settled her gaze on her best friend. "I have absolutely no idea!" she replied, her head shaking a bit. A delighted grin graced her face. The events of the last hour had been most odd!

Just the day before, she had received a short missive from Elizabeth Cunningham Statton, the Duchess of Somerset, imploring her to see to it the Duke of Somerset danced at least once during the Weatherstone ball.

I know this will seem awkward, but if Somerset does not ask upon your meeting him (and he had better, as I have ordered him to do so, and he knows what my retribution will be if he does not), then please offer your arm and insist he join you for a turn about the room. I would hate to think of him keeping company with a potted palm, and he would do that very thing as he is more bored by playing cards than by plant life. The children and I will join him in London the day of the ball (but I don't plan to attend as I expect to arrive too late). This will be my first Little Season in London in over five years, and I finally have my figure restored to the way it was when I married my duke. I have every intention of attending every ball! I so look forward to seeing you again, Sincerely yours, Beth.

To think, her older friend from finishing school, now a duchess and mother of four children, expected her to dance with her duke! So when Lady Elizabeth Carlington arranged her introduction to Jeremy, Duke of Somerset, and mentioned that the duchess expected her to dance with him, the duke's face had brightened, and then he had *laughed!* The kind of laughter that, despite the crush in the ballroom, was overheard by anyone standing within ten feet of them.

Suddenly mortified, Elizabeth gave the man a quick curtsy and was about to step away when he suddenly stilled her by cupping her elbow with his gloved hand. The kid leather was soft and warm against her skin as he slid his arm beneath hers, making it look to anyone who might be watching that Elizabeth had offered her arm to the duke.

"Forgive me, Lady Elizabeth, but I was expecting Beth's friend to be... well," he paused and lowered his face so that it was closer to the side of hers. "Not a woman of your beauty, certainly," he quickly explained, the mirth still evident in his dark blue eyes. Momentarily confused, Elizabeth searched the duke's face for some inkling that he was teasing her. But she found his manner quite sincere. "You see, my wife believes I am too shy to arrange my own dances," he added when he saw Elizabeth's expression.

"And you are not," Elizabeth stated, her momentary confusion dissipating as she regarded the handsome, young duke. Was he even thirty? No wonder Elizabeth Cunningham, the daughter of a viscount, found the man irresistible! Of course, when her friend had married him, he was merely the second son of a duke and not ever expected to inherit his father's title. But when a boating accident took the lives of his father and elder brother, Jeremy Statton was forced to take on the dukedom, and her friend was suddenly a duchess.

"I was at one time, I suppose," he admitted as he led them to the refreshment table. "But after five years in Parliament and five years of dealing with tenants, and five years of marriage, and four children, I find I can converse easily with just about anyone. Helps to be a duke, I suppose," he said as he handed her a glass of champagne. "You are allowed, I hope?" he asked before he placed the glass into her raised hand.

"I am," Lady Elizabeth replied with a nod as she resisted the urge to sound offended. The duke was not at all what she expected. He was far more confident than Beth had led her to believe. "Beth insisted I see to it you danced..." She stopped and inhaled sharply. "Forgive me, Your Grace. *Her Grace*," she corrected herself, her face coloring in embarrassment. How could she forget propriety so quickly? Just because she had known Elizabeth Cunningham as a viscount's daughter and not a duchess did not give her the right to be so familiar now!

"It's quite all right, my lady," the duke said with a wave of his bejeweled hand. "Beth has frequently spoken of you. She's very fond of you and wondered at when you might finally marry one of these..." He waved his arm in the direction of several young gentlemen grouped near the doors leading to the terraced gardens.

Elizabeth felt her face redden even more. "I've not yet been made an offer," she answered, keeping a smile pasted on her face.

There had been talk her first Season. A young earl seemed set to ask for her hand, and then *something* had happened. He had shown up at the last ball of that season with a rather plump young lady on his arm. The gossip had it they had married by special license, and that the earl had suddenly come into a good deal of money. Not particularly disappointed, since the earl didn't suit her, and even more important to her, he didn't seem to suit her father—even though her father never said anything to indicate he didn't want her marrying the earl—Elizabeth figured her second Season would provide more agreeable marriage opportunities. Indeed, there were more eligible gentlemen, but there were also more marriageable daughters of the *ton*. And the young baron who showed the most interest suddenly... did not. Her father finally admitted his complicity in the baron's abrupt disinterest, explaining that the young man's political future was cloudy at best and that his fortune was far too small to support a wife.

And now, in her third Season, Elizabeth was more mature and considered one of the most beautiful prospects. The Earl of Trenton seemed most interested in courting her. Now that they had danced several times, including a waltz earlier this evening, and he had taken her in his curricle for a ride through the park during the fashionable hour, Elizabeth was quite sure this was the Season she would become engaged. And she was quite sure Gabriel Wellingham, the Earl of Trenton, would be her husband. By Christmastime.

She could only hope they would never have to kiss one another.

As if toasting the thought, she took a sip of champagne.

The Duke of Somerset regarded her with a grin. "I have it on good authority a gentleman who is present this very evening has intentions of asking for your hand," he stated with an arched eyebrow, the look making his debonaire features seem a bit rakish.

"Indeed?" she answered, somewhat breathless at hearing a duke confirm what she had already suspected. *Gabriel will ask for my hand!* she thought with some relief. She finished off the champagne and a footman retrieved her glass even before she could look about for a place to set it down.

Jeremy smiled. "My Beth will be so thrilled. As a young matron who has already given me four children, she's feeling as if all her friends have forgotten her."

Elizabeth shook her head. "We have not," she replied quickly. "I will be sure to call upon her when she arrives in town. When do you expect that will be?"

The duke shrugged. "She arrived tonight, just as I was taking my leave. She will be very pleased to know you still hold her in high regard, so to prove it, I beg you pay a call on her tomorrow." He glanced about the room, aware of the orchestra beginning the next dance. "And now, my lady, it sounds as if the next dance is about to begin." He held out his hand, expecting Elizabeth to place hers in it. Elizabeth paused, a bit startled that he expected her to dance. It was the supper dance, after all, and he had not claimed it on her card, though no one else had, either. "It would be my honor," she breathed, suddenly aware that it was not only the supper dance, but a waltz!

The two stepped to the edge of the crowd surrounding the ballroom floor and were suddenly moving in time with dozens of other couples. A better dancer than the Earl of Trenton and much taller, the Duke of Somerset swept her about the room, his hold on her quite firm and his steps perfectly placed. It was a marvelous dance, and it left Elizabeth feeling as if she was being shown off to everyone in the room. The sensation of spinning was dizzying. The lights from the candles above highlighted the red in her auburn hair. And somewhere along the edge of the crowd, her future husband was probably watching her.

It could not have been a more perfect night.

And then she had been sent spinning into the arms of George Bennett-Jones.

What a very odd night!

Realizing she still held George's handkerchief, Elizabeth slowly spread open the white linen across her lap. "GBJ," she murmured as she studied the embroidered initials in one corner. "Who *are* you?"

CHAPTER 18
UNREHEARSED MANEUVERS
IN REVIEW

"I owe you a debt of gratitude, Your Grace," George said in a lowered voice as he stood next to the Duke of Somerset. They were near the entrance of the room that had been set up for cards, supposedly considering which game to join. "Your timing was impeccable, as was your placement. It almost looked as if we rehearsed it," he added, obviously pleased with the evening's second waltz. They couldn't have planned the maneuver any better, nor the fact that it gave George the opportunity to escort Lady Elizabeth to the supper. That she had so readily agreed still had George thanking his lucky stars.

"My pleasure, truly," Jeremy Statton replied happily, having a hard time keeping his grin in check. "The look on her face was..." He shook his head, apparently unable to come up with the appropriate words. "I shall have Beth in giggles when I tell her what we did. Hell, *I'll* be in good humor every time I think of it."

Alarmed by the thought the duke would share the details of their plot with his wife, George regarded his friend for a moment. "Do you think that's wise?" he asked aloud, his brows furrowed with worry. "What if Her Grace tells Lady Elizabeth? She'll think me a *rake*!"

The duke stifled a laugh as he used his embroidered handkerchief to dab at his eyes. "Trust me, Bostwick. There isn't a person at this ball who would ever mistake *you* for a rake," he said jovially. The laughter the man had been holding in was finally allowed to burble forth, and several card players turned in their direction to determine what the duke found so amusing.

Although the verbal jab was meant as a compliment, George felt it as if it had been delivered into his belly by a closed fist.

It was true, though, he knew.

No one in the *ton* would ever consider him a danger when it came to their wives or daughters. George Bennett-Jones could be trusted with any of them. Why, he had even overheard the Marquess of Morganfield tell Lady Elizabeth he trusted him with her.

Sometimes living an honorable life made for a milquetoast existence.

Or, perhaps not.

Perhaps it was that very trust that could work in his favor, he realized suddenly. For who would ever expect George Bennett-Jones to waltz off with their daughter in front of the entire *ton*? Or kiss her until she whimpered? Or do anything else the least bit scandalous with her? And with Lady Elizabeth assured he could be trusted...

Not certain he could behave in an aristocratic manner for the remainder of the evening, George made his excuses with the Duke of Somerset and took his leave. As he sat in his new town coach, he grinned the entire trip to Josephine's.

CHAPTER 19
LOVE AT FIRST SIGHT

*I*f there was such a thing as love at first sight, then George Bennett-Jones would have to admit he had experienced it first-hand. Aggravating, exciting, painful, unexpected, frightening and quite delightful, the sensation of being in love was so new to him, he hardly knew how to behave.

This sensation was nothing like what he felt for Josephine. His mistress didn't make his heart race—at least, not outside of the bed where they engaged in an occasional tumble. She didn't have him pining to see her. Or anxious to arrange a floral delivery from a local hothouse.

He wondered if it had been apparent to his peers at the ball that he was undoubtedly, unbelievably, unquestionably and hopelessly in love.

In a word, he was *doomed.*

Elizabeth Carlington. He spoke her name in his mind, allowing the shape of the words to form on his tongue and lips. And he remembered how she had said his name. *Gee-orge,* as if the word was made up of two syllables instead of just the one, so that from her lips, the name was almost... exotic. And her lips when she said his name, well, when she said *anything,* they were positively... He was glad he was in his town coach when he noticed the uncomfortable bulge in his breeches.

A vision of Lady Elizabeth came to him again. *How can a*

woman have such glorious auburn hair? he wondered, remembering how the reds and golds shone under the candlelight of the massive chandeliers that lit Lord Weatherstone's ballroom. It was her hair that made him glance in her direction the very first time he noticed her there. He hadn't had the chance to see her clearly the day he had discovered her shopping with Lady Charlotte. Her bonnet had completely hidden her gorgeous features while he held the door for her. And then to learn it was Lady Elizabeth beneath that bonnet had been a happy accident. Her maid had been flirting with his tiger, unaware of George listening to their banter from inside the town coach.

With his first sight of Elizabeth, George knew she was her own glorious sun, her smile and auburn hair radiating light and warmth as she moved effortlessly across the ballroom floor. Unfortunately, at the moment he saw her for the first time, her planet was Wellingham. With his butter blond curls, bright blue eyes and once boyish features finally hardening into handsome lines, the young earl was a perfect contrast to Lady Elizabeth's coloring. Given their families' status in the *ton*—her the daughter of a marquess and him the Earl of Trenton—they were a perfect match.

George found himself wondering when the betrothal would be announced.

And quite suddenly, a curl of jealousy formed within his belly. It was an unfamiliar sensation, one that had him feeling a bit annoyed and a bit off-kilter and just a bit... possessive. *What the hell is wrong with me?* he wondered suddenly. *I only danced with her.* And he planned to send a contribution to her charity, anonymously, if her father wasn't funding it as George suspected.

But there had been that wonderful conversation during the supper, and the look in her eyes when he had rescued her from the duke, and the way she had said, "George." A man could do no better than Lady Elizabeth Carlington, he had found himself thinking, just before the second waltz.

And the Earl of Trenton had apparently come to the same conclusion.

The thought again rankled George. Why should he allow the earl to court Lady Elizabeth unfettered? *I have as much right to court her as any other unmarried man in the ton.*

Well, he did if her father gave his permission. And if she allowed him to, of course.

George shook himself out of his reverie. *Court Lady Elizabeth?* What could he be thinking? Even if Josephine thought he needed to find a wife, did he really need to right now? Courting meant an eventual engagement which invariably led to marriage which usually resulted in a nursery full of children and a life of never-ending responsibility. He prided himself on having successfully avoided the state of matrimony for the nine years during which he could have been legally leg-shackled.

And who was he to think he could court Lady Elizabeth when the Earl of Trenton seemed ready to ask for her hand? George was merely a viscount. With a net worth maybe a third of the earl's, and an ugly puss for a face...

Well, *ugly* might be a strong word, he amended, remembering that Josephine thought him quite handsome when he smiled.

But he certainly couldn't hold a candle to Butter Blond's fair complexion, blue eyes, and those curls that seemed to have all the young ladies of the *ton* batting their lashes at him.

The Earl of Trenton was the epitome of what the ladies of the *ton* found most appealing.

And George Bennett-Jones was not.

CHAPTER 20
CONFESSIONS OF A MAN
IN LOVE

"Well?"

George looked up to find Josephine standing over him, her hands clasped together as if she were trying to keep them still. His mistress had been in her bedchamber, just about to retire for the night, when she had seen George's town coach from her window. She watched as it rumbled around the corner and made its way down the alley behind her townhouse, as if it were heading for the mews at one end of the street. Given his penchant for discretion, Josephine wasn't surprised when George entered her house through the back door, letting himself in with a key he kept hidden somewhere in the garden statuary.

Somewhat amused at her increasing impatience, George leaned back in the overstuffed chair in Josephine's parlor and took a slow sip of brandy. He was tempted to make her wait a good deal longer before he regaled her with stories from that evening's ball, but he wanted desperately to tell someone of his success. His friend Teddy was no doubt abed at this time of the night, given his need to be at the bank at an ungodly hour in the morning. And he knew Josephine wanted to hear about the ball from someone other than a Cyprian who might have been in attendance.

"I danced with Lady Elizabeth," he stated with a curt nod.

At Josephine's expression of surprise, he added, "The second half of a waltz. The supper dance, no less. I owe the Duke of Somerset a huge favor in helping arrange the situation to my benefit."

Josephine blinked, the curve of her lip slowly lifting into a tentative smile. "And?" she encouraged, wanting to know more.

"I escorted her to the supper." He wasn't disappointed when Josephine's face brightened even more. "I brought her a plate of nibbles and conversed with her and Lady Charlotte until the orchestra resumed their play." He took another sip of brandy, rather enjoying his mistress' reaction to his description of the evening's highlights.

"Go on!" Josephine nearly shouted.

George smiled, the expression making his eyes light up and his face lift into its most handsome visage. "I asked for a dance at Lady Worthington's ball and have been assured I will have *two* saved for me." He watched as Josephine took a seat in the settee directly across from his chair. "And I have reason to believe that one of those dances will not be for dancing, but rather for me to demonstrate the art of *kissing*." With that last comment, George finished off his brandy, giving Josephine a look of satisfaction that suggested he was a cat who had just been given a rather large bowl of cream.

Josephine's sigh filled the suddenly quiet parlor. "Indeed?" she replied, her smile quite broad. "Oh, well done, George," she said, quickly standing up and moving to place her hands on either side of his face. She kissed him on the forehead. "And do you think the two of you will suit?" she asked carefully.

Perhaps it was too early for George to decide if the daughter of David Carlington would make a suitable wife. If not her, though, Josephine was at a loss as to who else might. The other eligible young ladies of the Little Season were a collection of simpering idiots and three older girls who were clearly blue-stockings. Although George would probably do fine with a bluestocking, Josephine would prefer he marry a woman with better political connections in the *ton*.

"I think I may be in love with her."

The comment had been made in such a quiet voice, Josephine wasn't quite sure she had heard correctly. "Oh," she replied with a quick nod. "Well, that was... this is... a bit—"

"Unexpected, I know," George finished for her, a sigh escaping as he leaned forward in the chair. The smile he had displayed only moments before was replaced with a look of sadness. "Streater warned me, you must know. He said I would like her."

Catching her lip with a tooth, Josephine regarded George in surprise. "Did he now?" She took a breath and glanced off to one side. "I saw him today. At... At the bank. He looked... he looked as if he had never lost his arm," she stammered suddenly. "How can that be, George? And how does Mr. Streater know Lady Elizabeth?" she asked suddenly, turning to face him again.

George leaned back in the chair and closed his eyes, wondering at Josephine's discomfiture. He had never known her to stammer, never known her to seem unsure of herself, never known her to be anything other than a confident, proud consort. "He was her first... client, I suppose you would call him. For her charity. 'Lady E's Finding Work for the Wounded.' She negotiated with Whittaker for Teddy's position at the bank. And it sounds as if his artificial arm, which Lady E arranged to have made, is a success."

Josephine cocked her head to one side. "So, there is more to Lady Elizabeth than just a pretty face?" she commented lightly, wondering if the girl's father was behind the charity. David Carlington had complained on more than one occasion that supporting his wife's charities was a drain on his finances. Josephine made a mental note to ask the marquess when she next paid him a visit. A frown suddenly replaced her smile.

"What of Trenton? Was he there?"

The look of satisfaction on George's face was replaced with one of disgust. Rolling his eyes, he pinched the top of his nose with his thumb and forefinger. "Yes, he was there."

"Did he kiss her?" Josephine asked, her own expression one of worry. "Did anyone pay witness—?"

"Yes, and no. At least, not if you don't count me," George

replied with a self-deprecating smile. At Josephine's worried look, he smiled quite broadly. "Lady Elizabeth said his kiss was horrible." He watched in delight as Josephine's expression changed.

"Say it again?" she whispered.

"It was horrible. And he apparently licked her. Which only made it worse for him."

When he heard his mistress giggle, he blinked.

He had never heard Josephine giggle before.

She sounded like a young schoolgirl who had just been chased by the ducks on the Serpentine. "Oh, George. You really must warn me before you tell me such stories," Josephine admonished him, one of her arms wrapped in front of her waist as if she had to hold herself up.

George regarded her with a tightly controlled grin. "Which is why I'll be demonstrating the art of kissing at Lady Worthington's ball," he stated as seriously as he could given Josephine's reaction. "Lady Elizabeth will be my subject. I'm thinking the library will be a suitable setting."

He rather enjoyed watching Josephine then. Seeing her facial expression change from one of amusement to one of astonishment. Seeing her eyes suddenly regard him with newfound respect.

"Well done, George," she whispered, a grin still on her face.

Everyone thought they could trust George Bennett-Jones, Viscount Bostwick. It was past time he made his honorable trait work in his favor.

Standing up from the chair, George took Josephine's hand and kissed the back of it. "Thank you," he said before he kissed her cheek. "You made this evening possible, you must know." For a moment, he thought he might ask if he could spend the night, but the image of Lady Elizabeth appeared in his mind's eye and he thought better of it.

Giving Josephine a quick hug, George took his leave of her and headed to his townhouse in Park Lane.

CHAPTER 21
THOUGHTS ON A BALL
OVERCOME BOREDOM

The following day

George sat in the House of Lords, his periwig creating an itch he could not scratch, while he attempted to listen to the Lord Chancellor. He managed to follow the discourse for nearly a half hour before boredom forced him to glance around the chambers. Again. He noted that the Marquess of Devonville seemed especially attentive, his scowl suggesting he disagreed with what was being said.

The marquess had held court the night before in the card room at Lord Weatherstone's ball. He complained of being confounded by his daughter, Lady Hannah Slater. Due to two years of mourning—both her mother and then an aunt had died quite suddenly—she was finally having her first Season at the ripe old age of twenty. And despite being a beauty, she had yet to secure a husband from the half-dozen young gents who called on her. She claimed to prefer the company of one Harold MacDuff, an unfashionably large Alpenmastiff that followed her everywhere and left gobs of slobber in his wake.

"She insists she wants a man only with whom to have children," Lord Devonville complained as he lit his second cheroot of the evening. "Says that men only love their mistresses, and so she is only interested in a husband for the children he can give her."

George had listened intently, surprised that a woman of only twenty could already know what it took most women in the *ton* years to figure out—mistresses were a man's passion while wives were merely the mothers of their children.

Perhaps Lady Hannah's mother had explained it to her when she was younger.

But as George thought more about it, he knew he did not really *love* his own mistress. At least, not in the romantic, passionate way in which he thought Lady Hannah meant.

The way he felt about Elizabeth.

Josephine Wentworth had become his best friend and confidante, it was true, but he could not claim to be in *love* with her.

And he hadn't bedded his mistress in several weeks.

"It sounds as if your daughter knows you too well," the Earl of Torrington teased the marquess from his place at a card table. "And her dog is very intelligent."

Devonville pointed his cheroot in the earl's direction. "Damn you, Grandby, you know I never loved *any* of my mistresses," he shot back, although there was no animosity in the rebuke. The comment was followed by light laughter, but George noticed the look of hurt in Devonville's eyes as he resumed smoking. The marquess might have married for convenience, but, by the time he had lost his wife to a sudden fever, he dearly loved her.

And the man hadn't employed a mistress in a very long time.

George thought of Josephine and wondered when he might see her again. These days, to say he employed her as his mistress would be stretching the truth, he knew. At one time, he had looked forward to his twice-weekly visits with her. But after his uncle's death and his inheritance of the viscountcy, George found he looked forward more to the time they spent in conversation than the time they spent in her bed.

Now, during his visits, which tended to be during tea time, they met in her parlor and spoke of politics, gossip and the arts of seduction and sex. These last topics sometimes led them upstairs, where she tutored him in kissing, foreplay and how to make love while in a variety of positions. The last time he had shared her bed was more than a month ago, when she had taught him how to use his tongue on her most intimate parts in order to send her into ecstasy. Her lesson proved so effective she succumbed to *la petite mort*, leaving George wondering what he had done wrong.

Josephine was finally revived with the help of a vinaigrette he used so liberally the bedchamber smelled of the vile odor for the remainder of the night, forcing them to retire to another bedchamber. She explained what had happened, praising his lovemaking skills as she did so. Not quite sure he wanted his mistress to faint on him again, though, he had avoided bedding her in favor of conversation.

Armed with what he thought was enough information to get him through a *ton* ball or any society event, George agreed to Josephine's suggestion that he attend three events scheduled during the next week— Lord Weatherstone's ball, Lady Worthington's ball, and a tour of the latest acquisitions at the British Museum. He promised Josephine he would use those occasions to seek out and speak only with members of the fairer sex. He had also promised Josephine he would ask at least one lady to accompany him in his curricle for a drive in Hyde Park.

One down, two to go.

CHAPTER 22
SUITABILITY

ady Hannah Slater regarded Lady Elizabeth as she sat on the edge of the settee in the Devonville House parlor. She and her best friends had left the Weatherstone ball precisely at one and shared Hannah's coach for the short trip to the other end of Park Lane. "Are you quite sure you want to marry Trenton should he ask for your hand?" she asked. She did not seem the least bit pleased by Lady Elizabeth's declaration that she would be married by Christmastime. "You can put off marriage another Season or two. It's not as if you *have* to marry," she said in a very persuasive tone.

Lady Charlotte Bingham held her breath, waiting for Lady Elizabeth Carlington's eminent response. She expected Elizabeth to counter Hannah with a rather loud or emphatic argument as to why she *would* and *should* marry the Earl of Trenton. Elizabeth was, after all, a woman who knew her own mind and was quite good at getting what she wanted.

That is, if she still *wanted* the Earl of Trenton. There had been that awful kiss.

Some might consider her demanding, others thought her spoiled, her father once accused her of being manipulative, and her mother thought her too bold. But those closest to her knew she was merely determined to get what she wanted. She rarely spent her entire allowance on a shopping trip, and now she probably had none of it left given she was funding her own charity. She was a tireless worker when it came to her mother's favorite charities. And she never pitched a fit.

Until now.

"How can I put off marriage another year, Hannah?" Elizabeth nearly shouted. "I am one-and-twenty! Look at Beth Cunningham! She was... what? *Seventeen* when she married? She has four children and is only a year old than I am."

"You are not anything like the duchess," Charlotte put in, hoping to help calm the marquess' daughter. "Beth and Somerset were in love when he was still in school. Hannah is just concerned that you might not be getting the best husband in Gabriel Wellingham."

"He's an *earl*!" Elizabeth countered, as if the rank had everything to do with how to choose a husband. "There are currently no sons of marquesses of an age to marry—"

"I hear Leonard Blakely is considering marriage," Hannah said helpfully.

Charlotte's inhalation of breath was as loud as it could be. "Blakely is a pimply-faced bounder!" she exclaimed in shock, earning her a point in Elizabeth's estimation. The boy in question, a notorious gambler since the age of fifteen, was no doubt planning to marry in order to gain any dowry involved. Who knew what his debts would be before he reached his majority? "And I think he's only eighteen."

"—And as for dukes, I believe our fair Charlotte has claim to the only one to whom I would ever *consider* marriage," Elizabeth stated, continuing her rant despite her friend's helpful suggestions.

"I hear the Earl of Trenton employs a mistress," Hannah whispered, her face taking on a look of pain. It was her sincere belief that men only married for convenience and only ever really loved their mistresses. Despite having married friends who could readily dispute her belief and a father who insisted that her late mother was the only woman he had ever truly loved, Hannah held fast to her belief. When her mother died two years earlier, Hannah decided then that when she married, it would be for the sole purpose of having children. She was sure a husband would never love her for who she was, but would only marry her to gain her substantial dowry and a mother for his children.

Better that she accept that suit now than be disappointed once she was married.

Charlotte sighed. "I believe nearly every man in the *ton* has a mistress, Hannah," Charlotte countered patiently, wondering if her duke would ever employ one given his situation. Would any woman besides herself ever want to share a bed with a man who was so badly scarred? She doubted any of the high-priced courtesans employed by the rich men of London would do so. *Would a more desperate whore, though?* She had heard tales of prostitutes who would bed men infected with the French pox, their cases so advanced their faces displayed the ravages of the disease. She shivered at the thought.

"I overheard Father saying Trenton has *several,*" Elizabeth said in a quiet voice. Her comment was met with wide eyes from both of her friends. "But I do not know from where he learned of it."

Angling her head to one side, Charlotte took a deep breath. "At least you two seem to suit one another," she allowed, a tooth catching her lower lip, thinking it wasn't necessarily reason enough to marry the man.

"And that matters most, I suppose," Hannah said then, folding her hands together in her lap. From her perspective, it was reason enough to marry the man.

"Yes," Elizabeth agreed with a nod, as if she were reassuring herself. "Yes, it *does* matter. And if he or someone else doesn't ask for my hand this Season, I shall ask someone myself. I simply do not wish to be a burden to my parents any longer."

There was stunned silence for several seconds as Hannah and Charlotte shared expressions of disbelief. And when Elizabeth allowed a self-deprecating smirk to appear, all three women burst into laughter that could be heard throughout the entire house.

"Now that I have made you all laugh, I must take my leave,"

Elizabeth said as she stood up. "I promised Somerset I would pay a call on Beth today, and I must be back home for when Trenton fetches me for a ride in the park."

The trip to the Somerset's townhouse would have been faster had Elizabeth simply walked, but having left her lady's maid at Carlington House, she thought it best she go in the carriage in which she had ridden to Devonville House. Upon her arrival at the duke's London residence, a white townhouse facing the park, Elizabeth expected to have to wait in the parlor. She was rather stunned when Beth, Duchess of Somerset, joined her in the vestibule even before the butler could see to taking her parasol and bonnet. The sounds of children, screaming and crying, could be heard from the depths of the house.

"Oh, Lizzie, I cannot tell you how glad I am to see you," Beth said as she dipped a quick curtsy and kissed her friend on the cheek. "But we must hurry and be gone."

Elizabeth's eyes widened as she watched the duchess make her way through the vestibule and out the door. She turned to give the butler a questioning look, but the man's impassive expression gave no indication of what had happened. She turned around and stepped back out of the house. "What ever is wrong?" she asked as she watched Beth take a deep breath and let it out slowly.

Beth rolled her eyes as she continued to pull on a pair of gloves before opening her parasol. "Forgive me. I spent the entire day with those hellions in a traveling coach yesterday. Spent the entire night with a splitting headache. Thank the gods Jeremy knows what to do to help in that regard." Another roll of her eyes and a sudden blush were apparently supposed to be enough to explain what he had done to alleviate her pain. "I have had quite my fill of them and was ever so happy to learn you would save me from them today. Oh, how are you, Lizzy?" She hooked her arm into Elizabeth's and led them across the street.

Elizabeth wasn't sure if she should laugh or cry on her friend's behalf. "I am… confused," she finally replied, which had the duchess chuckling.

"How many offers are you considering?" Beth countered, as if they had been discussing the weather. "I'm sure we can make quick work of this and have you settled by Christmastime." She turned to regard Elizabeth as they made their way into Hyde Park. "That is what you want, isn't it?"

Nodding, Elizabeth wondered at how her friend seemed to know of her dilemma. They had exchanged correspondence, but she had been careful not to include too many details. She didn't wish to seem insipid to her older friend. An older friend who was already married and had been for so long. "It is. But I've had no offers. However, I have heard Trenton will ask for my hand. We're to go for a ride in the park this afternoon. During the fashionable hour," she explained. "Should he propose, I plan to accept."

Beth frowned, as if the news wasn't what she expected. "He's not the only one, surely," she said.

"If there is another, he has not made his intentions clear." She paused a moment, remembering George Bennett-Jones. She had promised him two dances at the next ball, although at no time did she get the impression he was interested in courting her.

Angling her head to one side, Beth finally murmured, "I suppose he wouldn't." When she felt Elizabeth's gaze on her, she added, "They don't all make their intentions known, Lizzie. Especially if they think you've already made a decision." She sighed. "I had it easy. Somerset and I were in love long before his father died. I was married when I had barely reached seventeen, and I was already with child…"

"What?" Elizabeth nearly stopped in her tracks at hearing her friend's confession.

The duchess rolled her eyes. "Lizzie…" She suddenly frowned. "Oh, I suppose your married friends haven't told you that most of them were familiar with the marriage bed before their wedding night."

"They have not," Elizabeth agreed, rather shocked by her friend's assertion.

"We're not supposed to, of course. We have to protect your delicate sensibilities." This was followed by a mutual giggle before Elizabeth suddenly sobered.

"Are you saying I will be expected to give up my virtue *before* I say my vows?" She could suddenly imagine the Earl of Trenton expecting such a thing. Why, what if he decided he didn't like her as a bedmate and didn't wish to marry her? He could break off the engagement and leave her ruined!

Beth glanced about the park, as if to be sure no one else was within earshot. "Don't tell anyone I told you this, but once you're betrothed, your future husband will expect to bed you."

"But… how?" Blinking, as if she didn't understand her friend's question, Beth gave a shake of her head. Before she could answer, though, Elizabeth added, "A chaperone wouldn't allow such a thing," she whispered. "He certainly wouldn't try something with a… lady's maid present, would he?"

Displaying an arched eyebrow, Beth said, "Once you're betrothed, you'll no longer have need of a chaperone. Your betrothed can do whatever he likes with you."

The implication of Beth's comment was quite clear, and Elizabeth's breath caught in her throat. "But if he breaks off the engagement, I would be left ruined!"

"Which is why a gentleman doesn't do such a thing," the duchess said firmly. "Should you change your mind, though, you're allowed to break off the engagement without any harm to your reputation." She dared another glance around where they walked. "There is a reason the first babe is always early and the rest are on time," she added with an arched brow, "So you cannot end an engagement if you're left with child, or you shall be ruined."

Elizabeth considered her friend's words as they made their way along the crushed granite path. "Do you like the marriage bed?" she asked in a quiet voice.

Beth allowed a grin. "Oh, I do, but then, I have a husband who is very generous. He delights in providing me pleasure."

She paused a moment. "Which is how I ended up with four hellions in only five years," she added with a smirk and no apology for the curse she used to describe her children.

"What if I hate it? What if... what if my betrothed isn't... generous? What if—?"

"Then find out before you marry him. Just be sure to use discretion. And insist he use a French letter so you won't be left with child." She paused a moment. "Or better yet, marry a man for whom you feel affection, and the rest will sort itself."

Easier said than done, Elizabeth almost replied. For at that moment, she didn't feel affection for the Earl of Trenton. Or any man, for that matter.

CHAPTER 23

A MARQUESS AND A VISCOUNT DISCUSS A CERTAIN CHARITY

ater that afternoon

"Lord Morganfield," George called out, hurrying down the steps to join the elder peer outside the House of Lords. When the marquess slowed his descent to allow George to join him, George added, "A word if I may?"

Morganfield regarded the new viscount with an arched eyebrow, the expression exaggerated due to the periwig he still wore. "Bostwick," he acknowledged George with a nod. "You look well. Becoming a member of the *ton* seems to agree with you."

George was careful to still his features; he had been nervous since the moment he decided he would ask the marquess for permission to court his daughter. Morganfield's comment was meant to draw a smile, but George would not allow one until he was sure he had something about which to smile. "As it always has with you, I am sure," George responded, allowing his lips to curve a bit.

They reached the last step and headed down the wide hallway toward one of the entrances to Parliament.

"It was noble of you to have escorted my daughter to the supper last night," Morganfield responded, wondering if George's request for a moment of his time might have something to do with her. Ever since Josephine Wentworth's last visit, he had been wondering if the viscount would approach him about his intentions with respect to Elizabeth.

George smiled then. "There was nothing noble about accompanying a beautiful woman to a ball's supper, my lord," George replied with a shake of his head. They passed through the wide entry doors, opened for them by liveried footman who stood at attention on either side of the entrance. Bright sunshine washed over them. "It was my pleasure, I assure you. She is an interesting woman—"

"Who I fear I may have spoiled rotten," Morganfield interjected.

"—Who knows her mind and is quite determined to accomplish something important," George continued, as if he hadn't heard the marquess. He was referring to her charity, of course, but wanted to discover how much Morganfield was contributing toward its goal.

Morganfield paused and then stopped walking. "You are sure... are we talking about *my* daughter?" he asked.

"Indeed," George answered, his brows furrowing and a wave of nervousness suddenly engulfing him. "Lady Elizabeth," he clarified with a nod. "I have a very good friend, a man who was badly wounded at Quatre Bras. Due to your daughter's contacts and money from her charity's coffers, he has been able to return to his old clerking position," George stated, watching Morganfield's face for evidence that he knew something of Elizabeth's charity. At the blank look the marquess displayed, George shook his own head quickly. "Never mind, my lord. I only asked for a moment of your time because I wished to request your permission to court Lady Elizabeth."

But David Carlington's curiosity was suddenly acute. "What did you say?"

Suddenly more nervous, George glanced around, wanting to be sure no one was eavesdropping on their conversation. "I wish to court your daughter," he said in a lowered voice, aware a flush of red was slowly rising to cover his face. He hoped the brim of his top hat was hiding the worst of it.

"Of course, fine, fine," Morganfield said with a dismissive wave of his hand. "What did you say about her *charity's coffers?*"

Stunned, George stared at the marquess. He had expected Morganfield to scoff at him. He had expected him to claim his daughter could marry no lower than an earl. Then he had expected an inquisition in response to his rebuttal, one he had carefully rehearsed, outlining how it was he would make a good and faithful protector, extolling the virtues of the newly remodeled Bostwick Place, enumerating the profits of his three gypsum mines, describing the new town coach in the renovated carriage house, explaining that he would take on the patronage of Lady E's charity...

"Which charity?" Morganfield asked then, apparently for the second time. "I'm aware she is involved with a few of Lady Morganfield's charities, of course," he added quickly, not wanting to seem ignorant of his daughter's activities.

George straightened, realizing just then that David Carlington knew *nothing* of Lady E and Associates' "Finding Work for the Wounded."

So, he's not an associate.

But if that were the case, where had the money come from to pay the bribe?

"I suppose Lady Elizabeth must receive a bit of pin money on a regular basis," George said, realizing there could be no other explanation for how she was funding the bribes. Her mother had her own charities to see to—it was unlikely she was funding Elizabeth.

The marquess blinked once, twice before his brows furrowed together. "I give her an allowance, of course. She gets twenty guinea or so every month during the Season, but I only do that because I require she pay for all her own purchases. She's not allowed to have any bills sent to me," he explained with a pointed finger that bobbed up and down to drive home his point. He seemed annoyed at having to explain himself. "Now, what is this about her *charity?*"

George debated with himself for a very long time before

reaching into his waistcoat pocket. He drew out the calling card he had taken from Teddy and held it out to the marquess.

Morganfield gave him a suspicious glance before turning his attention to the white pasteboard. "Lady E and Associates. Finding work for the wounded," he read aloud, his eyes widening as he noticed the address at the bottom of the card. "Good God, she's got an *office!*" the marquess exclaimed when he recognized where in Oxford Street the address was located. He stared at the card for a bit longer, shaking his head as he did so. Finally looking at George, he asked, "How long as she been... Lady E?"

Shrugging, George replied, "Not long, I think. I believe my friend was her first placement." He debated with himself as to whether or not he should mention the bribe. "I gather from your reaction that Lady Elizabeth has not approached you about... *funding* her venture."

The marquess seemed surprised by the query and then remembered George's earlier question about an allowance. "You gather correctly," Morganfield replied, his attention on something far away, as if he were just realizing something. "No wonder she didn't wear a new gown for last night's ball," he murmured absently, his attention still not entirely on George. "She had her mother quite vexed when she wore one from two Seasons ago. I, of course, didn't notice, but Lady Morganfield was quite sure some old biddy would, and then there would be a scandalous mention of it in the society pages of *The Times*. Can't have that, I suppose," he added with a hint of a scowl that soon turned up at the corners of his mouth.

"I suppose not," George replied with a shrug. His grin indicated he shared Morganfield's amusement at the dictates of women's fashion. If Elizabeth's gown had been from the last *century*, George was quite sure he wouldn't have noticed. After all, who looked at a woman's gown when she had the face of an angel and such gorgeous auburn hair? "With your permission, my lord, I will take Lady Elizabeth for a ride in the park this week."

Morganfield nodded. "Of course. If you're not already

aware, there are... *others*... who are interested." He said this last as a warning, his lips pursing when he considered the identity of one earl who was proving to be as irritating as Josephine Wentworth had promised. "I haven't arranged anything on her behalf. And unlike in years past, I don't plan to interfere with her choice this year." *Except maybe to have a certain earl embarrassed in chambers, if that can be arranged.*

George considered the comment. If the Earl of Trenton was successful in his pursuit of Lady Elizabeth, then her father would not interfere. *Damn*! But the marquess had apparently prevented past suitors from asking for Elizabeth's hand. So... why not now? Why protect her from fortune seekers for two years and then let her loose to make her own match?

And then a thought came to mind that had him reeling.

How had Lady Elizabeth managed to stay unattached for so long? Unless the marquess was still pulling the puppet strings, George could not imagine how the beauty could still be biddable.

Unless the marquess really had spoiled her. At the moment, George couldn't believe the young lady was spoiled.

"Thank you, Lord Morganfield. I shall take that into consideration," George answered. With a bow, he took his leave of the marquess and headed for Oxford Street.

CHAPTER 24

THE EARL AND LADY E
ENJOY A RIDE IN HYDE PARK

*M*eanwhile...

"My lady, you look especially fetching today," Gabriel commented as he completed his bow and reached for Elizabeth's hand.

Elizabeth regarded the earl with a smile. "As do you, Trenton," she replied, wondering if her choice of a dark blue carriage gown and matching pelisse might have been a bit too conservative for their afternoon ride in Hyde Park. The earl stood before her in a bright blue top coat, gold metallic waistcoat, and breeches so snug they showed... everything... in relief. She struggled to keep her eyes on his face as he lowered it to kiss the back of her hand, hoping he hadn't noticed that she had noticed the bulge beneath his waistcoat.

"Will your maid be joining us?" he asked as he glanced behind her and saw no one else in the vestibule.

"She will, of course," Elizabeth responded as she turned her head a fraction. Anna appeared from behind her, obviously having hidden herself behind the vestibule wall until summoned.

Surprised by the sudden appearance of the maid, Trenton's expression changed from one of mischief to all business. He held his arm out and turned as Elizabeth rested her hand on it.

Alfred opened the door, and they departed Carlington House.

Elizabeth was a bit disappointed when she first learned the earl hadn't driven himself. The barouche parked in front had both a groom and a tiger, neither moving to give up their seats as drivers. She noted the horses were both black and well matched in size. "Are they new?" she asked as Trenton handed her into the side of the barouche facing in the direction of travel. He then assisted Anna, who would be forced to ride backwards for their trip.

"To me, I daresay. Got them at Tattersall's last week. It seems Lord Brougham lost a rather large sum at the faro tables and had to give them over as collateral," Trenton explained as he stepped up into the carriage. Given his choice of sitting next to the maid or next to Elizabeth, he chose Elizabeth. He lowered himself into the squabs, not the least bit concerned that his thigh brushed Elizabeth's gown as he did so.

Stunned at the impropriety, Elizabeth thought at first she should feel some excitement at the intimate contact. She was quite sure he intended to touch her. *He is testing me*, she decided, wondering if she should feel flattered that he would show such interest so early in their relationship—never mind the horrible kiss he had bestowed on her. This was a courtship, after all. But as the barouche made its way to Rotten Row for the fashionable hour, she found she was annoyed with the earl. *How dare he?*

"I heard you had a bit of difficulty during the second waltz last evening. Had I known, I assure you I would have come to your rescue," he said as he moved his arm to rest on the top of the squabs behind Elizabeth.

Elizabeth feigned ignorance. "Trouble? Why, there was no trouble," she replied lightly. "Well, I suppose there was for the duke, since his shoe had to be repaired before he could continue to enjoy his evening."

Trenton's brows furrowed, "But... weren't you dancing with him when he... stumbled?" he queried, sure his sources had described the scene quite thoroughly. At least four people he spoke with claimed to have seen exactly what happened.

"I was, but George Bennett-Jones took up where the duke left off, and all was well." She said it as nonchalantly as she could, hoping to deflect the earl's interest in the matter.

"I was concerned for your welfare, my lady," he countered, leaning his head toward hers so that his lips were mere inches from her cheek.

Elizabeth dared a glance in his direction, careful to hold her head so she wouldn't be any closer to him as she did so. "That was very kind of you, my lord," she replied with a grin.

"And for your... reputation. I was quite upset to discover you supped with that viscount's nephew. You really should be more careful."

Trying very hard not to breathe, Elizabeth stilled herself as she considered the earl's words. *Viscount's nephew?* George hadn't mentioned his relationship to a viscount during the supper. "And why would that be? Mr. Bennett-Jones seemed every bit the gentleman." She considered his prospects and wondered if the best he could hope for was a modest inheritance.

So he probably *was* a cit. How else could he make a living?

"Well, he's certainly not good *ton*," Trenton commented as he inched closer to her. The barouche was stopped just outside the gates to Hyde Park, waiting in a rather long queue to enter and join the line of equipage and horses already in the procession. "I would, of course, have come to your aid, but I was forced to spend the time with Lady Winthorpe. She was distraught over the loss of her cat and simply could not be consoled."

Elizabeth once again struggled to maintain a calm air. Lady Winthorpe was a widow, notorious for her *affaires* with younger men of the *ton*. "How sad for her," she offered, affecting an appropriate expression of grief. "I do hope she is feeling better now."

Trenton shrugged. "When I left her, she was... much happier," he said with a hint of mischief. Stifling the urge to inhale sharply, Elizabeth turned to find Trenton smiling at her. "I am teasing, of course," he said as his white teeth gleamed in the afternoon sunshine. "But I am sure your thoughts were not very charitable just then," he added, his manner becoming a bit more serious. "Really, Elizabeth. Must you think the worst of us young bucks?"

Elizabeth? She hadn't given him permission to use her given name! Instead of admonishing him, though, she decided to join in his humor. "Given the behavior of so many young bucks, I could easily say 'yes' to your question," she replied with her own mischievous grin.

The Earl of Trenton was about to respond when male voices called out to him. And for the rest of their time in the park, various riders and passengers in other coaches stopped to talk or ask as to their health and about Lord Weatherstone's ball. The earl's manner was most jovial and cordial, especially to the demoiselles who seemed disappointed to see him in the company of a lady. By the time they had made their way back to Carlington House, Elizabeth was sure they had spoken with every gentleman and half the young ladies in London.

Every gentleman except for George Bennett-Jones, she realized.

She wondered where he might be at that moment. At a men's club? Perhaps he was looking at horseflesh at Tattersall's. Or was he fencing or shooting or... she remembered he would be at Lady Worthington's ball the following night. *I can ask him then.*

As they left the park, Elizabeth thought about her charity and wondered if the earl would approve of her venture. Trying to drum up the courage to ask, she turned a bit on the seat to regard her host. He seemed in the best of spirits. "May I ask your opinion of something?" she began, hoping her question wouldn't change his good mood.

"Of course," he answered, taking one of her hands in his and kissing the back of it.

Elizabeth gave him a tentative smile. "If I told you I was starting my own charity, what would be your... opinion of that?"

Trenton sat up straighter, his body turning so he was nearly facing her. "I... I rather think I would find it a worthy endeavor," he answered carefully. "Indeed, I've often wondered what a proper lady does with her time when she is not calling on others, or seeing to the guests who call on her, or coming up with fanciful menus for dinners," he commented. "A charity would seem a perfectly acceptable use of your spare time."

Nodding, Elizabeth gave the earl a tentative nod. "Thank you," she replied, not about to tell him what she had to do for her charity to succeed. At least he was amenable to the *idea* of her starting a charity. Perhaps she would admit to having already started it the next time they spoke.

When Trenton escorted her to the front door of Carlington House, he did so with a sweeping bow and a kiss on the back of her gloved hand. "I thank you for your company this afternoon, my lady. I do hope you'll save me two dances tomorrow evening."

Elizabeth grinned in reply, thinking about the two dances she had offered George. "I will see what I can do," she said in an exaggerated sigh.

Trenton nodded. "Until tomorrow night, my lady," he said as he bowed deeply. And then he was off, bounding down the stairs and nearly hopping into the barouche, looking every bit the rake Lady Elizabeth thought he might be.

CHAPTER 25
A CHARITY RECEIVES A DONATION OR TWO

The following morning Lady Elizabeth reported to her office to find two disabled soldiers waiting at the door along with a note from the solicitor, Andrew S. Barton, Esquire, from whom she let the space.

I have an envelope for you.

Telling the men she would be but a moment, Elizabeth hurried to the solicitor's office next door. She greeted the older gentleman and was given an envelope so thick it could almost be considered a package. Inside, a note, written in a scrawl that suggested it was penned by a man, said,

Keep up the good work. Should you need it, there is more where this came from. Simply let Mr. Barton know you're in need, and he will relay the message to me.

There was no signature.

A bit stunned, Elizabeth stared at the one-hundred pounds she pulled from the envelope. If ever there was a perfect time for a donation to arrive, this was it.

But who had left it?

The money couldn't have come from Theodore Streater. And she rather doubted Avery Whittaker would have sent it. He seemed too greedy to be charitable. The solicitor disavowed any knowledge of the envelope's contents, saying it had been delivered by a gentleman the afternoon prior.

One of those two men had to have told *someone* of means about her charity. Before she could leave Barton's office to return to her own, a liveried footman came in carrying a purse. "Lady E?" he asked, apparently having just come from next door and been told by the men waiting there that she was next door.

"I am," she replied.

"I am to give this to you. For your charity," the footman said as he held out the velvet purse.

Elizabeth paused before reaching out to take the purse, trying to remember if she had ever before seen the livery the footman wore. "Thank you," she said hesitantly, surprised at the weight of the purse. "And from whom does this come?" she asked in awe, hoping the servant would mention his employer by name. Through the fabric of the purse, she could feel large coins. Lots of them.

"I am not at liberty to say, milady," he replied with a shake of his head. He bowed deeply and took his leave of the office.

The solicitor eyed Elizabeth, a grin breaking out on his face. "Seems you have a patron or two, Lady Elizabeth."

She nodded in wonderment. "Indeed." A smile broke out when she realized she had absolutely no idea who could have sent the money. *I have anonymous benefactors!*

The realization buoyed her for the entire morning as she met with her new clients. For as disheartening as their tales were of being unable to find work, she was quite sure she would be able to secure positions for them both. Bribery was the key to finding work for the wounded, Elizabeth now knew, and she was quite good at getting what she wanted.

CHAPTER 26
CONTEMPLATING A KISS

ady Worthington's Ball

"I thought about what we talked of during supper at Lord Weatherstone's ball," Elizabeth spoke quietly from behind her fan, her eyes scanning the crowded ballroom as if she were looking for someone. Lady Worthington had to be pleased at the huge turnout, her brightly-lit ballroom a crush even before the first waltz.

George dared a glance in her direction, his posture erect. He moved his hands behind his back and clasped them together in an effort to quell his sudden nervousness. *She had thought about what they talked of?* A rush of heat suffused his face. He considered that the sudden lack of air in the ballroom could be explained by the number of guests in attendance, but he had to admit to himself it was because *she* stood so near to him. "We spoke of many things," he replied lightly, nodding to the Earl of Ellsworth and his countess as they passed in front of him.

Elizabeth took a deep breath, or at least as deep a one as she could given how tight Anna had tied her corset. The only benefit of a corset this snug was that it would keep her upright during the later dances.

Well, one of the benefits.

The other was quite evident to any man who dared to gaze at the space above the neckline of her bodice. She had worn the low-cut cream confection of silk and tulle on Lady Hannah's recommendation. The patronesses of Almack's might not approve of such a slim gown that hinted at the shape of her long legs and displayed nearly all of the tops of her breasts, but if ever there was a ball where it was appropriate, Lady Worthington's was it.

The admiring looks of her dance partners were more important than the opinions of Almack's patronesses just then.

Especially the look of the dance partner who stood next to her.

"I was thinking about *kisses*," she clarified, her fan closing as she turned to gaze at George directly. It was a bold move on her part, she knew, but she wasn't about to leave that night's ball without some of her questions answered.

George had to force his face to remain impassive. "Ah," he replied, the tip of his tongue touching his bottom lip. He met Lady Elizabeth's gaze and nodded. "And?" he prodded, a hint of a smile touching the corners of his mouth.

Elizabeth could feel the blush coming on even before she knew it colored her face. She resisted the temptation to reopen her fan and hide behind it. "I wondered if, perhaps, you would be so kind as to give me a..." She leaned in and lowered her voice, the line of her body suggesting she was trying to hear something he was saying. "Demonstration." She straightened and held her breath while she waited for George's reaction, tempted to claim he should forget what she had just said. This was a huge mistake. It was entirely inappropriate. He would think her fast! But she had given this a good deal of thought. She was determined to marry Trenton. This would just be a kiss. An opportunity to learn what a kiss was supposed to be like. Besides, when would she ever see George again?

George Bennett-Jones blinked once and forcefully closed his mouth. *A demonstration?* She could only mean one thing with her request. She was suggesting he... he kiss her. Which meant she would compare his kiss to the one she had experienced with Gabriel Wellingham behind the hedgerow in Lord Weatherstone's garden. It was *horrible*, she had said, the disgust in her voice more telling than the mere statement.

He could certainly do better than Trenton, perhaps enough for her to realize Trenton was not a good match for her. Swallowing hard, George reached down to capture the dance card and pencil that dangled from Elizabeth's wrist. "I see you still have two dances available," he commented, his manner suggesting he hadn't heard her comment. *She left me two dances as she promised!* He wrote his name onto both lines and raised his eyes to meet hers. "I am at your service, of course, my lady," he said as he bowed, his eyes twinkling and one edge of his lips curled up.

At that moment, the Marquess of Devonville approached and bowed to Lady Elizabeth. "My lady, I believe this is my dance," the debonair gentleman said as he held out his hand to take hers. The man might have been in his fifties and Hannah's father, but William Slater, Marquess of Devonville, was still an attractive man. His long hair was pulled back into a queue and held with a black ribbon, and his evening clothes looked as if they had been made by Weston himself. "Bostwick," he acknowledged, when he realized he had interrupted a moment between Lady Elizabeth and the viscount.

George nodded and gave the marquess a smile. "My lord," he responded as he gave a slight bow.

"Of course, Lord Devonville," Elizabeth said with a bright smile, not hearing the exchange between the two gentlemen. "I would have found you if you hadn't found me," she assured him as she gave George a curtsy and followed the marquess onto the dance floor.

Extremely satisfied with himself, George grinned and went off to find the refreshment table. A kiss was in his future, albeit a small one, he figured.

Now, where should he take her? The garden off the terrace would be too crowded with other couples expecting to engage in the same dalliance. There were alcoves off the ballroom, but anyone might see their departure from the ballroom floor, and Lady Elizabeth's reputation would be in ruins. He made his way out of the ballroom and down the hall, remembering the house to have a library somewhere nearby. Lady Worthington had hosted a *musicale* that spring, during which he and the Earl of Torrington had retired to the library for a drink.

The library was not far from the ballroom; George entered and looked around, deciding it would do fine for his needs. Checking the door handle, he found it didn't lock, though, and he wondered if that might pose a problem. Perhaps a lookout would need to be employed. And if he couldn't arrange one in the short time between now and their second dance, or rather their kiss, then proper position in the room would have to suffice.

George decided he would have to be sure he stood facing the entrance while Elizabeth's back would need to be oriented toward the door. Then he would nod and take her hand in his, holding her fingers a bit longer than propriety normally allowed, and be sure to kiss her knuckles completely—a brush of his lips would not suffice. He would lower her hand then, perhaps even keeping it in his grasp for just a moment more. Then he would use the forefinger of his other hand to caress her jaw and angle her head just so. Gazing into her eyes, he would pause before lowering his lips to hers.

It would have to be a tender kiss, almost a caress. He would explain himself as he made each move, he decided, ensuring it would be construed as a demonstration and not simply an opportunity for him to do what he had hoped to with Lady Elizabeth ever since their sudden dance at Lord Weatherstone's ball. And he would only use his lips to engage Lady Elizabeth— it would not be seemly to introduce his tongue during this demonstration.

As he made his way back to the ballroom, he remembered wondering if Trenton had used his tongue in his attempt at a kiss with the young woman. Perhaps it was *that* she found *most unpleasant*. George bristled at the mere thought of the earl engaging Elizabeth in such a manner, his usually calm temperament suddenly turning to anger. His frown must have been apparent, for Edward Bingham nudged him with an elbow. His daydream interrupted, George regarded the earl with surprise. "Ellsworth."

Bingham snorted. "You looked as if you wanted to kill someone just then," he chided the viscount, leaning back so his belly protruded in front of him. Had he been a member of the opposite sex, one might have mistaken him for a woman in the last stages of breeding.

George gave the earl a sideways glance. "Given the opportunity, perhaps I would have," he answered under his breath.

Bingham nodded in response. "Just be sure there are no witnesses when you do," he commented lightly before wandering off.

CHAPTER 27
A KISS IS NOT JUST A KISS

$\mathcal{E}$xcited, nervous and just a bit giddy, Lady Elizabeth downed her glass of champagne in just a few gulps. Lady Hannah arched an elegant blonde eyebrow. "Elizabeth!" she admonished her friend. "How many of those have you drunk?" she asked in a hoarse whisper. Lady Charlotte glanced about, hoping no one else had paid witness to her friend's action.

"Shush," Elizabeth replied with a grin. "That was only my second this entire evening. I am simply thirsty—"

"Then have a glass of punch," Lady Hannah offered as she turned to take one from the refreshment table. She started to give it to Elizabeth, but the older girl waved it off.

"I think not. I saw what Grandby poured in there," Elizabeth countered with a shiver of disgust.

Hannah sniffed the red liquid. She took a sip from the crystal tumbler and seemed to hold it in her mouth for a moment before swallowing. "I can't taste anything out of the ordinary. A bit too much orgeat..." She downed the rest of the punch and then shrugged as Charlotte and Elizabeth watched her. She refilled the glass and turned to smile at her friends. "What is it?" she asked as she saw their looks of surprise.

"Hannah! The Earl of Torrington poured an entire bottle of

Russian vodka into that bowl," Elizabeth whispered as loudly as she dared.

Her friend looked at the crystal cup and shrugged, taking another sip. Charlotte moved to the refreshment table and took a glass from the footman. Taking a drink, she found she couldn't taste anything out of the ordinary.

Elizabeth sighed, deciding the two couldn't get too tipsy on the punch. Her second glass of champagne had reached her knees, though, the sensation rather pleasant. She checked her dance card and took a quick look at the large clock that hung just above where the orchestra was seated. Two more minutes and she would meet George in the library. She and George had already danced once; it was during that quadrille that he had engaged in small talk and complimented her on the cream silk de Naples gown she wore. He had asked if he might take her on a tour of the British Museum in the morning, an invitation she accepted before she had a chance to give it any thought. Near the end of the dance, he explained where she should meet him for their next dance.

This dance.

He promised a better kiss than the one Gabriel Wellingham had bestowed on her.

Part of her wanted George to prove his point since that first kiss had been rather awful. But another part of her wanted George to fail in his attempt, for then she would be sure it was merely she who had to modify her expectations of what a kiss should be. Indeed, she could learn how to appreciate a wet, sloppy kiss if kisses were supposed to be wet and sloppy.

The licking, she wasn't so sure about.

"I must find Mr. Bennett-Jones for this dance," Elizabeth stated as she heard the orchestra begin playing. She moved away from her friends, and then, sure no one was watching her, stepped out through the nearest door. Having been in Lady Worthington's home several times, she knew exactly where to find the library. Making certain she wasn't seen, Elizabeth ducked into the room and quietly closed the door behind her.

Holding the handle to lock it, she was dismayed to find it did not have a lock.

"I'm afraid we'll have to make do without a lock."

Startled, Elizabeth whirled around to find George leaning against a library table, his arms crossed over his chest and his face sporting a mischievous grin. Her breath caught as she noticed the man wasn't as *unattractive* as she had first thought. In fact, with his sable hair combed into a perfect Titus style and the close fit of his evening wear and the grin that lifted his eyes, and indeed, his entire face, Elizabeth thought him rather handsome. "George!" she whispered hoarsely, meaning to scold him for startling her.

"I'm sorry, my lady," he said as he bowed. "I thought you would at least look about the room *before* you closed the door," he teased, but then his breath caught as he took in the sight of her again. Auburn curls atop her head were dressed with satin ribbons and mother-of-pearl combs, a single strand of pearls graced the base of her long neck, and the satin gown displayed the tops of her breasts and a rather deep cleavage.

Curtsying to his bow, Elizabeth nearly rolled her eyes. "It is I who should be apologizing, George. I do hope you have not been waiting long," she hedged as she moved to stand before him.

My whole life, he almost said. "Just a few moments. Enough time to read *The Iliad* and half of *The Odyssey*," he added as he waved toward a copy of Homer's epic poems left open on the table. Two glasses of champagne stood next to the book. "Will you join me in a toast?" he asked as he picked up the glasses and held one out to her.

Smiling at his attempt at humor, Elizabeth felt the nervousness leave her body. This was George. She had nothing to fear from him. He was just going to kiss her. "Of course," she finally said, moving a step closer to take the glass.

George's eyes closed for more than a blink, as if he were saying a silent prayer. "To the art of kissing," he stated, holding his glass out to touch hers.

He heard her slight inhalation of breath at his toast and wondered if she was shocked. As he took a sip of the champagne, he watched in surprise as Elizabeth drained her entire glass in a single gulp.

Handing the empty glass to him, she straightened. "An excellent idea, George," she said, the sound of his name on her lips much more intoxicating than the champagne.

George put down the glasses and angled his head to regard her. She was beautiful. Despite having danced with her earlier that evening, he had done so in a crowded ballroom and was well aware too many eyes were on them. He dared not stare for fear someone would realize how he felt about her. But now, here in the privacy of the library, it was just the two of them, and there was no one to witness his gaze, no one to pass judgement should his gaze linger too long.

Slowly lifting a finger, he paused before sliding the back of it along her jawline, barely touching her skin. He heard her breath catch and hold before he lowered his head over hers and slowly, very slowly, placed his lips over hers. He had planned to explain what he was doing every step of the way; for some reason, it seemed rather wrong to be describing what he was about to do. Actions spoke louder than words, after all.

And his actions were downright deafening.

Perhaps it was the effect of the champagne or maybe it was just the giddiness she had felt all evening, but Elizabeth took delight in the sensation of his firm lips, the wash of his warm breath over her cheek, the way his eyelids slowly closed over his eyes and the curve of his long dark, gold-tipped lashes as they rested against the tops of his cheekbones. Her first impression was to grin—the bare touch of his lips to hers tickled at first. And then he pressed a bit harder. His lips parted a bit more, and hers followed, not wanting to lose their lock on his. The light scents of amber and sandalwood touched her nose, enhancing the taste of champagne on his lips. A tendril of pleasure shot through her belly, surprising her so that, a bit unsteady, she had to reach up with one hand to grab his lapel for support.

Thinking she meant to push him away, George quickly ended the kiss, reluctantly pulling his lips from hers but then trailing featherlight kisses down along her jawline before he thought he really should pull away. A whimper of what sounded like despair made him pause. A hand pressed against his jaw to move him back to where her lips were suddenly on his, capturing them so he was forced to respond in kind. Her arms reached up to wrap around his neck while one of his encircled her waist. His other hand moved to the back of her head. Fingertips caressed the nape of her neck. The palm of his hand supported her head as he again moved to sprinkle kisses down her jaw, down her neck and to the hollow where her pulse beat so quickly, it seemed to vibrate against his tongue and lips.

So when George suddenly froze his movements, his body tensing, Elizabeth did the same. "What is it?" she whispered, surprised she could speak with any kind of coherency. But she had felt the vibration in the floor, too, and gasped.

"Follow my lead." George straightened but left the one hand on the back of her head. He moved his arm around a bit, ensuring his wrist was against her coiffure. Realizing almost too late her arms were still wrapped around his neck, Elizabeth dropped them to her sides.

The door to the library swung open and Lady Fletcher halted in mid-step. "Good God!" One of her hands had gone to her chest as if she were having an attack. "*George?* Is that you?"

"Oh, thank God, Lady Fletcher. I am so glad to see you!" George announced with what sounded like a great deal of relief. "Please, do come in. And close the door, won't you?" he added in a hoarse whisper.

Her back to the door, Elizabeth could only imagine what Lady Fletcher had seen upon entering. *Just what is George doing?* she wondered, still feeling his wrist pressed against her hair. *I'll be ruined!* Lady Fletcher wasn't the worst gossip in the *ton*, but she certainly had friends who were.

Lady Fletcher looked taken aback by George's pronouncement. "Whatever is going on here?" she asked as she shut the door, still stunned George hadn't moved away from the woman who stood in front of him.

"This dance, Lady Fletcher," George said in a voice that suggested he was complaining. "Just as Lady Elizabeth was going under this arm, my cuff link caught in her hair. I fear the poor girl will never deign to dance with me again. I thought if I could get us in here, I could get my cuff link released without ruining her curls, but I'm making a cake of it."

The older lady gave a very loud sigh, one Elizabeth hoped was of relief and not something else. *Like disbelief.* "Oh, please George, do stop moving, won't you?" Lady Fletcher scolded as she glided over to stand next to the two of them.

"How do you do, Lady Fletcher?" Elizabeth ventured, her voice sounding a bit uncertain. "I would curtsy, but I dare not make the situation worse than it is."

"You're excused, of course," the baron's wife said with a wave of her hand before she moved it out of Elizabeth's line of sight and to the back of her head.

Elizabeth could feel a bit of hair pulling and then a satisfied, "There!" before George's hand left the back of her head to fall to his side. She watched his expression change as genuine relief seemed to wash over his face.

"How can I ever thank you, my lady?" George said with such conviction, even Elizabeth believed he had snagged his cuff link in her hair. The man was a quick thinker on his feet!

"Yes, how can I thank you, my lady?" Elizabeth asked, moving a hand to the back of her coiffure to determine if she would need to pay a visit to the retiring room. A maid might really need to pin up her hair.

The older woman regarded the two of them. "You're very welcome, Lady Elizabeth. I once had my hair snagged by Lord Appleby's diamonds. They were far larger than yours, George," she added as she actually took his wrist in hand again and examined the cuff link through her lorgnette before going on. "Took down my entire coif. I had to leave the ball on account of his negligence."

"Oh, dear. That must have been awful!" Elizabeth

commented, a good deal of sincerity in her voice. She wondered if perhaps the lady's "entire coif" was really a wig that had come off. Considering Lady Fletcher's age, she decided that was exactly what had happened.

"Now, as for you, George, I expect a dance," Lady Fletcher stated with no hint of humor.

George nodded. "Of course, milady. Just name which one, and I shall be there with bells on," he said lightly.

"This one will do, actually." She turned to Lady Elizabeth. "May I suggest you make your way to the retiring room, dear girl? I believe you're in need of a repair," she added with a wave of her lorgnette.

Realizing she was being dismissed, Lady Elizabeth curtsied to both Lady Fletcher and to George. "Thank you again, milady," she said before hurrying from the room, still so surprised at having someone walk in on them, she hadn't had a chance to even *think* about the kiss.

The kiss!

Or was it many kisses? she wondered. How long had she stood there engulfed in the pure delight of those all-consuming kisses? George's lips had been warm and not wet, and possessive but not overly so, and so light and deft as they trailed along her skin, sometimes barely touching her and other times suckling her so she nearly cried out from the pleasure of it. George hadn't been boasting when he claimed there was an art to kissing.

The man was a master!

And he hadn't licked her. At least, not like Gabriel had. George's tongue had barely touched the hollow of her neck as her pulse pounded against the skin there.

And then they had been interrupted.

She suddenly felt bereft at not knowing what he would have done next. Would his lips have captured the skin there and suckled and supped until she really did cry out? Her entire body trembled at the thought of it. Her breasts suddenly felt heavy. And a deep craving developed deep inside her belly.

What has George Bennett-Jones done to me?

He had held her as if she were a fragile doll, his fingers

caressing the nape of her neck so that shivers of... even now, she felt the flesh on the back of her neck quiver at the thought of it. She paused and backed up against the hall wall, took a deep breath and let it out very slowly. It took a very long time, but when she was sure she was no longer under George's spell, she hurried off to the retiring room.

CHAPTER 28
AN AUNT'S ADVICE

George regarded Lady Margaret Fletcher with an arched eyebrow. "Your timing was... probably perfect, Aunt Maggie. Thank you again for agreeing to guard the door," he said with a sigh. He hoped his face wasn't red with the embarrassment he felt. To be caught with his hand in the biscuit jar, or in this case, his cuff link in Elizabeth's hair, was still mortifying. Despite the realistic way in which he'd covered his illicit kisses with the marquess' daughter, he had a feeling Margaret Fletcher wasn't fooled. His mother's sister was perceptive, and she could be a gossip should a topic strike her interest. He had only asked her to stand near the library door so that he might have "a chance to talk to Lady Elizabeth in private." The request had been immediately granted, the Amazon of a woman taking great delight in being somehow involved in her nephew's assignation with a marquess' daughter.

"Nonsense, George," she answered with a wave of her fan, a rather happy expression crossing her matronly face. "It was positively exciting to know that my nephew might actually be kissing Lady Elizabeth in the library during a ball!" Her face took on a more serious expression. "I just couldn't stand out there another moment. You *were* kissing her before your cuff link ruined everything, I hope?" she stated suddenly.

His mouth opened in astonishment as George realized if he

denied the kiss, he would leave Aunt Maggie quite disappointed. But he couldn't have the woman telling every other woman in the *ton* her nephew had stolen kisses during Lady Worthington's ball! "Aunt Maggie!" he chided her. "I have no intention of exposing Lady Elizabeth to gossip that could hurt her chances of a advantageous marriage," he admonished as he pulled his topcoat sleeves into place.

"Oh, poppycock, George," Lady Fletcher replied, waving her closed fan and soundly whacking his arm with it. "I certainly wouldn't tell anyone any such thing. I just want to know for *myself*," she claimed in a lowered voice, her nose quite high up as she made her statement. "Besides, if the gossip did hurt her chances of a marriage with that Wellingham boy, well then, all the better for you, right?"

George's eyes widened. The woman was... well, *right*, actually. Although he had no intention of using gossip to influence who Lady Elizabeth chose for a husband, his aunt had managed to put into words what he had only briefly—very briefly—thought about in how he could win Lady Elizabeth's hand in marriage. "What have you heard about Trenton?" he asked, more because he wanted to know what the wags were saying than to deflect her attention from the possibility he had kissed Lady Elizabeth.

Lady Fletcher straightened to her nearly six-foot height. "Well, that Lord Trenton plans to ask for Lady Elizabeth's hand, of course," she answered in a matter-of-fact tone, as if *everyone* knew the engagement was imminent.

Damnation, George thought in dismay. If his aunt had heard the gossip regarding the Earl of Trenton, then there was no doubt Gabriel Wellingham had voiced his intention to ask for Lady Elizabeth's hand in front of witnesses, probably at White's. "I have heard as much," he admitted, sighing. He raked his fingers through his short hair and quickly used them to smooth it back into place.

His aunt sighed as well. "She seems like a good match for *you*, George."

The words were all the encouragement he needed right then.

With the embarrassment of his aunt's interruption—he secretly wondered why she had seen fit to burst in on them, unless she had come in to warn them someone was coming—he had considered giving up his pursuit of Lady Elizabeth Carlington. But now that Lady Fletcher had given her opinion, he was suddenly as determined as he had been after the Weatherstone ball. "Thank you for saying so," he murmured. "She has agreed to join me for a tour of the British Museum tomorrow morning." He considered telling his aunt more, but thought better of it. "I... We should be getting back to the ballroom," he said by way of an excuse to end their discussion, "If we're to dance any of this dance."

As he held open the library door for Lady Fletcher, he realized he had not only managed to avoid a confession, but he had also pleased his aunt. He thought their discussion could not have gone better.

CHAPTER 29
THE AFTERMATH OF A KISS

Thirty minutes later

"There you are!" Lady Charlotte exclaimed as she watched Lady Elizabeth make her way toward her and Lady Hannah. "Did George ever claim his dance with you?" she asked then, remembering how he had requested they save dances for him. "He is very proficient at the country dances. And elegant. He holds himself as if he were to the manor born," Charlotte added, her eyebrow arching as if she was daring Elizabeth to counter the assessment.

Elizabeth smiled as she reached up to touch the back of her coiffure. The maid on duty in the retiring room had done a quick but adequate job of getting her hair back into place. She had missed a cotillion in the meantime, though, and hoped that whomever had requested the dance on her card would have forgotten. "He is, indeed," Elizabeth agreed with a nod. "I just came from having my hair repaired. What have I missed?" she asked, surprised to find Hannah and Charlotte standing almost exactly where she had left them. Had they noticed she and George weren't in the ballroom for the dance before the quadrille that had just ended? Given the crush, though, she knew they wouldn't have been able to *see* any of the dancing.

"Ten minutes of tedious cotillion?" Hannah replied with a

wan smile. Her short gasps for air suggested the cotillion was a bit more taxing than tedious, though.

"Oh, dear. Someone needs a really good kisser." Elizabeth inhaled sharply. "*Dancer*, I meant to say," she corrected herself, shocked that she said aloud what she was merely thinking.

Charlotte grinned. Hannah's eyes widened in delight. "Elizabeth!" they both chorused and then burst into more giggles.

Elizabeth couldn't help but join in the merriment. She felt positively giddy. Everyone should have to experience the kind of kisses George had bestowed on her in the library. George's kiss, or kisses—she wasn't quite sure where one ended and the next had begun or if it had all been just one long, luxurious trip to heaven—had been everything she had hoped for and more. She was sure there was even a moment when he tried to end it and she shamelessly refused to allow it by recapturing his lips with her own.

A few days ago, the news of Trenton's plan to ask for her hand in marriage excited her, even thrilled her.

Now, she wasn't so sure.

After Gabriel Wellingham's attempt at a passionate kiss in the gardens during the Weatherstone ball, she thought only to tolerate horrible kissing for the rest of her life. And then George Bennett-Jones made it perfectly clear that kissing was an art form. Who knew the mere press and suckling of open lips and the touching of a tongue against skin could incite such sensations? Such feelings of... *intimacy?* For he had kissed far better than she had ever imagined was possible.

And they might still be kissing if it hadn't been for Lady Fletcher's arrival.

Thank goodness George could think fast! She had been a bit confused by his proclamation that he was glad to see the matron, but his plea for help had apparently convinced Lady Fletcher they were in the library simply to remove his cuff link from her hair. The woman had given no sign she thought anything untoward. And she knew George—she had called him by his given name when she walked into the library! Elizabeth was getting the impression that many in the *ton* not only knew George but found him to be trustworthy, too.

If they only knew what he was capable of, they might change their good opinion of him!

So it was a surprise, when later that night, she returned from having danced a cotillion with the Earl of Trenton to find her friends waiting for her with bated breath.

"He asked about you," Charlotte whispered, her comment a bit breathless. She had just completed the cotillion with George as her partner before rejoining Hannah on the sidelines.

"Who asked about me?" Hannah asked, still catching her breath after having to endure the same dance with Charlotte's father. Although the man tried hard, he couldn't seem to keep the appropriate rhythm for any dance. At least he had only stepped on her foot once, and realized it quickly enough so as not to scuff her satin slippers too much.

"Not you," Charlotte said with a shake of her head. "Elizabeth."

Elizabeth, who had been watching Gabriel escort Lady Wadsworth to her husband, still had her attention on his departing figure. She finally turned to regard her friends. "He who?" she asked, her gaze returning to watch the earl make his way across the ballroom floor. Gabriel Wellingham was confident, she noticed, and perhaps a bit vain. She just then remembered a comment he had made during their dance. *I don't wish to dance with girls who are prettier than me.* She had thought then he made comment in jest.

Now she wondered if he was serious.

You are the exception, of course, Trenton had added quickly, as if he had noticed her sudden look of offense. And then he had smiled that perfect smile, his perfect white teeth gleaming under the hundreds of candles that lit the ballroom. His apple green satin topcoat and breeches were daring, but the color was no doubt chosen so he would stand out from the scores of gentlemen dressed in black evening clothes. From the back, though, with his blond curls and green satin, he could easily be mistaken for a woman if one didn't see any of him below his waist.

"George! A rather good dancer, I must say," Charlotte whispered hoarsely, glancing about to be sure no one was eavesdropping.

Elizabeth's head snapped around. "What did he ask about me?" She had finally recovered from the man's kisses, although it had taken the time in the retiring room to have her hair repaired and a bit more champagne before her lips stopped quivering and her knees were able to support her again.

A rather wicked grin spreading over Charlotte's face, the blonde looked to her right. The man in question was leading Lady Morganfield onto the dance floor for the evening's second waltz. Elizabeth followed her friend's line of sight and spotted the pair as they faced each other to bow and curtsy. Hannah grinned. "And now he'll ask your *mother* about you," she said in delight.

"What did he ask?" Elizabeth repeated, trying hard not to watch as George led her mother in the waltz, a dance at which he seemed to excel. Her mother was positively beaming.

She wondered if her father was watching.

Charlotte leaned in and repeated what George had asked. "What led Lady Elizabeth to found her own charity?"

Frowning, Elizabeth seemed startled by the question. *He knows about my charity?* "Does he find my charity... offensive?" she asked, immediately deciding she did not like George Bennett-Jones. The memory of his kiss in the library nearly changed her mind just as quickly, though.

But Charlotte's eyes had widened and she was shaking her head. "Oh, quite the contrary. He thought you very brave to take on a subject he said others in the *ton* shunned," she explained quickly. She wasn't about to add that she found George Bennett-Jones rather intriguing, as if she should know him from somewhere. He seemed to know all about the Wainwrights and the part of Sussex near Kirdford where their duchy was based. He was attentive, polite, not the least bit vain, and he spoke with an ease suggesting he rubbed elbows with the *ton* on a daily basis.

At this bit of news, Elizabeth considered her friend's words. Her opinion of George Bennett-Jones flipped again. "Indeed?" she replied, her ire gone as quickly as it had appeared. "Then, I wonder if he might be inclined to donate funds," she added. *And why might he consider her* brave *to have started her charity?* she wondered.

Charlotte considered how to reply. "It seems he has a dear friend who has benefitted. Someone who lost an arm in France during the war," she recited, just then remembering Elizabeth's mention of her charity's first beneficiary when they were shopping. "He could read and write, but no employer would grant him a position because his right arm was missing. Then you stepped in and found him a position as a clerk at the Bank of England," she hurried on, retelling the story George had told her during their dance, remembering the details matched exactly what Elizabeth had described.

Elizabeth stood still for a very long time as she realized two things at the same time. One hundred pounds and a purse full of guineas had been given to her charity—anonymously. Theodore Streater's friend had paid for her bonnet as a thank you gift. Could *George* be that friend? And one of those anonymous donors?

Charlotte leaned in, remembering the best part. "Then he implied you would have had to *bribe* a man at the bank in order to secure the position. Just like you said you had to! I told George if that were necessary, then you would have done so out of your own pin money—"

"You *told* him that?" Elizabeth whispered in surprise, her hand going to her mouth.

Lady Hannah inhaled sharply. "I do not know how you can give up nearly every penny of your allowance to fund such an endeavor," she put in, glancing about when she heard the orchestra tuning for the next dance.

Shrugging, Elizabeth gave her friend a wan smile. "Father helps, of course, but it's not really his passion," she lied. "He must appear to fund the charities that my mother favors," she added as an excuse, apparently glancing around the ballroom in order to locate her next dance partner. She rather hoped she could get a glimpse of George while she was at it, but Lord Henley had moved to her elbow to claim the dance, and the opportunity was lost. *So, George knows of my charity. He approves. And he may be one of my anonymous donors.*

I wonder if Gabriel will be of the same mind?

The thought was a bit disconcerting as she left the ball that night.

CHAPTER 30
A PROPOSAL OF SORTS

he following morning
Excited and a bit nervous, George steered his curricle around the corner to Carlington House. Elizabeth had agreed to accompany him on a tour of the British Museum, the venue to which he had promised Josephine he would escort a young lady. His attendance at the two balls earlier in the week had proved far more entertaining and satisfying than he could have imagined. To meet and dance with Elizabeth Carlington, to have the honor of escorting her to supper and then to be invited to kiss her nearly senseless... how could a morning trip to tour the museum even compare?

What was Josephine thinking?

But the morning would be spent in the company of Lady Elizabeth. He would have her all to himself. Never mind the hordes of people who would be in the museum with them. The latest exhibition was proving popular with the masses.

The front door opened even before he reached the top of the steps. A butler, sporting an expression of suspicion, regarded him for a moment.

"George Bennett-Jones to see Lady Elizabeth," he said as he clasped his hands behind his back.

Opening the door a fraction more, Alfred stepped aside and allowed him into the vestibule. "Wait here," he intoned, his manner suggesting he rather doubted Lady Elizabeth would ask that he be escorted to the parlor. George merely nodded and waited, his gaze taking in the recently remodeled vestibule. *Tasteful*, he thought, and rather conservative. As in his recently renovated vestibule, one large piece of artwork graced a wall, but the space lacked a live plant and fresh flowers. The wall covering was a rich, dark green moiré patterned silk that tricked the eye, changing its shape as his gaze traveled over the fabric. His eye was still being tricked when Elizabeth appeared from the hallway.

"George," she said as she moved to stand before him, a vision in a sapphire pelisse over a lighter blue gown. "I hope you haven't been waiting long."

His heart racing, George bowed over her hand and kissed the back of it. "My lady," he replied as he lifted his head and took in the sight of her. Her deep blue, wide-brimmed hat displayed more of her auburn hair than a bonnet might. "I've only just arrived." He had to suppress a grin when he realized the butler hadn't found her to let her know of his arrival; she must have come from another part of the house. "Shall we?" he asked as he indicated the front door.

"Of course," she replied, pulling on a pair of gloves as she moved to leave the house. "My maid, Anna, will have to join us, of course."

"Of course," George replied as he held the door for her and the petite girl that followed. He hurried to walk beside Elizabeth, offering his arm as he did so.

"'Tis a beautiful day," Elizabeth murmured as they reached the curricle.

George tossed a coin to a small boy who held the reins. "Because you are in it, my lady," George replied in a voice that couldn't be overheard by her maid, handing her up into the open carriage.

Awestruck, Elizabeth watched as George helped Anna into the back seat. She wondered for a moment if she should be concerned that he would be so overt in his compliment and then decided she rather liked it. He had said it so quickly and with such ease, it couldn't have been rehearsed. She found she couldn't look away as George then walked around to the front of the horses, stopping in front of them so that he could give them each half an apple. He stepped up into the curricle and took up the reins with practiced ease. As they were about to enter traffic, he paused. "Did you wish to bring a sunshade, my lady?"

Startled at her oversight, Elizabeth turned to find George gazing at her. There was concern in his expression, she noticed, making her suddenly aware of him in a way she hadn't thought of George before. *He is a very polite man.* A frisson shot through her belly. *A gentleman who cares for my welfare*, she thought. "No, but thank you for asking, George," she replied, her face coloring up.

George nodded. "Very well." And then they were off, the curricle speeding through the light morning cart traffic and passing the occasional town coach on its way to Montague Place.

Although not sitting as high as she did in Gabriel's phaeton, George's well-sprung curricle proved just as exhilarating. She dared a glance at the way he held the ribbons, his control confident but firm. The matched Cleveland Bays seemed pleased to be able to move quickly, their canter sometimes becoming a gallop when they had the streets to themselves. Before long, they were pulling up in front of the huge museum, it's gray stone exterior set off by dark red roofs.

George nodded to a curbside tiger who immediately took his reins and the coin George offered him. Hurrying to the other side of the curricle, George at first offered one hand, and then, when he determined how far his passenger would have to step in order to get down, he lifted his other arm.

Elizabeth stepped down carefully, finally allowing George to grasp her waist and lower her until her feet touched the walk. That moment, when she was suspended in mid-air, her only support his hands on either side of her waist and one of her hands on his shoulder, Elizabeth felt as if she were weightless. She tried to imagine Gabriel lifting her down from his phaeton, wondering how it would be to have the earl's hands on her waist as she floated down.

In her reverie, she hadn't noticed George moving to assist Anna, who shyly thanked him and moved to stand behind her mistress.

George offered Elizabeth his arm, smiling as he did so. "We may have to wait a few minutes in a queue before being allowed to go in," he said in apology. "The Bassae Frieze is proving to be a popular exhibit."

Elizabeth nodded her understanding. "My father mentioned it is quite spectacular."

Not surprised to learn Lord Morganfield had already visited the recently acquired frieze, George dared another glance in Elizabeth's direction. "So, his lordship saw it but did not take you along?"

Elizabeth smiled at the comment. "He took my mother, of course. I was..." She paused, wondering if she should admit she was at her charity's office. He knew of the charity; Charlotte had made that quite clear during Lady Worthington's ball.

Noticing her hesitation, George leaned his head down a bit and whispered, "Working, perhaps?"

A shiver passed through Elizabeth at the sound of his whisper. The words could have been a taunt, a tease of sorts, given those in the *ton* weren't supposed to perform work of any kind. But the manner in which he had made the comment was more of a compliment—an acknowledgement that what she did was important. "Yes, I suppose it could be called that," she agreed. They entered the building and moved toward the long room where a series of marbles were on display. "It doesn't seem like... *work*, though. The time flies by whilst I'm there. And there are so many that need help. I want to help them all, but—"

"In just helping *one*, you have made a tremendous difference, Lady Elizabeth," George interrupted. Had she been allowed to say what he thought she might, he was sure she would express a feeling of impotence—that despite her best efforts and all the money she could ever receive from patrons, there would always be more crippled soldiers than jobs that could accommodate them. George knew she could never be allowed to think that what she did was hopeless.

"Have I?" she asked, pausing to look up at him.

"Indeed," George replied. "Teddy Streater is right as rain. I never thought he would be the same as he was before... before the war," he got out, the comment catching in his throat just a bit. "And his new arm is quite impressive," he added, leaning closer and lowering his voice. "One must watch him very carefully to see that it isn't real."

Elizabeth beamed in delight. She hadn't seen Theodore Streater since the day she had secured his position at the Bank of England. "I should like to make his acquaintance again, George," she replied. "Do you suppose you might be able to arrange it?"

Smiling, George nodded. "Of course, milady," he answered, thinking if she agreed to be his wife, then Teddy would stand with him at the wedding. She could see him then, although that might be too far in the future.

George guided Elizabeth and her maid to the entrance of a hall that contained the twenty-three panels that made up the Bassae Frieze. Apparently taken from the Temple of Apollo in the Arcadian hills in Greece, the series of marbles depicted the Amazonomachy and Centauromachy battles. They had been imported and set up around the perimeter of their own room at the museum, although it was difficult to tell if the panels were in any kind of order.

As George wound them through the crowds of morning patrons, he wondered if the sight of nude statues would offend Elizabeth. They turned to look upon the first set of statues in the collection. George held his breath for a moment, not sure if he should have warned her about the state of undress of the figures represented in the friezes.

"Oh," Elizabeth breathed as a hand went to her mouth. Anna was a bit more vocal in her surprise, though, quickly clasping a hand over her mouth to stifle a shriek. A naked warrior looked as if he was being attacked by a Centaur, one of his arms missing. What could have been a headless woman in a robe was next to the Centaur, and beyond that was a robed man, his head also missing.

George could feel Elizabeth's eyes on him as she first studied the statuary and then him. *Is she comparing what she sees to me?* he wondered. The statues were larger than life-size, so he hoped she would take *that* into account as she compared all the body parts. At least the warriors that still had complete sets of genitalia weren't too well endowed.

"It's too bad so much is missing," Elizabeth said in a hoarse whisper. Blinking, George wondered if she was referring to those specific body parts or the statuary in general. "And it appears as if the marble was colored at one time."

He led them through the hall, where friezes were displayed end-to-end around the entire room. They occasionally stopped to view a particular frieze, especially if it was more complete. Anna seemed most disturbed by one of the Amazons, who had apparently been killed and was being taken from the battle, her torn gown leaving a naked breast on display. George kept part of his attention on Elizabeth, wondering what she was thinking as she took in the same scene. "Are you all right?" he asked her *sotto voce*.

Elizabeth glanced up at him, her face flushed. "I am," she replied with a nod. "It's all so very... powerful. The carving has captured so much movement and emotion."

A bit relieved at hearing her description, George relaxed and moved them to the next section. And so it went for another hour as they walked around the room, weaving their way through the crush of people, before exiting the hall and moving on to the Towneley collection. There they walked around the Discobolus, a marble of a discus thrower.

"His head looks as if it had to be reattached," Elizabeth murmured, trying to keep her gaze from settling on the naked man's genitalia.

George angled his own head and nodded. The seam where the repair had been made was quite evident. "And he's looking in the wrong direction," he whispered, moving so his lips had to be close to Elizabeth's ear as he made the comment. "His head should be pointed back, so he's looking at the discus."

"Oh," she replied, giving the statue another look, her own head angling to mimic the discus thrower. "I see what you mean," she murmured. They passed by a few more Grecian statues, of gods and goddesses in various poses, a Roman caryatid, a cupid, a satyr and a nymph, a bust of Homer, the head of Clytie, a large vase, a Venus, a sphinx and a marble of two boys quarreling over a game of knuckle bones. George allowed his gaze to settle on Elizabeth as she moved from each display, wondering what she thought of the statuary.

When they finally took their leave of the museum, George escorted her on his arm. "I do hope you enjoyed the morning," he spoke as he assisted Elizabeth into the curricle. "I found the exhibit quite interesting."

Elizabeth afforded him a smile. "It was indeed."

Once Anna was seated in the back, George hopped up and took the reins from the boy who held them. "Any trouble?" he asked the youth as he fished another coin from his pocket.

"No, sir," the boy answered, shaking his head. "But a gentleman asked me to give this to Lady E," he said as he produced a wrinkled pasteboard from his pocket.

George heard Elizabeth's inhalation of breath. He realized too late why she should be surprised. Other than the few who she had helped or done business with while setting up her office, who knew of her real identity?

She reached over and took the card from the boy, nodding as she did so. "Thank you," she said before she read the bold text.

Waiting patiently—George figured Elizabeth would offer the name on the card if she wanted to—he touched the crop to the back of the horses and merged the curricle into traffic.

"Do you know Mr. Avery Whittaker at the Bank of England?" Elizabeth suddenly asked, her attention on some-thing far ahead of them. Her brows were furrowed, as if she were deep in thought and not quite sure of something.

Turning his head to regard his passenger for a moment,

George shrugged. "I know *of* him, but haven't had the pleasure of an introduction." When she didn't reply right away, he asked, "Is something amiss?"

Elizabeth half turned toward him, the card still gripped in her gloved hands. "He was the man I paid so Mr. Streater could gain back his old position at the bank."

"Go on," George replied carefully.

"He has written here that he has another position available."

George considered the way in which she made the statement, as if it bothered her somehow when she should have been happy to know she could help another unemployed man. "That's good, right? You can place another wounded man into employment."

Despite knowing that George knew of her charity, Elizabeth was still surprised at his comment. "Yes. Yes, it is," she replied softly. She was sure the position would require another bribe, though. How many other positions would Mr. Whittaker have in exchange for a bribe?

"Or, perhaps it is not," George said suddenly. He reconsidered the situation. Was Avery Whittaker looking to make a windfall on the bribes Lady E would be willing to pay to place her clients? "Do you consider Mr. Whittaker an honorable man?" he asked then, keeping his eye on traffic and glancing in her direction when he could afford to do so.

Elizabeth sat very still for a long time, not immediately responding to George's question. "My impression of him was not... favorable," she admitted, turning her attention to George. She watched his profile as he expertly drove the equipage through the busy traffic. When he glanced again in her direction, she almost looked away, not wanting to be caught staring at him. But she was caught. She held his gaze for a moment before George had to look away so he could steer them around a costermonger selling oranges at the edge of the street.

"Then do not do business with the man," he said with a shake of his head. "There are plenty of other employers who may not require payment for their positions. Or, at least not twenty guineas." He continued driving the curricle around various slower vehicles until they were on a wider street that afforded them more room.

"Could we... could we go for a walk, George?" she asked, her manner still suggesting she was pensive.

"Oh, course, my lady," George said, a grin lifting his eyes. They were off at a fast clip, passing carts and horses and carriages on their way to Rotten Row.

Once in Hyde Park, George maneuvered the curricle onto a side lane, parking it under a large oak that provided a patch of shade for the horses and for Anna, who dozed in the back seat. He jumped down to the ground and quickly hobbled the horses before moving to the other side of the curricle.

Elizabeth's hand trembled as she placed it into George's hand. A look of concern passed over his face as she stepped down from the curricle. "Is there something wrong, my lady," he queried, his brows furrowing in concern. Aware that her half boot didn't yet have a solid purchase on the curricle's upper step, he reached over with his other hand to place it at her waist. Just as she slipped, he let go of her hand and caught her waist in both hands as she fell. He slowly lowered her to the ground, surprised she didn't seem to notice her precarious situation. He held her until he was sure her feet were on the ground.

She suddenly let out a startled gasp.

"Lady Elizabeth?" he added quickly, seeing her lower lip quiver as he let her down. He was about to offer his arm but instead stood facing her. He gave a quick glance in the direction of Anna, noting her closed eyes. She was resting against the squabs, oblivious to her mistress' distress. He quirked a brow at Elizabeth, wanting her to at least say *something* before he moved to escort her along the tree-lined path.

"Forgive me, George. I just... I am..." She paused for a moment and then looked up at him, her eyes bright. "I am nervous," she blurted, her face pinking with her admission.

Taken aback, George stared at her for a long moment. "I assure you, Lady Elizabeth, you have no reason to be nervous. We are just going for a stroll." He stopped when he noticed her attention was not on him, but her face had turned that beautiful shade of pink she seemed to display when embarrassed. Leaning so his forehead nearly touched hers, he added, "And, I promise, I will not attempt to steal a kiss."

That comment got her attention.

Elizabeth's face turned up suddenly, so her parted lips were mere inches from his. "You won't?" she questioned, the tone of her voice indicating disappointment. Her eyes were wide, their aquamarine coloring clear in the autumnal midday light.

Now truly confused, George pondered how to respond. If she wasn't nervous about the prospect of him kissing her, what had her so addled? "Well, that is, unless... unless you *want* me to. And then I shall happily oblige you, of course." He lowered his voice to a whisper. "Though I would recommend we wait until we are out of your maid's line of sight before doing so."

Her face brightening, Elizabeth nodded and moved to put her hand on his arm. "I apologize, George. I am not nervous about kissing, truly." They began walking, George's eyebrow arching up at the comment. "It's just that, I wish to speak with you about a topic of some... delicacy." There was something about having seen so many naked bodies that seemed to have emboldened her—even if they were carved in marble and missing several parts.

Now *George* was suddenly nervous. He waited a moment before saying, "Go on."

There was a moment of silence as they walked the crushed granite path, the only sounds coming from bird song and the crunching under their feet. And then the sound of Elizabeth's deep inhalation of breath came followed by an apology. "Forgive my impropriety at asking this, but... do you... frequent brothels?" The last part of the question came out quickly, as though if she thought too much about what she was going to ask, she would think better of it and not ask at all, and then later regret not asking.

Amused and a bit relieved, George forced his lips into a thin line. "I do not," he stated evenly, his head shaking just a bit. He wondered if it was a sigh of relief he heard coming from Elizabeth or merely her labored breathing.

"Do you employ a mistress?"

His amusement leaving him as suddenly as he felt it, he again replied, "I do not." When Elizabeth looked up, her face showing her surprise, he added, "I did until very recently."

Elizabeth continued to look up at him. "Did you... tire of her?" There was a hint of concern in her question, as if she was worried about the fate of the mistress.

Taking a deep breath, George was tempted to rebuke her for the improper questions, but something about her nervous behavior had him curious about her motivation for asking the questions in the first place. "Not at all. Our relationship simply... changed, I suppose," he said, a bit of sadness sounding in his response. Figuring she would ask how, he continued, "We are the best of friends now. I take tea with her a couple of times a week, and we discuss all sorts of topics. She is a very intelligent woman," he explained quickly, not wanting Elizabeth to get the wrong idea. "And she is older and far wiser than me," he added with a quirk at the corner of his mouth.

He watched as Elizabeth regarded him from the corner of her eye. "Oh," she finally replied. George thought she might change the subject, but then she asked, "Then, are you looking for a new... lover?"

George suddenly stopped walking, forcing Elizabeth, whose arm was hooked into his, to spin around and end up face to face with him. *Is that what she thought?* That he was seeking a mistress and had *her* in his sights?

And then another possibility formed in his mind.

Was she *offering* to be his mistress? Was there something about seeing statues of naked men that caused this proper young lady to suddenly become wanton? Even statues that were missing vital parts?

If so, he might have to consider taking her to the museum every time they went for a ride.

He brought her hand up to his mouth and kissed the back of it. "I suppose you could put it in those terms," he answered carefully, "Although I believe in my case, the proper term is 'wife'."

He wondered at the look of relief on her face.

"Now, you must answer a question for me," he ventured carefully. "You have been extremely nervous and very quiet since we left the museum. And now, as well. Why?"

Elizabeth took a deep breath and looked around him, noting that her maid couldn't clearly see them from where she rested in the curricle. "I have been led to believe by some of my older friends' comments that... marital congress is most unpleasant," she whispered, deciding not to consider Beth's comments to the contrary.

George's eyebrow cocked up nearly into his hairline. "Indeed? How unfortunate for them," he responded, the comment out of his mouth before he had a chance to think about how it would sound.

Her eyes widened. "Is it... supposed to be?" Her voice was breathy, and her hand shook in his, her nervousness now more apparent than ever. From what Beth had said, she should look forward to sexual congress, as long as she had a generous husband.

George took a deep breath and pondered how to respond, not realizing that she hadn't yet answered his question. "From what I understand, and I can only provide hearsay because I am a man, after all—"

"Of course," she was nodding, her expression indicating she was hanging on his every word.

"—I have heard a woman's first time experiencing sexual congress can be... unpleasant." He closed his eyes tightly, aware that his face had taken on a shade very close to the color of her hair. "But then, thereafter, it should be a very... pleasant, indeed, a very pleasurable experience," he clarified, his voice dropping to barely a whisper. "If it is not, then their husbands are not doing right by them in the bedchamber. Or whatever room they frequent when engaging in intercourse," he added, noting her widened eyes at his clarification.

The slight breeze brought the scent of jasmine to his nostrils, and he was aware that it had to have come from her. There was no jasmine anywhere near where they stood. The heady fragrance must have addled his brain even more than their topic of conversation, for the next words out of his mouth were, "Of course, it is possible for a woman to be thoroughly pleasured without involving intercourse." He immediately wondered why he would even put voice to that option.

And then he heard her response and realized why.

"Oh," she breathed, her head nodding, the swath of auburn hair visible at the base of her hat showing golden and red. "I see. Will you... I mean, if you are so inclined, do you suppose you could do that? With me? To me?" Her lower lip quivered as if she might cry. "I wish to *know...*"

There was a moment when George Bennett-Jones thought he had died and gone to heaven, his first and only wish for the past few days to be given the opportunity to bed the beautiful Elizabeth Carlington. To think a simple trip to the museum and the sight of naked men carved in marble could cause such curiosity in a lady that she would ask to be given a demonstration of pleasure!

What she was suggesting was wholly inappropriate. *Wasn't it?* He was suddenly uncertain, not having covered this kind of situation with Josephine. Certainly, if a lady was asking— begging almost—to be pleasured, wasn't it acceptable for him to oblige her? For him to accommodate her request?

At the moment, he wanted nothing more than to accommodate her right then and there. He could easily unfasten part of her bodice until he could slide his hand beneath the fabric and fill it with one of her breasts, tease the nipple until it was ripe and ready for his tongue and teeth, pleasure her until she either begged for more or felt sated enough to tell him to stop.

And if she begged for more?

A lady wouldn't do such a thing, of course.

If she were his wife and begged for more, well, he could kneel before her, slide a hand lightly up the inside of her calf and thigh until he could use a finger to part her curls and touch the feminine folds that protected her womanhood. And then he would simply add a finger or two and tease the nub therein until it was swollen and throbbing and she was no longer able to stand on her own. Then he would capture her limp body in his arms and gentle her back to reality. Slowly. Kissing her lightly and whispering assurances in her ear as his lips touched the delicate lobes.

When he was sure she was brought to rights, he would calmly refasten her bodice and thank her for the opportunity to do her bidding. Then he could say he was looking forward to pleasuring her as often as she wished since she was his wife.

If she wasn't his wife? *She's not my wife.*

She would have to agree to be his wife.

Wouldn't she?

I have permission to court her, but does she know that?

He really shouldn't agree to her request, but if he didn't, would she seek such knowledge elsewhere? From Trenton? The thought had him deciding he had to do whatever he could to see to it she decided in his favor.

Perhaps he should suggest a night she would find a bit too daring, too salacious in the hopes she would think better of her request and beg him to forget she ever asked. Not that *he* would ever be able to forget such a request. Or forgive himself for giving her the out if she took it. This was his opportunity to court her, after all. He might only have this one opportunity to prove himself.

And then the reality of her request hit him in the gut so hard, he nearly doubled over.

Yes, he was sure Josephine's instructions had helped him to become adept enough to pleasure the marquess' daughter, probably enough that she would feel thoroughly sated. But he would be unable to take her as he truly wanted, *as his own*, as his one and only lover for the rest of their lives. Gabriel Wellingham was about to make an offer of marriage, and despite her comment about his awful kiss, George was quite sure Elizabeth would accept the earl's suit over that of a viscount's.

Unless I convince her otherwise.

In the course of pleasuring her, of kissing her lips and breasts and suckling her nipples and stroking her womanhood until she sobbed from the intense sensation of her body's release, he could not take her maidenhead.

He would have to leave her a virgin for her future husband.

He cursed his need to remain honorable over all else. Once again, he nearly cursed at how his honor forbid him to simply take her right then and there.

A feeling of pain mixed with jealousy gripped him. He knew he could no longer deny what she meant to him. He wanted this woman for himself. *She could be my wife*, he thought again. It was true he wasn't as rich as Trenton, certainly not as handsome as the Butter Blond, but he had a title with a decent income. He knew he could keep a promise of fidelity.

And he was quite sure he could keep her satisfied in their bed.

I want her as my wife.

The devil!

What the hell had happened to him in the past five days? He had managed to avoid the Marriage Mart for nine years and suddenly, in five days' time, he had allowed this woman, a marquess' daughter, to captivate him in a way no other had ever done before. This wasn't simple lust he felt. Oh, he wanted very much to bed her, to bring her to ecstasy over and over until she cried out his name in that amazing way she said it. He wanted to bury himself inside her and spend an entire night— no, *every* night—taking his own pleasure at the very second after he was sure she had shattered into a billion tiny pieces of pure pleasure. The very thought of it had his cock straining against his buckskin breeches. Had they been anywhere but in the middle of Hyde Park, he might have stripped her bare right then and there, determined to prove to her that he would make a better lover than any of her other suitors.

Certainly a better lover than Butter Blond.

The mere thought of Trenton in bed with Elizabeth caused him anger. And grief. "May I inquire, my lady, as to who else you might have directed this same... request?" George stammered.

Had she asked Gabriel Wellingham? *God, no!* George could

only imagine the earl taking a great deal of delight in accommodating her request. He would take a great deal more than that if he were given the chance, George thought with derision. Elizabeth's evident nervousness suggested she had broached the subject with only George, but he wanted to be sure.

Elizabeth's eyes widened, her sudden indignation quite apparent. "How *dare* you?" she countered angrily. *This was a mistake! Oh, what have I done?* she thought quickly, wondering what she could say now to leave George with the impression she was simply testing him, or teasing him, having a bit of fun at his expense. But her sudden angry outburst precluded either of those choices now.

The pink flush that infused her face was so sudden, George had to blink to ensure he had actually witnessed the change in her complexion. "Pardon, my lady, I only ask because I am... concerned... for your reputation," he countered, his voice so quiet Elizabeth could barely make out his words.

She sighed heavily and tore her gaze away from his, squeezing her eyes shut. "I just... I just want to *know*. Father said you could be trusted..." She broke off the comment, her eyes showing surprise when she heard the irony in her words. She shook her head.

At first, George took umbrage at the comment. Why was it everyone in the *ton* found him so damned trustworthy? But he quickly realized how the perception could be put to good use. Put to use proving to Elizabeth that he could pleasure her. Prove to her he was worth consideration as a potential husband. If he wanted her as his wife, he had better start courting her, after all.

"I *can* be trusted," George declared with a nod. "I will, of course, accommodate your request, my lady."

Elizabeth blinked. "You will?" she responded, her eyes once again wide. The aquamarine pools threatened to swallow up George until she suddenly looked away. "Oh, whatever have I done? You must think me... a *wanton!* Please, can you forget I ever asked...?"

He reached out with his own gloved hand and cupped the side of her face, turning it so her eyes finally met his. *No, I can't!*

he almost said in response, thinking of barn doors and horses and how his cock was hardening. "Milady, I would be *honored* to make love to you," he murmured, surprising himself when he noticed he was saying the words out loud. "But I promise when I do so, I will leave your virtue intact."

Lady Elizabeth's eyes widened, her sudden inhalation of breath causing her bodice to rise in turn. "You... you would?" she whispered, her parted lips appearing as if they were begging to be kissed, the tops of her breasts appearing as if they were begging to be caressed.

George was nearly forced to close his eyes. If she agreed to his terms, those breasts would soon be his to pleasure. Nodding, he stepped closer. "But, Lady Elizabeth, I can only do this if you can make me a promise," he stated as he took one of her hands in his.

Elizabeth watched him, her eyes locked on his and her breath held. "Go on," she responded, finally inhaling.

"When Trenton offers for your hand, as I am led to believe he will do in the next day or so, please think of your future happiness... and not just the money or his title," he stated as he held his head high. "And know that should you decide not to accept his suit, I will offer for you. And I promise you right now, that should you agree to be my wife, I will *never* take a mistress nor employ a lady of the evening. As my wife, you will be honored and cherished for the rest of our days."

Awestruck, Elizabeth stared at him for several seconds. She wanted to protest—of course, she would consider her alternatives before simply agreeing to wed Gabriel Wellingham! Actually, she already had. But until she discovered just how pleasurable—or not—lovemaking could be, she suddenly didn't want to make a decision about marrying *anyone*. Even by Christmastime.

Please, think of your future happiness.

What an odd request from a man she had only met a few days ago!

Odd, and yet so sincere.

Realizing she needed to respond in some fashion, Elizabeth

took a deep breath. "I will, George. I promise," she finally said with a nod.

George did his best to keep his eyes from widening and a cry of delight from escaping his lips. He nodded in turn, his plans forming quickly in his head. "I will send an unmarked town coach to your house at six o'clock this evening. Say you are having dinner with a friend and leave your maid behind. We'll share champagne in the library when you arrive. Dinner is at seven. Wear your choice of garments, but know that I shall remove every one of them before the clock strikes ten. I shall see to it you are thoroughly pleasured by midnight and allow you to rest undisturbed until one. Then I shall help you to get dressed and personally see to it you are returned safely to your home by two."

George ended his quickly made up itinerary and then thought he should at least give her an out should she change her mind. She was a woman, after all, and once she gave this assignation some more thought, she would probably wish she had never brought it up with him. "Should you change your mind, simply decline the coach when it arrives.

"Regardless of what happens, I will not change my good opinion of you."

Sometime during his description of the night's schedule, Elizabeth felt her breasts grow heavy, their nipples becoming hardened pebbles. Somewhere deep inside, desire bloomed. She felt moisture form at the top of her thighs, tendrils of heat coiling in her abdomen. And she seemed to have difficulty breathing, although that could have been due to how tightly Anna had tied her corset that morning. *I shall remove every one...* She glanced up at him, her sudden intake of breath sounding as if she were offended. "If I am to be... naked," she said the word very quietly, "What about you? Will you remove your clothes as well?"

George struggled to maintain his pleasant look as he felt a wave of embarrassment wash over him. "Have you ever seen an unclothed man?" he asked, the words so quiet she had to lean in toward him to hear them. "Besides the statues we just saw at the museum, of course," he added in a somewhat louder voice.

She stared at George for a few seconds, a memory of seeing her father atop her mother flash before her eyes. They had both been naked—her mother's long legs wrapped about her father's hips while his body bowed over hers, supported on arms that were taut, his face straining as if he were in agony. She had heard her mother's moans from outside the room and thought perhaps she was in pain. But when she had opened the door and peaked through the crack, she understood almost immediately what she was witnessing. Her father's movements suddenly stilled and he groaned loudly while her mother mewled in delight, her face full of joy. "I saw my father once," she whispered with a nod. "Quite by accident," she added, her face turning a deep pink with the admission.

George nodded, silently wondering how *that* had happened. "I should not wish to... frighten you by having you see me." He paused a moment and then added, "Although I have a very... fit body... and—"

"Which is quite evident to anyone who sees you in evening attire," Elizabeth put in quickly, thinking perhaps it was better that George *not* be naked.

What if I cannot keep my hands off of him?

George's expression turned to one of delight. "Why, thank you, milady. I do believe you have justified every pound I have spent at Weston's with your compliment."

Elizabeth gave him a nod, her thoughts going back to her original query. And his quick reply. Everything he claimed he would do that evening was so wrong, and yet, she was... *curious.* She felt desire. Perhaps not for him, exactly, but desire to know more about what happened in a bedchamber late at night. *I shall see to it you are thoroughly pleasured by midnight.* And yet, he promised he would leave her virtue intact.

How could that be?

He said he would make love to her, but didn't that imply... something *more* than the kissing and touching she was imagining? Something didn't quite make sense in all this, and she struggled to think while her body wanted his hands, his lips, his body all over it.

She would be pleasured, but what of George? He had just promised she would be left with her maidenhead intact. Other than seeing her naked, what could he possibly gain by agreeing to her request? Was seeing her naked... enough? "You make a very generous offer, George," she finally answered, stepping forward to place a hand against his cheek. A hint of stubble was already apparent despite the early hour. "But what of you? Of your... pleasure?"

Stunned that she hadn't dismissed the entire idea outright, George placed a hand over hers, lifting it so that he could gently kiss the palm. "Just hearing you say my name when you are in ecstasy will be pleasure enough for me," he replied, his voice husky at the mere thought of her naked body next to his. Leaning down, he kissed her lightly, using just his lips.

Elizabeth returned the gentle kiss, wanting it to become something far more intense, more powerful, more punishing in the hope it could soothe the ache that had infused her body. How could she wait until *tonight*? How could she survive the overwhelming desire that was coursing through her body right now? But George finished the kiss as lightly as he had begun it, pulling away ever so slowly. He turned to lead them back to the curricle, but just as she was placing her hand on his arm, he pulled her into his arms and hugged her body to his as tightly as he could.

As Elizabeth wrapped her arms around his neck and returned the hug, the feel of his hot, hard body against the entire length of hers made her feel as if she was being branded. The even harder bulge digging into her belly made her wonder if she might have some control in all of this; his body's response was a reaction to *her*, she realized. But before she could truly enjoy the moment, George had pulled away and was straightening his coat and sleeves.

"I... I apologize, milady." His eyes were downcast. *How could I allow myself that impropriety?* Wasn't it bad enough that he had not only agreed to her request to know *more*, but that he had described an evening of what some would consider debauchery?

He was going to remove every stitch of her clothing! *I'm a heathen.*

"Please, do not," Elizabeth replied quickly, her head shaking with her words.

"I promised I wouldn't steal a kiss." *I am going to hell.*

Elizabeth had to stifle the urge to throttle him. "You cannot steal what is freely given," she countered, her manner suggesting she might suddenly be a bit perturbed with him.

A bit taken aback at her sudden ire, George considered her comment and wondered if he had annoyed her enough that she would call off the assignation. When she didn't offer further comments, George finally nodded, holding his arm for her. "Thank you, milady." *Maybe I won't go to hell.*

They returned to the curricle in silence, waking Anna as they climbed up. And for nearly the entire ride back to the Morganfield House, they said not a word, but Elizabeth's mind was in a whirl.

Whatever was I thinking?

Obviously I was not thinking, she corrected herself, for *had* she truly thought this through, she would have come to her senses and, when George asked why she seemed so nervous, she could have blamed it on the possibility that they might kiss while on their walk along the secluded path. Asking the man for a demonstration of kissing, as she had done two nights ago, was one thing. Asking to be pleasured just to discover what it was like to be pleasured—before she was suitably married—was ludicrous.

Curiosity killed the cat. *What will it do to me?*

As if in reply, a frisson coursed through her entire body. She gasped, stunned that the mere thought of George touching her would have such an effect on her.

But one thing—no, two things—had been made perfectly clear during their discussion.

First, George Bennett-Jones was an honorable man.

He was not going to seduce her because he *could*. He was going to do so because she asked it of him.

What else would he be willing to do for me? she wondered. Did she have some kind of tantalizing effect on the man? *You can trust George...*

Second, in a surprise she couldn't have seen coming, at least not this soon in her relationship with him, George had said that if she didn't accept Gabriel Wellingham's suit, then he planned to ask for her hand in marriage.

She remembered her conversation with Beth. At the time, she had only danced and supped with George, never considering him a contender for her hand. He hadn't seemed interested in her in that way. After their intimate kiss at Lady Worthington's ball, and the discussion they had just had, she decided he was courting her.

If she compared the two men, she would have to seriously consider George's suit.

To be fair to Gabriel, though, he was an *earl*, she considered. And he was rich as Croesus. What did Mr. Bennett-Jones have to offer? She didn't even know what the man did to earn his money! He exuded self-confidence in a way that surprised her, given he was not a particularly handsome man. And he behaved as if he were a gentleman, a man of means. He had to be fairly well-to-do; his fine tailored clothing (he had said something about spending money at Weston's) and new curricle with its matched Cleveland Bays were evidence of that. And he had mentioned his home in Mayfair.

She would be there tonight.

She would see first-hand how he lived, how many servants he employed...

Her stomach took a tumble and she gasped. *His servants!* Should any of them gossip, and servants always gossiped, she would be ruined!

George reached out a hand and placed it over hers. "What is it?" he asked, concern etching the brow she could see as he kept his eyes on the road, expertly weaving the curricle in and around the traffic outside the park.

Elizabeth glanced around, surprised they were already out of Hyde Park and in Oxford Street. Turning to see if Anna was still sleeping, she leaned over so that her lips were near his ear. "Do you employ servants?"

His eyes widening a bit, George took her meaning almost immediately. "An entire household staff of ten, of course, but I will see to it that not even my butler, Elkins, will be in residence this evening. Your reputation will be quite safe, I assure you," he murmured, realizing he was going to have to invent an evening's entertainment for his servants to go out and enjoy while he saw to Elizabeth's. He wanted desperately to kiss her then, to assure her somehow that she had nothing to fear. He half expected her to change her mind, to apologize and request he forget their entire conversation.

But Elizabeth Carlington wasn't a typical lady of the *ton*, he was finding.

"I will provide a chaperone in the carriage, but she is of utmost quality and will be discreet." At least, he hoped he could convince Josephine to be a chaperone. *What will she think of this arrangement?* He wondered if his mistress would scold him for having proposed such an assignation. "Do you know how you will... take your leave?" he asked then, realizing he had given her instructions and no opportunity to argue or counter what he had said.

Sighing, Elizabeth thought of Beth. Certainly the duchess would agree to be her excuse for the evening given their conversation in the park.

This is what you want. This is what you desire. Don't think too much.

"I will say I plan to dine with a good friend, who is providing a coach and a chaperone. I will be home late," she recited, as if she did this sort of thing every week. "See you at breakfast tomorrow morning."

George dared a glance at her and smiled. His suddenly handsome visage caught Elizabeth by surprise. "Tonight, then," he said in a whisper as he handed her down and escorted her to the front door of Carlington House before heading back to the curricle to assist the maid.

Aware that Alfred had opened the door behind her, Elizabeth stood on the top step of Carlington House and watched as George escorted Anna to the house. *An honorable man,* she thought again. "Thank you for a lovely morning," she said when George bowed over her hand.

"You're very welcome, Lady Elizabeth," he replied, aware of Alfred's scowl as the butler stared down at him. "I look forward to our next encounter. Until then," he said as he tipped his hat. "I wish you a very pleasant day."

CHAPTER 31

ARRANGEMENTS FOR AN ASSIGNATION

Once he took his leave of Carlington House, George headed straight for Josephine's townhouse. He found his mistress at home, in her bath, in fact, preparing for an evening at the theatre. While George described what had happened in the park and his intention to prove himself to Elizabeth that very evening, he knelt behind the copper tub.

"What are you doing, George?" she asked, sitting forward in the tub so that her breasts were pressed against her bent knees.

"I wish to help you with your hair, of course," he answered in surprise. "You... you've allowed me to in the past."

Josephine gave him a smile and reluctantly leaned back. As he rubbed rose-scented soap into her hair, taking care to gently massage the suds through the long strands before pouring a pitcher of warm rinse water along her hairline, she sighed. "You'll make your wife an excellent lady's maid," she teased, closing her eyes as a curtain of water streamed over her face.

"You once told me having your hair washed by me was the most sensuous feeling you ever experienced," he countered in a quiet voice, his hands squeezing water out of her hair before he refilled the pitcher and repeated the rinsing. "I told Lady Elizabeth I would ask for her hand if she didn't accept Trenton's suit."

Josephine turned to regard him, obviously disappointed he

would couch his proposal in such terms. "Indeed?" she replied. "Why give him the opportunity at all?"

"It has to be her decision, Josie, which I hope to sway in my favor tonight." He told her of his plans for the evening, only half-believing Lady Elizabeth would get into his coach and appear at his door.

As he expected, Josephine seemed somewhat surprised and rather pleased by the young lady's request, immediately offering her assistance in planning the execution of the evening. She insisted on being involved, reminding George he needed a wife and this was an opportunity for him to court a suitable woman.

Once she was out of the tub and wrapped in a dressing gown, she outlined the details for the evening, from the menu planning to arranging how George was going to return Elizabeth to her home by two in the morning.

But the details for *how* he would go about fulfilling Lady Elizabeth's request were left up to George. He couldn't help but notice Josephine's lack of advice in that regard. She lectured him at length about making sure he kept a pleasant expression on his face. Warned him that, despite how passionate he might feel about the lady, he would have to maintain control of himself. "If you are successful in pleasuring her—if she even allows you to touch her most intimate places—she may very well offer her virtue," she had said by way of a warning.

George scoffed and replied, "Only in my very best dreams."

"Women can become quite wanton when they're given half a chance," Josephine countered, her arms crossing in front of her chest. Alarmed by the comment, George swallowed. Hard. His mistress couldn't help but notice. "Sensuality is not a sin, George," she said with a shake of her head. "If she believes she is committing a sin at any point during the evening, then you have lost." And then she scolded him before reminding him Lady Elizabeth's motive for agreeing to the evening's itinerary was borne of curiosity. "She has heard stories and wants to discover for herself if the claims are true," she explained patiently, remembering her own thoughts on the subject when she was still a virgin.

When she was but seventeen, her mother, a courtesan of some skill and repute, tutored her and her sister in the arts of seduction and pleasure. When it was time for them to make their debut, it was her mother who chose their first protectors.

Her sister left England with a French paramour, an older gentleman who claimed he would continue her education and see to it she was compensated generously.

For Josephine, her mother selected a member of the aristocracy, the son of an earl. The gentleman had been kind that first night, and very generous with his gifts, but his preference for bedding virgins meant she was soon dismissed with a modest settlement and replaced by another courtesan's daughter. Her only other protector before George was another member of the aristocracy, an earl who set her up in a small townhouse near Berkeley Square and kept regular appointments over the course of their five years together. It was under his tutelage that she developed an interest in politics and current events, realizing her lover appreciated their conversations as much as her skills in bed.

His unexpected death meant a few months of uncertainty, and a few months to spend time at home. Time to get reacquainted with those from her youth. And the realization that a man to whom she had once promised her affection was the man with whom she wanted to spend the rest of her life. The man she wanted to marry, should Jack ever make his way in the world and be able to support a wife. But it would be years before he would be able to do just that.

Bereft and fearing for her own future, Josephine returned to London and made discreet inquiries that led to her introduction to George. Their contract was negotiated and paid for by George's uncle, the viscount whose title he had inherited earlier this year. The older man explained he was hiring her because he didn't want his nephew—his only heir—employing whores or otherwise fathering bastards.

The implication was clear to her; she was not to allow a pregnancy, and should one occur, she would be required to end it.

Josephine regarded George for a moment. "If you intend to ask for her hand, you must be sure her thoughts of you promise more than what the earl has to offer. Now is the time to tell her you have a title. Even though Trenton is rich and has a better title than you—" she began, as if he didn't already know how much better Gabriel Wellingham looked on paper—and in the looking glass—than did he. "—I have it on good authority that he lacks certain... *skills*," she hinted, her eyebrow arching suggestively.

The comment captured George's full attention. "What do you know?" he asked, his nervousness about the upcoming evening suddenly gone.

Josephine regarded him for a very long time. "He pays three mistresses, one of them quite a lot more than he should have to," she said with a shake of her head. "Refuses to learn the very basics and sees only to his own satisfaction." This last was said with a bit of derision, as if providing reciprocal pleasure was required along with the coin paid for the privilege of a tumble.

"Why didn't you tell me I didn't please you?" George asked suddenly. "Back in the beginning?" Their arrangement had been in place for some time before she hinted he needed to be a better lover.

Caught off-guard by the question, Josephine regarded him a moment. But then her eyes closed and she sank into the chair next to his, her face softening. She reached for his hand and gripped it. "Because you did. In other ways. Truly." At his look of disbelief, she added, "Because, afterwards, you held me. You spoke sweet nothings, and you stroked my hair. You stayed in my bed far longer than you had to." Indeed, there had been many times when he simply slept with her the entire night, so when they awakened, they could continue making love. Those were the times she cherished most, for it was by the first light of day when George looked his best and seemed happiest. "You... loved me, I suppose." She swallowed hard then, her eyes brightening with unshed tears. Looking away quickly, she took a deep breath and then slowly returned her attention to him. "A woman can overlook quite a lot when she feels... loved."

George was up and out of his chair and lifting her into his arms almost before she had finished her admission. He held her tightly to his body, one arm around her shoulders and the other around her waist. "Oh, Josie, can you ever forgive me for what I'm about to do?" he whispered, his words nearly lost in her hair. He felt her head shake against his shoulder.

Josephine pulled her head away so that she could see his face. "I will never forgive you if you do *not* try for her hand," she countered, a wicked smile replacing the sad visage she had displayed only moments before. "What kind of tutor would I be if my student didn't succeed at my speciality?"

George stared at her for a very long time. "You really *want* me to marry her, don't you?" he asked then, his brows furrowing in confusion. Another thought intruded. "But, I will continue to be your protector even after I am wed—"

"No, you will not."

Josephine's voice sounded almost foreign to his ears; the emphatic statement was delivered with such finality. Confused, George stepped back. "But, if I am not your protector..."

Josephine interrupted him again. "I have already made arrangements for my future, George."

An expression that could only be described as pain crossed George's face before he looked away. *Arrangements? When? And with whom?* Had she done this all behind his back?

His mistress allowed him the moment before she reached out to place a hand on his arm. "Once you inherited, I knew you would need to marry. And marry well. I have seen to it I will have a new protector once that—"

"And I have no say in the matter?" he countered in a voice that was suddenly filled with anger. The look of astonishment hid the other emotions that immediately joined his anger.

"No, you do not," she answered calmly, steeling herself for a row she was sure was about to erupt. They had never fought before. They'd had disagreements on occasion, friendly arguments about politics or his choice of clothing for a weekend in the country or her thoughts on whose social entertainments he should attend. But they had never yelled at one another. Never turned their backs on one another or slammed doors or thrown *objets d' art* at the walls or each other.

"Josie, how could you?"

The woman took a deep breath and held it for a moment before finally saying, "I know you, George. Unlike every other titled man in this town, you will honor your marriage vows. And you would feel beholden to me and feel so guilty, you would continue my allowance for the rest of my days, but I will not be a kept woman—"

"You're my *friend,* damn it!" George shouted, the hurt he was feeling in his chest so acute he thought he might be having an attack of some kind. At the sound of his voice, so loud in his ears, he shut his eyes tightly. *We've never raised our voices at one another*, he thought, stunned he could be acting so poorly toward a woman he was sure he once loved.

"You pay me quite well for the privilege," Josephine responded too quickly, her own voice so quiet he almost didn't hear her words. She regretted them immediately, her hands coming up to cover her mouth even though she knew it was too late. "I did not mean that," she rushed to say, tears pricking the edges of her eyes. How could she say such a thing to a man who only wanted the best for her? Who had seen to her every need for eight years?

Most mistresses could hope for a protector for a year, perhaps two, before having to arrange a new one. She had been blessed when George's uncle had insisted on her being hired as his mistress. He had to have made a discreet inquiry of the Earl of Staffordshire as to her suitability, and the earl's response must have been positive since there were no other living clients to recommend her. And the contract had been quite generous, considering she wasn't a celebrated courtesan. She wondered then if her lack of notoriety was more valued by the viscount than her other talents. She never guessed the arrangement would last eight years!

"Josie," George sighed, the sting of the simple statement hurting almost as badly as the thought of losing her completely. He gathered her into his arms and held her tightly. "Oh, Josie.

He is a duke, no?" he whispered, his lips kissing her hair. "Nothing less than a duke for you, I should think," he added, finally pulling away to gaze at her.

Josephine's eyes were wet with tears. She had never allowed him to see her like this—so sad, so vulnerable. "No, George," she replied with a small shake of her head. "He doesn't even have a title," she added, sniffling.

In the middle of retrieving his handkerchief from his waist coat pocket, George paused and regarded the woman with a frown. "What do you mean?" he asked, finally offering her the linen cloth. "What are you saying?"

Josephine hadn't intended to tell George of her plans to marry the man she had loved when she was a younger woman. The man to whom she had promised her affection all those years ago. Had her father lived through the winter of influenza that ravaged their village when she was seventeen, she wouldn't have made the trip to London in search of her mother. She wouldn't have been tutored by her mother and then been seen by the son of the Earl of Staffordshire and been made an offer she couldn't refuse. An offer that resulted in a career as a mistress, such as it was. But now her childhood lover had made his way in the world. He was ready to take a wife.

And he still wanted her.

"I have accepted an offer of marriage from my first... love," she finally replied, a sense of relief flooding her as she heard the words spoken aloud.

George stared at Josephine for a very long time. "First love?" he repeated, as if he couldn't quite comprehend her statement. At her nod, he closed his eyes. "And... you love him still?" he asked, his eyes remaining shut until he realized he had to open them in order to see her nod in response.

"I have since we were... twelve, thirteen, perhaps," she explained quietly. "We have remained in contact all these years. I was sure he would find someone else, but it turns out, he is a very stubborn man," she said before a sob took her breath. "He still wants me to marry me. He would have wed me after the earl died, but he couldn't support a wife back then."

George inhaled, then let his breath out slowly. "Does this man know you are my mistress?" he queried, not sure what he thought about Josephine returning to a man who had apparently held a candle for her all these years.

Josephine couldn't meet his gaze as she shook her head. "He thinks I have been a servant in a nobleman's home," she replied, her head falling against the small of his shoulder. His arms moved to embrace her, to comfort her as her body shook with another sob.

"Which you have been, I suppose," George said, stroking her face with a finger. He kissed her forehead and then sighed. "I shall miss you terribly," he stated, fighting to keep his composure when he felt tears fill his eyes. He blinked them back and took a deep breath. "Will you go back to Yorkshire then?" he asked, realizing there was no point in arguing about her future when she had already seen to it.

Raising her face from his shoulder, she shook her head. "Jack's business is in Oxfordshire, but he wrote that he would like us to find a house in town, too."

Although a bit confused, George nodded. "And what exactly is his business?"

Josephine took a deep breath. "Wool," she finally said with a nod.

George blinked once. Wool meant sheep, and sheep meant... a shepherd. George couldn't imagine Josephine, a woman who was so worldly—so interested in politics and current affairs—with a man who was a shepherd. "Sheep?" he clarified, thinking she was trying to make her Jack sound as if he had a better station in life. *As long as he's not a tailor.*

"Well, he used to tend them when we were children. His father had quite an extensive herd, you see," she explained quickly. "But Jack figured out a way to make a better weaving machine that turns the wool into a very fine fabric."

"Indeed?" George replied with a furrowed brow. "Does he have one of these machines in actual operation?"

Nodding, Josephine said, "Over a hundred of them in his building in Oxford. He employs several hundred people to operate them and keep them in working order. And several clerks to keep track of the business."

Well, the man sounded like he could be quite wealthy. "The Luddites haven't burned him out, then?"

Cocking her head to one side, she gave George a look of derision. "Jack saw fit to hire people who lost their positions at the factories where the first frames were installed, insisting he wanted only experts to create his superfine," she explained patiently. "It struck me as very wise of him to play on the egos of mere factory workers like that. He makes them feel important. And he pays them more than they made when they worked on looms."

Wise, indeed. "And you love him?" George stated more than asked. He stood very still as he waited for her response.

Knowing she would hurt him with his answer, Josephine returned her head to his shoulder. "I always have, George," she said quietly. "Just as much as I do you," she added as she leaned her head back so that she could see his face.

George nodded, although he had a hard time believing the last statement. *Was it possible for a woman to love two men at the same time?* "Do you suppose I will ever be allowed to meet the man?" he asked, his gaze capturing Josephine's. At her suddenly arched eyebrow, he added, "I think I would be more *accepting* of your arrangement if I at least... knew the man."

Josephine gave him a brief nod. "He cannot know, George," she whispered, her head shaking almost imperceptibly.

Pressing his lips into a thin line, George regarded her for a very long time. "Then he won't," he agreed, hugging her body to his own as if it would be the last time they embraced.

And with that hug, George understood why Josephine was so insistent about helping with the evening's plan, for now it was more important than ever he convince Elizabeth Carlington to be his wife. Josephine had a future planned—and it didn't include him.

CHAPTER 32
MEETING A MISTRESS FOR
THE VERY FIRST TIME

*S*uddenly nervous and wondering for at least the tenth time that day what she was thinking when she made the scandalous request of George Bennett-Jones, Elizabeth took a quick look in the cheval mirror. She might have been wearing a dinner gown, its peacock silk overskirt shimmering in the early evening light from the nearby window, but with only petticoats and a pair of pantaloons and stockings and without a corset or even a chemise beneath, she felt almost naked.

She could simply send a note of regret with whomever was in the coach when it came to fetch her. It was a woman's prerogative to change her mind, after all. But what a coward she would seem to be if she backed out now! And she might be many things, but "coward" was not on the list. What if George had had plans and suddenly changed them to accommodate her request? But, no, *he* had been the one to set the time and place. She had merely made the request, and implored him as a friend to consider it. But come to think on it some more, she hadn't really *begged*. She had merely told him what she wanted.

And not in her typical Elizabeth Carlington manner.

She had been so nervous she could barely walk and breathe at the same time. That George had agreed to her request had surprised her; she expected him to request some time to think on it before giving her an answer, and then, after an interminable two or three days, probably give her his regrets, saying he could not in good conscious do something so salacious to a lady of the *ton*.

And the biggest surprise of all—he intended to ask for her hand in marriage if she didn't accept the earl's suit!

Did he say that out of a sense of honor? For what he planned to do to her went far beyond kissing—it would be considered ruination by anyone. According to Beth's words, though, if the two were betrothed, then what they were about to do would be perfectly normal. Expected, even.

"A town coach has arrived, miss," Anna said from the doorway. "Looks to be fairly new." She gave her mistress a quick look and added a hairpin where a curl threatened to come loose. "What will you take for a wrap? It may get a bit chilly later, and I think it's about to rain."

Anna always thought it was about to rain. Trouble was, she was usually right. This was England. And it rained more often than not.

Flutterbies were circling inside Elizabeth as she considered what to wear over her gown. "My mantle with the hood," she replied finally, knowing it would seem redundant to wear the peacock-feathered bonnet and her hood over it, but hiding her identity might prove more important at two o'clock in the morning than any fashion *faux pax*.

"Very good, my lady," Anna said, coming out of the dressing room with the long wool cape. "Are you going to the theatre then?" she asked, as she helped drape the mantle around Elizabeth's shoulders.

"That's the plan, although with the Duchess of Somerset, who knows? We may end up spending the evening playing cards. No need to wait up. I can undress myself."

With that comment better matching what she had written to Beth in her earlier correspondence, Elizabeth took her leave and boldly walked out to the waiting coach.

It was a beautiful town coach—unmarked, shiny and jet black with no evidence it had ever been used before this evening. A footman held the door open for her as she joined a woman she expected to be one of George's maids. Instead she found a very attractive woman in her mid-thirties, dressed in an expensive carriage gown of green wool and sporting a very fashionable matching hat with green feathers. Elizabeth took the seat opposite the woman, in the direction of travel, settling herself into fine leather squabs and sighing. The trip to George's house would be very comfortable.

The woman's expression was friendly as she regarded Elizabeth.

"How do you do?" Elizabeth said a bit uncertainly, wondering at first if she was climbing into someone else's coach. Then it dawned on her. As a member of the *ton*, Elizabeth would be expected to make the first introduction, even though the other woman was obviously older. "I am Elizabeth Carlington," she said as she held out her right hand and gave the woman a tentative smile.

The woman took her hand and shook it, her eyes taking in Elizabeth without seeming to do so. "Lady Elizabeth," she nodded in turn, her head cocking to one side. "Forgive me, but you are at least as beautiful as George described," she said with a bit of awe in her voice. "I thought he was exaggerating." She had seen Elizabeth many times over the years, of course, but not like this. Not since her coming out. Not since she had changed from a girl fresh out of the schoolroom into a woman.

Elizabeth's mouth formed an 'o' as she heard the words and realized the identity of the woman. "Are you... Josephine, perhaps?" she ventured carefully, studying the elegant visage before her.

Shutting her eyes for an instant, Josephine sighed. "I apologize, my lady. I have been so nervous about meeting you, I've forgotten my manners. I am Josephine Wentworth," she admitted with a nod, her air of confidence momentarily gone.

"Oh, please call me Elizabeth. George told me you are his best friend," she insisted as she leaned forward a bit. *I've seen this woman before!* "Pardon me, but haven't I seen you at the house? In conference with my father, perhaps?" she asked, trying to remember the circumstances. *In the study.* She was dressed in widow's weeds, saying something about an earl while her father sat behind his desk and drank brandy. *In the morning.*

A bit wary, Josephine regarded the younger woman with a look of surprise. "George said that?" she asked in a quiet voice. She tore her gaze from Elizabeth's for a moment, not quite sure what to say. The young lady seemed friendly and approachable, though. "As to my visit with your father, I was simply there to warn him about a potential political opponent. Politics are a... hobby of mine," she added, not expecting Elizabeth to understand.

Elizabeth noted the woman's sudden change in comportment, the way she worried the fabric of her gown between her gloved fingers, the way her eyes had trouble focusing on her. *Have I embarrassed her?* "George also mentioned your prior relationship with him," she offered carefully, her voice as neutral as possible. George had said he was no longer employing a mistress, which meant he was no longer employing *her* as a mistress. And the woman had been in her home, conversing with her father. Apparently not in the capacity of a mistress. *Politics are a hobby...*

All the air seemed to go out of Josephine just then, her beautiful features showing disappointment. Elizabeth thought the woman might cry. "I apologize. Perhaps I misunderstood..."

"You did not," Josephine hurried to interrupt her. Her head was shaking from side to side. "It is time for George to marry, and as much as I adore the man, and I do very much, I am far too old and set in my ways to consider him for a husband," she explained, a brittle smile on her lips. "Perhaps you will allow me to continue as his friend... that is, if you end up becoming his wife. I do hope you won't banish me..."

"Of course not," Elizabeth interrupted, a bit surprised at the mention that she might become George's wife. *George must have told her everything! Which means he is truly serious about asking for my hand if I do not accept the earl's suit!* "He values you. Values your friendship and your opinions very much. I would hope we could... be friends," she added, wondering if her words sounded terribly naïve to the woman who was obviously far more worldly than she.

And whatever was she thinking to say they could be *friends*? Josephine Wentworth was a mistress! Although, perhaps she wasn't well known as a mistress, Elizabeth considered. She certainly looked respectable, what with her beautiful carriage gown and bonnet and a pretty face that didn't sport much in the way of cosmetics.

But now wasn't the time to be thinking about the mistress. She needed to know more about George! "Might I ask a question about George?" Elizabeth asked, thinking that the woman before her probably knew more about the man than anyone else.

A wan smile appeared on Josephine's face. "Of course. I expect you have dozens. George said you'd only just met a few nights ago."

Elizabeth reeled at that. It *had* only been a few nights. Two balls at which the worst and most wonderful things had happened. "Did George tell you why I am visiting him at his house tonight?"

Sighing, Josephine caught a lower lip with a tooth. "He said you had a curiosity about pleasure and that you were coming for dinner."

Elizabeth could feel her face heat with embarrassment. "Oh, dear," she replied, her eyes flitting nervously around the coach. "Do you... think me wanton? For wondering about... about pleasure, I mean?"

The former mistress smiled sadly. "No, my darling. I should be worried if you did not."

Well, this was unexpected. "And, does *George* think I am wanton?"

Josephine shook her head. "I rather doubt it. One of the reasons he is so enamored with you is that you are not a frail, fraidy kitten. You apparently know what you want and are willing to go after it," she added, daring Elizabeth to counter the assessment.

"I assure you, I have *never* done anything like this before," Elizabeth breathed, her nervousness returning. "I just... I do not want to go through life wondering what might have been if I end up married to a man who kisses like a dog and employs multiple mistresses."

Josephine sat up straighter, obviously surprised by the bold comment. Of course, she knew the identity of Elizabeth's subject. "Oh, my. You're not speaking of the Earl of Trenton by any chance, are you?" she asked, her expression taking on a painful grimace.

Her own eyes widening, Elizabeth nodded. "Why, yes. There's been talk he plans to ask for my hand. Although my father says he has not yet asked his permission to do so."

Shaking her head in disgust, Josephine pretended to be interested in something outside the coach. "One of my friends is a mistress to Trenton. I would never put up with him myself, for I cannot tolerate lickers..." She paused, and Elizabeth heard her quick inhalation of breath. "I apologize."

"Please, do not. Tell me what you were about to say," Elizabeth insisted. "I must know of his proclivities. I already know about his... wet kisses," she said with a hint of disgust.

Attempting to stifle a chuckle, Josephine rolled her eyes. "There are times—and places on your body—where you will find it is... appropriate for a man to... lick you. Trenton does not seem to have those sorted just yet. Which is why his three mistresses tend to keep him talking as much as possible so there is little time for him to engage in kissing and such," she added with a hint of delight. Oh, what tactics mistresses could employ to tolerate their protectors!

Elizabeth stared at the older woman. "Oh, dear," she finally breathed, a feeling of unease crawling through her. The coach suddenly stopped, and from the gentle bump she felt, she knew the driver had dismounted. She could hear the click of his heels on the cobbles as he walked to the door. Staring at Josephine, Elizabeth could feel her confidence waning even before the door opened.

Josephine saw Elizabeth's discomfort and leaned forward to take one of the younger woman's hands in hers. "He will not hurt you. He will not take your virtue. He just wants to give you what you want. What you asked for," she said in an urgent voice. "And I beg you, please, do not hurt him."

Elizabeth had to force her mouth to close upon hearing Josephine's last words. *Do not hurt him?*

I have no intention of doing such a thing!

CHAPTER 33
WELCOME TO BOSTWICK
PLACE

The door to the coach opened. Taking a deep breath, Elizabeth nodded to George's best friend, pulled her mantle hood over her bonnet, and stepped out of the coach. She waited for Josephine to step out of the coach, but the driver was already closing the door. When Elizabeth turned around to face the house, she gazed up in astonishment. In the center, an arched portico was supported by two Grecian columns, their alabaster finish so bright and untouched by soot, Elizabeth thought they must be new or, at the very least, recently cleaned. Brass fittings on the forest green painted door were polished to a sheen, the lion's head of the knocker reflecting the light from the gas lamps on either side of the doors. The sense of newness was pervasive, even the cut stone steps beneath her feet seemed as if a mason had placed them only last week and she was the first to step on them.

Had the house just been built?

She was sure she would have noticed its construction when on her carriage rides to Hyde Park. No, this house had been here all along, perhaps in a shabbier state, she thought as she regarded the potted topiary trees flanking the front doors. Even their spiral design was perfect in scale and trim, making her think a gardener had been on duty only moments ago. Everything about the exterior of the house suggested its owner came from wealth or had inherited an estate worth thousands. *George must be rich.* A quick look around the nearby homes confirmed she was still in Park Lane. George Bennett-Jones was indeed rich if he could afford a townhouse here in Mayfair! Or, perhaps he merely let the property. Even so, the rent would be exorbitant!

Before she had reached the wide landing at the top of the three steps, she noticed the large pots of topiary trees were flanked by smaller pots of colorful flowers. Aware of the coach pulling out of the drive, she turned to watch it leave, suddenly wondering if the coach belonged to George or to Josephine. A town coach was expensive. Extremely expensive. And that one was so new, she was probably only one of a few to sit in its plush leather squabs.

The door opened to reveal a brightly lit vestibule, its golden walls shimmering with candlelight. It wasn't until she was over the threshold that she perceived the man at the door was not a butler but George himself, dressed in dark superfine and sporting a cravat that was so perfectly tied, she was tempted to hook a finger into the knot and jerk it apart. The thought brought a smile to her face, one that George countered with his own.

She walked to him, glided by him as he stepped aside to give her room, and turned to curtsy when he shut the door and bowed.

"Welcome to my home, Lady Elizabeth," he said quietly, closing the front door before he reached down to take her gloved hand and brush his lips over the bent knuckles. "May I take your mantle, my lady?" he asked then, watching Elizabeth as her eyes darted about the entry.

George was impeccably dressed, she decided, her gaze taking in the long dark blue satin dinner jacket over a silver waistcoat topped with a black silk cravat. His breeches matched the dinner jacket and ended where silver stockings began, their fabric straining due to his muscular calves. Aware of his gaze on her and not wanting him to think she was staring, she redirected her attention to the accoutrements of the well-appointed entry, occasionally glancing in his direction as if she didn't believe what she saw.

George found her gaze amusing at first, her eyes so wide and innocent. *But what does that make me?* He wondered if he had grown horns and a tail ending in a trident.

He very nearly moved his hand to his head to check.

Elizabeth absently removed the catch from the frog at her throat. Lifting the hood from over her bonnet, she pulled the mantle from around one shoulder. "Yes, thank you. Could you please let Mr. Bennett-Jones know Lady Elizabeth has come to call?" she said lightly, hoping a bit of levity would help her retain a sense of control. She would need to cling to that little bit of control to get through the night.

Smiling in that way Elizabeth found made him look so handsome, George lifted her mantle from her other shoulder and had to close his eyes a moment. Her teal gown, the perfect contrast to her auburn hair, was cut low in the front to reveal her deep cleavage and was just as low cut in the back, its deep v ending in the middle of her back. The tiny matching bonnet, adorned with peacock feathers, was pinned at a fashionable angle in the mass of curls. He knew almost immediately the bonnet was *the* bonnet—the one he had purchased on her behalf, he hoped without her knowledge.

Or her father's.

"I would, my lady, but I have strict instructions from Viscount Bostwick to take you to the library for champagne," he said with a hint of mischief.

"You have a ..," she paused as she continued her survey of the elegant vestibule, her eyes taking in the painting on the ceiling, the gilt edging on the moldings, the alabaster columns that stood on either side of the wide opening to the main hall, the Aubusson carpet covering the entire floor. She had made a complete turn of the room while taking it all in. "... A very beautiful home," she breathed as her gaze finally settled on him. She blinked, though, at realizing what he had just said. "Viscount Bostwick?" she repeated, a look of confusion settling on her face. "Who…?"

George bowed. "At your service, my lady," he replied with a grin. Having hung up her mantle, he had reappeared from behind a wall that displayed a huge oil painting of what very well could be the West Sussex countryside. "My home is made more beautiful by your presence, my lady," he added as he moved to stand in front of her, a slight smile keeping his face friendly and handsome. *Keep your expression light or you'll scare her to death*, he remembered Josie saying.

Elizabeth blinked. "I didn't know. No one said. You never—"

"Does it make a difference?" he asked in a quiet voice. He suddenly shook his head. Of course it makes a difference. He was a peer. Had he been anything less in social standing, she would never consider his suit. "Perhaps we can pretend for just one night that we are simply two people who wish to spend time together," he proposed.

The comment seemed sincere, as did the look in his eye as he regarded her. "Very well," she replied as she gave a quick glance down the great hall. "Is your butler otherwise detained?" she asked, her nervousness suddenly returning. George looked larger somehow, more imposing, certainly more confident than he had in the ballroom or in the park. But he also appeared approachable, his dark blue top coat and breeches the perfect enhancement for his bronzed skin and sable hair and blue eyes. She hadn't noticed his eyes before, hadn't even realized he had blue eyes. They weren't light blue like Gabriel's, but a darker blue. Deeper. A color she could spend several minutes trying to define as she stared up at him.

George held her gaze while wondering what she was thinking. "As I promised, I have seen to it the staff is away for the evening," he answered lightly. "I sent them on a bit of a holiday, actually." He didn't add that she had no reason to be concerned about gossiping servants. For an assignation such as this, it was imperative that no one know of her presence in his home. Had he not trusted his coachman as much as he did, he would have had Elizabeth picked up by a hired coach. Josephine insisted on the new town coach, though, reminding him that he was competing with Butter Blond for Elizabeth's hand.

He could only hope Josephine's presence in the coach hadn't been a mistake.

CHAPTER 34
A DINNER TO REMEMBER

*E*lizabeth placed her gloved hand on his arm. *How can his arm be so warm?* she wondered as she walked alongside him, her gaze trying to take in the elegance of his home. The ornate floral arrangement on the round table in the vestibule, the columns that stood on either side of the entrance to the hall, the endless length of Aubusson carpet on the floors, the rich moldings along the walls and carved balustrades on the edge of the stairs. Carlington House was certainly well appointed, with rich fabrics and tasteful wall coverings and furnishings, but George's house was somehow more... more *everything*. Newer, perhaps. Not as lived-in as her own home, and yet it felt more welcoming. "Truly, you have a beautiful house," she breathed again, her head tilting to take in the myriad paintings that lined the walls.

George turned his head and found his lips mere inches from hers. "Because you are in it," he replied without pause.

Thinking he might be teasing, Elizabeth stared at his eyes, saw the desire there, saw his lips hovering so close, and decided he wasn't teasing. Without realizing quite what she was doing, she lifted her head just a bit more and raised her free hand to cup the side of his face. Her lips collided with his, her mouth open and inviting and tasting of mint. But the kiss was quick, meant to greet him and to let him know she had not changed her mind and, perhaps, to remind him that *she* had a bit of control in all this. She allowed a wan smile. "You are too kind," she murmured, finally responding to his compliment. Motioning toward what she figured was the library door, George nodded and led her into the brightly lit room.

Too kind? George thought suddenly. He had spent the afternoon designing just how this was going to work. This was his only opportunity to court her, to convince her he would make a better husband than Butter Blond, to make her feel as if she were the only woman in the world, the only woman for him. And after only a walk from the front door to the library, she had him so addled he wanted to do nothing more than undress her right there and then and ravish her until she agreed to be his wife.

And then he would really ravish her.

"Oh, George, what an amazing library," she cooed as she turned around slowly to take in the accoutrements of the room —the towers of books, the coffered ceilings, the astrolabe on the edge of a walnut library table, the overstuffed chairs set next to a massive stone fireplace where bright flames danced and logs crackled and popped. This wasn't at all like the stuffy library at Carlington House, with its dark woods and even darker fabrics. This was warm and inviting. One could pick out a book, sink into one of the comfortably plush chairs, and simply get lost in a story.

When she had made the entire turn of the room, she found him holding two champagne flutes. *Deja vu*, she thought, remembering another library and two glasses of champagne in the Worthington house—only the night before.

Had it only been last night?

She took one of the glasses and held it up in a sort of salute before taking a long drink. One of George's eyebrows arched up. She took note, stopped nearly in mid-gulp and slowly pulled the glass away from her lips. His attention held as the rim left her lip, a droplet of champagne resting there until the tip of her tongue captured it.

The thought of her tongue tip sliding over his body came

unbidden, forcing George to take a quick breath and hold it, forcing him to stay very still or risk losing control and taking her into his arms and forcing his own tongue into her mouth.

Holding the half-empty glass up near her shoulder, Elizabeth wondered if George would admonish her for drinking too much or too fast. "It's very good," she murmured, indicating the glass she held.

George's lips curved and he moved a step closer. He held out his glass as if to look at the liquid with lamplight behind it. "All because of the bubbles," he said quietly, forcing Elizabeth to set her gaze on his glass. "When you drink champagne, small sips allow the bubbles to rest on your tongue, to tease it into tasting the unique flavors before they float away. Then, when you swallow, you do so of only a bit of the liquid, and those bubbles continue their magic as they slide down your throat." His gaze had moved from the liquid in his glass to her, his eyes following the column of her neck down a bit before he glanced back up at her. "If you haven't eaten anything recently, then within minutes, your knees may feel a bit giddy, and after a few more, *you* may begin to feel that way, too." This last was said with a hint of humor, his eyes sparkling nearly as much as the champagne. He finally took a sip, and Elizabeth could tell he was holding it on his tongue before he finally swallowed. She watched, mesmerized, as his throat moved.

She had been holding her breath as she listened to George described the effects of champagne. Despite having drunk several glasses the night before, she had never given much thought to how she was supposed to drink champagne—slowly, taking small sips at a time. Her knees were already feeling a bit weak—she was nervous again, and she thought if she drank the champagne quickly, it would help calm her for the dinner to come. Now she considered that if she didn't sit down or at least lean against something solid, she was afraid she might just sink to the floor. Glancing down, she found the floor covered in a colorful patterned carpet. Perhaps she could simply lower herself to sit on it, as long as she arranged her skirts to keep her ankles covered.

George regarded her with a mischievous grin and stepped forward, offering his arm. "I do believe milady is in need of some supper," he said as he noted Elizabeth's quick placement of her hand on his arm. A jolt shot through him as she gripped his forearm, her gloved hand taking purchase as if her life depended on it. With his free hand, he took up the silver bucket containing the champagne bottle and held it in the crook of his arm.

"That sounds delightful," Elizabeth responded with a nod, allowing him to lead her up the stairs. "How long have you lived here?" she asked as she continued to survey her surroundings. Everything around her looked *rich*. The colors, the woods, the fabrics, the carpets. Everything looked expensive and new and carefully maintained. There was nothing old or stuffy about the place. Nothing that suggested anything but the paintings were from the prior century.

"Just since August," George replied lightly. And when Elizabeth expected him to say that he had purchased everything in it since then, he added, "My uncle lived here prior to his death. I was his only heir, so I inherited everything last January. Including his title." He paused in the double wide opening to a large room. "I thought we would be more comfortable having supper up here," he stated as he led her through the doorway and then closed the doors behind him. A massive fireplace, in the center of the long back wall of the room, and several lamps throughout the space gave the apartment a golden glow. Elizabeth glanced about, not even realizing until her second look that a massive canopied bed was situated at one end of the room. The velvet drapes were closed on the side of the bed facing them.

"Is this... your bedchamber?" she asked with a hint of alarm, her heart suddenly pounding in her chest. She took a quick drink of champagne hoping to quell her nervousness.

"My apartment, yes," George amended, hoping he hadn't miscalculated by having their dinner brought here instead of to the dining room downstairs. He thought that room too spacious for an intimate dinner.

The apartment was sectioned by furnishings, one area set up with an escritoire and desk chair, another with a settee, chairs, and small tables, a breakfast table with two dining chairs were positioned next to a serving buffet, and, at the far end of the room, the bed with a bench at its foot, a large wardrobe, a cheval mirror and two large dressers. Beyond that, there was a door that she thought probably led to a bathing chamber.

"It's beautiful," Elizabeth spoke finally, her eyes still surveying her surroundings before they returned to find his watching her. She swallowed the rest of the champagne in her glass.

George refilled her glass even before she could ask for more. "Thank you," he said quietly. He took a sip of champagne.

Elizabeth remembered the bonnet she wore and thought it best to remove it before they sat down to dinner. She pulled a couple of pins out of the velvet and lifted it from the mass of curls atop her head. Setting it on a small table, she turned to find George still watching her. He was holding a chair for her at a table set for two. Covered serving platters filled the table, leaving little room for anything but essential dinner accoutrements.

She took the proffered chair and placed a linen napkin from her place setting across her lap. In a moment, George was sitting across from her doing the same thing. He poured wine as he commented on the weather, topped off her champagne glass as she replied, and regarded her for a long moment before realizing he was staring. *Serve dinner*, his practical self ordered, his other self a bit preoccupied with the female he found across the table from him.

The beautiful woman he hoped to one day marry.

George lifted the lid from a serving platter, revealing a variety of sliced meats and cheeses. Another platter featured a display of fruit, artfully cut and arranged in an arc that resembled a rainbow. Given the scent of fresh baked bread that hovered over the table, Elizabeth reasoned the small loaf of bread was still warm. "May I serve you?" he asked, noticing Elizabeth's curious glance at the array of foods.

The question forced her to look at the wide display of foods and wonder if he meant more by the question. "I'd like that, George," she replied with a small smile, lifting her plate and holding it near the meats. "It all looks... delicious," she commented as she watched him place several thin slices onto her plate.

"I hope it's to your liking, milady," he replied, serving himself a few slices before he reached over to cut the bread.

Sighing, Elizabeth shook her head. "There's really no need for you to call me that, George," she said.

George regarded her for a moment. "You don't strike me as a Liz or an Eliza," he commented with a shake of his head. He saw her shudder as a grin broke out on her face.

"No. And Beth will not do, either," she murmured as she shook her head and took a bite of meat, her manner suggesting she was finally becoming comfortable in his presence.

Cocking his head to one side, George thought for a moment. "Because it is the name of a best friend? The Duchess of Somerset, perhaps?" he put forth. Elizabeth would be but a year or two younger than Jeremy Statton's wife, Elizabeth Cunningham Statton.

Elizabeth's expression of astonishment was quickly replaced with one of suspicion. "How... how did you know?" she asked. She began eating in earnest, knowing she had drunk too much champagne on an empty stomach. Not only were her knees feeling weak, her head was buzzing just a bit, too.

Deciding it couldn't hurt to admit he was a friend of the duke, George shrugged. "I have known Jeremy since our days at Eton," he said in an off-hand manner.

"*Jeremy?*" Elizabeth repeated, her response suggesting she found his use of the duke's first name a bit too familiar.

George shrugged. "Excuse me, *His Grace*," he amended, giving her a grin. "I have known him too long, I suppose. And as the second son, he wasn't supposed to become a duke. Besides, the use of titles among friends seems... pompous, somehow," he said by way of explanation. "And he does not always behave as you would expect a duke to do," he added, his grin widening.

"Whatever do you mean?" she countered, her suspicion replaced with outright curiosity.

Wondering if he should admit to the ruse that led to her to being thrown into his arms the first time they danced, George shook his head and drained his champagne glass. Pretending he didn't hear her question, he said, "Although he was a rather good sport about allowing me to dance with you."

Elizabeth stared at him for a moment, suddenly sober. *"Allowing* you to dance with me? Whatever are you saying, George?" she asked as she helped herself to some of the cheese. She made a sound of appreciation as her lips captured the golden cube.

George had to close his eyes for a moment. The desire to kiss those lips didn't pass, but at least he could dampen it by not looking at them. "I asked him to... share... some of his waltz with me," he said very carefully. "He was most accommodating and, I thought, a good sport about appearing as if he had broken his shoe heel in the process." Holding his breath as he waited for her response, he finally looked up to see her staring at him.

She swallowed the cheese. "You... *planned* that? He... he tossed me to you... deliberately?" she questioned, her brows furrowing as she remembered how she ended up in George's arms, how easily he had taken up where the duke had left off, how powerful a dancer he had been to be able to keep them twirling in the circle of waltzing couples and yet carry on a conversation as if nothing untoward had happened.

George reached out to place his hand over the one she had left on the table. Her eyes locked with his as if his touch shocked her. "*Toss* is probably a poor description of what had to be a very coordinated effort on both our parts," George started to explain in his own defense. "The placement had to be perfect, the execution very precise. I had to be sure no harm would come to you—that no one would think *you* had caused the duke's stumble. If anyone noticed what happened, His Grace had to appear to be the one at fault."

Elizabeth sat very still for a moment, her expression not indicating if she was shocked or amused or angry or ambivalent. "But... but *why?*" was her only response.

George blinked. Once. Twice. He sat back and considered her query. "I wanted a dance with you, Elizabeth."

Slumping against the back of her own chair, Elizabeth regarded her host in disbelief. "George!" she said as she suppressed a smile. "I suppose I am flattered." The champagne was obviously having an effect on her ability to think straight. She rather liked how he said her name. As if it was a prayer. "Why didn't you just ask me for the dance?"

Stunned by her simple question, George took a deep breath. "Well, I was sure your card was full. And I knew His Grace planned a dance with you," he said lamely. "I... I do apologize..."

"Oh, nonsense," Elizabeth interrupted with a wave of her hand. She reached for another piece of cheese. "It was rather an exhilarating experience. And it's certainly a unique way of introducing yourself to a lady," she said, giving George the impression she was impressed by the stunt. "I don't recommend you do it to meet others, though, George. I don't think that most ladies would find it as... *flattering* as I do at the moment," she admitted with a prim smile. She closed her lips around the piece of cheese and savored the flavor, making a small sound of appreciation.

At hearing she was flattered, George felt a great deal of satisfaction at that moment. His loins stirred at the sight of her lips, and he struggled to maintain control. Wished he were that piece of cheese. "I promise I shall never attempt such a feat again," he murmured, helping himself to a strawberry and pretending it was a part of her as he slowly chewed it.

Elizabeth smiled then, a brilliant smile that displayed perfect white teeth. The ease of their conversation had her realizing they were talking in a manner her father would never allow in the dining room at Carlington House.

Needing to get his attention onto other less arousing thoughts, George changed the subject. "It would seem you have many friends who have already married," he said as he poured a bit more wine into their glasses.

Elizabeth regarded a cube of fruit, the honey and lemon glaze making it sparkle in the candlelight. "I suppose so," she returned as she gave his comment consideration. "And a few who are not. I haven't been in a hurry to get to the altar." She popped the fruit into her mouth and nearly closed her eyes as she savored the flavor and texture.

George picked up his wine glass. "Any particular reason why not?" he asked lightly. "I admit, I... I haven't exactly been in a hurry myself," he confessed, hoping she wouldn't ask why.

Of course, she asked why.

"And why not, George?" Elizabeth straightened, her posture suddenly making her appear as if she ruled a country. And making the tops of her breasts mound a bit above the edge of her bodice.

George did his best not to glance directly at her bosom. He shrugged. "Until very recently, I... I haven't needed to, and to be honest, I didn't wish to."

Elizabeth held very still as she replayed his words in her head. "And yet, earlier today, you said you would ask for my hand if the earl didn't. Were you sincere in your comment?"

Taking a sip of wine while he considered his reply, George regarded her over the rim of the glass. Perhaps it was just the champagne that emboldened her, but he rather liked her forthrightness. When he set down the glass, he nodded. "I was. I still intend to, in fact."

Elizabeth nodded, not giving any indication if she was startled or otherwise affected by his answer; she allowed only an air of ambivalence. "What, pray tell, has happened to make you change your mind about marriage?" she asked, half-expecting he wouldn't answer her query, half-expecting he would insist on hearing her answer before providing more of his own. So Elizabeth was surprised when George reached over the table and took one of her hands in his. Shocked by the impropriety, she was tempted to pull her hand away. But she was mesmerized by his long tapered fingers as they gently lifted hers.

"You helped my friend get his job back at the bank," George stated. Teddy Streater had known that night at Angelo's. *You'd like her*, he had said, in that way Teddy had of knowing things he shouldn't, or meddling in affairs about which he shouldn't know anything. "I saw you dancing. I heard you laugh. I met you. We danced. We ate supper. I kissed you. We rode in the park. You kissed me." He sighed heavily and gave a another shrug with one shoulder, hoping she wouldn't require further explanation.

The comments, delivered as if they were a checklist of his requirements to find a suitable wife, had Elizabeth setting her fork on her plate and straightening in her chair. "But, you know nothing about me!" she countered, a bit perturbed at herself for sounding ungrateful at hearing his kind words. She pulled her hand away in the process of crossing her arms, the movement enhancing her décolletage even more.

It was suddenly apparent to George that she was *not* wearing a corset.

"My father says I'm a spoiled brat," she claimed, as if that would be reason enough for him to reconsider her for matrimony.

George leaned forward, resting his elbows against the edge of the table as he clasped his hands together. "He mentioned that," he acknowledged with a nod. When she reacted, her face a mix of surprise and anger and disappointment, one hand formed a fist where it rested on the table. George placed his hand over it as quickly as it formed. "Perhaps I find your desire to get your own way merely a sign of a woman who knows what she wants," he countered.

"Is that... is that what you believe?" she asked, momentarily at a loss. She was rather surprised by his insight. Of course, she wasn't spoiled; her father had been quite firm about limiting her allowance and those with whom she could socialize.

How could George know so much about her already?

And when had he spoken to her father?

George allowed a smile, the expression creating crinkles on either side of his eyes and laugh lines on either side of his mouth. *He is handsome*, she decided. Something deep in her belly flipped, forcing her to slide a hand down the front of her dress to quiet the turmoil.

"Yes, that's what I believe," George answered with a nod. He regarded her for a moment. "And now, in the interest of fairness, you must answer the same question," he urged, his voice not the least bit demanding. In fact, his lip curved a bit, suggesting he was amused by their exchange.

Sighing, Elizabeth closed her eyes for a moment. *What harm would it do to tell him I'm not married because no one has offered for my hand?* Everyone believed she was the recipient of multiple offers every Season. How she had managed to avoid the offers she had heard were coming was beyond her. It was why she secretly hoped her father might be interfering at just the right moment to steer unsuitable gentlemen away from her and her dowry. She secretly prayed that was the reason, for if it was due to something else, that something else would be *her*, and she couldn't bear to think that men somehow found her wanting. Or undesirable. Or spoiled. Or possessing some other trait that was somehow *wrong* for a gently bred female of the *ton*.

Unbidden tears pricking the edges of her eyes, Elizabeth looked up to find George staring at her. Concern was evident in his eyes. And before she quite knew what was happening, George was out of his chair and pulling her up from hers, his arms wrapping about her shoulders and pulling her body against his. Arms like steel bands held her against his solidity. She knew she should rebuff his attempt to... to do whatever it was he was doing in holding her so tightly, so that the entire front of her body was pressed against his, so that she could practically feel his heartbeats beneath her head, so that she was left feeling not the least bit inclined to rebuff anything he did. Instead, her hands automatically pressed against his chest, her head leaning into his shoulder.

"I didn't mean to pry," he said in a very quiet voice, one hand moving to the back of her head as if to provide support.

Elizabeth relaxed into his arms, melted against his body, and luxuriated in the scents of sandalwood and amber and in the warmth of his arms around her. *Would a married couple hold one another like this?* she wondered. A flash of seeing herself doing it while lying down, on a bed, shot through her mind, and her belly seemed to flip again. Was that George she was holding? Or was it Gabriel?

"I have never been made an offer of marriage," she murmured, a sob carrying the last of her comment so it came out in a bit of a stutter. She felt George stiffen, felt his arms lessen their hold just a tad.

"Indeed?" he replied, his voice indicating his surprise at the comment. "Had you made it known you weren't entertaining offers?" He stepped back a bit, concern still evident on his face as he helped her to sit down again.

"No," she replied, fighting to keep a tear from escaping her eye.

"I suppose *you* didn't need to," he countered, as if he knew exactly why she hadn't been made an offer.

"And just what does *that* mean?" she asked, suddenly a bit indignant. Her spine had reasserted itself, and she found she could sit up on her own just fine.

The problem was, she wore no corset, and her suddenly erect posture only enhanced her barely contained bosom so George couldn't help but notice. He kept his eyes locked on hers, swallowing hard. Once dinner was done, he would be working to free that bosom from its bodice, and after that, he would be fondling and kissing and... He shook himself and remembered Elizabeth was waiting for a reply. "Your father will ensure you marry well," he said simply. "And to a man meeting his approval."

Elizabeth gasped. George seemed to voice exactly what she had hoped was the case. She was certain David Carlington had run off one of her would-be suitors, but she hadn't been so sure about the other two. "Do *you* meet his approval?" she asked then, her voice so quiet George almost didn't hear her.

George looked down at his plate, wondering how much he

should tell her. He had asked for permission to court Lady Eliz-abeth, and the marquess had been almost flippant in the manner in which he gave his permission. At the time, Lord Morganfield had been far more concerned about Lady E's charity and the money to fund it. But then, after yesterday morning's parliamentary session that included a rather uncom-fortable exchange between Butter Blond and the marquess, Morganfield had approached George and stated, without preamble, "You have my permission, and you have my blessing." That last comment had surprised him. It implied he already had the marquess' permission to court Lady Elizabeth *and* to marry her should she agree to his proposal.

Had Josephine provided assistance he wasn't aware of in helping obtain Morganfield's permission? If she had, he found he didn't mind so very much. He knew the marquess and Josephine had spent countless hours discussing politics. Those discussions would have no doubt included talk of logical marriages, strategic alliances, profitable mergers. "I believe so, yes," George finally answered, his eyes finally coming up to meet hers.

A bit surprised by this bit of news, Elizabeth decided she would ask her father when next she spoke with him. She wondered what her father would admit to having done on her behalf.

Or his.

In the meantime, a quick glance at the empty dishes in front of her told her dinner was over. And that meant that if she allowed it, George would begin the ministrations he promised would bring her pleasure. She could back out, of course. Ask forgiveness for his having to dismiss the entire household staff for the evening. Beg his pardon for having to arrange a coach and chaperone to see her here and home again. And George had promised he wouldn't think any less of her if she changed her mind.

But her curiosity was piqued. Her belly flipped at the mere thought of his hands on her body again, as they had been just moments before. There had been a sense of power, but power mixed with gentleness in how he held her against his solid form. And Elizabeth *wanted* to know more. Much more.

When she shook herself from her reverie, she looked up to find George standing next to her chair, his hand held out to her.

"If you still wish it, Elizabeth, I would like to see to your comfort and to your pleasure."

CHAPTER 35
PLEASURE FOR PITY SAKE

A sense of euphoria filled Elizabeth as she regarded George. Perhaps it was the champagne, maybe the wine, surely the food, and definitely the conversation that had relaxed her to the point she was looking forward to whatever George had in mind for her. He had made promises as to her virtue. He was a gentleman. She was sure she could trust him to keep his word.

And then his lips covered hers in a kiss that was light and delicious. Before she could even think about returning it, or at least participating, his lips had moved to her jaw and then to the column of her neck while his hands barely touched her shoulder and the back of her head. At first, he sprinkled light kisses here and there, and then his lips took purchase near the hollow of her throat.

George moved his hands to her waist, lifting and moving her until she was in front of an upholstered chair near the fireplace. He slowly lowered her until she was completely seated, his mouth never leaving her neck. He continued lowering himself until he knelt in front of her, his lips slowly letting go so that she gasped as she fell back into the chair padding.

Undoing his tailcoat buttons, George quickly doffed the garment and set it aside, hoping Elkins wouldn't chide him too badly if he happened to be the one to find it discarded on the floor. Elizabeth no longer seemed so nervous, but he could tell her body thrummed when he reached down and lifted her slippered foot to his thigh. Her leg quivered beneath his fingers as he used his other hand to slowly remove her kid leather slipper.

Her short breaths and the crackling of the fire were the only sounds in the room as he moved his fingers up the side of her calf, around the back of her knee—she inhaled sharply then—and up the outside of her thigh, the pad of his fingers seeking the ties of her garter. The ribbon gave way quickly. His other hand joined the first, sliding up the inside of her leg before reaching beneath the stocking top. Slowly, he unrolled the silken sheath, down her thigh, over her knee, around her calf. Once it was down to her ankle, he raised her foot to his mouth and placed his lips over the space just above the ankle bone, gentle suckling the tender skin as Elizabeth inhaled and then softly moaned.

He dared a glance up to find her head back, her throat fully exposed, her breasts barely contained by the low-cut bodice of her gown. Wanting desperately to claim the hollow of her throat where her pulse was visible, George instead concentrated on her foot, removing the stocking completely. He used his fingers to slowly stroke the sides of her foot before placing it on the floor. George moved his attention to the other foot and repeated his slow, deliberate motions, all the while aware of the quiet moaning and quick breaths that emanated from Elizabeth.

Once her second stocking was off her foot, he placed a hand on the front of one of her calves, capturing the edge of her hem and pushing it up her leg until it crested her bent knee. The gown, petticoats and pantaloons were bunched up, hiding him from her suddenly opened eyes. His lips captured the inside of her knee, kissing it quickly before her reflexes jerked it away in response. Given the extra room between her legs, his head moved up her leg a bit more, his kisses grazing the soft, tender skin of her inner thigh.

Elizabeth whimpered, her control slipping away with every touch of his lips—and she was still in her gown! She took a deep breath and let it out slowly, only then aware that one of her hands was being held in his. Leaning over it, he reached out with his lips and pulled a small finger into his mouth, suckling it until a smile appeared on her lips. Elizabeth forced herself to sit upright and then leaned over to press her lips against his forehead.

George looked up then, the very slightest of smiles curling the corner of his mouth. Elizabeth regarded him a moment, deciding he was rather wicked when he was like this, worshipping her hands while playing the devil with his touching and kissing. She closed her eyes, expecting him to kiss her lips, but he instead used the opportunity to stand and to draw her up and out of the chair. He had her turned, her back pressed to the front of his body before she could even open her eyes in surprise.

"You must tell me to stop if you should feel the least bit... uncomfortable. Or, if you think you're about to faint," George spoke quietly, his lips barely touching the skin beneath her ear.

Elizabeth started. "Faint?" she repeated, an inhalation of breath joining the word as his lips moved to her earlobe and bit gently on the flesh. She turned in his arms so she faced him again. "Why ever would I... faint?" One of her hands reached up to grip his shoulder, as if she needed it for support.

George paused in his nibbling and straightened a bit, although Elizabeth's hand on his shoulder stayed where it was. Her eyes found his, a hint of worry evident in their gaze. He wondered how to answer. He could be blunt and simply tell her he expected to bring her to ecstasy at least a few times and she might be overcome by the excessive pleasure of it all.

But to do so would be boastful of his newly learned skills.

And what if she didn't respond as his mistress had?

Josie was experienced in matters of a carnal nature. As experienced as she was at giving pleasure, she also knew how to allow his touch and tongue and lips to bring her pleasure, how to open herself to the possibilities of further pleasure, even when she claimed to be sated. "The French call it *la petit mort*," he finally stated quietly, his expression remaining impassive.

Elizabeth's French lessons slowly resolved the meaning of George's words. *The little death.*

Perhaps the little death came from being so out of breath from the incredible sensation you simply fainted. The mere thought of such pleasure sent a delightful shiver through Elizabeth's belly. Her eyes widened suddenly in response, in understanding of what she'd just felt—arousal—and the cause of it—mere words spoken by a man that, until this moment, she'd considered a means to an end.

Unbidden thoughts of Gabriel Wellingham surfaced just then. With his appreciative glances and flirty words, he had made her feel as if he desired her. But at no time had any of his words caused this kind of response in her. Never had she experienced *arousal* with him—even when she thought of him while she lay waiting for sleep to take her late at night.

When Elizabeth's thoughts returned to George, her full attention on his face just inches from her gaze, her body responded again. This time she couldn't ignore the pleasant shivers, the exciting frissons that coursed through her entire being. He was looking at her as if he were memorizing every inch of her, as if he hoped to read her thoughts by studying every detail of her face. He must have known, somehow, that his mere suggestion of her possibly fainting would cause these skitters of pleasure beneath her skin.

Didn't he? If so, it didn't show on his face.

How could he know?

George noted her widened eyes and sought to alleviate any fears he might have caused with his comment. "Should you be so overcome by pleasure you do indeed faint, I promise I shall not take advantage of your situation. Other than to... hold you," he added hesitantly. If she did faint, he had no intention of leaving her side. He could only hope that if she did faint, she would do so *after* he'd removed her gown and other clothing so he might use the time to memorize every inch of her body.

The thought of her naked body in his arms sparked his own arousal, his hardening manhood suddenly uncomfortable behind the placket of his breeches. He grimaced, annoyed his body would betray his desire so early in the assignation.

Elizabeth nodded, her gaze still on him. A series of pleasant contractions skittered through her, causing her to inhale sharply. Mistaking the pained expression etched on his face as concern for her, Elizabeth nodded. "I shall try my best to remain conscious. I shouldn't want to miss anything, after all," she said demurely, a nervous grin appearing.

George regarded her for a long moment, heartened she could exhibit a sense of humor at a time when he knew she must be at least as anxious as he was.

And then his lips were on hers, claiming them in a gentle kiss very much like the one they had shared in Lady Worthington's library. Elizabeth leaned into the kiss, feeling a shock of excitement when her bosom lightly touched the front of his waistcoat. At the same moment, the tip of his tongue moved to separate her lips. Her surprise was swallowed by his tongue and his mouth, their movement over her lips and inside her mouth making her dizzy with excitement. Moving her hands to his shoulders, she first gripped his waistcoat and then used her palms to support herself; otherwise, her body would simply fall against the front of his, and wouldn't that be too wanton?

The sensation created by one of his fingers caressing her jawline had her arching back so her throat was fully exposed to his touch. Wrapping an arm around the back of her waist to prevent her from falling, George pulled away from the kiss enough to move his lips down her neck and to the hollow of her throat. He was aware of her hands around his neck, holding on as if her life depended on it. And when the fingertips that caressed her cheek moved down her neckline, pausing to trace the line of the fabric along the tops of her breasts, he felt the jolt that nearly knocked her out of his arms.

He took the opportunity to turn her around. Before she could utter a protest or ask what he was about to do, his lips were on the back of her neck, one arm wrapped around her waist, another undoing the hooks down the middle of her back. As the fabric spread apart, he moved his kisses lower, following the bones of her spine until he'd run out of hooks. Placing the palm of his hand very slightly against her inward curve of her back, he slid it up and out along the back of her shoulder, feeling her shivers beneath his fingers as the gown was freed from one shoulder. At that moment, he confirmed she wore no corset.

And no shift.

It was nearly his undoing.

His manhood sprang to life against the placket of his breeches, straining the fabric. He took a breath and steadied himself, forcing himself to concentrate on freeing the long sleeve of her gown from her arm. His finger drew down her skin, gently pulling silk past her elbow and over her hand. Her body felt almost boneless as it leaned against the front of the hard lines of his torso, her auburn curls tickling his jaw. He was sure she could feel his manhood pressing into the base of her spine as he shifted behind her to remove the other sleeve. As if in slow motion, Elizabeth raised her free hand to place it against the space just below her breasts, apparently to hold up the gown as her arm slipped out of the other sleeve.

George drew his finger back up the outside of her arm, eliciting a sigh from Elizabeth. Her head was resting against his shoulder, and he used the opportunity to capture her earlobe with his tongue and pull it between his teeth. The sudden inhalation of her breath brought the tops of her breasts into view, forcing George to close his eyes and concentrate on suckling the soft skin of her ear and undoing the buttons of his waistcoat.

With that task completed, he moved his lips to follow her hairline to the nape of her neck while he shrugged out of one side of the waistcoat. That done, he moved his free arm to grasp her around her middle, where her arm held up the gown. He let go of her with his other arm. The waistcoat joined the tailcoat in the neat pile he'd created below. He wrapped his arm about her shoulders, sliding the tips of his fingers over the lines of her collarbone, around the hollow of her throat, and down the center of her bosom until they disappeared in her cleavage.

She was aware of the gown's silk slipping from her breasts, of its cool slickness sliding down over her stomach, of his lips nipping at her shoulder and his hand cupping her breast. The sound of her gasp nearly brought her back to her senses, but then he'd captured a nipple between his thumb and middle finger, held it gently while barely rubbing it with the pad of his forefinger. She was lost again as his ministrations sent shivers of delight through her breast.

Her other breast, suddenly heavy and tipped with a hardening nipple, filled his other hand as he slid it up from her waist and cradled it. A thumb passed over the engorged tip, once barely making contact, and the second time pressing it and then circling it until it was round and red. The jolt of electricity that passed through her breast forced her back against the front of his body. The fabric of his shirt seemed to chafe the skin of her back, the wool of his breeches scratching through the thin fabric of her pantaloons.

With her head still against his shoulder, his lips took purchase along her jaw and the skin just below it. There were sounds of whimpering, of sighs and mewling Elizabeth barely registered came from her. When one breast was suddenly released from his hand, she caught a glimpse of herself in the mirror and watched as the hand slid down the front of her body and disappeared beneath the gown. The tapes of her pantaloons suddenly loosened, and the fine lawn slid down her legs to pool at her feet. After another moment, the petticoat joined the pile, the swishing of the soft fabric over her legs and her sudden inhalations the only sounds in the room.

George could feel her labored breathing, hear her soft moans, feel the entire weight of her body pressed against the front of his. Her legs seemed as if they were no longer able to hold her up; she would slide down to the floor if he didn't get her onto the bed. He slowly pulled his hands away from her and caught her body in his arms. He carried her the few steps to the large bed—his bed.

Elkins had pulled the curtains around the side of the bed facing the room and turned down the linens, leaving the expanse of white linen the perfect canvas onto which to place her. Although she still held her gown clutched to the front of her body, she had done nothing to re-cover her breasts. As for the rest of her body, George knew there was nothing beneath the silk but her bare skin. One of her arms lay splayed to one side. He reached down and wrapped his hand around hers, lifted it to his lips, and brushed his lips over the bare knuckles. Elizabeth's quick inhalation of breath matched the frisson he felt shoot down her arm.

She gazed up at him through long lashes that nearly hid her eyes. Finally able to catch her breath and allowing her vision to clear, Elizabeth sighed. "That was... amazing," she murmured, noticing for the first time he now wore only his linen shirt and breeches. "Will you... stay with me while I rest?"

George blinked and straightened, momentarily confused by her question. Then he was amused when he understood to what she referred. *I shall see to it you are thoroughly pleasured by midnight and allow you to rest undisturbed until one.* "My lady, I haven't yet begun to pleasure you," he responded with a devilish half-smile that made him look enticing, handsome even.

Elizabeth stared back. "Oh," she breathed, her eyes widening as she realized the implication of his statement.

George nearly drowned in their aquamarine depths. Aware he was staring, he nodded and said, "I will be but a moment." He forced his gaze away and moved back to the chair. He turned down the flame in the main lamp and then sat down to take off his shoes and stockings. Having no intention of being naked himself, he thought only to get himself comfortable enough to perform the ministrations he thought would prove his skill.

He wondered at Elizabeth's comfort. She hadn't made a single protest as he'd removed her shoes and stockings, nor had she put up a fuss about his having unhooked her gown or about nearly removing the last vestige of covering she still held clutched to her bosom. Well, by the time he was done—he had over two hours before midnight would strike—she might yet remove the gown of her own accord. He had decided he would not take it from her unless she asked for him to do so.

With any luck, she would beg him to remove it.

Although the flames in the fireplace were dying just a bit, when he thought about adding another log, he decided against it—the extra light would counter his efforts to relax her enough for what was to come, and the room seemed especially warm already.

Or perhaps it is just me who is too warm.

There was still a good deal of champagne in the bottle, although the ice around it had mostly melted. He refilled her glass and took it to her, noting that she supported herself on one elbow and let go of her gown to take the champagne. Refilling his own glass, he took a long drink of it and looked about the room, very aware her eyes followed him. He finally moved back to the bed, raising one leg so he could sit on the edge of it and support most of his weight on the foot that remained on the floor. Elizabeth's gaze followed his movement, her body backing up into the middle of the bed as he did so, as if to give him room to join her there.

"The first time I saw you dancing, you were waltzing," he said in a very quiet voice, so husky he almost didn't recognize it as his own. "Your gorgeous hair was all sparkling with the light from the candles in the chandeliers, and you had a brilliant smile on your face, as if you were having the best night of your life. And it was at that moment that I..." He looked away for a moment, leaving her hanging on his last word. She pushed herself up so that her arms were straight and slightly behind her, the gown barely perched on the tips of her breasts. "I wanted so badly to be a part of your... of your night." He'd nearly said 'life' just then, but thought better of it.

No need to frighten the woman just yet.

"So, you can imagine my delight when you were thrown into my arms and danced the rest of the waltz with me. You dance beautifully, by the way" he said, before drinking the last of his champagne. "And then you agreed to attend the supper with me. I thought I must be the luckiest man in the world."

At some point in his confession, Elizabeth had raised a hand to cup his cheek. He leaned into it and closed his eyes, covered her hand with his own, and then pulled her hand away so he could kiss the palm. His tongue trailed up to her wrist and his lips kissed it, forcing Elizabeth to take a sharp breath when the unexpected sensation of pleasure shot up through her arm. His other hand had moved to support her elbow, where his lips fluttered like butterfly wings over the delicate skin. George heard her whimpers, felt the ripples under her skin and carefully repositioned his body so that he could reach her lips with his own.

The kiss was ever so gentle at first—barely a whisper of a touch before he pressed the tip of his tongue against her teeth. She moaned and slowly lowered her upper body back down to the pillows, the strength in her arm suddenly gone. As George deepened the kiss, he moved a hand to stroke her other arm, his fingertip trailing up the inside of her wrist to her elbow and on to the soft, silken skin under her arm.

When his thumb brushed against the side of her breast, she jerked, the reaction causing George to pause a moment and finish the kiss. His lips worked their way down her jaw to her neck and then to her throat, where his tongue found the round hollow and seemed to take delight in feeling the source of her light moans and whimpering. He brushed his thumb against the side of her breast again, teasing and testing to determine if she would deny him. When her chest lifted just a bit from the bed, he slid his hand higher, using his thumb to brush over the nipple. The ruched bud was already erect, already aroused and ready for his lips to suckle it. He wanted to hear his name spoken in her velvet soft voice as he took her to her first level of ecstasy.

Her eyes, if not already closed, were nearly so, the lashes seeming to rest on the tops of those beautiful cheekbones. His lips finished the work his tongue had started on her throat, moving ever so slowly down the front of her body. When his lips reached her collarbone, he let his tongue lave across it as his chin caught the edge of her bodice.

As he moved lower, the upper edge of the fabric caught on

her erect peaks, chafing them so Elizabeth's body nearly came off the bed, her fists struggling to hang onto the soft mattress. His mouth covered her nipple, sucking it until it was between his teeth and then gently biting it—not too hard, for fear she would deny him any more of her body. Her cries were louder, no longer whimpers, her breaths short, quick gasps as his mouth lifted and let go of the nipple. Reaching out with his tongue, he laved it across the hardened bud. Elizabeth's chest came up from the mattress, as did her hands, and her fingers buried themselves in his hair.

"Ge... orge!" she cried out, drawing out his name as she writhed beneath him. Her hands had moved down to the sides of his body, clutching at the linen of his shirt, pulling it out of his breeches in handfuls as he moved his mouth to the other nipple. He cupped the breast in one warm hand and lifted it up, his lips kissing and suckling as he did so, barely aware she had managed to get his shirt up along his back. And then he felt her warm hands, her fingers, her nails gripping his back, scraping and gripping and leaving little half-moon brands in his skin. He let go of her nipple and groaned, suddenly aware of his own body's reaction to her arousal. With her writhing, her gown had moved down to her hips. Gasping for his own breath, George lowered his head against her belly, the tip of his tongue circling her naval and the soft flesh around it while the hair on the top of his head tickled the underside of her breasts.

"Take it off," he heard from somewhere above. His tongue slowed its descent and he wondered at the words. "Get it off, *please*," she was whispering, begging as her fingers fumbled and clutched at her gown. Suddenly understanding, George moved a hand beneath her bottom and lifted her hips as he gently pulled on the fabric. He wanted to jerk the gown free, tear it from her body in a fit of lust, but the litany of *maintain control* echoed in his mind.

How the hell am I going to manage it? he wondered.

CHAPTER 36
THE REVERENCE IN
PLEASURE

She should have felt chilled. Should have felt vulnerable. She should have felt embarrassed at her nakedness.

I should be feeling ashamed of myself!

But Elizabeth felt none of those as George's gentle touches pushed her gown down past her hips, exposing her most intimate places, his fingers barely making contact with her flushed skin as he complied with her request.

My request! My demand!

Where his fingers touched her, she felt a soft warmth, a caress of heat that enveloped her. She had expected his hands to be rough and harsh, impatient, commanding and demanding as he undressed her, as he drew them around the curves of her breasts, down the sides of her torso, around her hip and over her bottom, down the length of her thighs and over the slope of her calves. Instead, they had been patient, reverent, so very careful, as if she were made of fine china and might shatter should he press too hard.

He had warned her. He had said he would have her undressed by ten. *How could he have known? How could he know she would simply give in to his seduction?* A thought struck her and she inhaled sharply.

Perhaps this wasn't the first time a woman had asked him to do this to her!

How many others had he pleasured like this? How many others had succumbed to his gentle caresses and begged him to undress them? Did he do this often? "George?" she managed, her hoarse whisper nearly caught in her throat, her body still shivering as if it were cold.

George stilled his hands where they were at her feet, her clothes draped over one arm as if he were a lady's maid about to hang her gown in the clothes press and take the rest to the laundry. "Yes, milady?" he answered in a whisper. He set her clothes on the back of a chair and moved quickly to the head of the bed. She reclined near the middle of the mattress, her auburn hair spilling over the pillows to create a halo of curly silk around her head. She was watching him through lowered lashes, her mouth slightly open, her entire body naked. Until that moment, he didn't realize just how much he had been craving her, that he had been a man starved for her kind of sustenance, and here she was, bared and spread before him like a banquet. It took every bit of willpower he possessed not to rake his eyes over what he knew must be a beautiful body, to concentrate his attention instead on just her face, on just those aquamarine eyes barely visible through the curtain of her lashes.

"How many women have you seduced like this?" she whispered, reaching up with a finger to capture the knot of his cravat. The perfectly tied mail coach knot was undone in an instant, the ties spilling down to graze over her dewy skin.

Taken aback by the question, George blinked once, twice as he tried very hard not to notice the ends of his black cravat puddle onto her midriff and drape over one breast. "I have... never done this before," he replied with a shake of his head, the motion causing the linen fabric to dance over her skin.

Elizabeth's first reaction was to call him out as a liar, but then she noticed his fingers were shaking just a bit. Indeed, his hands were shaking, quivering, making her realize something.

He was just as nervous as she was.

For despite not being cold, her entire body shook, vibrated, shivered. Surely not from fear; she had nothing to be afraid of with George. Anticipation, perhaps. She grasped one of the ends of the cravat and gently pulled it so that George was forced to lower his head until the length of fabric unwrapped itself from around his neck. "But you... you knew I would beg you to remove my gown. How did you know?"

Lowering himself to sit on the edge of the bed, George shrugged and tried hard to avoid the sight of his cravat spilled over her body. At that moment, he decided he would never again complain to Elkins about having to wear one, as long as it was *this* one. "I didn't," he claimed, his shoulders slumping with the admission. At her look of disbelief, he added, "I thought when you heard such a warning, you would... withdraw your request to have me pleasure you," he returned quietly.

This is unexpected! "And then I did not," she whispered, her arms suddenly moving to cover her breasts, despite the cravat already doing a fine job of it. Her right knee bent slightly and crossed over her left leg so that her mound was hidden from his view, should he even look there. A flush of pink suffused her entire body. *What was I thinking? What must he think of me?*

"And when you did not," George continued, a wan smile touching his lips, "I felt so honored... I *feel* honored—"

"Honored?" she interrupted in disbelief, raising herself onto one elbow and leaning toward him.

George took in the sight of her then, his cravat no longer covering any of her as it slid off the curves of her body. He reached down to capture a hand in his, to raise it to his lips and kiss the back of it, closing his eyes as he did so. "That you would give me such an opportunity to spend time with you," he murmured, not letting go of her hand. "That you would ask me to pleasure you. That you would give me the chance to prove myself in the bedchamber. At least, as much as I can without ruining you completely," he added as he gazed at her. He kissed her hand again, this time turning it over in order to place his lips against her palm.

Elizabeth regarded him for a very long time as he held her hand. *He is honored.*

His schedule had promised she would be *thoroughly plea-sured by midnight.* Without loss of virtue. How could he expect to bring her such pleasure if he had no intention of performing sexual intercourse? The very thought of his naked body atop hers—anchored to her by her legs wrapped around his thighs—came unbidden, and a pleasant sensation passed across her belly. The sudden hitch in her breath broke the momentary spell. "Do you... do you still wish to do so?" she whispered, her breaths coming a bit faster, her swollen breasts suddenly aching to be touched, to be kissed and suckled again.

"God, yes," George blurted, his free hand raking his hair into spikes as a grin split his face.

Elizabeth nodded and raised herself so she reclined on one straight arm. "Then look at me, George. All of me. And tell me, truthfully, you must be truthful about this or I shall never speak to you again. Are my breasts—?"

"Perfect," George interrupted, his head bobbing up and down. "Beautiful—"

"Look at me, George!"

Her plea startled him, forced him to look at her as she lowered herself to the bed, to gaze at all of her in her naked glory, all at once and then in little bits as he took in the sight of her long legs, the curve of her hips, the indentation of her waist, her very swollen breasts as they parted slightly from the middle of her chest, her one arm draped over her stomach while the other rested, bent, on the linens, her collarbone where it crested, her shoulders as they curved and dipped and joined her long neck. When his eyes finally locked with hers, he stayed very still, wondering what she would have him do next.

Elizabeth stared back at George, a truth becoming quite apparent to her as he gazed at her. She had expected him to look upon her nakedness with lust, to see something akin to evil in his eyes as they traveled over her exposed flesh. Instead, she found his gaze one of reverence, as if he worshiped the very sight of her.

Perhaps he felt affection for her. *That's the reason he agreed to this arrangement. He plans to ask for my hand in marriage.* He would do anything for her, she realized.

She just needed to ask.

Reaching for the tail of his shirt, she lifted it. "Take this off, George," she demanded, her voice quiet but commanding. Pausing only a moment, George pulled the linen from his body and tossed it aside.

He could hear her inhalation of breath as she took in the sight of his bare chest, his muscular shoulders and arms, the dusting of dark hair covering his chest. But her eyes didn't suggest she was frightened by the sight of him. In fact, she seemed somehow emboldened, knowing that he would do whatever she demanded. "Touch me, George. Make me... feel something."

God, she is naked, George thought suddenly, remembering his vow that she would be so before ten. And he wasn't far behind. He paused for only a moment before joining her on the bed, his hand very lightly skimming the surface of her skin, his finger pads and palm sliding along the planes of her body. All of her body. He heard her soft gasps as his hand smoothed along her hip, over the top of her thigh and then over the velvet soft skin between her thighs. He could bring her to the next level of ecstasy in just a few minutes!

Using his open hand, he gently lifted one of her legs so her knee bent slightly. When he moved his hand to her other leg, the bent leg fell to the side. Using the pads of his fingers, he barely stroked the delicate skin of her inner thighs, felt the shivers beneath and the quickening as her hips tensed. Slipping his hand between her thighs, his fingers parted the soft curls covering her mound and slid between the feminine folds. Her entire body jerked in response, a shriek escaping her lips.

George paused the movement of his hand and then slowly, very slowly, drew his middle finger along the moist cleft, up and then back down. Her hips seemed to angle to follow his finger, so he rested the palm of his hand on her mound to hold her down as his finger stroked harder. Elizabeth cried out, her breaths coming in pants. He slid his entire hand between her thighs, felt her wetness, felt the molten heat spreading as he softly rubbed her swollen womanhood. When his movements quickened, Elizabeth whimpered, clutched the bed linens in one hand and George's arm in the other in an attempt to hold herself down as her body arched into his touch. Capturing the tip of one breast in his mouth, George laved his tongue across the hardened nipple.

Elizabeth nearly screamed. Her body, bowed and taut and aching for release, gave way to a wave that crashed through her entire being. His name came out as a strangled plea. And when the wave crashed again, she whimpered and clung as tightly as she could, afraid she would be swept away from reality should she let go.

George lifted his head from her breast, amazed at how large and firm it appeared in its flushed, aroused state. He stilled his hand, held it against her engorged womanhood for a moment longer before carefully sliding it up and away from her body.

Elizabeth whimpered at the renewed stimulation and then whimpered again at the loss of his touch, pulling her knees together as she seemed to melt into the mattress. George lowered himself to the bed, straightening his body alongside hers. He gathered her boneless body so it rested against his, the side of her face pressed into the small of his shoulder. He could feel the pounding of her heart against his chest.

Kissing her hair, he closed his eyes and took a deep breath, inhaling the scent of jasmine. Smiling, he slid a hand along her arm, down her back, over the curve of her bottom and back up her body, gentling her to a state of peace and calm.

It had been so easy to pleasure her. So satisfying to know that simple kisses and gentle strokes could bring her to ecstasy. He wanted nothing more than to do it again. Every night. *Every day!*

He glanced toward the clock and smiled to himself.

He had plenty of time.

CHAPTER 37
TURNING THE TABLES
IN BED

*E*lizabeth was aware of his warm hands caressing her skin as she allowed herself to be held against George's body. One of her hands rested in the crisp curls that dusted his chest, the beat of his heart creating a tattoo beneath it. She was sure hers was doing the same against his ribs. She had believed the pleasure she experienced earlier was as intense as it could be—how could it be possible to feel such amazing sensations?—and then George had assaulted her senses with a level of ecstasy from which she didn't want to recover. She could stay like this all night, all limp and sated and floating between sleep and consciousness, unable to think about leaving the bed and getting dressed.

She did want to address the issue of George's breeches. They were still on his body, the wool chafing the tender skin of her inner thighs where her leg draped over one of his. And barely containing what she just then realized was his arousal. "George," she whispered, her hand skimming down his chest to the top of his breeches. She felt his reaction in the sculpted abdominal muscles even before she heard his sharp intake of breath.

A hand was suddenly covering hers. Although she couldn't see his face, she felt his discomfort. "Yes, my sweet?" he whispered, bringing her hand to his lips so he could kiss the palm.

Elizabeth bit her lower lip. "You simply must remove your

breeches," she whispered. He had lowered her left hand back to his chest where he still held his hand over it, but at her insistent comment, he gripped her hand tighter.

"I must?" he responded, not expecting such a demand.

She could feel his pulse increase. She smiled at her ability to discomfit him so. "Yes. They're most uncomfortable. I don't know how you can even *wear* them," she spoke softly. Raising herself so she was supported on one elbow, she caught and regarded George's panicked gaze in the dim candlelight. One of her breasts rested against his chest while the other rested on the hand that held hers.

George stared at her for a moment more before nodding. "Perhaps you should... look away, milady—"

"George, you remove those breeches right now, or I shall remove myself from this bed," Elizabeth stated in no uncertain terms.

The buttons were undone in an instant, George not remembering a time when he had unbuttoned them quite so quickly. His engorged cock sprang free as he hooked his thumbs into the waist of both his drawers and the breeches and lifted his hips. Pushing the offending garments over his buttocks and down his legs, he bent and kicked until he could toss them aside, all the while holding Elizabeth's startled gaze. *Maintain control,* he thought as he remembered he was naked, for the first time, with a woman who wasn't Josie. Or his childhood nurse.

He thought about reaching for the bed clothes and covering himself before Elizabeth could get a good look. *Coward!* Instead, he lowered his back into the pillows and then locked his hands behind his head, his elbows thrust out on either side of his head as he allowed a smirk to form on his lips. "As you wish, milady," he murmured.

Elizabeth forced herself to look, really *look*, at George's body. He was spread out like a lounging statue before her, his taut, muscled body lean and sculpted, like one of the marbles she'd seen at the British Museum just that morning. But another statue came to mind, one far better sculpted and closer in comparison to the body she was admiring. "You have a body like David," she murmured, her hand hovering just above his abdomen. She pulled it away when his stomach seemed to cave in suddenly.

"David?" he repeated, his brows shooting up his forehead as he suddenly performed a sit-up. "David who?" Her father's name was David, but certainly she wouldn't refer to Morganfield by his given name.

Elizabeth pulled her gaze from his bobbing cock, her brows furrowing as she considered the question. "I... I don't know. I don't think he has a last name," she replied with a shake of her head. "His..." She pointed at his manhood. "...Isn't nearly so... large, of course, but—"

A strangled curse erupted from George and forced her to return her attention to his face. "You've seen a naked man? Besides your father?"

Elizabeth waved a hand in the air, as if it wasn't important. "When I saw my father naked, he and mother were... well, making a bit of noise one afternoon in their bedchamber, and I peeked in. So it wasn't such a shock when I saw David."

That cursing sound came out of George again.

"I think it must have been a shock for Hannah, though. I thought she would faint. And then she couldn't keep her eyes off of him!"

She let out a shriek as her body was suddenly brought down to the mattress and George was over the top of her, his eyes wide and... was that *hurt* she saw in them?

"Who is *David?*" he whispered hoarsely, the words a struggle to get out around the extreme jealousy he was experiencing.

Elizabeth's mouth opened quite wide as she placed a hand against the side of his face. "Michaelangelo's David, of course," she murmured, a smile of delight curving her lips. "I saw the statue when Hannah and my parents and I were in Italy to visit Mama's family." She felt the fire and anger drain from George as he seemed to slump onto her, his erection cradled by her belly.

"You little minx, you," he said as his own lips curved.

"I meant it as a compliment," she countered with a whisper.

George regarded her for a very long time, his eyes locked

with hers in shared amusement. But after a few moments, he became aware of how his entire body was atop hers, aware of where their skin touched, how her breasts were mounded from the weight of his chest on them, of his turgid manhood pressed into the soft flesh of her belly, how his thighs straddled hers, of her toes where they rested against his calves. He slowly took inventory of all his parts and her parts and desire overwhelmed him.

His mouth settled onto her willing lips and he kissed her slowly, kissed her until he felt her need for him through her very being. Lowering his lips to her jaw, he trailed a line of kisses down the front of her body, a few here, a few there, occasionally allowing them to suckle a breast, kiss the tip of a nipple, glide over a rib. When he heard her breathing change, felt her body become taut, he pushed himself lower, bringing his legs to rest between hers as he continued his descent. His kisses brought out whimpers, driving him lower along her body.

Elizabeth's whimpers turned to sobs, to pleas for him to take her. He moved his body farther down the bed until he could see the soft, moist folds between her thighs, feel the wetness as he drew a finger down the moist cleft. Before he could repeat the stroke, Elizabeth's body arched up and she cried out, his name suddenly a plea. Circling his thumb into the soft, wet flesh of her womanhood, George slowed his breathing and waited. Her quickened breaths, her tensing body told him she had to be close to her ecstasy. Simply watching her made his cock throb, his own release almost eminent. He had never been so close to orgasm and yet not been inside a woman.

"Take me, George. Please. I beg you," she whispered hoarsely, her head tossing from side to side.

George heard her plea. He had promised her he would not hurt her, though. He could not take her maidenhead. Not tonight, at least. Perhaps not ever if she chose the earl over him.

The thought of Trenton helped him to regain control of his body.

He placed his head between her legs, moved his hands to cradle her bottom and gently lifted her hips. Her legs spread apart, and suddenly, she was all his. He lowered his face to the soft curls as he used a finger to gently part her feminine folds. His mouth kissed the swollen flesh, his tongue stroking and circling.

He first felt her recoil in surprise at the assault of his tongue on her womanhood, and then he was aware of her trying to force herself harder against his mouth. Lifting and tilting her hips until she felt his hand cover her mound to hold her down, she began mewling. When his thumb pressed against the aching bud he had aroused with his tongue and thumb, Elizabeth inhaled sharply. George gently licked the space beneath the bud, inciting another gasp and a whispered "yes." Knowing she was as ready as she would ever be, he laved his tongue across the swollen center of her womanhood—once, twice—and then his lips took purchase on it and suckled it.

Her back arched up, her chin tilted so her head was thrown back to expose her throat, and her hands clutched the bed linens as if to keep her body anchored to the bed. George could feel her entire body shatter beneath him. But it was the sound of her voice, crying out his name, the sound of her ecstasy, his very name, drawn out in several syllables in the form of a prayer, that made George realize his own release could not be stopped. He hauled his body up and over hers, his rigid cock seeking her sheath. Sliding it along her wet folds, desperate to bury it inside her but knowing he could not—he had *promised* her he would not—he growled as her hot, slick vulva surrounded him, cradled him when her knees lifted and pressed against his hips, slid along the entire length of him, up and back down his hardened shaft as she lifted and lowered her hips. When Elizabeth's body again shuddered beneath his and her fingernails branded his back with half-moons and her voice cried out his name again, ecstasy took him, the intense darkness and bright lights and extreme pleasure engulfing everything around and inside him.

Only she could do this to him—make him *feel* like he hadn't felt in his entire life. Make his body ache for her touch and her lips and those fingers that were hot and searing against the skin of his back. His voice forced out a strangled, "Oh, God,... Elizabeth… I… I love you," before his seed spilt onto her belly. Suddenly drained of strength, his body collapsed onto hers. He buried his head between her neck and shoulder and allowed a blanket of darkness to cover him.

The sensation of warm arms wrapping around his back, of fingertips stroking his flesh, of lips kissing his ear, brought him back from sleep. He listened intently at first, aware his breathing had finally returned to normal. He wondered if Elizabeth was all right.

And, for just a moment, he wondered *where* he was.

"George?" It was a barely audible whisper, said against the whorl of his ear and followed by the sensation of a tongue licking his earlobe.

George slowly lifted his head, careful not to put more weight on the feminine body he was squishing into the mattress. *How long did I sleep?* he wondered absently, suddenly embarrassed he had passed out on her, his hard body pressing her deep into the bed. The sight of Elizabeth in the waning light from the fireplace made him grin. Her bee-stung lips were smiling, and her hair was splayed out in a jumble of curls across the pillow they shared. "Are you… well?" he whispered, his voice still husky.

She turned her head to look up at the canopy, moving bits of her body one after the other as if they had been momentarily removed from her and she had just managed to put them back into place. "I think so," she whispered, a giggle escaping her throat. "But, are you? You looked as if…"

Nodding, George lifted himself onto one elbow. "I was not in pain, I assure you," he answered in an amused whisper, knowing she probably thought he was experiencing extreme discomfort when his own body had come apart into a billion pieces. He surveyed the bed. And then he surveyed Elizabeth. Her luscious body, with its creamy white skin and full breasts and slight belly, was posed as if she were a goddess in a painting. She had managed to pull her knees together; they rested off to one side so that her mound was nearly hidden from his view. At the sight of his semen gleaming on her belly, he flinched and caught her gazing at him. "I apologize, milady. I didn't intend to take my own pleas—"

Reaching out with a finger, Elizabeth placed it over his lips to stop his comment. "Do not. Please," she struggled to get out, her eyes clear and her voice quite steady.

George regarded her for a very long time, realizing she had aged just a bit with this experience. She seemed more—more sure of herself, more assertive, more of a *woman*—and he found he rather liked her better this way. "Did my demonstration...was it what you... expected?" he asked, not sure, other than simple curiosity, what her motivation had been when she made the request of him to pleasure her.

As a blush suddenly colored her upper body and face, Elizabeth lowered her eyes. "I had no idea, George," she murmured, a finger reaching up to trace his jawline. "My mother once told me that intercourse was like a massive tickle, but that is... a *massive* understatement. I cannot describe it, and I cannot believe that I could ever experience it again," she murmured, her voice barely audible, the tone of it suggesting she had accepted a fate that didn't include the possibility of such pleasure. Ever again.

George stared down at her. "Every night, should you choose," he answered quickly, chiding himself that he would seem so eager. "And," he paused, leaning in to kiss her cheek, "There is *more*."

Her eyes widened. "Oh, my God," she breathed. "You didn't..?" she started to ask, her brow furrowed in confusion. She stared down at the wetness on her belly, sure he had simply pulled out of her as his orgasm took hold of his body. She had overheard gossip that suggested some men did that, so as to lessen the chances of getting their mistresses with child.

"I promised I would leave your maidenhood intact, and I have done so. It is yours to give to your husband." *Whoever that will be,* he thought reluctantly, a sudden pain slicing though his middle at the thought that she would marry someone else. Butter Blond. *God, no.*

Instead of appearing relieved, Elizabeth seemed somehow

disappointed, her eyes downcast as she turned her body on the bed so she lay on her side. George kissed her shoulder. "I also promised I would allow you an hour to rest. I shall take my leave of you and return—"

"You leave this bed, George Bennett-Jones, and I shall never speak to you again," Elizabeth countered angrily, her body suddenly raised and supported on one elbow while her flushed face turned to regard him. Her entire body trembled.

At that moment, Elizabeth wanted nothing more than to pull George down atop her, to feel the length of his body against hers, to hold him and kiss him and stroke him until sleep took them for the rest of the night. There was desire, certainly, but also a need for closeness, a need to wake up in his arms, to somehow guarantee that what had occurred this evening really had *happened* and wasn't just a figment of her overactive imagination.

George froze and stared at her in shock. He watched as her sudden anger dissipated as quickly as it had appeared, though, and she seemed to crumble back onto the bed under his gaze. "What is it, Elizabeth?" he whispered, slipping an arm beneath her body and pulling it toward him. With his other hand, he wiped away the evidence of his orgasm from her belly and wondered if the chambermaid would notice the stain on the linen where he cleaned his hand.

Whatever tension had been in her body the moment before was suddenly gone; she felt limp as he positioned her on top of his chest and hip, pulling one of her legs to rest between his. Her whole body still shivered. There was the sensation of moisture on his shoulder. Placing a hand against the side of her face, he felt a hot tear. "Are you hurt?" he asked in alarm, wondering if he had done something wrong. Thinking she was cold, he reached down, grabbed at the edge of the bed linens and pulled them over their bodies.

"No," she whispered, one of her arms reaching around his chest to anchor herself more firmly to him. The trembles slowly subsided as George ran his hand up and down her arm and then tucked the linen and coverlet around her shoulders.

"Tell me, please," George said very quietly, part of him marveling at the way he was able to hold her entire body against his. He had expected she would want him out of the bed, that she would want privacy after their lovemaking. Josie never stayed long, hurrying off to the bath to clean herself and to remove the vinegar-soaked sponges she inserted before their time together.

"Do you think me wanton?" Elizabeth had closed her eyes in an effort to concentrate. She was aware of George's heartbeat, of one arm around her waist, of the hand that held the linen against her shoulder, of the feel of his chest and hip beneath her body, of his engorged manhood resting against the top of her thigh, of the gentle rise and fall of his chest with each breath he took.

God, yes! Wasn't it every man's dream to have a beautiful woman ask him to bed her? But that didn't necessarily make the woman a wanton. *Unless she makes it a habit of asking several men for the favor.* "Since you said I am the only one you have asked to pleasure you, then no," he countered quietly, his head shaking just a bit on the pillow.

When he didn't elaborate on his answer, Elizabeth continued to stare at him. "How can you not?" she asked, the tone of her voice suggesting he *should* think her wanton.

"Because, my sweet, being sensual is not the same as being a wanton. And you are... a very sensuous woman." He took the opportunity to kiss her, his lips capturing hers in a light caress that made her body shiver again. "And one apparently suffering from the cold," he added as he turned on his side and rolled her so he could tuck her back against his chest and the front of his thighs against the back of hers. He tried not to think of his arousal as it rested against her bottom.

Elizabeth allowed him the intimate contact, a sigh escaping as she realized how much warmer and safer she felt. How much she craved his touch. She wasn't cold, really, but she had no idea why her body thrummed as it did. She only knew she had to stay pressed against George for as long as he would allow her to do so.

She wasn't aware of time passing or of falling into a dream-filled sleep.

When George was sure Elizabeth was asleep, he reluctantly climbed out of the bed. Glancing at the hearth, he saw the two basins of water Elkins had left warming there. He wet a flannel and cleaned himself, hoping he wouldn't remove the musky scent of Elizabeth as he did so. He wanted to smell it again and again as he slept later.

Sleep? How would he be able to sleep after a night such as this? To have lain with the woman of his dreams, to have pleasured her and been pleasured so thoroughly by simply rubbing his shaft against her—how could he ever hope to sleep again? Just the thought of her body still in his bed made his entire body thrum.

She has to marry me.

If she didn't, he would be left feeling bereft and quite sorry he hadn't taken the opportunity to ruin her when he had the chance. He had no intention of considering any other woman to be his wife. If Elizabeth denied his request for her hand, he would simply live out his days without a wife, without an heir. The viscountcy could revert to the Crown...

Why the thought of Prinny gaining the Bostwick viscountcy should bring George to his senses, he didn't know. But it did.

She has to marry me.

CHAPTER 38
AFTER ECSTASY, REALITY

ware that the comforting warmth at her back was gone, Elizabeth woke from her dreams of being pleasured. *George!* she thought happily, remembering the feel of his hands and his kisses and his tongue as he pleasured her. She watched his silhouette from where she lay on the bed. *God, he is somehow handsome,* she thought. He, with a fencer's grace and a body finer than any of the Grecian marbles, with his manhood still erect, looking like a sword, ready to impale her and promising even more pleasure than what she had already experienced. He, a master of kisses to make her knees weak and her head spin, George Bennett-Jones was the man she should be marrying, she acknowledged.

Somewhere deep inside, the flutterbies suddenly flipped. Her heart tightened. And Josephine's words came back to her. *He just wants to give you what you want. What you asked for.*

And he had!

But she was the daughter of a marquess. Could she marry a viscount? Even if she loved him, and she could not say yet if she did or did not, she was expected to marry well. She was sure her mother would prefer she marry a marquess or duke. As for her father, she had no idea. Would a viscount do?

If Trenton could never pleasure her the way George had tonight, at least she had experienced sexual pleasure.

She would remember this night for as long as she lived and not have to wonder what she might have missed. At that last thought, a feeling of emptiness slowly settled over her.

When he was done cleaning himself, George picked up the other basin and a flannel and moved to the bed. Wetting the cloth, he reached over to wipe Elizabeth's body. One of her hands reached out and rested over the top of his hand. "What are you doing?" she demanded, gasping as she felt the warm, wet flannel touch her still-sensitive skin. Her eyes were bright in the dim light, as if they were lined with unshed tears.

"I need to... I wish to clean..." He stopped, not sure what to say to explain himself. He moved the cloth over her belly, gently washing her creamy white skin, removing the evidence of his orgasm from her skin and the lingering dampness from between her legs. When he completed his ministrations, he leaned over her body and kissed her belly and her breasts and finally her lips. Before he had finished, she was weeping quietly. "Why are you crying?" he asked in a hoarse whisper. "Did I... did I hurt you?"

Elizabeth moved a hand to her cheek, pulling it away and staring at the palm as if she, too, was surprised by her tears. "No, George," she whispered as she shook her head. She sniffled. "I've no idea why I'm suddenly a watering pot," she added. She had an idea, though. A thought that perhaps this would be the only time in her life she would experience such a glorious experience. She couldn't imagine Trenton showing her such attention. Worshipping her body as if she was a goddess.

But what if he would? What if his skills in bed were equal to George's? She could imagine the earl's response should she make the request of a pre-marital assignation like this one. He would no doubt welcome the opportunity to bed her. Bed her and take her virtue knowing he would be marrying her by Christmastime. She sighed and was wondering which man's offer she would accept when she noticed George's look of worry. "What is it?" she asked.

A quick glance at the clock told George they hadn't much time. It was already a bit after one. *I promised to have Elizabeth home by two!* "I must get you dressed," he murmured as he left the bed again. He moved toward the pile of clothes near the chair and quickly pulled on his breeches, fastening the buttons in quick succession. He tossed his shirt over his head before hurrying to the bed. He reached down to lift her, but Elizabeth waved off his assistance.

"I can manage," she whispered, flicking the remaining tears from one cheek with a finger. George shook out her gown and held it for her. She pulled it on in silence as he recovered her stockings.

"May I be of assistance?" he asked quietly. At her quizzical look, he added, "It seems only fair given I removed them," he said as he held up one of the stockings.

Elizabeth regarded the rolled stocking he held and then moved to take a seat at their dinner table. "I suppose I should insist," she replied, a wan smile appearing.

His own smile tentative, George knelt before her. He kissed the back of her fingers as he waited for her to extend a bare foot. Elizabeth pulled up the hem of her gown so a foot barely appeared. She watched as George placed the stocking over her toes and very slowly unrolled the silk onto her foot, over her ankle and up her calf. When his fingers reached the back of her knee, she inhaled sharply. George looked up to find she had leaned her head back, her face displaying a look of pure joy made golden by the light of the fire. "What is it, my sweeting?" he whispered, keeping his fingers firmly in place at the back of her knee.

"It's nothing," she replied, lowering her head until her eyes opened and regarded him with an impish grin.

Not believing her, George very lightly stroked the back of her knee again, all the while pretending he was pulling the stocking over her bent knee. He felt her leg shiver and heard her slight inhalation of breath. "You would make a fine lady's maid," she said in a teasing voice.

George grinned as he repeated his caresses with the other stocking, all the while wondering what Elizabeth thought of their night together. He placed her slippers back on her feet and stood up. "I rather doubt that. I have never done this before," he said as he moved to refasten the hooks at the back of her gown.

Stifling a gasp of surprise, Elizabeth regarded him with a glance over her shoulder. *Josephine was his mistress; certainly he would have had to undress her.* But, perhaps not. "Please, do not fasten all of them," she said suddenly, referring to the hooks he was securing at her back. "I have to undress myself," she added as she felt his fingers against her bare skin and another frisson pass through her body.

He stopped fastening the hooks and wondered at the hitch in her breath, wondered what she was thinking as she went about gathering up her things and retrieving stray hairpins from the bed. *Had she made some sort of decision then?*

He tucked his shirt into his breeches and reached for his waist coat, buttoning it as quickly as he could given his fingers didn't want to be doing this. They wanted to be undoing the hooks on the back of Elizabeth's dress. They wanted to be sliding along her skin, over her breasts and down her belly and between her thighs and into the warm, wet sheath that promised... he shook his head to clear it.

Trenton would ask for her hand any day now. *Does she regret having asked me to do this?* he wondered suddenly, afraid that perhaps he had made a huge mistake in introducing her to the wonders of sensual pleasure. He pulled on his top coat, still lost in thought. Now that she knew what sensations she could experience with him, did she realize they might not be the same with a different man? With a man who didn't care if he provided pleasure in return for the pleasure he took from her?

George picked up the bonnet from the table where she had carefully placed it earlier that evening. *Teal velvet with peacock feathers.* Yes, this had to be the bonnet he had paid for that day at Neville Peabody's shop. He traced a finger tip along the edge of the feathers, remembering the afternoon he had discovered her shopping with Lady Charlotte. And when Neville had mentioned Lady Elizabeth's purchase, he had thought immediately to pay for it on her behalf.

"A bit jaunty, I suppose," Elizabeth murmured as she

watched George regard her bonnet. He seemed to be studying it quite intently, as if he recognized it.

"Yes, but..." he started to respond and then turned his attention to Elizabeth. "It suits you. Perfectly. I knew it would..." He stopped speaking suddenly and bit his lip. The expression on his face was one of contrition, as if he already knew he had been caught at having done something wrong and would have to own up to it.

Elizabeth's quick inhalation of breath confirmed she had heard and understood what he was talking about. "You're the one who paid for the bonnet." It wasn't a question, merely an acknowledgement. "George! I went back to the shop and tried to pay for it before Mr. Peabody could send the bill to my father," she said, a bit breathless. "Why, George? Why would *you* pay for my bonnet like that? It was most... *improper*," she said, her breaths coming in short little gasps.

George thought she might hyperventilate if he didn't act immediately. The bonnet still clutched in his hand, he moved toward her and placed his mouth over hers, his free hand moving to the back of her waist to pull her body hard against his. Although she was obviously surprised, Elizabeth soon allowed the kiss, indeed, even returned it a bit before George slowly pulled his lips away. He left his forehead pressed against hers, though, his eyes closed. "You did a great service for a good friend, my lady. I meant nothing more than to thank you for the consideration and graciousness you showed Mr. Streater."

Elizabeth's eyes opened wide as she remembered Charlotte talking of her charity during the Worthington ball. She pulled her head away from George's so she could see his face. "So, you didn't intend it as a gift for... gifting's sake?" she half-asked. *Who am I to question George's propriety when I have asked him to demonstrate the pleasures that can be had in a marriage bed?*

"No, my lady," he answered with a shake of his head. "Although I would welcome the opportunity to bestow gifts upon you when the circumstances allow it," he hinted, hoping she might agree to be his wife when he proposed the following afternoon. *Always promise her more*, Josephine had said, when instructing him about women.

Elizabeth ignored the statement. "And how is it you are such good friends with Theodore Streater?" she asked, taking her bonnet from George. She had wound her hair into a simple bun while George rolled her stockings onto her legs. Now she began pinning the bonnet onto the bun, taking great care to set as many pins as she could find into securing the bonnet in place.

George couldn't help but notice how she deliberately avoided responding to his last statement. "We met at Angelo's Academy. He is one of my fencing partners," he said with what could have been a shrug.

Surprised at their association, Elizabeth thought a moment. "You mean, you... *were*... fencing partners," she tried to clarify, thinking that a one-armed man would be unable to continue in the sport. She had seen swordplay. She had watched fencing matches. It always appeared as if a man needed two arms—one to hold the weapon and one to balance his movements.

But George allowed a wicked grin as he shook his head. "We are still. He is a formidable opponent. I see to payment of his dues at the academy since he has been unable to afford such luxuries." Even though he never considered that what he did for his friend was anything more than what any friend would do for another, perhaps he could impress her with his own charity as it related to Teddy.

But Elizabeth's stance suddenly softened and she lowered her chin. "It's very kind of you to do so. He is... he seems like a good man," she said quietly.

"He is," George confirmed with a nod. "Now, my lady, if you are ready—"

"Why *me*, George?" she asked suddenly. Her face was tilted up as she regarded him. When she saw his brows furrow, she continued, "There are at least a dozen young ladies looking to marry this year, George. Two of them have dowries far larger than mine and another two or three are far more beautiful to look upon than I am. There must be dozens of eligible daughters from wealthy families looking to marry. Why me, George?"

George stared at her, one brow furrowed in consternation at her words. He couldn't tell her she was his mistress' first choice for him. He couldn't tell her Teddy thought her perfect for him. And he certainly couldn't tell her, despite his intention to avoid the matter entirely, he had fallen heels over head in love with her when he had first laid eyes on her. "My lady, if I wanted to marry a milk-and-water milkmaid, I would have already married." The retort came out more forcibly than he intended. He noticed her surprised look as she leaned back a bit at his words. She didn't step away, though, holding her ground as if she was prepared to argue her point further.

He doesn't think me insipid, Elizabeth thought, her head still held in that angle that made her appear every bit as stubborn as she was. Which meant he had a completely different opinion of her. "Pray tell, George. What is it about *me* that would compel you to offer for my hand when we have only known one another a few days?" When George didn't reply right away, she inhaled sharply. "Or... perhaps I should wonder why you think it necessary to ask for my hand? For I must assure you, I do not think you should feel honor bound to do so..."

In an instant, George took hold of one of her hands, lifting it to his lips to place a kiss on the palm. "You are a beautiful woman, milady—"

"There are dozens of beautiful women in the Marriage Mart...," she interrupted him, her retort spoken with a roll of her eyes.

"Who knows what she wants—"

"Because I'm a spoiled brat, George!"

"—And is willing to take risks to see to it she gets it," George continued as if he hadn't heard her comment. He had one arm around her waist now, pulling her body closer to his.

"I can be very stubborn," she countered, her hands moving to grip his upper arms. *Don't you realize I cannot marry you?* "I am fond of you George, and so grateful... but I'm quite sure I am expected to marry a man of higher rank than you. Besides..." She shook her head. "However can you claim you wish to ask for my hand?"

George closed his eyes and touched her forehead with his own. He barely heard anything after *I am fond of you, George.* If necessary, those words would sustain him for a long time. As to how to respond to her question, he knew exactly what to say. "I want our children to be compassionate. I want them to realize what a privileged life they lead compared to the lives of others. I want them to learn that from *you.*"

Elizabeth stared at George, her eyes wide with surprise at his words. *Our children,* she heard over and over in her head.

Our children. I want our children to be compassionate.

He truly has given this some thought, she realized. Not knowing what else to do, she pulled her head away from his and kissed the corner of his mouth.

George regarded her for a moment, hoping she understood his meaning. He knew no other way to get his point across. "We really... we really *must* be going," he whispered then, not wanting to let go his hold on Elizabeth. *We would be going back to my bed, if I wasn't so damned honorable!*

Elizabeth nodded. "I am ready," she announced with a sigh, her hair sporting the ornate peacock bonnet. She pulled on her gloves. *He really does love me. Damn him!*

George looked at her then, studying her face and noticing the wetness on her cheeks, the brightness of her eyes. "Why the tears, Elizabeth?" George asked quietly, his concern evident as he took her hand and held it in his.

Elizabeth shrugged and ducked her head away for a moment. "I honestly don't know," she replied with a shake of her head, her gloved hand reaching up to wipe them away. "I didn't know I was crying."

I want them to learn that from you.

George nervously glanced at the clock on the mantle. One-forty. They needed to leave now if they were to get to her home in time to meet the two o'clock deadline he had promised when they had set up this assignation. "Are you ready?" he asked, his gaze taking in her suddenly worried expression and tense stance. "Let us go."

Was he joking? The man had her thoroughly discombobulated! His touch had been magic—every body part he had caressed with his fingers and his lips and his tongue and even just his breath still tingled—his kisses had been electrifying, his soft words had been comforting and enticing. She had experienced pleasures she had never dreamed could be possible, and was now barely put back together. And, on top of that, George had spoken of children, *their* children, and held her as she imagined a loving husband would hold his wife.

How in damnation was she supposed to go back to her home and pretend that none of this had happened?

"I... suppose," she finally answered, her eyes finally meeting his when she was sure she had her reticule in hand. When he offered her his arm, Elizabeth regarded it for a long moment. She looked back up at his face and sighed. "Oh, George," she whispered, her entire body suddenly pressed against his, her face resting in the small of his shoulder and the peacock feather in her bonnet colliding with his nose. Instinctively, his arms wrapped about her shoulders. "Thank you," she murmured into his coat, the scent of sandalwood and amber teasing her nose as the steel band of his arms embraced her. It would be so easy to simply stay there for the night. If George would allow it, she would gladly remove all her clothing and lie with him.

The morning would come soon enough, though, and if she wasn't at Carlington House when breakfast was served, there would be hell to pay. "I shall never forget this night as long as I live," she vowed as she finally pushed herself away.

George allowed a smile as he reveled in her having held him. "Nor shall I, my lady," he replied, again holding his arm for her. This time she took it, and they left the room and descended the stairs.

George left her at the bottom of the stairs so he could retrieve her mantle from the vestibule. When he returned, he helped drape it over her shoulders. "I must be sure no one sees you," he murmured as he led her to the door at the back of the house. "Should I tell my coachman to go to the front or the back of your house?" he asked as they strolled through the long hallway. "I will, of course, accompany you. For your safety." *And because I don't wish to part from you just yet.*

Elizabeth barely registered his question, her senses all so much more... *alive* than they had been before. Things were brighter, more colorful. Sounds were easier to hear, and there were more of them. She could smell citrus and sandalwood and the scent of musk. The feel of the superfine wool under her fingers was somehow enhanced. She drank in sight of the portraits and moldings framing the hallway, the ornate dining room off to one side of the hall, and a beautifully decorated salon off to the other side. Near the back of the house, a parlor, golden from the candle lamps and fires lit within, looked out over a garden illuminated by a gas lamp.

She was sure she wouldn't have noticed any of it before.

"The front, of course," she finally answered, her voice quiet in the empty house. "I am expected, having spent the evening with my friend, Her Grace, Duchess of Somerset," she explained, her face lighting with a tentative smile.

George allowed his own smile, secretly glad that if anyone must know of this evening besides the two of them and Josephine, Beth Stretton would be the one. The woman would be most discreet. "And does Her Grace know you have spent the evening with her?" he asked, wondering how many others might know that Elizabeth Carlington was planning to spend an entire evening, unchaperoned, in his company. He opened the back door and led her down several brick steps and into the garden.

Sensing his concern for her reputation, Elizabeth gave him a smile. "She is the only one," she responded, her eyes flitting about the path they followed. Mums and pansies bordered the paved walkway, their colors skewed by the gas light. "We are playing cards and trying on gowns," she added, the activities sounding so... girlish. A frisson passed through her body as she considered what this night meant for her.

George opened the back gate and the door to the coach. "It sounds as if you are having a delightful evening," he replied, handing her into the coach. He climbed in after her, hoping he might sit on the same side of the coach as she.

He was not disappointed.

Elizabeth had moved to the opposite side of the coach, leaving plenty of room on the bench seat for him. Settling into the squabs for the short ride to Carlington House, George reached out a hand to cover one of hers. "Did I satisfy your curiosity?" he asked in a hoarse whisper. He leaned over and placed a kiss on the side of her head, just as the coach began its short journey.

"Indeed," Elizabeth breathed in reply. She could feel her face flushing as she remembered some of the things he had done to her that evening. Her body responded with a shiver, and she leaned closer to George. "And yet, you claim there is *more*. How can that be, George?" she asked, her head held low. She had come to realize she could ask him anything and he wouldn't seemed shocked by the query. How different George Bennett-Jones was from men in the *ton*!

And how unfortunate she would not learn of the "more" from him.

George sighed as he squeezed her gloved hand. "If we are married, I shall make love to you as often as you'll have me. The first time..." He paused and allowed his head to drop backward as he considered what to tell her.

"I have heard it can be painful," she stated, her eyes looking up to meet his. How bad could it be with George, though? She imagined he would be careful. He would be slow and deliberate and ask after her health.

He nodded, the movement nearly hidden in the darkness. "But I can make it less so," he claimed in a quiet voice. "And see to it you experience a wondrous pleasure even more complete than you felt tonight." Boasting might not be his forté, but this was his last chance to stake his claim and make Elizabeth see the advantage of marrying him instead of Butter Blond.

"And you?" Elizabeth countered quickly, aware their ride was nearly over.

George furrowed his brows and regarded her for a moment. "Me?" he asked, not sure of her meaning.

"What will *you* experience?" she asked patiently.

He thought at first she referred to the sensations of a man's orgasm and then wondered if perhaps she was asking what he would experience the first time, should he be the one to take her virtue. "I honestly do not know," he breathed in astonishment. "I have never... I have never bedded a virgin," he added with a small shake of his head.

Elizabeth stared at him for a very long time, surprised by his admission. So, he was not an experienced man, she decided, leaning over to rest her head against his shoulder. A wave of tiredness swept over her as his arm wrapped around her back and pulled her closer to his warmth.

"May I kiss you?"

Suddenly nervous and not quite sure why, Elizabeth lifted her head from his shoulder. Her eyes went wide at the sound of his voice. He seemed... sad, somehow. She didn't answer but angled her face so his lips could take hers. They were firm and warm, pressing gently against her own lips and then sliding ever so carefully across them. The kiss turned hard and possessive before his lips finally captured her bottom lip and nipped it as he pulled away. In the darkness, she could barely make out his eyes as he did so, but she thought she saw a hint of sadness there.

"You honor me, my lady," he whispered, his ungloved hand cupping her cheek and his eyes taking in all of her.

Elizabeth slumped against him, a frustrated sigh escaping. "Oh, George. When I asked if you would show me what pleasures might be possible, I had no idea... I didn't know it could be... like it was." She struggled to get her words out. "And I cannot even admonish my married friends for not having told me, for then they would know that I..."

George embraced her tightly. "Shhh," he whispered into the side of her head. "Will there be anyone awake when you arrive?"

"There shouldn't be. I told Alfred not to wait up. Why do you ask?" she asked, her awareness of his body so near it made her own thrum again. *What has he done to me?*

George gave her a look of chagrin, only noticeable due to the light streaming in through one of the coach windows from a gas lamp they passed on the way to Carlington House. "Anyone who looks at you will *know*," he said in a low voice.

Elizabeth's eyebrow became an elegant arch. "Know... what?" she wondered, a bit of alarm in her response.

George sighed. "That you've been kissed. Thoroughly... kissed."

Elizabeth swallowed as she regarded him. Then her hand reached up to her mouth, her fingers gingerly touching the swollen flesh. "Is it truly that evident?" she countered, one finger tracing the line of her lip.

George inhaled sharply at the sight of her finger outlining her cherry red lips. "God, yes," he murmured, smiling as he said it. The coach ground to a halt, forcing him to shift her body so she didn't end up sliding to the floor of the coach. "Forsham will open the door and hand you out. I will wait until I know you are safely inside," he explained quickly. "And, if it is agreeable with my lady, I will call on you later this afternoon," he stated, getting the words out as fast as he could for fear he would lose his nerve.

Elizabeth considered his request. He had said he would ask for her hand in marriage. She wondered if he would do so once he spent more time considering their evening together. Perhaps the viscount would change his mind and decide he preferred a woman who was more reserved. More refined. Perhaps this evening had been a test, and he had been waiting for her to turn demure and refuse his overtures and claim her request had been a mistake.

But he had said, *I love you*, she remembered. In a moment of passion, yes, but still, he had said those words with such conviction!

Our children.

"I will see you this afternoon then," Elizabeth replied before kissing his cheek and giving him a quick hug. The door was opening; she had only a second to get to her feet and rearrange her skirts before Forsham would hand her down.

Instead of moving to the door, she leaned over George and held her face very close to his, willing him to kiss her one last time. He did so, wrapping an arm around her neck and pulling her down so he could deepen the kiss. Then it was over as quickly as it had begun. She stepped down from the carriage and hurried up the front walk to the double doors of Carlington House. George watched from the coach window, noting how Elizabeth opened the door herself and slipped in, turning once to give him a wave before shutting the door.

Although the sound of the door closing didn't reach his ears, the sound of his heartbeat was suddenly very loud in George's ears.

CHAPTER 39
ONE LAST MOMENT WITH THE MISTRESS

George took a very deep breath and settled back into the squabs, a combination of emotions vying for his attention. He was relieved, for the evening had gone better than planned. Except for that moment he had lost control and nearly buried himself in Elizabeth, he had managed to leave her virtue intact. No other man would have resisted the temptation.

Lady Elizabeth hadn't been as reserved as he expected, and he wondered if he should be concerned she allowed him to undress her so readily, allowed him to touch her and kiss her in places that would make most women blush in embarrassment. Her soft whimpers and his name spoken in soft whispers brought him a deep sense of satisfaction.

Despite his nervousness—and he *had* been nervous—he had been able to bring her to the brink of ecstasy and push her over the edge until she was breathless and boneless and sobbed his name in that way she had of making it sound like the most wonderful moniker a man could have. And he had done it again and again, the last time resulting in his own release that had been such a surprise, he had said words he never thought he would say aloud to anyone but Josephine.

I love you.

The thought of Josephine brought him up short. He suddenly wondered about the time she and Elizabeth had spent together in the town coach. What had his mistress thought of her? The two had been together at least fifteen minutes in the coach; perhaps Josephine had learned something that could help him in his pursuit of Elizabeth.

The coach slowed and finally stopped. A quick glance showed he was already back at his townhouse. Glancing at his Breguet, he was stunned to find it was only a quarter past two. He climbed out of the coach and gave a wave to his coachman, who directed the four horses to head for the stables behind the house.

The familiar scent of Josephine's perfume tickled his nose as he opened his front door. Dressed in the same carriage gown she had worn when she set off in his coach to fetch Elizabeth, she slowly rose from a chair in the vestibule. "Josie," he breathed, rushing to wrap his arms around her.

Josephine allowed the hug but did not return the gesture. "How do, George," she said with a slight smile. She regarded him as he removed his arms from around her shoulders. "Well?" she demanded, a bit breathless. When George didn't immediately respond, she added, "Was she everything you... expected?" *Wanted? Dreamed of?* She had spent the entire evening thinking about George and Elizabeth, wondering how the two fared in each other's company. Wondering if Elizabeth had even made it through dinner, let alone the champagne in the library. Although she desperately wanted to know, Josephine had stayed away until just after two, deciding it was better to give George the benefit of the doubt.

"Oh, God, yes," he answered without pause. "I love her, Josie. I do. I... " He shook his head as if to clear it. She seemed to wilt before his eyes. "I apologize," he said then, scrubbing his face with his hands, ashamed he could be so insensitive to Josephine. She was his mistress. He had loved her all the years they had been together.

"George! There's no need to apologize," she admonished, placing a gloved hand on his arm. "I merely stopped by to see if I might be of assistance in getting Lady Elizabeth home. But I suppose you made your ridiculous deadline," she teased, unable to resist the jab at him for keeping his word as to when he would return Elizabeth to her house. Josephine angled her head to one side as she watched her protector begin to pace across the vestibule.

"We did," George acknowledged, nodding. "And it was not ridiculous. It was... appropriate," he explained lamely, trying to keep his memories of the evening from becoming jumbled. There was so much he wanted to remember. So much he wanted to replay in his head, if for no other reason than to be able to relive those moments over and over again. Even if Elizabeth didn't agree to marry him, he would forever remember this night. He thought perhaps the memories could sustain him for the rest of his life. "How... how did you get here?" he asked suddenly, not having seen a carriage in front of his townhouse.

"Clarice dropped me on the way from the theatre," she said with a wave, referring to a discreet courtesan with whom she occasionally attended social functions. "She confirmed Gabriel Wellingham will be asking for Elizabeth's hand tomorrow... or rather, later today," she stated, a sense of urgency in her words. She told herself the news was the real reason she had stopped by this evening, although it was really curiosity about how George had fared with his assignation.

George stilled and took a deep breath. He nodded, as if he had come to the same conclusion. "Short of ruining her completely, I have done all that I can," he said finally. He knew then he really meant it. What else could he have done to court Elizabeth Carlington in the short amount of time he had had? He had danced with her, supped with her, taken her on a ride in the park, kissed her, taken her to the museum, kissed her again, and made love to her in every way but the way in which he truly wanted. "I shall call on her later this afternoon. I told her... I said I would ask for her hand if she doesn't accept Trenton's suit. I should know by then if she has accepted his offer."

Josephine crossed her arms and let out a very unladylike snort. "George Bennett-Jones! Why not go as early as you can? Before Wellingham is even out of bed?" she asked, suddenly angry. "I have it on very good authority the marquess is an early riser, and I rather think the rest of his household is as well."

Surprised by her outburst, George warily regarded his mistress for a moment before replying. "I want her to have the choice, Josie."

His mistress shook her head and crossed her arms, obviously annoyed. "She will still have the *choice*, George," she admonished him. "Some of these young ladies don't make a decision on the day they are asked. They expect to have three or four offers before the end of the Little Season! And then they decide!"

"Which is why there is no hurry, Josie," he interrupted, his voice kept deliberately quiet. He wondered at the sense of calm that had settled over him. If he closed his eyes, he could see Elizabeth as she was when she was beneath him, naked and open and begging him to take her, her swollen lips eager to kiss him and her fingernails laying claim to the skin of his back. And he could still remember that overwhelming and sensational feeling as his body reacted to hers. He had never experienced anything like it with Josephine. *Never*.

So now, as Josephine admonished him for not taking the initiative and being first to ask for Elizabeth's hand, he felt a great deal of satisfaction in what he had accomplished this evening. He wasn't about to allow Josephine to ruin his good mood. But even as he basked in his success with the woman he hoped would be his wife, he watched Josephine as she seemed to deflate before his very eyes. "What is wrong?" he asked suddenly, hurrying to provide support with an arm and shoulder.

Tears pricked at the edges of Josephine's eyes. "Oh, George," she sighed, her head shaking as he took her back to the chair she was sitting in when he first arrived. "I truly can no longer be your mistress," she whispered, a tear escaping her eye and slowly rolling down her cheek.

George furrowed his brows, more concerned about her saddened state than the words she spoke. "What has happened?" he asked, kneeling in front of her while clutching one of her gloved hands in his. Had his assignation with Elizabeth bothered Josie more than she would admit?

"I received a note from Jack. He is due to arrive in London the day after tomorrow." She lifted her head to meet his gaze and then could not. "I thought... I thought I had more time—"

"Whatever do you mean?" George asked then, his worry increasing. Something was wrong. He couldn't remember a time when Josephine had shed a tear about *anything*. Pulling his handkerchief out of his waistcoat pocket, he placed it in her hand and closed her fingers around it. "Josie, tell me what is wrong."

Josephine sighed, using the handkerchief to dab at the corners of her eyes. "He wants me to accompany him whilst he looks at townhouses... he is prepared to buy one here in London—"

"That's wonderful! You'll be in London. I can still see you on occasion," George reasoned, his expression especially happy. "In a social setting, of course."

"He wishes to live part of the time here in town—"

"Show him yours," George stated firmly. "Tell him... tell him you just inherited it."

"Inherited it?" Josephine replied in surprise, her head shaking quickly. "From *whom*? He knows my father had nothing..." Her voice trailed off and her eyes fell to gaze at the carpet, as if she was embarrassed at her admission.

"Does Jack know about your mother?" George asked gently.

George watched the younger daughter as she seemed to crumble before his eyes. In all the years George had known Josephine, he had never seen her so unsure of herself, so lost. She had always seemed confident and strong, as if she could rule a country. She had taught him that trait. Instilled in him the need to exude confidence, to appear friendly and approachable, to carry himself as if he were to the manor born. The change in the way others regarded him was a revelation. From the piste to his place in the House of Lords, his peers seemed to regard him with respect while never becoming too formal with him.

"I told him... I told Jack she had gone to London to care for a family member," she whispered.

George thought for a moment. "Does he know she has since died?" George knew Josephine's mother lived in town when he first took Josephine as his mistress. He had never met the woman, and when she died a few years later, Josephine had kept the news to herself for a very long time.

"No," she breathed, her head lifting until she was seated quite upright in the chair.

"Then you inherited the house from her... or her family," George stated firmly. "Now, is your wardrobe in order?" he asked then, recalling that he rarely saw her in anything other than an occasional day gown and apparel appropriate only for a bedchamber.

The change of subject was a surprise to Josephine. "Of course," she replied, a bit indignant. "Your generosity has seen to that."

George nodded then, as if acknowledging her compliment. "So, your having inherited a house and some funds from your mother or a member of her family is not so unbelievable. "Your name is already on the title. I saw to that years ago. It's in my study. I know exactly where it is." He stood up as if to go get it, but Josephine held on to his hand.

"George!" she protested. "I cannot take your *house!*" she countered, surprised by his generosity and even more surprised that the house was his to give. She had always thought it was merely leased for her use.

"But, you must," he insisted. "You cannot turn down a wedding gift, after all," he reasoned, his face brightening with his quick thinking.

Josephine moved to get up and then decided to keep her seat. *He was giving her the house! Had given her the house.* The house she had grown so fond of over the course of their eight years together. The house that held her favorite memories and everything she could call her own. George was giving it to her!

"Here 'tis," George announced as he returned from his study, holding out the title to the townhouse.

Finally reaching for the document, Josephine caught his hand and kissed the back of it. "Are you quite certain?" she asked, sniffling and trying very hard to maintain her decorum.

George smiled, making him look every bit as handsome as she had ever seen him. "I am positive," he answered with a nod. "I've never had need of it, and I know you have grown fond of it." He sighed, a sense of overwhelming satisfaction settling over him. He wondered if this was how Elizabeth felt when she was successful at placing a wounded soldier in a position.

Closing his eyes, he thought of their last moments together in the coach, remembered Elizabeth's last kiss, how desperate she had seemed when she turned back to him and kissed him. *Hard.* A last kiss? Or simply the last kiss of an evening's togetherness?

Josephine was right, he decided. The woman could no longer be his mistress. And he found he no longer wanted her in that capacity. "You are welcome to spend the night here, but I must insist you take one of the guest suites," George said very carefully. "I do not think it proper for either one of us to be sharing a bedchamber this evening."

And he certainly didn't want her to see the state of his apartment at the moment.

Josephine smiled and nodded. "Thank you, George. A guest suite will do fine." With her tears wiped away, she allowed George to escort her up the stairs. It would be the last evening she would spend in his home with George as her protector, with him as her employer. In just over a day, Jack would claim her, and her new life would begin.

She found she could hardly wait.

CHAPTER 40
DECISION DAY

he following day
He had kissed her as if it would be the last time he ever did so. Elizabeth remembered the sad look in his eyes as he had watched her step down from the carriage, as if he never thought to see her again. As promised, he had returned her exactly at two o'clock, the bells of a nearby church tolling the hour as she lowered her face to his. Lips parted, she had leaned over him until George had been forced to return what started as a gentle kiss and then had become... something more. She had wanted to throw her arms around him, beg him to take her back to his townhouse, back to his bed and to the promise of... *more*.

Her entire body shivered, and she sighed.

"Are you well?"

Elizabeth gave a start as she realized her mother was staring at her. "Pardon?" she replied, her voice a bit breathy.

Lady Morganfield angled her head as her eyes lit up with amusement. "You must have had a grand time with the duchess last evening. And you look as if you're still there, wherever it was," she added as her grin widened.

Swallowing, Elizabeth considered her mother's comment. Her maid, Anna, had mentioned she looked—how had she put it?—*Brighter.*

"You must have slept especially well last night. Your complexion is the best I've seen it in weeks."

One of Elizabeth's hands lifted to her cheek as she glanced down at her breakfast plate, her cheeks growing warm under her mother's scrutiny. She hoped the woman couldn't tell she had been pleasured within an inch of her life just barely seven hours ago. In response to that thought, a delightful shiver coursed through her belly, and she nearly cried out at the sensation. George wasn't even touching her, and yet she could still feel the effects of his fingers, his lips, his tongue all over her body!

Her mother was expecting a reply, she remembered, and she struggled to pull her mind into the breakfast room and the conversation she was supposed to be having. Lord Morganfield, wondering at the sudden silence, closed his newly ironed copy of *The Times* and regarded his daughter with a questioning look.

"Why, thank you, Mother," Elizabeth replied lightly, allowing a brilliant smile to appear. "I did sleep well. I think it helped that Beth and I spent the evening at their townhouse instead of going out."

Lady Morganfield's eyebrow arched. "I thought you planned to attend the play at the Drury Lane Theatre," she countered, a bit of disappointment in her voice. "I was hoping for your review this morning. Your father and I may attend this evening." She pretended to ignore her husband's quick shake of his head in her direction; he would go only if she insisted they do so. To make it up to him, she would show up at his bedchamber door wearing his favorite lace and feather confection shortly after their return.

Adeline Carlington had become quite good at encouraging her husband to be social outside of their home this past year. And in the spirit of good sportsmanship, he had allowed it.

Elizabeth shrugged. "We were planning to do so, but Beth... I mean, Her Grace... had the latest *La Belle Assemblée*, and we ended up spending the night drooling over all the fashion plates. And she allowed me to try on several of the new gowns she had from her modiste for the winter season. The new fabrics are just splendid!" The reasons she listed for not attending the theatre nearly matched what she and Beth had discussed the day before when they devised the plot to help her escape Carlington House at six o'clock. She had sent a note this morning letting Her Grace know she had arrived home safely and that she would tell her more when next they met.

But she had no intention of telling her what had *happened* at George's house.

Her father was still regarding her, his expression, as usual, not giving away his thoughts on the subject. It was one of the traits that made him an effective politician. "Father, what is it?" she finally asked, wondering if he could read her mind and knew everything that had happened to her the night before. She could feel her cheeks redden, sure he knew *everything*.

He placed the paper on the table. "There is talk Trenton will ask for your hand," he replied, neither the tone of his voice nor his expression indicating whether he was pleased or not about the subject.

"Oh?" Elizabeth replied, her eyes widening as sudden panic coursed through her. She hadn't given the earl a single thought since late last evening. How could she when George had done such amazing things to her, leaving her brain so addled she could barely think?

Lady Morganfield straightened in her chair and gave Elizabeth a tentative smile. "And?" she questioned with a hint of tease in her voice. When Elizabeth didn't answer right away, her mother's expression brightened. "Oh, this explains why you're so discombobulated this morning. Trenton will probably come calling this afternoon!"

Elizabeth's eyes widened. "Oh, God, I hope not," she blurted, her stomach threatening to send up her breakfast.

Her mother's expression changed to one of grave concern. "Why, daughter, whatever is the matter?" She got up and moved to the other side of the table, reaching her arm around Elizabeth's shoulder.

Elizabeth was aware of her father's eyes studying her, his face changing to show... concern, was it? Or disappointment? Or was that... *hope?* If only he would tell her if he approved of Trenton or not!

"I don't know," she replied. It was as truthful a statement as she could make at the moment. "I suppose I am just... nervous," she offered. She didn't want to tell her mother that Gabriel Wellingham kissed like Lady Hannah's Alpenmastiff. She couldn't admit that what was done *before* intercourse was far more pleasurable than a massive tickle. She couldn't even imagine anything *beyond* what she had already experienced!

Adeline Carlington gave her daughter a brilliant smile and kissed her cheek. "Of course, you are. You're about to be proposed to by one of the richest men in all of England!" she gushed.

David Carlington rolled his eyes as he resisted the urge to share his opinion of the earl. At some point, it would be appropriate to do so. Just not now.

CHAPTER 41

CHARITY MEANS WORK IN MORE WAYS THAN ONE

*L*ater that morning
Lady Elizabeth entered her office in Oxford Street and was relieved to see that both Augustus Overby and Nicholas Barnaby, her new clerks, were busy at the library table. Her desk, completely free of papers only the morning before, was now covered in small stacks of the stuff, leaving very little room for writing correspondence.

Both men jumped to their feet, although Mr. Overby did so a bit slowly, his leg having been damaged by a mortar in the battle at Quatre Bras. They bowed to her quick curtsy and said their greetings.

"Good morning, gentlemen," she said with a smile, her expression faltering when she saw all the papers. "Oh, my," she breathed, moving to look more closely at the top sheet of one pile.

"We were quite... busy yesterday," Mr. Overby said in an apologetic tone. His responsibility to the charity was to locate employers willing to hire ex-soldiers. His method for doing so included combing the news sheets for listings of positions and meeting with shop owners and warehouse foremen about positions that might not be publicized. "Once you placed those five men a few days ago, word started spreading."

"Indeed," Mr. Barnaby added, hurrying to stand on the

other side of the desk. "If I might explain, milady," he added, a tooth catching his lower lip. His job was to meet with applicants, write down their personal and past-work experience information, and collect any characters they might have from prior employment. Judging from the amount of paperwork now covering her library table, it was evident he had earned his first day's wages.

Elizabeth raised her eyes to meet his troubled expression. "Are all these... applicants?" she asked. *Whatever happened while I was at the museum with George?* She had to force down the bit of panic gripping her.

Mr. Barnaby was suddenly behind her, pulling out the desk chair and indicating she should sit down. She did so, thanking him as he moved to stand to one side. "Not exactly, milady," he said with a hint of reassurance. "The stacks on the left are the positions Mr. Overby found available to be filled. Most are employers who are willing to hire ex-soldiers in exchange for certain... guarantees." He straightened the stack in question.

Guarantees being bribes, Elizabeth thought with a roll of her eyes.

"Some are simply employers who have warehouse positions. They usually require a more able-bodied man, but allowances can be made—"

"Should there be some sort of *guarantee*," Elizabeth finished for him.

Mr. Barnaby reluctantly nodded, the air seeming to leave his lungs. "Yes, milady. And this stack on the right," he said as he leaned over the desk and picked up the sheath of papers, "are the applicants that stopped by yesterday hoping to have an audience with you."

Elizabeth took the papers and leafed through them, counting nine in total. "My. You were busy yesterday. I suppose I should get started then," she said, the panic quickly subsiding. *I can do this.* Glancing quickly at the addresses of the applicants, she wasn't surprised to see they lived in close proximity to one another. "And while I do this, I need you to go to this hotel where most of these men seem to reside. Gather them up and see to it they go to this tailor's shop." She handed him a pasteboard calling card, along with the purse containing the coins the footman had dropped off earlier that week. "Give them fare for the hackney, and go with them if you're able. They're to have a suit of clothes made. See to it the tailor is paid fairly. Once that's done, I'll get them to one of these employers."

Mr. Barnaby regarded the pasteboard and hefted the purse, quickly realizing the coins inside were not mere farthings. "You *trust* me with this, milady?" he asked, his expression one of surprise.

Elizabeth regarded him for a moment. "It seems I do, Mr. Barnaby. Please do not do anything untoward with the money. Remember, your pay is commensurate with your work performance." Although her words held no menace, she hoped she made her point quite clear.

Nodding his understanding, Mr. Barnaby pocketed the purse as best he could, took the list of applicants Elizabeth handed him, and bade them both farewell.

For the next two hours, Elizabeth studied the positions available as well as the applications, matching each man to a job that would best suit him based on his prior experience and particular disability. Meanwhile, Mr. Overby continued his search of the newspaper listings, occasionally using a scissors to cut out a promising position. Elizabeth sometimes asked about a certain applicant, while he countered with questions about suitable employers.

Once she had completed her first task, Elizabeth lined up Mr . Overby's latest job opportunities on one side of her desk, readying them for the next set of applicants she knew would be along soon. Satisfied she had done all she could for the day, she took her leave of the office, entrusting it to Mr. Overby's care, and headed for home.

Elizabeth might have stayed longer—she *wanted* to stay longer—but according to her father, an earl would be showing up at her home at any moment to propose marriage.

She wouldn't be able to accept his suit if she wasn't there.

CHAPTER 42
PROPOSAL INTERRUPTED

*D*espite having been warned that Gabriel Wellingham, Earl of Trenton would be paying a call on her that day, Elizabeth was dismayed when the butler, Alfred, knocked on her bedchamber door and announced him. She had only been home a few minutes! "I have put him in the parlor, milady," Alfred said with the kind of stoicism only those in service seemed to exhibit. "Should I ring for tea?"

Elizabeth caught her image in the looking glass over the vanity. *Frightened*, she thought suddenly. *I look frightened. This will not do.* Tea made everything just a bit better. It certainly couldn't hurt. "Please, do, Alfred. I'll be down in a moment." Straightening in front of the mirror, she regarded her image a moment. Her maid had done her hair in a rather fetching tumble of curls atop her head, a teal ribbon woven through the strands in a perfect contrast to her auburn hair and a near-match for her eye color. The dark mint muslin day gown she had just pulled on set off her complexion in a way that pastel gowns simply couldn't. *But am I beautiful?* she wondered, thinking Lady Hannah was, because she looked like a fairy princess, and Lady Charlotte was because... she just was.

How does a man decide if you are beautiful? she wondered, remembering George's comment from the night before. Was it her hair color or her eyes or the shape of her face? She touched a finger to her lips, a memory of George's last kiss making her eyes close as she relived it over and over in her head. The mere thought of his touch made her breasts feel heavy, her feminine core ache for him.

She shook herself, remembering it was *Gabriel* who waited for her downstairs. He of the blond, curly hair and sky blue eyes. He of the ten-thousand pounds a year and who knew what kind of inheritance? *Why couldn't he be George?* But the sudden thought of George with blond curls caused a giggle to burble forth. Elizabeth saw her joy reflected in the mirror. She could do this. Taking a deep breath, she hurried from the room and headed for the parlor.

When she entered the brightly lit room—the sun was obviously shining, although she hadn't noticed when she had returned from her office—she found Lord Trenton leaning against the fireplace mantle, one hand hidden behind his back. *He's wearing a puce topcoat*, Elizabeth thought suddenly. And wearing the color quite well, although the fit of his coat seemed a bit snug. He didn't immediately look up or at her, his attention instead on a miniature in a gold gilt frame.

"Lord Trenton," Elizabeth said, greeting him with a light voice. At least, she hoped it was. Her heart was pounding so hard she could barely hear herself speak.

"Ah, Elizabeth," he said, a smile showing off his perfect white teeth and forming a dimple in one cheek.

Did I give him permission to use my given name? Elizabeth found herself wondering again, bristling at the way he said it. Not like a prayer, the way George said it, but rather as if it were a stodgy, old-fashioned name that had to be bitten out as quickly as possible.

Gabriel hurried to stand before her and took her hand as he bowed to her curtsy. "You look as beautiful as ever," he said, his gaze pausing on her décolletage as it swept up her body.

"Thank you, milord," she replied with a nod, a sense of... *disgust* suddenly replacing the joy she had felt only moments before. "Tea will be here in a moment," she added, now wishing she had turned down Alfred's suggestion. Moving to the velvet settee, she took a seat and arranged her skirts. "Please, do sit down," she offered as she waved toward the nearest chair.

Gabriel took a quick glance at the proffered chair and returned his attention to her. "I was hoping we might... talk," he said, his other hand coming from behind his back to shove a handful of mums toward her.

Elizabeth suddenly sneezed. "Oh, of course," she managed, as she gingerly took the flowers from his grasp. Gabriel's eyes flicked toward the door where a footman hovered.

Taking his meaning, Elizabeth held her breath a moment. "Mr. Thatcher, could you please see to some water for these flowers? And close the door?" she called out, shoving the bouquet of golden blooms into a nearby vase.

Surprised at the request, the footman glanced about before he took the vase of flowers from her and took his leave of the room. He closed the door behind him.

Satisfied they were now alone, Gabriel took a deep breath and positioned himself directly in front of Elizabeth. "Elizabeth. I am sure you must know why I..."

The parlor door opened, the tea cart rolling in ahead of a maid. Gabriel sighed loudly and stepped back to allow the cart to pass between them.

Pursing her lips to stifle a grin, Elizabeth nodded to the maid. "I can serve, Rose. Thank you."

Reluctantly, Rose made her way out of the room, not bothering to shut the door as she left.

"Tea?" Elizabeth asked as she lifted the pot and prepared to pour a cup for the earl.

The Earl of Trenton seemed to have a debate with himself, his attention again on the open door. "Uh, no, thank you," he responded, his anxiousness suddenly noticeable.

"A biscuit, perhaps?" Elizabeth offered, lifting the plate of lemon confections from the cart. *He is squirming*, she thought, surprised a man who displayed such confidence in a crowded ballroom could be *nervous*.

Gabriel regarded the biscuits and then shook his head. "No.

None for me, thank you," he replied, waving his hand as if the plate were offensive to him.

Shocked he would turn down both the tea and the biscuits, Elizabeth angled her head. "Something else, perhaps?" she asked. "I can have Cook make you something," she suggested. It was only polite to at least accept tea, she considered. *Although, he looks like he needs a brandy!*

His eyes rolling skyward, Gabriel took another deep breath. "No, thank you, Lady Elizabeth. As I said, I..." He stopped and glanced back toward the open door. He lifted a finger and then moved to close it himself.

A bit alarmed, and suddenly aware they were *alone* behind closed doors, Elizabeth set aside her tea cup and straightened on the settee. "My lord, whatever is *the matter?*" she asked as Gabriel repositioned himself, although he couldn't stand directly in front of her as the tea cart took up some of the space. An image of the night he kissed her suddenly filled her mind's eye.

Was Gabriel about to try to kiss her now?

"Is it true, milady, that you have let an office in Oxford Street for the purpose of performing... *work?*" he finally got out, his arms crossing in front of his body. His head was shaking as if he knew it couldn't be true.

"I have let an office in Oxford Street for the purpose of doing *charity work*, yes," Elizabeth responded demurely, wondering where he had learned of her charity's location.

Gabriel's eyes widened, but the response left him speechless for a moment. "Oh," he finally said, straightening. "That's... very noble," he offered, apparently not prepared for the answer to be what it was. A bit of air seemed to go out of him. "And, have you done this charity *work* for a long time?" He seemed to have great difficulty with the word *work*, as if saying it was somehow foreign to his lips.

Elizabeth poured herself a cup of tea. "Not long at all. But I take great pride in having been able to help those who have already benefited," she offered with a smile. She deliberately kept her answer vague, hoping the earl wouldn't press her for more details. What could she tell him? She had only placed six soldiers into various positions and, as of this morning, nine others were pending. That didn't sound particularly successful.

The earl seemed placated by the answer, but he still seemed ill at ease. And agitated. "My lord, what has upset you so? Please tell me, what is wrong?" Elizabeth pressed. Perhaps she had guessed wrong, and the earl would not be supportive of her charity.

"Nothing is *wrong* exactly," he replied a bit curtly, shifting his shoulders in the rather tight-fitting top coat he wore. The dark puce, Elizabeth suddenly decided, was a color that did little to enhance the earl's current complexion. One of his hands was gripping his hip while the other was raised, as if he wished to make an important point.

Elizabeth wondered if he took that stance when he was speaking in chambers.

"Well, there is something *wrong*, but it has no bearing on my presence here," he said, his manner suddenly a bit cross.

Elizabeth's eyes widened at his odd response. *Why is he so agitated?* Even in his current state, he was as handsome as she had ever seen him, his blond curls a bit wild about his face, one lock curling on his forehead. *Will he always be more beautiful than me?* she wondered.

What had he said? *My own beauty requires a woman with at least as much to match my own.* Surely, he had said it in jest.

Or had he?

Would he always dress better than she did? She thought of the other men she had seen that week. George wouldn't be caught dead wearing puce. Or apple green. He wore impeccably tailored suits in dark superfine and conservative waistcoats. He wasn't flamboyant. *Please think of your future happiness... and not just the money or the title*, he had said just yesterday. He'd had the same mistress for eight years and was quitting her to marry. Quitting her because he intended to honor his marriage vows.

At the thought of the mistress, one of Josephine's comments about Trenton's mistresses came to mind. And certainty suddenly washed over her.

She could not marry this man.

It didn't matter if he was an earl, or if he was rich as Croesus, or blond and blue-eyed or that he dressed better than she and all her friends combined.

I cannot marry this man.

Before she quite knew what she was saying, the words were out of her mouth. "Oh, dear, did one of your mistresses quit you?" she asked, in a manner suggesting she was truly concerned, a sympathetic smile touching her lips as her head angled to one side.

"Yes, damn it, and she was..." Gabriel stopped speaking and stared at Elizabeth, shock evident on his suddenly flushed face. "How did... what do *you* know of my mistresses?" he demanded, his brows drawn together to form a single line on his forehead. The expression gave him a comical look, one that Elizabeth promised to remember for the rest of her days. How had she not noticed this level of vanity before? How had she been able to ignore his quick anger and the sense of entitlement he seemed to exhibit when around others?

Classically handsome men were obviously given too much latitude. They didn't have to *work* to earn the consideration of an unattached female.

And having buckets of blunt didn't help the matter, either.

"Oh, goodness, *Gabriel*," she said as she waved her hand in a dismissive motion. "You're an *earl*. Let's see. You're left with, what? Just the two now?" Elizabeth countered, not allowing the earl's apparent surprise to affect her own rising disgust. She rather liked addressing him by his given name just then, too, especially in a tone that was almost a scold.

Gabriel's mouth was open in surprise and something else. "How... how *dare* you?" was all he could say in response.

"They must cost you a *fortune!*" Elizabeth continued, as if she hadn't heard his admonishment. "And I don't know *how* you can keep them all *satisfied*," she continued, just then noticing the earl's reddened face. She certainly felt satisfied at the effect her words were having on him. "Oh, wait, you *cannot*. That must be why the one quit you," she stated in the same sweet tone she would use if she were discussing the weather. "Now, tell me Gabriel, why was it you've come calling?"

"Why, you little..."

Elizabeth was on her feet in a instant. "Don't you *dare!*" she interrupted him, her own rising anger so quick it surprised even her. *You disgusting rake*, she wanted to add, but thought it would be too unladylike to say aloud. Why discussing mistresses was somehow acceptable in her own mind could have only been because she had been in the presence of a perfectly acceptable one the evening before. The mistress who had seen to it she had the ammunition she needed at this very moment to most thoroughly discomfit the earl. *Brava, Josephine!*

Gabriel jumped back a step, startled she would stand up to him. "Milady, I..." He paused, noticed her expression, one that suggested he would be better off taking his leave of Carlington House or risk being hit by a flying *objet d'art*.

Such as the porcelain figurine that graced the table next to where she stood.

"I have an appointment," he stated suddenly, his gaze flitting to the figurine and back to Elizabeth. "Thank you for the... hospitality," he added, backing his way toward the door, visibly swallowing. "I will see my way out."

Elizabeth's eyes shot daggers before she called out, "Really, Gabriel. You need to *smile*. You have no idea how *lucky* you are at this moment."

Lucky she didn't have a loaded pistol.

Lucky there weren't any servants to see how she had given him the cut direct.

Lucky he wasn't about to be betrothed to a woman who knew what she wanted in life and went after it.

After a hasty bow, the earl did indeed show himself out the door, a tentative smile pasted on his face.

A moment later, Elizabeth was aware of the front door closing rather loudly.

She stared at the parlor door, a bit shocked at what had just happened.

Stunned at what the earl had nearly said. *Bitch?*

And even more stunned at what *she had* said.

Sinking into the velvet settee, Elizabeth hung her head and placed her suddenly trembling hands on either side of her face. "Oh, what have I done?" she asked, tears pricking the edges of the eyes. "What have I done?"

Gabriel Wellingham couldn't get out of Carlington House fast enough. Once he was through the front door, he paused on the stoop and took a deep breath before descending the stairs to his phaeton. His smile wasn't one of mirth or pleasure, but one forced by the last words he had heard Lady Elizabeth state before he removed himself from the parlor. *You need to smile. You have no idea how lucky you are at this moment.*

Indeed, he was lucky he had avoided asking a *shrew* for her hand in marriage! How had he misjudged her so? He thought she would be the perfect accomplice in his ploy to embarrass the Marquess of Morganfield. A beautiful, brainless woman more concerned about appearances and money than her father's political career. A year or two of political maneuverings, social set downs and manipulative gossip, and he would have taken the place of the disgraced marquess in Parliament, the man's daughter an unknowing patsy standing by his side.

But what else had her words threatened would happen if they did wed? Her parting shot was a warning, to be sure. Would she go public with what she knew of the mistress that had quit him the night before? Not that his having a mistress, or two or three, was somehow scandalous. But perhaps she knew of what he had *discussed* with his mistresses. They were always so eager for him to talk, asking him leading questions about the proceedings in chambers, asking him about his political views, asking him what he thought of various and sundry aspects of life so there was barely time for a tumble or two, and certainly no time for kissing.

Nearly stopping in his tracks, Gabriel had an epiphany. *Spies!* he thought. His mistresses were *spies*, sharing the information he was freely imparting to them with... who? *The French?* Other members of Parliament? Elizabeth?

Gabriel vowed to end his contracts with both mistresses that very night. An expensive endeavor, he knew, remembering how much in pin money and rent he would need to pay to end the liaisons, but it was necessary.

He wasn't about to suffer the same embarrassments he knew his rival had suffered so many years ago at the hands of a mistress who sold his secrets to the French. Better to sit quietly in chambers and allow the older lords to direct the proceedings. He could be patient, at least until another daughter of the *ton*, one whose father was somewhat powerful, appeared on the Marriage Mart in the next year or so. Then he could use her to gain the political power he so desperately wanted.

CHAPTER 43
REGRETS

ord Morganfield paused a moment before stepping over the threshold of the parlor. The rich scarlet and sea foam green upholstery fabrics were well suited to the darker cherry wood finishes of the furniture his wife had so carefully chosen when she had redone the room years before. The year he decided he rather loved her, preferred her, in fact, to his long-time mistress. The year she had borne his son—the heir to his title.

The boy was off to Eton now, presumedly getting an education, although David Carlington's own time there had been spent in pulling pranks and avoiding getting caught while doing any number of things he shouldn't have been doing. Thank the gods those days weren't well documented; otherwise, he would not now be enjoying his career as a powerful member of Parliament.

But, at the moment, he stood in the doorway of his parlor in Carlington House gazing at his eldest, his daughter of one-and-twenty, who at breakfast had seemed somehow *different* from every other day they had shared the morning meal—he reading *The Times* and her occasionally conversing about Society events and the latest fashions from Paris with her mother.

Never *gossip*, though, he realized suddenly.

Her mother might have enjoyed sharing the latest *on-dit*

about town, but Elizabeth didn't seem to share in the fascination of other people's foibles and failures. She was more practical about everything, sure of what she wanted and usually quite good at getting it.

Not spoiled, necessarily, but determined. *Perhaps Bostwick knows her better than I do.* He shook his head. *Not better*, he argued with himself. *Perhaps he just knows a different side of her.*

She was a daughter he could be proud of, he thought, remembering her commitment to her favorite charities, practical charities that didn't necessarily attract the attention of the other ladies of the *ton*. And to the charity she had started with her own funds—a charity that, according to his sources, had already seen at least six clients placed into employment at a cost of nearly seventy pounds.

She didn't behave like a hoyden—well, at least, he certainly had never *heard* she indulged in such behavior—and after being in Society for three Seasons, it seemed she had decided it was time to accept *someone's* offer of marriage. At eight-and-twenty, the Earl of Trenton would seem the perfect match for an only daughter.

But not to him.

To Morganfield, Trenton came off a bit of a self-important ass, too rich and too beautiful to be taken too seriously, too vain to want as his son-in-law, and too eager to achieve political power. Wellingham had made a rather brusque remark to the marquess during the Weatherstone ball, implying that he had decided on Elizabeth because she was beautiful, and his own beauty required a woman with at least as much to match his own. Could the man be so addle-brained as to actually believe what he espoused?

But then the impertinent Trenton hadn't even asked his *permission* to court his daughter.

And this afternoon, at exactly the moment it was fashionable to pay an afternoon call, the ass had shown up at his front door with flowers and a ring in hand, asking to see Elizabeth— "alone, if it can be arranged"—and asked for her hand in marriage.

At least, that's what Lord Morganfield *thought* had happened.

He didn't know exactly what had transpired, which is why he stood in the doorway to the parlor watching his beautiful daughter do a perfect imitation of an afternoon shower. It dawned on him that he hadn't seen her cry in a very long time, and he suddenly wondered if she shed tears of joy or of sorrow.

It was always very difficult to determine until such time as the tears stopped flowing.

When Elizabeth finally looked up from her tear-soaked handkerchief and saw him regarding her, she let out an "Oh," and stood up so quickly she nearly lost her balance and fell back down on the settee.

He hid the sudden grin that he felt tugging at the corners of his mouth and entered the room. Wrapping his arms around her shoulders, he hugged her and rubbed her back until her sobs subsided and he heard her whispered, "Oh, Father."

Sorrow, then. "Shh," he whispered, kissing her temple and then her forehead as he pulled away. "Your mother used to cry like this," he said quietly, as he led her to his favorite wing chair and pulled her onto his lap. She let out another "Oh," but he wasn't sure if it was in reaction to her being pulled down onto his knee or surprise that her mother used to cry. "She always felt much better afterwards," he added, when she finally turned her tear-stained face to his. He took a deep breath and let it out. "I am ready now. You can tell me what happened," he added, as if he'd had to gird himself for whatever bad news she had to share.

Elizabeth nodded and took a breath. "I may have done something truly terrible," she said, a sob interrupting the "truly" so that it came out in two parts.

Lord Morganfield sighed and leaned back into the chair. "Was it illegal?" he asked.

Her eyebrows furrowed as she considered the question. "No," she replied in a whisper. Her eyes suddenly widened. "Worse, I should think."

Morganfield's own eyes widened, and he held his breath. "Go on."

"I allowed Gabriel to kiss me at Lord Weatherstone's ball," she blurted, holding her own breath as if waiting for her father's rebuke. She was nearly blue in the face before she decided he wasn't going to throttle her.

"And?" he finally prompted, withholding his opinion that the Earl of Trenton did indeed warrant arrest and possibly transport, but not because of a kiss.

"He kissed like Harold!" Elizabeth proclaimed with a suitable degree of disgust, hoping the analogy would help to get her point across.

At first, she thought she succeeded.

"*Harold* kissed you?" the marquess queried.

Elizabeth sniffled. "Harold is always kissing me. He's very affectionate," she added, suddenly feeling her father's knees shift dangerously beneath her.

David Carlington blinked once. "Who is this Harold?" he asked, his eyebrow still rather high.

"Harold MacDuff," she replied quite matter-of-factly.

"Harold MacDuff?" he repeated, his eyes darting back and forth, as if he was having a hard time remembering if he had ever met someone—anyone—by the name of Harold MacDuff.

"Hannah's Harold," she clarified, suddenly realizing her father didn't remember having met Harold.

Her father stared at her for a very long moment. "Does this Harold... also kiss Hannah?" he asked, his eyes darting about as if he were trying to follow the path of an annoying fly.

"Oh, all the time. He's very affectionate."

The knees under her jerked enough that Elizabeth felt she had to move to the ottoman in front of the chair or risk being dumped onto the floor. "And Hannah *allows* this?" her father asked, the cocked eyebrow nearly into his hairline.

He was hoping that, with time, feeling would come back into his knees.

His legs had gone to sleep.

"Well, of course. I think she's rather *indulgent*, actually. She allows him to sleep in her bed with her."

Lord Morganfield made a rather rude noise in his throat, and his other eyebrow joined the first in elevation. "Indeed?"

"I suppose it's rather nice in the winter to have such a large, warm body to snuggle up to," she commented lightly, thinking just then how wonderful it would be if she and George could share a bed in the winter. Or anytime, really. *Naked, in bed with George.* A frisson passed through her that made her suddenly feel rather warm and wonderful.

The marquess took a deep breath just as Adeline Carlington peeked into the parlor. "There you are," she said with a bit of relief, her smile growing as she realized she had found both her husband and her daughter apparently having a heart-to-heart talk. "I suppose I'm all on pins and needles," she said brightly, her Italian accent barely evident. Then she noticed her husband's obvious discomfort and her daughter's tear-stained face. "Oh, my. Whatever's happened?" she asked as her look of happiness was replaced with one of concern. She wrung her hands together at her waist.

"Harold MacDuff, it seems," her husband replied, not yet able to stand up, a courtesy he usually performed when his wife, or any woman, for that matter, entered a room.

"Harold?" Adeline repeated, her eyebrows lifting. "Whatever has he done *now?*"

"He's kissed our daughter!" the marquess nearly shouted.

Adeline's face brightened again, displaying her straight white teeth. "Oh, he does that all the time," she said with a wave of her hand. "He's very affectionate. I don't allow him to kiss *me,* of course, but I do let him lick my hand now and again. He never could hold his licker." She tittered when she registered her clever pun.

A growl sounded from David, Marquess of Morganfield. "Who *is* this Harold MacDuff? And where do I find him?" Duels might be illegal in England, but at the moment, he didn't care. He only wanted to get his hands on the man who had taken the liberty of kissing his daughter. And licking his wife.

Adeline frowned at her husband's reaction. "He's more of a

what, really, darling. Harold is, oh, what *is* he again?" she asked as she turned to Elizabeth.

"An Alpenmastiff," Elizabeth said with a nod. "I was just telling Father that Butter Blond—I mean, Lord Trenton—kisses just like Harold."

They both turned to the marquess to find his head in his hands, a mournful moan emanating from him.

Her mother suddenly straightened. "Butter Blond?" she repeated, at which point Lord Morganfield slammed his hand down on the arm of his wing chair.

"Enough!" he yelled, causing both women to jump a bit before landing quite suddenly with rather startled expressions on their faces. "Enough about Harold whoever. How many times has *Butter Blond* kissed you?"

Adeline's moment of shock passed quicker than Elizabeth's as the parents both turned to their daughter. Her mouth had formed a perfect 'o,' and the look on her face showed her fright at having upset her father. "Forgive me. I know it's a horrible nickname, but it... it so *suits* Gabriel," she said as her shoulders fell and her gaze lowered to her father's feet. "And just the one time," she added, remembering the rest of her father's query.

Adeline sat down in a chair next to her husband. "You call Gabriel 'Butter Blond'?" she queried, her lips pursing in attempt to prevent a grin from appearing. Lord Morganfield leaned back in his chair and allowed a burble of laughter to escape. "Do you use that expression as a term of endearment, my dear child?" he asked before another chuckle erupted.

"No, of course not," she replied with a shake of her head, wondering if her father would require a trip to Bedlam. "George mentioned it during Lady Worthington's ball, and it just seemed such a suitable nickname..."

The marquess regarded Elizabeth with a smile and a nod. And then another as he remembered how their conversation started. "So, Gabriel Wellingham, the Earl of Trenton, kisses like an Alpenmastiff, does he?"

Elizabeth sighed, her shoulders slumping. "Yes."

Adeline gasped.

"And he licks like one, too," Elizabeth added, a shake of disgust accompanying her comment.

Adeline nearly fainted.

Lord Morganfield glanced in her direction and rolled his eyes. *At some point, this tidbit of information about Trenton could be helpful.* Perhaps in the political arena, although he couldn't quite figure how. He thought for a moment. *Lord Chancellor, I move the Earl of Trenton's point on the matter be stricken from the record. The man kisses like Harold MacDuff and licks like him, too!* It might make for a moment of humor— everyone knew they could use a bit more of *that* in chambers... He shook himself out of his reverie to find his daughter's eyes wet with tears. "I take it you didn't accept Trenton's marriage proposal," he stated with a curt nod.

Elizabeth shoulders shook with a sob. "He didn't actually *ask* for my hand. I think I... I may have offended him. But I wouldn't have accepted if he had asked." She dared a glance in her mother's direction, afraid her words might have her mother fainting for certain. Adeline merely angled her head to one side and seemed deep in thought.

Her father inhaled and let out the breath in a very slow, satisfying sigh. "Thank you for deciding to turn him down," he said then, his own arms braced on the arms of the wing chair as if he had to ground himself.

Elizabeth's eyes widened again as she watched her father's reaction. "You're not... disappointed in me?" she whispered then, swallowing a sob.

"No," he replied rather quickly. "I am rather proud of you, in fact. But you simply must tell me why, because I'm sure I'll be asked at least a dozen times at White's tonight," he paused and glanced at his wife. "Or the theatre, and I should like to have the answer straight from your lips so that I might provide a suitable response." He secretly thrilled at how Adeline's eyebrows lifted when he mentioned the theatre.

Sighing, Elizabeth stared at him for several seconds, trying to decide if she could tell him the real reason. But she couldn't tell him about George. Not yet, anyway. "I don't think you can tell the gentlemen at White's why I turned down the earl," she responded finally. At her father's suddenly serious expression, she added, "It was mostly because he kisses like Lady Hannah's dog."

Morganfield furrowed his brows when he realized she was serious. "You truly turned down Trenton because he kisses like an Alpenmastiff?" he asked in astonishment, his amusement growing by the moment.

Not able to help herself, Elizabeth smiled, putting a hand over her mouth to hide it. "It was quite... wet and slobbery, and then he *licked* my cheek..." Her body shuddered as she remembered the experience. A sound of disgust escaped her, causing her to shake even more.

Her father was grinning like she had never seen him grin before. "And this all happened during Weatherstone's ball?" he asked. At Elizabeth's nod and an expression that made her look as if she had swallowed the cook's concoction for coughs, Morganfield slowly nodded. "That wasn't the *only* reason you turned him down, though," he stated quite emphatically.

Sighing, Elizabeth rolled her eyes. "When I asked if he was agitated because one of his mistresses quit him, which I only guessed at and got quite right, he grew quite upset. He still has *two* of them! He must have to pay them a fortune to put up with his awful kisses. It's a wonder he's still rich!"

Lord Morganfield stared at his daughter, his mood suddenly serious again. "You asked him about his *mistress?*" he repeated, his head suddenly shaking from side to side. A look of... was it disappointment? Astonishment? Or *pain*, perhaps, crossed his features. "You cannot..." He paused and took a breath, sitting up a bit straighter in the chair. "It's not done, Elizabeth," he spoke quietly. "It's simply not done."

Worrying the edge of his thumbnail between his teeth, he considered what a mistress had cost him early in his career, both politically, because she had been a spy of sorts, and privately, because Adeline remained so emotionally distant those first few years. He had felt as if he had no one to turn to when his world had come down around him. He had had no one to blame but himself—well, he could blame the courtesan who relayed his pillow talk to a political enemy, but it was he who shared information with her he had no business sharing with anyone outside of chambers. "But, I see your point," he added, his attitude softening a bit as he pulled his thoughts to the present. He sighed rather loudly. "You must know, had you accepted the earl's suit, I would have had to disown you," he said without a hint of humor. The idea of Trenton as his son-in-law had been so abhorrent, he could barely tolerate the thought of his daughter *dancing* with the man, let alone kissing him!

Her eyes wide again and wet with tears, Elizabeth sniffled and stared at her father. "Why didn't you tell me that? You knew he was going to propose. You told me at breakfast!"

Morganfield allowed a sigh. "I wanted you to make your own decision. I trusted you would make the right one," he replied. "Besides, it sounds as if you sent him away in a most satisfying manner."

Elizabeth considered how she had sent him away. It had been satisfying at the time, but now she couldn't help but think she had been a bit too spiteful.

The marquess took a deep breath. "Gabriel Wellingham is a threat to this country, my dear child."

Shocked by her father's pronouncement, she said, "Oh. I do hope you mean... politically, and not because he is a spy for the French or an assassin out to kill Prinny or some such."

"Wouldn't surprise me in the least if he were," her father retorted, his manner still suggesting he was serious. "Wouldn't necessarily oppose the assassination, though," he added under his breath.

Elizabeth pretended not to hear her father's last comment. "Then, I suppose I am... rather *glad* I did what I had to do." She paused a moment. "Mother, I do hope you are not disappointed in me."

Adeline rolled her eyes. "I was hoping for at least an earl for you," she replied, although there wasn't a hint of sadness in her words.

Elizabeth regarded her father for a moment more, feeling

not the least bit chastised by his words about mistresses. Lady Hannah might be able to abide them when she married, but Elizabeth had decided that whomever she married would not employ one. "Politics aside, Father, why *did* you want me to turn him down?" she asked then, realizing there was more to his dislike of the earl than to what he had just admitted.

Morganfield leaned back into the chair and took a deep breath. "A matter of honor, I suppose," he answered with a sigh. "He didn't ask my permission to court you, and *he* didn't tell me he was planning to ask for your hand."

Elizabeth blinked. "He... He didn't? Then... how did you *know* he would do so today?"

Her father shook his head. "Gossip, my girl. I heard the gossip," he murmured, disgust still evident in his voice. He took a deep breath. "So, do *you* feel better?" he asked, his own mood lightening. "Because I certainly do."

"Oh, much," she replied with a nod, grinning as she wiped away the remains of her tears. Elizabeth thought a moment, a sob racking her body and causing her to hiccup. She regarded her father, saw that he seemed... happy. "When you first came in, you said you had news," she remembered suddenly. "Was... *that* your news? That you were going to disown me?"

Her father smiled. Noticing hers had become a bit drippy, he held out his own handkerchief. "No, Elizabeth. Actually, I was going to let you know about *another* suitor for your hand," he stated, leaning back in his chair. "In the event you needed a choice, although it's apparent you didn't. I don't suppose *he's* kissed you?" he asked rhetorically.

"He who?" Elizabeth asked, afraid he might be referring to someone other than George. George had been the only other man who had ever kissed her.

Kissed her senseless. Kissed her *everywhere.*

The troublesome frisson shot through her again, and she chastised herself for allowing herself to remember just how delicious those kisses had been. Especially with her father sitting directly in front of her. Her face took on the pink shade that obviously displayed her embarrassment.

"Bostwick," the marquess stated simply.

Elizabeth blinked and regarded her father for a moment, recognizing the name from when George had used it the night before. "Bostwick?" she repeated. Had George asked her father's permission to court her?

"Yes. Lord Bostwick," he clarified, wondering at his daughter's expression. "The viscount?" he added, thinking that would clear up any confusion. "You had *supper* with him at Weatherstone's ball," he stated rather loudly. "He took you for a *ride* in the park. You *danced* with him at Lady Worthington's ball. *Twice*, if I remember correctly. And you went to the museum with him yesterday," he added, his expression suggesting that if she was trying to deny her association with the man, he wasn't going to have any of it.

Elizabeth allowed a grin. "*George*, you mean," she replied, drawing out the word into the two syllables that made the name sound like so much more than it was.

"Bennett-Jones, yes," her father insisted, his brows furrowing into a single line. Under different circumstances, he might have thought his daughter's imitation of one of Lord Everly's tropical fish was rather amusing. At this moment, he did not.

"I take it his original introduction didn't include that little snippet of a title?"

Elizabeth regarded her father for a moment. Until last night, George had *never* given her a hint he was a member of the *ton*. Never *once* had he said anything about being a viscount. Or being related to one. But then, none of those around the man had said any honorifics to suggest he was, either. Everyone called him "George." When Lady Fletcher had caught them kissing in Lady Worthington's library, she had called him "George." As had several gentlemen they had come in contact with during the ball. "It did not," she finally said, her teeth catching her lower lip.

Lord Morganfield nodded. "Well, the man has always been a most honorable gentleman. He asked for my permission to court you a couple of days ago. After a session of Parliament," he stated evenly. "He's not nearly as rich as Trenton, of course, but still worth about a third of that, I should think."

"Oh," Elizabeth answered, rather startled at the news. She wondered if a third of "very rich" was still... rich.

"Especially since he owns some gypsum mines down in Sussex. Most of his lands are down there."

"Lands?" Elizabeth repeated in disbelief. "Not 'land'?" She swallowed, took a deep breath and swallowed again.

A third of "very rich" was indeed *rich*.

Her father smiled then. "You look as if you might swoon."

Elizabeth stared back at him then, her mouth finally opening to speak, but nothing came out.

David Carlington regarded his daughter for another moment, wondering at her odd reaction. She had done *something*, he knew, he just couldn't quite figure out what it was. "Did *he* kiss you?" he asked then, the tone of his voice almost hopeful.

Elizabeth swallowed, realizing she needed to admit that she had, indeed, been kissed by George Bennett-Jones. And kissed him back. "Yes. Yes, he did," she answered slowly, as if she were reliving the entire moment in the library when he had bestowed that very first kiss on her. "Well, I *asked* him to kiss me, actually."

When she didn't elaborate, her father leaned forward. "And?"

"Oh. He's very good... at kissing," she replied, her face taking on a pink glow. She was sure her father had already determined that. Honorable man that he was, George had probably asked her father's permission to kiss her. And her father probably allowed it so someone in his sphere of influence could attest to being better at something than Butter Blond. *But that's just ridiculous*, she decided and returned her attention to her father.

"And?"

Elizabeth blinked at her father, not sure what he wanted to her to say. "And?" she countered carefully. She was not about to admit she had been naked with him, too!

Suddenly alarmed, the marquess leaned forward in his chair. "Did Lord Bostwick take your virtue?" he whispered hoarsely.

"He most absolutely did *not!*" she nearly shouted, forcing her father to sit back in the chair and regard her with a bit of shock. "It isn't his... or anyone else's... to *take*," she added. "At least,... not yet," she said in a quieter voice, suddenly wondering when George might come to ask for her hand.

George!

He said he would come ask for her hand if he discovered she wasn't betrothed to Butter Blond. How long would that take? Gossip seemed to travel fast in London, but apparently not fast enough.

Her father nodded his head then and settled back into the chair, not particularly satisfied with her response. "What else?" he asked then, knowing if he kept at it, she would admit to the *something*.

Elizabeth sighed, realizing she needed to tell her father more. "He paid for my bonnet. The one with the peacock feathers," she admitted finally, as if that would help her father to remember a bonnet he had never actually seen.

Her father regarded her for a moment, his expression not changing. "Was he... *with you* when he paid for the peacock?" he asked, his brows furrowing suddenly. If so, a shopkeeper had seen them together and witnessed an improper purchase.

Elizabeth shook her head. "Of course not! He wasn't even *in* the shop!"

The marquess struggled to maintain decorum as he tried to figure out how George Bennett-Jones would have paid for his daughter's bonnet without actually being *in* the shop. "I suppose you can guess my next question," he stated, his face taking on a rather stern appearance. As frustrating as it was to have a conversation with Elizabeth, he usually found it more fun to pretend he couldn't follow so she would have to over-explain herself. Unfortunately, at the moment, he really couldn't follow her train of thought. *I've been derailed,* he thought suddenly, wondering how it was he could sit in chambers day after day and comprehend everything that was said when he rarely dedicated more than half an ear to it, but spending a few minutes with his daughter required all of his concentration and powers of deduction beyond those of a Bow Street Runner.

Elizabeth blinked once. Twice. "Oh," she said, as she understood his meaning. "Well, he had to go into the shop to pay, of course, but he wasn't there when I bought the bonnet. But I think it must have been him who went in as Lady Charlotte and I were taking our leave of the place. And when I went back to pay for the bonnet, because I didn't pay for it when Lady Charlotte was with me because I'm always a bit embarrassed about paying for fripperies when Charlotte is with me because she always just puts it on her father's account, and I cannot do that because you give me an allowance so that I can pay for things directly," she paused to take a breath while David Carlington fought the impulse to growl at her expense. "So, once I dropped her at Ellsworth House, I had the driver take me back to the shop..," she paused when she noticed her father's increasingly strained expression as he followed her explanation.

"Well, don't stop now," the marquess insisted. "This is all starting to make sense in some twisted, torturous way."

Thinking she should feel a bit offended, Elizabeth straightened on the ottoman. "When I spoke with Mr. Peabody about the bill, he said it was already paid. And when I asked who would do such a thing, he said he was sworn to secrecy and would not reveal the person's identity."

Her father's eyebrows became one. "So... how is it you know that *Bostwick* paid for it?"

Elizabeth took a deep breath and let it out slowly, realizing she would need to divulge certain secrets if she was to answer *that* question.

Or she could parry.

"Mr. Neville said it was purchased as a 'thank you' gift."

When she hesitated to say more, her father arched an eyebrow. "And why would Bostwick have need to thank my daughter, I wonder?" he said *sotto voce*. His gaze on her hardened. "Enlighten me, daughter."

Elizabeth's eyes widened. "I helped a friend of his gain suitable employment at the Bank of England," she blurted out. At least she didn't have to admit to having spent the evening in the presence of George. Naked.

Ah, now we're getting somewhere, the marquess thought as he settled back into his chair. "Through your charity, perhaps?" he half-asked, a smirk replacing his threatening look from a moment ago.

"Yes," Elizabeth breathed, her eyes widening again. "How... how did you know?"

Even before she had the words out, her father had retrieved her calling card from his waistcoat pocket. He held it up by one corner. "Lady E, I presume?" he countered, the expression on his face not giving away whether he was pleased or not at having identified the owner of the moniker.

Stunned that he had one of her cards in his possession, the air seemed to go out of Elizabeth. She slumped on the ottoman. Closing her eyes, she nodded. "I discovered the only way some soldiers can get back their old positions of employment—the ones they had *before* they went off to war and got wounded—is through bribery."

David straightened in his chair at this tidbit. *Bribery?*

"I thought to use my allowance to pay for everything. And it was enough to let an office and cover some initial expenses, but the bribe I had to pay Mr. Whittaker at the bank took most of the rest of my funds."

"How much?" her father asked, his hands clasping between his knees as he hid his growing alarm at her comments.

"Twenty guineas," Elizabeth replied, thinking she was prepared to argue it was necessary.

David Carlington resisted the urge to growl again. *Twenty guineas!* How dare someone demand a bribe in exchange for hiring a war veteran! "Whatever possessed you to think you could...?" Her father stopped and lowered his gaze to the floor between them. When he looked back up, he found Elizabeth staring at him, her wide eyes again wet with tears, her lips sealed together into a straight line. "Why did you... find it necessary to even *start* this charity?" he demanded then. His initial perturbation seemed to evaporate with the question. How could he find fault with her for possessing the wherewithal to actually start such a venture? Without his help? Without benefit of his name and his financial assistance? He had been quite helpful with Lady Morganfield's charities, even if they were essentially duplicates of other *ton* ladies' approaches to helping war widows and orphans. As far as he knew, someone benefitted from the money he gave his wife to use for her causes. He never asked for an accounting of how the funds were spent.

"I saw a need. None of the other charities seemed to benefit the men who actually *fought* in the war against France," Elizabeth stated simply. "Are you..." A sob interrupted her query. "Are you angry with me?" she finally asked, her tears threatening to spill down her cheeks anew.

Her father's brows furrowed. "No," he said with a shake of his head. "Quite the contrary, pet," he said, the term of endearment something he hadn't used with her since she was in leading strings. "It's just that, you really should have a chaperone when you're in your office. Or when you meet with these employers. What if someone threatened you? Or—"

"I have Mr. Overby and Mr. Barnaby," she replied quickly.

David Morganfield regarded her for a moment longer. "Your husband will insist on protection," he stated in a quiet voice. *Because I'll demand it of him*, he added to himself.

Elizabeth's quick inhalation of breath and suddenly down-turned eyes spoke volumes. Given the events of the afternoon, there might not be a husband, especially not the one she had envisioned for herself since that first ball of the Little Season.

David Carlington had obviously underestimated his own daughter. "I haven't given you much in the way of pin money. How, exactly, are you funding this little venture of yours?"

Elizabeth remembered she hadn't told him about the donations. "When I arrived at my office a few days after I placed Mr. Streater, a patron had left an envelope for my charity that contained a hundred pounds—"

"A hundred pounds?" the marquess repeated in shock. *Good grief! She already had donors to her charity!* "I suppose that made my sack of sovereigns look like pin money," he said under his breath.

And then he realized the identity of her other patron.

Bostwick!

Gasping, Elizabeth straightened and regarded her father in disbelief. "You? *You* sent the footman with the purse?" she asked, her face brightening. "But... but I didn't recognize his livery," she said in a whisper.

"He was a courier from Parliament," the marquess commented in an off-hand manner.

Elizabeth blinked. Her father had arranged for funds to be delivered to her charity! "Oh, thank you, Father," Elizabeth said brightly, her hands clasping together as if she were about to pray. "You'll be happy to know I was able to place two gentlemen as clerks with a trading company in Wapping with some of the funds you donated. The rest is being spent this very moment on a tailor. He's making suits of clothing for some of my newest clients."

The marquess nodded absently, his mind still on Bostwick. The man was definitely serious about marrying Elizabeth. He was honorable. He was devious. He was apparently a good kisser. He could certainly afford Elizabeth. And her charity. "Very good, pet," he said quietly, his head bobbing up and down. "I... I am very proud of you," he added as he reached over to take her hands in his. "I do hope you'll consider Bostwick's offer of marriage. He may not be as handsome or as rich as Butter Blond, but I think you two will suit one another far better."

Elizabeth stared at her father for several moments, surprised by his comments and even more stunned when she realized they had never spent this much time together in conversation.

Ever.

"Thank you, Father," she replied.

The butler appeared at the door and cleared his throat.

"My Lord. There is a George Bennett-Jones calling for Lady Elizabeth," he said, a bit of revulsion in his voice.

The marquess stood up and smoothed his coat sleeves. "That

would be *Lord Bostwick* to you and most of the *rest* of London," he stated emphatically, not adding anything about the man becoming his son-in-law sometime in the near future.

With any luck, next week.

The butler's eyes widened a fraction and quickly returned to normal.

Returning his attention to Elizabeth, her father said, "It's up to you, my dearest. I trust you will make the right decision." He turned to the chair where Adeline sat, and, reaching down, scooped her up into his arms. She let out a squeak of surprise, but quickly wrapped her arms around her husband's neck. "I'll see to your mother." With that, he left the room carrying his wife, who, when David wasn't looking, winked at her daughter.

As she watched her father and mother leave the parlor, Elizabeth felt a bit of outrage and nearly stamped her foot. Just how could her father think she would allow a man to bed her?

Even if she *had* almost allowed it?

Had even encouraged it!

In those moments of pure bliss, when his lips and hands and tongue had pleasured her until she had shattered, she had begged George to take her virtue. And despite her pleas, her quiet whimpers and her wanton behavior the night before, George had kept his word and left her virtue intact.

A man of his word. A man of honor.

She whirled around, looking for a mirror, sure her face was tear-stained and hoping she could do something about it before George appeared. This was not the way she planned to meet him! And the butler was still waiting on a response. "Tell him... Tell him I'll be but a moment," she started to say, but George was already there, standing behind the butler, looking as if the world had ended.

"George!" As she hurried up to him, the butler moved away quicker than she had ever seen him move.

George Bennett-Jones, Viscount Bostwick, reached for her hand and brushed his lips over her knuckles, his face so drawn and sad he looked a bit like a hound dog. Had she been able to see his lips at that moment, Elizabeth would have seen them tremble, would have seen the tears pricking the corners of his eyes.

And she would have taken him in her arms and consoled him and assured him he was the only man for her.

But Elizabeth was curtsying, her head tilted down a bit. She had barely straightened when he released her hand. "You came!" she said with a smile, her tears starting anew.

"I have," George acknowledged with a nod. "I merely wanted to wish you happy, and I would like to thank you for... allowing me to at least try for your hand," he said rather quietly. Never once did his eyes make contact with hers. "Good day," he added, before quickly turning on his heel and walking out of the parlor.

So struck was she by the tone of his voice and the words he had said, Elizabeth stood quite still for several seconds. The sound of the front door closing was the same sound she heard when her heart seemed to stop beating.

Thud. Just like that.

George was gone.

CHAPTER 44
A PROPOSAL IN REVERSE

*W*ondering if perhaps the events of the last minute had been a figment of her overactive imagination, Elizabeth looked about the parlor. Surely George hadn't just come in and wished her happy and given her some message of thanks! Her father had barely left the room with her mother, and they were no doubt at that very moment taking advantage of their togetherness somewhere upstairs.

Was George about to propose? If so, had he changed his mind at the last moment, deciding she wasn't worthy of him? She shook her head. She was the daughter of a marquess. Her dowry was quite substantial—at least, her father must have thought so. He frequently complained about it being a potential drain on the marquessate finances.

George said he came *to wish her happy*. But one didn't do that unless they were attending your wedding.

Or knew you to be engaged to marry.

Elizabeth's eyes opened in astonishment, her attention going to the door when Alfred suddenly appeared.

"There is a Miss Wentworth to see you, milady," he intoned with the voice he used when he thought the visitor was a *very important person*.

Elizabeth took a deep breath, holding it a moment. *Thank*

goodness! Josephine would know what to do. "Please, send her in," Elizabeth ordered, her subsequent breaths coming too fast. The hand George had kissed went to her breastbone.

Josephine Wentworth, dressed in a dark blue wool carriage gown and pelisse, stood on the threshold of the parlor.

"Oh, dear. He thinks me *engaged!*" Elizabeth whispered.

"He does, indeed," Josephine agreed with a solemn nod. As she took in Elizabeth's tear-stained face and the wet handkerchiefs the poor girl held wadded up in one of her hands, Josephine angled her head. "I see you've been playing at being a watering pot."

Nodding, Elizabeth curtsied and tears began pricking the corners of her eyes. "I could have positively *drowned* all the plants in this room," she replied, desperate to keep the new tears at bay. "Oh, Josephine, what have I done?" she cried, large tears once again escaping to stream down her face.

Josephine hurried to stand before Elizabeth, her own handkerchief held out as she regarded the girl. "I take it... you're *not* engaged?" the older woman asked with a knowing smile.

Shaking her head from side to side, Elizabeth sniffled. "I told my father I couldn't marry Butter Blond because he kissed like Harold MacDuff. And it was quite apparent Gabriel has no intention of giving up his mistresses," she added, her disgust increasing. "He still has *two* of them," she added with a good deal of emphasis and lot of disgust.

The older woman gave her a wan smile. "They'll be giving *him* up before he gets a chance to do so," she whispered hoarsely. "They cannot tolerate his kisses, either," she added with a wink. Sighing, she angled her head to the other side. Her expression sobered. "George assumed you had accepted the earl's suit. We saw him take his leave, and he was displaying an expression that would suggest he was successful with his proposal."

Sniffling, Elizabeth nodded. "I figured that from what George said when he came in. He didn't even give me a chance to tell him I didn't." She sniffled again, her heart so heavy she thought she might die.

Josephine took a deep breath. "I gather from all these tears that you do feel some sort of affection for my George?" she asked then, her gloved hand resting on the side of Elizabeth's arm. There was something very maternal in the way she regarded the crying woman, as if she had done it many times.

"Oh, very much so," Elizabeth agreed with a nod. "I think... I think I may be... in lo... love with him," she whispered, her lower lip trembling. "Is... is that possible after only a few days of knowing someone?" Her eyes lifted to meet Josephine's.

"I certainly hope so," the mistress replied happily. "Come, take a turn with me, won't you?" she added as she held out her arm. Elizabeth hooked her arm into Josephine's and they began a slow walk. "I have known George a very long time," Josephine told her as she led Elizabeth out the parlor door and down the hall toward the vestibule. "Eight years now."

"Eight years?" Elizabeth repeated, drying her eyes on the handkerchief the older woman had given her. "Is he... is he as considerate as he seems?" she queried, trying hard to suppress her sobs. They had stepped into the vestibule, and the butler was seeing to the front door.

"Oh, even more so," Josephine replied, patting the back of Elizabeth's hand with her assurance. They stepped out the door and made their way down the steps to the walkway. "I have been quite stern with him about how to treat others," she explained with a nod. "How to treat a lady. How to kiss a lady." At this comment, Elizabeth nearly stopped in her tracks.

"He is a very accomplished kisser, I think," Elizabeth said without the least hint of embarrassment at knowing such a thing. She allowed herself to be led down the walk to the town coach that waited at the curb. The driver—Elizabeth thought surely it was the same driver who had picked her up the night before—jumped down from his perch and opened the coach door.

"How to make love to a woman," Josephine went on, her voice lowered a bit as she stepped into the coach and then motioned for Elizabeth to join her.

"Then you've taught him quite well, for he was..." She

stopped when she saw that George Bennett-Jones was *in* the coach. "… Amazing," she finished, her quiet voice suddenly very audible in the close confines of the elegant space. "Good afternoon, George," she said with a sad smile, wanting desperately to sit next to him. But Josephine had taken the seat across from him and motioned for Elizabeth to sit next to her.

As he tipped his hat, George shot a look at Josephine that suggested he was most displeased with her—a look that suggested he would be speaking with her in private later. "My lady," he offered quietly.

"Oh, George. Or, *my lord*, I suppose I should say," Elizabeth corrected herself, her eyes widening.

"No," George said quietly, his head shaking from side to side. "Please, do not."

Elizabeth inhaled, her brow furrowing. "Why ever did you leave so quickly?" she whispered. "You didn't give me a chance to explain. And you didn't propose!"

His lips pressed together in a thin line, George regarded her. His expression didn't give any hint of the turmoil he felt inside. He was sure he had steeled himself quite adequately for what he was sure would be the outcome of today's proposal. Of course, Elizabeth would accept the earl's offer. Why had he allowed himself to hope it could be any different?

Trenton was young, he was handsome, and he was rich.

The fact that he kissed like an Alpenmastiff couldn't weigh much in the decision as to whom Elizabeth would marry. *Could it?* "Would it have made a difference?" he asked finally, his entire body seeming to deflate in front of her. He could barely get the question out before having to swallow quickly.

"Yes, of course," she said, and then remembered her father's comment. "I had a rather odd conversation with my father just now…"

At this, George lifted his eyes to her. "Oh?" he replied, his curiosity piqued.

"When I was explaining why I couldn't accept Gabriel Wellingham's offer for my hand. You see, Trenton never actually *asked* for my hand, and I thought to be sure of a couple of things before I told him to get out." She stopped and sighed. "Oh, I didn't really say it like that, of course, but I truly didn't wish to further associate with the earl," she said quite firmly. "Nor will he with me."

George sat up straighter at this news.

Had he heard her correctly?

"You did not..?"

"No," she replied with a shake of her head. "I do not feel affection for him, and I do not wish to marry a man who kisses like an Alpenmastiff. And licks like one, too," she added, her face screwing up into an expression of obvious disgust. "Nor do I wish to marry a man who is more beautiful than I am and who keeps three mistresses. Well, *two*, now that one has quit him," she quickly amended. She took a breath and let it out slowly. "You see, my friend, Lady Hannah, insists men do not love their wives if they have mistresses, and I should like it very much to have a husband who respects me enough to honor his marriage vows."

Stilling himself as the meaning of her words took hold, George regarded her carefully. "So, does this mean…?"

Elizabeth saw hope spring to the viscount's eyes, saw his face change from the drawn, sad visage to one more familiar to her.

He is a handsome man when he smiles, she thought.

And he was someone she could imagine sitting with at breakfast every morning, and spending time with in the library before dinner, and lying atop of, naked, every night just before sleep took hold. She suddenly pushed herself off the coach seat and knelt before him. "George Bennett-Jones, would you do me the honor of being my husband?" she asked quietly, placing her hands over those he held clasped together in his lap.

There was a long moment of stillness, when no sounds could be heard, not even the slightest breath. She felt his hands fall apart beneath hers, felt his open palms catch hers and his fingers tighten around her hands. "I want very much to be your wife," she added, her eyes filling with tears again. Tears of fear, she knew, since, for whatever reason, it was possible George no longer wanted her as his wife. And if that were the case, then she at least had only one witness to her impropriety. For when did a woman ask a man for his hand in marriage? She certainly had no intention of doing so when she entered his coach!

Elizabeth waited patiently as George regarded her, his fingers gently kneading hers as he held her hands.

"God, yes," he answered suddenly, pulling on her hands so she pitched forward. His arms were around her then, pulling her up and onto his lap and into his embrace that left his head planted against one breast and her arms wrapped about his neck. "By special license, if you prefer," he murmured, holding her hard against him.

By special license!

"I don't suppose it could be today?" she asked, her voice barely audible as a sob shook her body.

Her mother would never forgive her.

She felt more than heard George's quick inhalation of breath, felt his arms tense as he tightened his hold on her.

"I would like nothing more," he whispered, his head turning so his words could be heard despite his head still being pressed against her bosom. "But I would like to remain in your mother's good graces, and I rather doubt she would ever forgive me for depriving her of seeing you properly wed."

Adeline Carlington hadn't exactly voiced specific plans for her daughter's wedding; at least, if she had, Elizabeth hadn't been present. Other than her dowry, she couldn't remember her parents mentioning anything having to do with her eventual marriage. "Perhaps we can do it twice then," Elizabeth murmured, a good deal of mischief evident in her eyes. Then her brows furrowed, forcing a little wrinkle to appear between them. "You said you would ask for my hand today. What made you change your mind?" she asked, a bit indignant with her query.

George was attempting to shake his head as he gazed up at her, but her hold on either side of his face made doing so a bit difficult. "I assure you, my lady, I never changed my mind about wanting to marry you," he whispered, his voice sounding hoarse. "But I saw Trenton leave your home earlier this afternoon, and for a moment, he had a huge smile on his face. I took it to mean you had accepted his offer."

Her expression going from concern to shock, Elizabeth considered the terms under which the earl had left the house that afternoon.

First, he was probably fearful for his life. Had there been a pistol available, she would have shot him. Not so much now, of course, as she gave it some more consideration.

It would have been a waste of a bullet.

Second, Trenton was no doubt shocked at her behavior. He had every right to be surprised by her pointed questions about his mistresses. *It's just not done,* her father had said. Well, perhaps not, but it surely gave her a good deal of satisfaction to see the earl so... discomfited.

Some of those blond curls probably popped out of place!

And last, Trenton was probably feeling relief at her having dismissed him before he could ask for her hand; indeed, he was most certainly relieved he wasn't going to marry the daughter of a political opponent.

Or he was just relieved he wasn't going to marry *me*, she considered.

Then Elizabeth remembered something from earlier that afternoon; she had *told* him to smile.

"I told him to smile," she announced in a loud whisper. "Because he was lucky he wasn't going to be married to me."

George's brow furrowed at her comment. He thought back to earlier that afternoon when the young earl had left Carlington House. He had seen the earl from across the street. Watched as the pompous, overdressed peacock made his way to his high-perch phaeton. Frowned as the earl set the horses to a run straight from the curb.

Now that George gave it some more thought, despite the pearly whites put on display by the smiling Butter Blond, the

Earl of Trenton wasn't necessarily *happy* as he descended the steps and made his way to that sporty phaeton parked in front of Carlington House. The smile had changed to something more like a grimace.

What a fool he had been not to immediately appear on the steps and offer for Elizabeth's hand! All the grief—yes, it had been grief he had felt, thinking he had lost the woman he had loved from first sight—could have been avoided had he just had faith enough in Elizabeth to know she would choose him over Butter Blond.

"Oh, but I am lucky because I am going to be married to you," George sighed, burying his face into the space between her breasts. He took a deep breath, inhaling the scent of jasmine and listening to the beat of her heart. *She is going to marry me.* "May we marry tomorrow, perhaps?" he asked, his voice suddenly quite clear.

Elizabeth gave him one of her brilliant smiles. "I... suppose. Oh, we will be the *on-dit* for weeks to come, you realize," she scolded him. "Everyone will think I *had* to marry you," she teased, kissing his forehead and moving her hands to either side of his face.

"I do not really care about Society at the moment," George said as he kissed one of her collarbones.

The sound of a throat clearing brought them both to their senses. "Really, George. You're behaving like a libertine," Josephine announced from her side of the coach.

Having forgotten Josephine was even *in* the coach and suddenly quite embarrassed, Elizabeth took the opportunity to slide off of George's lap and sit next to him, her hands moving back to grasp his. "I beg forgiveness. I am just as much at fault as he," Elizabeth admitted as she noticed Josephine's amused expression.

The older woman didn't truly mean to admonish the couple, it seemed. But it was awfully rude to be kissing and pawing at one another in front of a third party. Even if she was George's ex-mistress. "Will you be a witness at our wedding?" Elizabeth asked then. "You are George's very best friend."

Josephine gave a wan smile, tears pricking the edges of her eyes. "Of course," she murmured quietly, wondering how she would tell Jack when he arrived that their first order of business as a betrothed couple would be to attend a wedding. And then attend their own. "I wouldn't miss it for the world," she added, before she allowed her own tears to flow freely.

CHAPTER 45

LOVE AMONG THE FEATHERS

*D*avid Carlington stared at the silk fabric canopy above his head. His wife, Adeline, lay nestled against him, her head resting in the small of his shoulder while one satin and feather clad arm lay draped over his bare chest. Her hand still gripped a small ostrich feather whose tendrils of fluff caressed his other shoulder. Some of her dressing gown lay haphazardly across his body. At the moment, the feather trim was tickling a certain body part into remembering what he had been doing just moments before.

And what Adeline had been doing with that ostrich feather before that.

With any luck, she would be doing it again in short order.

Having a wife like Adeline was like having a mistress, he mused, thinking of how enthusiastic she was in their marriage bed, how imaginative she was when it came to pleasuring him, and how agreeable she was in most every other matter.

Which had him suddenly wondering how she had thought to use an ostrich feather to tease him on this occasion. "Sweeting," his whispered, moving the hand that was wrapped around her waist lower so it cupped her bottom.

"Hmm?"

"From where did you get the idea to bring *this*—" he moved

his other hand to touch the hand that held the feather "—to bed?" he asked, his voice kept to barely a whisper.

He felt more than heard a chuckle burble up from his wife. "Miss Wentworth," she whispered back. David's eyes widened, although Adeline's face was still nestled into his shoulder so she couldn't see his reaction. She felt his body stiffen though, and she grinned. "Really, David. I wondered how long it would be before you finally *asked*. I might have been born in Italy, but it doesn't mean I was born knowing how to do these things to you."

Her husband's body remained taut. "How... how long have you and Miss Wentworth...?"

"Ever since she started coming to the house to meet with you," she murmured, finally raising her head and resting it on his chest.

His body still ready for flight, David took a deep breath and let it out slowly. "She's been... giving you lessons?" he queried, his face screwed up in a comical expression that made his wife chuckle again.

"My, but you have an active imagination, my darling," she purred, enjoying his nervousness. "*Lessons* is not what I would call her... suggestions," she said, with a small shake of her head. "She merely tells me a thing or two, or if I'm not here, she writes a note before she leaves the house. She's very creative."

Finally relaxing back into the pillows, David took another deep breath. "Why?" he asked, thinking this had been going on for... for eight years!

Adeline lowered her head back into the small of his shoulder, pondering how to explain she wanted her husband all to herself, that she never wanted to discover or be told by a gossiping hag he had taken another mistress ever again.

Especially after what had happened with his last mistress.

"I will not share you with another," she stated firmly. "So, I will do what I must to keep you in my bed."

David's hold on her tightened as he raised his head from the pillow. Her words had come out as a threat of sorts, and yet it was *she* who was willing to do what was necessary to ensure his fidelity.

As long as he didn't keep a separate mistress, Adeline Carlington was the perfect wife.

"If you didn't already know, please take my word that I have not bedded another woman since..." He allowed the statement to trail off, not wanting to say the name of the mistress who had betrayed him, and certainly not wanting his wife to know she had been Josephine Wentworth's sister. "Nor will I, Addy," he added, as he cupped the side of her face with a hand. Leaning down, he kissed her eyelids and lips to seal his promise.

Adeline returned the brief kiss. "I know, David," she replied with a nod. Perhaps there was a bit of relief in her words, as if she had suspected what he said to be true but wanted to hear the assurance aloud. She rolled back against him, returning her face to rest against his chest and kissing the space between two ribs.

David could feel her smile against his skin. "I suppose we could go to the theatre tonight," he murmured, as he drew two fingers through her thick, dark auburn hair. He didn't really *want* to go to the theatre, but there was a price to be paid for being pleasured to within an inch of your life.

"Oh, let's not," Adeline whispered, her head barely moving. Her arm moved down his body, though, so the ostrich feather ended up covering most of his abdomen and the tops of his thighs.

David felt her lips kiss the side of his chest again as her words sank in. "Really?" he replied in disbelief.

This was a first.

"Are you... feeling all right?" he asked, his brows furrowing as he moved to lift his upper body from the bed.

"I am fine," Adeline answered lazily, pressing her hand into his belly so the feather tickled him in several places and forced him to fall back into the mattress. "I just want to spend an evening here at home. And I think our daughter may wish to talk a bit about whatever has happened with Gabriel. And George." This last was said with a hint of surprise.

The marquess sighed, his thoughts reluctantly returning to Elizabeth. With any luck, she was at this very moment a betrothed woman. Hell, if George had any sense, he would have procured a special license right after he had permission to court Elizabeth in the hope she would would marry him. The couple might be standing before a *magistrate* at this very moment.

He could only hope.

"I know you had your heart set on her marrying an earl, but do you suppose you could be amenable to a viscount as a son-in-law?" he asked carefully, his fingers moving from her hair to her jaw.

Adeline yawned. "I suppose. Don't discount a viscount, especially if it's George," she added sleepily, as she remembered the words Josephine had written on her last note. "He's an excellent dancer. And I've been dying to get into Bostwick Place to see how the renovations turned out. I heard he spent a fortune."

David rolled his eyes. "He had to. I don't think his uncle spent a pence on that place the entire time he was alive. Somewhat of a miser he was after his wife died," he murmured.

"A molly *and* a miser?" Adeline countered, a grin appearing as she wiggled the ostrich feather and watched as her husband's hardening cock appeared between the tendrils.

"You minx!" He captured the hand that held the feather and took it from her. Then he turned the frond onto his giggling wife's well-endowed front as she rolled away from his side, dragging the undressing gown from the front of his body. The feather trim tickled his torso, reminding him of why he thought his wife a perfect mistress. Lifting himself over her, he leaned down to kiss her. "Will you be heartbroken if there is any chance our daughter forgoes the big church wedding?" he asked. *And saves me the expense while she's at it.* Somehow he knew that even if he could get Adeline to agree to forego a formal wedding, she would change her mind once the afterglow of lovemaking had dimmed.

He felt Adeline's legs open for him and all thoughts of a wedding and its associated costs left his head.

"I'm a mother. Of course, I will be heartbroken," Adeline

replied with a pout. But then her devilish grin made David realize she wouldn't be *too* heartbroken. "As long as you console me often, I think I shan't mind too much," she added, first wrapping one leg and then the other around his thighs. Her chest lifted from the bed as he impaled her.

"How about if I just tickle you?" her husband replied, the words coming out as a growl.

In only a few moments, she was laughing and gasping for air.

CHAPTER 46
A WALK IN THE PARK

*A*s they strolled along the familiar path in Hyde Park, Elizabeth noticed George's smile, his lips apart just a bit so his straight teeth showed, the crinkles on either side of his eyes deepening but at the same time lifting his lids so his eyes were more open.

"You're smiling," Elizabeth commented as they took a turn along the path they had walked just two weeks before, the one on which she had asked him if he would accommodate her wish to know *more*. Most of the trees had begun to display their autumn colors, the leaves turning gold and red under the cooler blue sky. There was no sign of rain clouds nor did the air smell as if there would be showers anytime that day. It was a perfect day for a wedding.

"I am," George replied, his smile broadening. "I have it on very good authority I am handsome when I smile," he stated, patting the gloved hand she had looped through his arm and giving her a wink as he did so.

"You look... happy," she replied.

George's lips were on her forehead in an instant. "That's because I am," he replied, his grin broadening. He tamped down the bit of nervousness he felt when he thought of what was to come at eleven o'clock that morning.

"You're about to be leg shackled. How can you be happy?"

she asked, an eyebrow angled up. There wasn't a hint of amusement in the query, but her eyes gave her away.

He laughed loudly at her comment, causing Elizabeth to finally smile.

He should be nervous.

He should be panicked.

He should be running from the park as fast as his long legs would carry him.

But a sense of calm settled over him as he considered his betrothed's question. "You see, there is this gorgeous woman I saw at a ball last week who was literally thrown into my arms, and then she asked me to kiss her, and then begged me to bed her, and then pleaded for my hand in marriage. Any man in his right mind would be smiling, given those circumstances," he claimed with a good deal of amusement.

"I didn't *beg* you to bed me!" Elizabeth countered indignantly, realizing with a bit of embarrassment that everything *else* he mentioned had indeed happened. She covered her mouth with her free hand as she looked about them, hoping no one was within hearing distance.

George leaned over, removed the hand from her mouth, and kissed her quite thoroughly. "Ah, but you will. I hope," he added, as a look of doubt suddenly crossed his face.

Elizabeth smiled. "Tonight, I will. When all the wedding guests have gone home and we're back at your house."

"Our house," George interrupted, his forehead touching hers as he closed his eyes. Despite Elizabeth's desire to get married the very day she had proposed, they had agreed to wait ten days.

Her father was sure he had convinced Adeline Carlington to accept a quick marriage by a vicar, but once she had dressed for dinner after their tryst, she begged him to allow her to arrange a simple church wedding. David Carlington reluctantly agreed, gave her a ten-day deadline, and dispatched a footman to Bostwick Place with a note.

Since Elizabeth had to maintain longer office hours— her burgeoning charity experienced an increase in clients as well as patrons over those next few days—she was happy to have the distraction, and she allowed her mother to make all the wedding arrangements.

She and the two men she had employed from the start—the "bees", she called them, since both their names ended in "by"— simply couldn't keep up with the number of applicants, locate enough positions, and meet with all the employers they needed. Just two days ago, the increased workload made it necessary for her to hire two more of her clients— a negotiator experienced in employment contracts as well as another clerk.

Word of her charity had reached *The Times*. An article praising her work had appeared yesterday—not in the Society pages, as a lady of the *ton* might expect her charity to be mentioned, but as part of the London news. Elizabeth wondered if perhaps her father was behind the story, and then thought it was more likely Josephine would have had a hand in its appearance.

Josephine's engagement was announced the same day as her own. Her affianced, Jack Theisen, was a distinguished-looking man nearly six inches taller than his bride-to-be. He saw to it she was rarely out of his sight once he arrived in London. Jack loved the townhouse Josephine claimed to have inherited from her mother, but he insisted they needed a larger house in town, one in which they could entertain his business clients and hold balls and host his extended family when they came to visit. Although the hunt was still on for such a dwelling—he was hoping for something in Cavendish Square—the handsome couple had said their vows before a vicar the day before and were happily ensconced in the townhouse until further notice.

Elizabeth secretly hoped they would make an appearance at her wedding. She had made sure an invitation was sent, not bothering to tell her mother the identity of Mrs. John Theisen.

"I think it's time we make our way to St. James," George murmured quietly. "Your mother will think I've whisked you off to Gretna Green."

Elizabeth nodded and quickened her step on the crushed granite path. George had arrived at Carlington House earlier that morning driving his own curricle, the equipage decorated with silk streamers and flowers. George requested to see her, sending a note with Alfred asking if she would join him on a ride in the park before heading for the church.

Her hair already done in a tumble of curls and ribbons, Elizabeth had just finished donning a gold silk de Naples gown her mother had insisted she wear for the occasion when the note was given to her. Afraid to open it at first—had George changed his mind?—she read it and nearly wept.

My beautiful Elizabeth. Please join me for a ride and a walk in the park. I know it may seem selfish, but I want nothing more than a few moments alone with you this morning so that I may bestow my wedding gifts upon you. Yours for the rest of my life, George.

Elizabeth had jumped at the chance to take her leave of the chaotic house to spend a few minutes alone with George. "If Gretna Green wasn't so far away, I would *insist* we go there instead," Elizabeth said with a wink.

Who knew her mother would be able to put together a complete church wedding in less than a fortnight?

Elizabeth had been secretly glad to spend her days at her office, seeing to new clients, while her mother met with the florists who would decorate the church, and the cooks who would see to the wedding breakfast, and the printer who created the invitations that were sent with great haste to family and friends.

Before they were back at the curricle, George stopped and turned to face Elizabeth. He glanced around quickly, wanting to be sure they were in the same place they had been when Elizabeth asked him to pleasure her, the same place where he had kissed her when he promised he wouldn't take her virtue, the place where he felt as if their courtship had begun.

"My lady, I was wondering if—"

"Kiss me, George," Elizabeth interrupted, her manner suddenly tense.

George blinked, but knew better than to argue. He lowered his lips to Elizabeth's, bestowing a light and short kiss before pulling away. Seeing her almost immediate look of disappointment, he whispered, "If I kiss you the way I truly wish to kiss you right now, *everyone* who comes to our wedding will know I had my way with you this morning."

Elizabeth inhaled. "Oh. Of course," she responded, sighing heavily. "So, does this mean you'll have your way with me... later?"

Smiling, George nodded. "I should hope so." If he continued to look into her eyes, he knew he would get lost. "In the meantime, I was wondering if—"

"May I have my way with you then, too?" Elizabeth interrupted, her lips curving up.

Fighting the flush he felt creeping up his neck and face, George nodded. "Of course, milady," he responded, not adding that she could have her way with him just about whenever she wanted. "I was wondering—"

"I must admit, I have been quite looking forward to it," she said, her face taking on the beautiful pink glow that announced her embarrassment.

George's smile was as wide as it had ever been. "My sweet, if you don't stop thinking about *later*, you're going to swoon in front of the wedding guests," he warned in a good-natured voice. When he saw the pink glow darken, he added, "I was wondering..." He stopped, thinking she might interrupt him again. When she merely gazed at him as if she were hanging on his every word, her eyes suddenly curious, he continued, "Would you like to open some of your wedding gifts right now?"

Elizabeth blinked. *Some?* She glanced around, her curiosity increasing when she saw no evidence of a gift. "Yes, of course, George," she replied, her voice so quiet it was almost a whisper.

Reaching into his coat pocket, George pulled out a slim pasteboard box and handed it to her. She took it, hesitating briefly as she did so, her eyes locked onto George's. Removing the lid of the box, she gasped when she saw a black velvet lining upon which sat a necklace of aquamarine gemstones. The stones were strung on a tiny gold chain. "Oh, George!" she breathed. "It's so... elegant. So beautiful. It's perfect!"

He lifted the necklace from the bed of velvet and wrapped it around the column of her neck, moving to stand behind her as he did so. Once the clasp was secure, he returned to stand in front of her, smiling as he confirmed the stones were the same color as her eyes. "When I asked your mother what color gown you would be wearing this morning, she wondered why I would wish to know. I showed her the necklace. She assured me this would be a good match to the gold. She was right, of course," he explained, reaching out to touch the stone that hung just above the center of her bodice. "Which means this should match as well," he added, as he pulled a smaller box from the other pocket of his topcoat.

Elizabeth's mouth dropped open, her gloved hands moving to frame her face. "George!" She reached out with one hand to lift the lid, revealing the matching bracelet, its aquamarine gems smaller versions of those in the necklace, strung on a similar tiny gold chain.

George fastened the bracelet around one of her wrists, kissing the inside of it when he finished. He stood back to regard the jewels. "There are more, of course, but..."

"More?"

A mischievous grin passed over his lips as he remembered her saying the same word the night he had pleasured her. *Always promise her more*, Josephine had said all those weeks ago, before he had begun to even think about finding a wife. George sobered. He nodded. "I thought it best to ply you with jewelry."

"But, *why?*" she asked as she studied the stones on her bracelet.

"I'm afraid the renovations to the mistress suite at Bostwick Place are... unfinished. And I've been told they won't be complete until you choose the colors you want."

Inhaling sharply, Elizabeth angled her head to one side. "There is a mistress suite?" she repeated. She hadn't remembered seeing evidence of one that night she had been in George's house. And, as to their living arrangements, she hadn't even given them a single thought. Anna had packed most of her clothes and slippers in trunks and helped some footmen to see to it they were carted to Bostwick Place. The maid seemed especially happy to make the move with her mistress.

It seemed there was a tiger for whom her maid felt a special fondness.

"Through the dressing room and bath beyond my room," George commented. "I do hope you'll be amenable to sharing my apartment with me until..."

"If you think we're sleeping in separate beds anytime soon, George Bennett-Jones, I shall never speak to you again!"

Eyeing his wife-to-be as if she had announced she loved him out loud, George stilled himself and then took a deep breath. "I have no intention of allowing you to sleep alone, my sweet," he replied, with a shake of his head. Before Elizabeth could give him any kind of rejoinder, he wrapped his arms around her shoulders and pulled her hard against his body, his lips capturing hers in a kiss that was as demanding as it was possessive.

Caught off-guard, Elizabeth could only allow the assault of his lips on hers, returning the kiss once she had gathered her wits. Her arms reached up to his shoulders, her hands to the sides of his neck, as a faint hum came from somewhere in her throat.

When the kiss ended, it was because George pulled away, his forehead left resting on hers. "Now, *everyone* will know I've kissed you this morning," he murmured with a sigh, seeing her bee-stung lips in their reddened glory.

"And not a single person could find fault with that when they see your wedding gifts," Elizabeth replied, her eyes closed, her long lashes curled atop her cheekbones. "Oh, I do... I do love you, George," she whispered. "Or, should I be calling you 'Bostwick' now?" This last question had her eyes opening to see a grin replaced with a grimace.

"You call me 'Bostwick,' and *I'll* never speak to you again," George replied in warning. "Which will be very difficult since I love you very much and intend to prove it at every opportunity."

"You can prove it right now by getting my daughter to St. James," David Carlington, the Marquess of Morganfield, interrupted in a gruff voice.

The couple whirled toward the carriage way to find Elizabeth's father on a high-perch phaeton. A bright cherry red phaeton. The black horse in front of it was barely reigned in, as if he had been forced to come to a sudden halt.

Elizabeth's astonishment was evident in her wide eyes. "Father? Is that... *yours?*" she asked as she took in the sight of the Marquess of Morganfield sitting high on the rather sporty equipage. The gleaming metal attested to either its very good care or its newness.

David Carlington straightened on the seat and regarded his daughter. "Indeed, it is," he remarked with just a hint of pride. "And you can be my first passenger if that rake you're about to marry will provide some assistance in getting you up here," he added in a tone that suggested he wasn't necessarily teasing.

"Ah, the man impugns my honor," George claimed in exaggerated offense, his grin belying his words. Although he could have taken offense at his future father-in-law's comment, George thought it better to make light of it. If he protested, it might make his guilt at the way he had gone about courting Elizabeth more apparent. He turned to her. "Are you game?"

Elizabeth turned her attention to him, her eyes still wide. "Oh, could I, George? I've never been. There's never any room for a chaperone," she explained when she saw his look of surprise.

George smiled at her enthusiasm. "I'll help you up. And should you decide you enjoy it, we'll take ours the next time we come to the park."

She was halfway up to the bench seat when she paused and looked down at George, balancing with one hand in his while her other was held by her father. "Ours?" she repeated. Her father pulled her onto the seat, the swish of her skirts affording George a tantalizing view of her ankles and petticoats.

"I apologize for our tardiness, my lord," George offered as he checked his Breguet and found it was still well before eleven. "She nearly had me talked into taking her to Greta Green," he added in a teasing voice.

"George!" Elizabeth exclaimed, the name coming out in far more than the two syllables she usually used to say it. Then she realized her intended was merely teasing.

Morganfield grinned at his future son-in-law. "Get thee to the church, Bostwick, or *I* shall never speak to you again."

"Yes, my lord," George replied with a curt nod, jumping up into his curricle. He pulled out into the lane and was soon following the phaeton as it made its way to St. James' church.

CHAPTER 47
WEDDING NIGHT WONDERS

*N*ight had already fallen by the time George maneuvered the curricle to the curb. Elizabeth, her head resting in the small of his shoulder, was asleep. A groom was soon seeing to the horse as George lifted his wife from the seat and carried her up the steps of Bostwick Place. Elkins opened the double doors even before George was on the landing, stepping aside with a poorly suppressed grin curving the corners of his mouth.

"My lord, my lady," he spoke quietly, not wanting to waken the new mistress of the house.

George glowered at his valet's use of titles but found he couldn't stay annoyed. "I think breakfast will be late. Very late. We should like to take it in the apartment, of course. And do be sure there's chocolate for the viscountess," George said in a quiet voice, his gaze lowering to Elizabeth's face. Her eyes were open, the aquamarine irises full of mischief, and an impish grin was forming.

"Chocolate sounds like a perfect way to start my first day as a wife." She reached out her right hand to Elkins. "I am Elizabeth... Bennett-Jones," she offered, nearly using her maiden name before she caught herself.

His face coloring at finding his master's new wife introducing herself from such an awkward position, Elkins took the proffered hand and shook it. "Elkins, my lady. At your service. I will see to it the staff is prepared to meet you properly on the morrow, my lady," the valet said as he released her hand.

Elizabeth nodded. "Thank you, Elkins. You may retire for the evening."

The valet's eyes widened. He glanced up at George, surprised he was already being dismissed. George grinned. "You heard the lady," he said as he turned and started up the stairs, giving his new wife a smirk as he did so.

Elkins stood at the bottom of the stairs and watched his master as George carried his viscountess up the stairs. "Good night, my lord. My lady." When they had disappeared into the hallway above, he made his way to his quarters. If Viscount Bostwick didn't require him until—how had he put it? *Late*, he had said—then perhaps it was time to make the acquaintance of the new upstairs maid. He was quite sure she had been flirting with him during the servants' night out at Vauxhall Gardens. Her services wouldn't be immediately required in the morning, after all.

"Since you dismissed my valet, I do hope you intend to help me undress," George said as he allowed Elizabeth to reach down and open the doors to his apartment. When her hand let go of the door handle, she reached up to put her finger into the knot of his cravat. With a slight jerk, the perfectly tied length of linen loosened from around his neck.

"Of course, I intend to. In fact, I plan to have you undressed and ready for me before I take off a single item of clothing," she claimed.

George paused before taking her into the apartment. "Indeed?' he replied, carrying her to an upholstered chair. He was about to set her down in front of it when she shook her head.

"No, George," she whispered. She used her head to motion toward the cheval mirror.

"As you wish, my lady," he replied. Elizabeth could feel his pulse rate increase as he strode toward the mirror, all the while keeping an eye on her. One of her hands was at his back, while the other was wrapped over his shoulder and around his neck. When he reached the space in front of the mirror, the very space where he had held her facing the mirror while he undid the fastenings of her gown that first time, he regarded her for a moment. Lowering his face to hers, he kissed her, a short, sweet kiss that was merely a harbinger of things to come.

She extricated herself from his hold, her feet barely touching the ground before she pulled the cravat from around his neck. She moved her fingers to undo his topcoat buttons, making quick work of them. George stood still while she pushed the garment off his body. Then she went to work on the buttons of his waistcoat. Even before he could pull off the waistcoat, she had started on the fastening of his breeches. Pulling his shirt fabric from around his waist, she splayed her fingers and moved her palms over the warm skin beneath his shirt.

Having promised he would maintain control for at least a while, George found himself succumbing to his wife's ministrations. Her deft fingers were making quick work of his clothing, and now, as her hands pushed against his chest and slid over the planes of his body, he found himself wondering how much longer he would be able to maintain any semblance of control. "My lady," he murmured, leaning over to kiss her forehead. "I cannot keep my hands from you any longer," he intoned, his lips still pressed against her face.

Elizabeth giggled. "Then don't, my lord. I order you to ravish me this very minute," she whispered, the hint of seduction lacing her words. Elizabeth shrieked in delight as her body was suddenly surrounded by his arms, his fingers pulling apart the fastenings of her bodice while his lips worked their magic on her earlobe. In only a moment, yards of golden silk hid her from view as George pulled her gown over her head. She felt the ties of her corset loosen, and in mere seconds, the offending garment was suddenly open and falling off her body. Her chemise followed in short order so that she was left wearing only her jewelry, gloves, stockings and slippers. Elizabeth inhaled sharply as he lifted her in his arms and laid her out on the bed, where the downturned linens left a wide expanse in which to place her nearly naked body.

George kicked off his shoes, jerked his stockings off his legs and pushed his breeches and drawers to the floor as he watched her nudge her slippers from both feet and toss them aside. The sight of her clad in only stockings, gloves and gemstones was intoxicating. He climbed onto the bed, holding his naked body suspended over hers. "I love you," he whispered. His lips captured hers, his kiss one of passion and promise.

Elizabeth wrapped her arms around his neck, returning the kiss, her body writhing beneath him so that he wanted nothing more than to bury himself in her. But he knew he would hurt her in doing so. Better to pleasure her until she was in ecstasy and then take her virtue, he decided.

He slid one hand along the length of her body as he kissed her. When it slid over her mound and through the dark curls between her thighs, her lips pulled away from his in a soft gasp. "George!" she whispered, his name coming out in a long, low groan.

Smiling to himself as he felt his own body respond, George pressed his hand against her, his middle finger sliding along the wetness between the warm folds. Her womanhood was there, already swollen and ready for his magic touch. He stroked it, circled it with his thumb and flicked over it with the edge of a finger before gently sliding the same finger inside her. Seeking the sensitive flesh inside with the pad of his finger, he watched as Elizabeth's body bowed beneath him, her eyelids so heavy they nearly covered the aquamarine of her eyes.

She arched back, gasping and moaning, begging him to take her. While sliding a second finger into her, George lowered his lips to one breast, covering one nipple to suckle and nip the engorged nub. He felt her body shiver, shake, shudder before he slowly removed his fingers and used their moistness to tease her engorged womanhood to the very edge of ecstasy. Lifting his body on his other arm, he positioned himself over her and between her legs as they parted and lifted to wrap around his thighs. When he was sure she was cresting a wave of pleasure, he allowed his sword to seek out the warmth and wetness of her sheath.

She surrounded him, pulled him in before he stilled his movement. She was so tight around him! He could hear her inhale as he filled her, as he stopped when he felt the barrier of her maidenhead. His mouth lowered onto her other breast, teasing and nipping at her nipple until Elizabeth's cry of his name filled the night. Then he pulled out of her a bit and plunged his turgid manhood into her as far as he dared, biting his lip as he felt and heard her sudden inhalation of breath at what must have been the pain. He stilled himself again, moved his hands to cradle her face. Kissing her lips and the corner of her mouth, he whispered, "I'm so sorry."

Elizabeth squeezed her eyes shut as she felt him penetrate her completely, the sense of fullness nearly as overwhelming as the wave after wave of pleasure had been just a moment ago. If there was pain, she was unaware of it, her very being having left her body to hover above, to watch as George kissed her, as he held himself so still inside her, as he buried his head into the space between her neck and shoulder, as his tongue barely touched the tender skin beneath her ear and his lips took purchase on her earlobe.

When she felt his words in her ears, she opened her eyes and inhaled as if she had been holding her breath for too long, her mind suddenly at one with her body again. "George," she whispered, drawing out his name and leaving her lips curved up in a seductive smile.

What had he said?

She was sure he had said something. She had felt his breath, his lips against the whorl of her ear. "Say it again," she breathed, her hands sliding up the sides of his torso, under his arms, up to his shoulders and around his neck.

"I love you," he whispered as he lifted his head, his torso

held suspended over hers by his bent arms. Before she could respond, his lips covered hers in a thorough kiss. And then he began to move. Instinctively, Elizabeth clenched down on his retreating manhood, not wanting it to leave her body, not wanting the sense of fullness to disappear.

At George's rather loud growl, she let go and was rewarded with his hardened manhood filling her again. And she moved to meet him, lifting her hips so that he was buried even deeper in her. A chuckle burbled up from his throat as he steadied himself. "You minx," he said as he caught sight of her mischievous grin. Then he was pulling out and thrusting into her, over and over in a rhythm she matched with her hips meeting his. And then she became aware of the throbbing deep inside. Of the sensations his thrusting sword created at her very core. Of the sounds of his panting as his rhythm quickened. And when the waves started rolling, she arched her back and cried out his name.

George intended to still himself, to watch as Elizabeth was taken by the waves of pleasure, to be sure she had come to completion. But seeing her ecstasy, feeling her sudden tightening on him, the way her body seemed to capture him and hold on and pull him deeper inside... it was too much. The spasm of the climax caught and shattered him. A growl and a whisper of "Elizabeth" were his only sounds before he collapsed onto the lush body beneath him.

Clinging to his back with her fingertips, Elizabeth held on as if her very life depended on it, for she was sure if she let go, her body would simply break apart and fly away on the slightest breath, on George's breath as it washed over her neck and shoulder and her breasts. With the last vestiges of the pleasure waves coursing through her, she took a deep breath and sighed it away. Turning her face to where his rested on the pillow next to hers, she kissed George on the forehead. "You are the master of the understatement, George," she whispered, a slow smile forming.

His body quite boneless as it lay sprawled over hers, George stirred enough to gaze at his wife through heavy eyes. "Hmm?" he managed, wondering what she meant.

"You said there would be '*more*'," she replied in a teasing voice. She felt his body tremble with a suppressed chuckle.

"My lady, you have barely experienced the 'more'," he whispered before falling into a satisfied slumber atop his wife, a smile still on his lips as he imagined Elizabeth's facial expression.

Sliding her suddenly limp legs down the sides of George's thighs while making sure he was still firmly inside her, Elizabeth sighed. "I was glad to see Mr. Streater looking so well," she murmured. Her first client had stood with George during the ceremony, acting as if he had been their matchmaker. In a way, he had been, she supposed.

"Hmm," George managed. "Beth looked as happy as the day she wed Jeremy," he commented, not adding that it was probably because their four children had been left at their townhouse with a nurse. "As did your other friends. I rather imagine Lady Charlotte will be a duchess before long."

"Hmm," Elizabeth murmured. "I think her duke will be out of hospital soon," she agreed. "But Hannah still doesn't yet have any prospects." The words were said with a hint of worry.

"She will," George replied, thinking there were a few eligible peers still in need of a wife. "Probably before we return from our wedding trip." His eyes suddenly opened, for at no point in the past two weeks had they discussed a wedding trip.

He was about to ask Elizabeth where she might like to go when she stirred. "Can we forego a wedding trip?" she asked in a whisper, the fingers of one hand spearing his hair so her nails scraped his scalp. She grinned when she felt his body shiver atop hers.

Blinking, George wondered if she could read his mind. "Completely?" he asked, a hint of surprise coloring his voice.

"Well, at least for now. I don't wish to leave this bed," his wife replied.

"Ever?" he teased.

"Ask me again in a couple of days," she murmured. "When you're sure you've gotten a child on me."

Not about to argue—the woman always seemed to know what she wanted and was quite good at getting it—George settled in for a quick nap. "As you wish, my lady. I am yours to command."

Grinning, Elizabeth closed her eyes and decided she rather liked the "more."

EPILOGUE

"There is a Mrs. Jack Theisen calling, my lord," Alfred announced from just inside the threshold of his master's study.

David Carlington looked up from the ledger spread open on his desk blotter, an ink-filled quill poised over it. A look of concentration etched his face as he tried to recall if he had ever met a woman by that name. "Who?" he asked finally, after searching his memory in vain for any familiarity with the moniker.

His hands behind his back, the butler seemed a bit unsure of what to say. "My lord, the last time she called, she was Miss Josephine Wentworth," he said, in a very dignified manner.

The man was certainly less sure of himself then he had been a few weeks ago, the marquess thought in amusement. David straightened, replacing his quill in the pot to prevent a drop of ink from spoiling his otherwise pristine page, an accounting of the costs associated with his daughter's wedding.

Despite his fears that the fête would cost a fortune, he was quite surprised to discover his wife's indulgence hadn't been one at all. The wedding and breakfast feast had cost far less than her last ball, in fact. And his new son-in-law's insistence that Elizabeth's dowry be directed to her charity instead of to George was a nice surprise, as well.

When he had personally delivered the donation to her charity at her office, the look on his daughter's face had been so precious, so genuinely thankful and happy, he thought he might have to make it a regular practice to deliver his donations in person.

David shook himself from his reverie and wondered what news Josephine could be bringing. Perhaps she only meant to thank him for allowing his daughter to marry George. It had been her idea, after all.

He remembered their last meeting—was that in August? Sighing, he braced his hands against the edge of the desk. The woman had not been mincing words when she said she intended to marry someday. "Send her in," he said to Alfred, as he stood up from his desk and made his way to stand in front of it.

Josephine entered slowly, her very new and fashionable bright red carriage gown and pelisse at odds with the widow's weeds she had worn for their last meeting. Her hat, featuring a small brim in the back that widened around the front, was adorned with several red fabric roses and a few feathers.

The sight of the feathers brought back memories of his recent afternoon with his wife. He felt a sudden flush heat his face as he moved forward, and surprise when Josephine performed a perfect curtsy. Reaching for her gloved hand, he lifted it and brushed his lips across the knuckles. "My lady," he intoned, using the words he would use for any lady of the *ton*. "How very good to see you again," he offered with a low nod.

Surprised at the formal greeting the marquess afforded her, Josephine had to bite back a chiding retort. "And you, my lord," she said instead. "You are looking... rather flushed and very... happy?" she guessed, her perusal of him not the least bit subtle.

David smiled, his head cocking to one side. "Indeed," he answered simply. He waved to the chair next to where he stood. "Join me in a brandy?" he offered, realizing immediately this wouldn't be like their other meetings.

Josephine couldn't suppress her amusement. "It's barely half past ten, Morganfield," she replied with a shake of her head.

"And I cannot stay. But thank you for the offer. I merely wished to convey my congratulations on you getting your daughter settled so quickly."

The marquess regarded her a moment. "I think you had far more to do with that than I did," he returned, a sigh escaping him as he leaned against his desk and crossed his arms. "Mrs. Jack Theisen, is it?" he said, remembering the butler's introduction. "That was quick."

His guest had to suppress a snort. "I hardly think thirteen years is quick," she replied with a shake of her head. "But I believe the phrase is, 'better late than never'." After a pause, she added, "I wanted to let you know that I won't be paying you these visits any longer. I am a married woman now. It seems my husband is truly a captain of industry and quite well regarded in Oxford. Jack is also looking forward to spending a good deal of time here in London. I would rather there not be a hint of scandal due to my... interest... in politics, or because I made my living as... as a mistress." She didn't add, *to your new son-in-law*," although she knew very well the marquess knew by whom she was formerly employed.

She also didn't add a plea that he pretend not to know her in the event they should cross paths in the future.

The marquess reluctantly nodded his agreement to her terms. "A shame, Josephine. I find our chats are always a source of such good information." He paused a moment, not wanting their exchange to become more awkward than it already was. "Would it be acceptable for Adeline to invite you and your husband to our next ball? I expect she'll be hosting one during the next Season. She usually does."

Her eyes widening at the implication of his query, Josephine stared at David for several seconds. "That would be... quite an honor, I should think," she answered, her steely reserve breaking down just a bit. She swallowed hard, overcome by his overture.

"I'll see to it," he replied with a nod. "And will you give my regards to Mr. Theisen? I am somewhat familiar with his success in the textile business. I think congratulations are in order."

Josephine's eyes darted to one side as she considered his comment. "I will, of course, my lord," she replied stiffly.

My lord? Christ, the woman never addressed him by his title! And if she was severing her ties to him, was she also going to cease her *suggestions* to Adeline on how to please him in their bedchamber? The woman had been responsible for rekindling the flames of passion he had felt for Adeline.

So, it wasn't exactly panic he experienced at the thought of Josephine no longer being in their lives, but he certainly recognized the disappointment he felt.

"My lady," he countered, his demeanor suddenly rather serious. "I find that I cannot accept your... resignation... from your duty to your country. Or to my wife," he added, hoping he didn't sound as selfish as he felt just then.

Josephine blinked in surprise. "My lord?" was all she could manage in response.

David shook his head. "If you think that just because you're married to a... what did you call him? Oh, a 'captain of industry', that you can be relieved of your duty to keep me informed as to your analysis of the political landscape, then you are sorely mistaken, my lady. In fact, I'll need to have your husband call on me so that I may make my position on the subject quite clear. I want there to be no misunderstanding on his part."

Rather shocked at his statement, Josephine stared at the marquess for several seconds. "Are you... threatening me, my lord?" she stammered, her heart pounding so hard she could barely hear her words. She had always displayed more self-confidence in David Carlington's presence than she ever felt, but at the moment, her confidence was crumbling before him.

"No!" he replied in a manner that suggested he was annoyed. "I'm merely telling you that I expect you to continue to keep me apprised as you have for so long. And I intend to be the one to tell your husband of your value to me. My lady," he added.

There was a hint of a twinkle in one eye, just enough that Josephine determined he meant no threat at all, but merely wished to acknowledge her importance to him. "When should my husband call on you, my lord?" she asked, her heart rate nearly back to normal.

"At his convenience, of course," Morganfield responded with a nod. "I should like to share a cheroot and a brandy with him, should he be inclined to accept my hospitality," he explained, his arms crossing his chest again. "Is that acceptable to my lady?"

Josephine allowed a smile and a roll of her eyes. Should her husband be inclined to agree with Morganfield's request for her continued services, she would be able to continue her daily research into politics and current events. She couldn't imagine why Jack wouldn't agree, but she was quite sure he would be very surprised when the Marquess of Morganfield informed him of what she had been doing for the past eight years. And now her meetings with the marquess wouldn't have to be so clandestine. "Very, my lord," Josephine replied with a nod. "Do let Lady Morganfield know I paid a visit, won't you?" she said quite sweetly as she curtsied.

David bowed quite low. "Of course. Oh. Did you wish to leave her a... message, perhaps?" he asked suddenly, a hint of humor to his query.

Mrs. Jack Theisen regarded him as a slow smile spread over face. "Yes, actually. Could you let her know I said, 'ice and mint', my lord? She'll understand," Josephine said as she gave him a wink. She turned and left the study, her carriage gown skirts swishing with her exit through the door.

David Carlington stared at her retreating back, her last words echoing over and over in his mind. "Oh, my," he whispered, before he fainted dead away.

EXCERPT

Read on for an excerpt from Linda Rae Sande's Book 2 of
"The Daughters of the Aristocracy"
The Grace of a Duke

Stunned at how quickly she had been escorted to the study, Charlotte made sure to afford the Duke of Chichester her very best, deepest curtsy followed by a brilliant smile and the words, "It is so very good to see you again, Your Grace."

Although a simple nod of his head would have sufficed, Joshua bowed, his vision taking in the woman he had often dreamed of having as his own. She seemed even more beautiful than when he had last seen her. At a ball, no doubt, her honey blonde hair shimmering under the candlelight of the ballroom, her infectious smile wiping out the glumness felt at his continued losing streak in the card room.

He rather doubted her comment, knowing that to see him now was not nearly as pleasant as it had been before the fire. He still had the strong jawline and a wider than normal nose for an aristocrat, and his features were balanced by broad cheekbones and a mouth that smiled easily.

At least, it used to.

With a leather mask covering most of the left half of his face and the side of his head to just beyond his ear, he looked as if he was about to attend a masked ball. If one looked closely, it became apparent that his left eyelid was pulled a bit, misshapen by the tight, scarred skin under the mask. "And you, Lady Charlotte," he answered, his face seeming to brighten where it was visible. He stepped forward and took her hand in his, lowering his lips and lightly brushing them over the knuckles. "I am honored that you have come."

A shiver passed through Charlotte's hand as she felt his warm lips actually touch her. To see him up and about, apparently in charge of ducal matters, was a huge relief. And to see that his scars were easily hidden by the mask he wore meant he was probably back to living a somewhat normal life. If she didn't know that the entire left side of his torso and arm had at one time been engulfed in flames, she would not know it from looking at him now. He leaned a bit to the left, no doubt due to what the doctor had explained was a tightening of the skin when it healed. If he was following the regimen recommended by the doctor, though, eventually he would regain full use of his arm and upper body, perhaps even regain the feeling in the damaged skin.

Gates cleared his throat and Joshua tore his gaze from Charlotte for a moment. "Yes, Gates?" he prodded, wishing the butler would leave them alone. He then felt a bit of panic at the thought that he would be left alone with *her*.

"Your Grace, your cook is in need of a menu for this evening's dinner," he intoned, using a quiet voice and a manner suggesting he had made the query earlier and, now that they had a guest, dinner would need to be more than a casual affair.

Joshua closed his eyes for a moment, a small headache suddenly forming at the front of his head. He used his right hand to rub his temple. He had forgotten to do menus for the week and then put off requesting anything in particular because, well, it was just Garrett and him eating in the dining room these days.

Charlotte noticed his discomfort. "If I may, Your Grace?" she offered quietly.

He opened his eyes, wondering at first what she meant, and

then realized with a sense of immense relief she might be about to save him. "Please do," he replied, his voice an exaggerated plea despite his not knowing exactly what it was she was offering.

Turning to the butler, Charlotte thought for a moment. "Let us start with walnuts and coffee in the library. Then, at the table, let us do a beef broth soup followed by a plate of cheese and breads. Leg of lamb with mint sauce and herbed new potatoes, and whatever vegetable is ripened in that beautiful garden I saw as we drove up. For the fish course, sole in a light butter sauce, and for dessert," she paused to regard Joshua for a moment, "Chocolate bread pudding with just a small dollop of vanilla crème."

Eyes widening, Joshua listened to her recite the menu. *My favorite meal*, he thought, wondering how she could possibly remember—if, indeed, she ever knew. He nodded at Gates' questioning glance in his direction. "What she said," he spoke quickly. "And could you have Mrs. Gates bring tea, please?" As he hoped, the butler bowed and left the study.

"Thank you," he said as he regarded Charlotte, a bemused expression on his face. "You have saved me from my cook's wrath."

The brilliant smile reappeared. "You are most welcome, Your Grace."

Joshua nodded, suddenly ill at ease. "Have you just come from London?" he asked, hoping there was more to her visit than just condolences for his departed family.

Charlotte nodded. "Indeed. I hope I've not caught you at an inopportune time," she spoke quietly, and then glanced at a nearby settee as if to suggest they be seated.

"Please," he said as he held out an arm. Once she had taken her place on the deep green velvet upholstered settee, he took the adjacent chair to her left, wanting to be sure the right side of his face was most visible to her. It wasn't just vanity that had him sitting to her left, though. The hearing in his left ear was still somewhat lacking, although a nearby doctor had assured him it would probably return in time.

"If it would be more comfortable for you, please feel free to remove your mask," Charlotte suggested, her hands folded loosely in her lap. The deep blue of her gown set off the creamy skin of her face and neck, and it's snug fitting bodice showed off just a hint of décolletage. "Your scars do not offend me."

Surprised by her suggestion and even more so by her statement, Joshua shook his head. "I could not," he replied sternly. "Certainly not in the company of such a beautiful woman as yourself."

Stunned by the comment, both by the compliment and by the realization that he seemed to have forgotten she had already seen him in a much worse state, Charlotte stilled herself.

Perhaps he doesn't remember, she thought suddenly. "As I recall, Your Grace, you were in hospital for nearly a month," she said quietly, not wanting the footman near the door to overhear her comment.

Joshua turned his head slightly, eyeing her with a bit of suspicion and wondering when a footman had come into the study. *Or is he always there?* he thought absently. *Like he's become part of the furniture.* "Twenty-nine days," he affirmed with a nod, his lips forming a straight line that suggested he was not the least bit pleased she knew anything about his time in hospital.

To remember those days was to relive a kind of torture he couldn't wish on his worst enemies. To remember those days meant he had to admit that, whenever he had been conscious, he had wished he could simply die. The pain had been excruciating. Death would have been a welcome respite. "And from whom did you learn this information?"

Charlotte lowered her gaze, wondering if she should admit her part in those first few hellish days of his hospitalization and the even worse days that followed. "I was... there, of course," she said in a whisper, forcing Joshua to lean in closer. He caught the familiar scent of jasmine, and as much as he wanted to inhale deeply, he forced himself to remain still. "I was already volunteering in the children's ward several days a week. Once you were brought in, I made it clear to your physician I be employed to see to your care."

Joshua's brows knitted together, the implication of her statement slowly sinking into his brain. *Christ, she's probably seen everything!* Every last gruesome burn and the raw wounds he sported for so many weeks after the fire. And, yet, here she sat, as if he had only been in hospital recovering from a fever. "But, why?" he asked aloud.

Lady Charlotte's eyebrows shot up. "We were... we are betrothed now."

Although he heard the words, Joshua didn't immediately comprehend them.

"I wanted to be sure you received the very best care. Sometimes those with burns are treated..." Charlotte paused, not wanting to say, "Horribly," but knowing it was what she had witnessed while volunteering at hospital. "Poorly," she finally finished, trying to hide the awkwardness of her statement with a shrug.

Suddenly very self-conscious, Joshua shifted in his chair. "So, you are aware of the... extent of my injuries," he countered in almost a question, his eyes not making contact with hers. *Betrothed? Matrimony?* Given the events of six months ago and the subsequent work he'd had to do to recover and then see to the recovery of the Chichester duchy, the very *last* thing he was considering was marriage.

I cannot allow this woman to think she must marry me!

ABOUT THE AUTHOR

A self-described nerd and lover of science, Linda Rae spent many years as a published technical writer specializing in 3D graphics workstations, software and 3D animation (her movie credits include SHREK and SHREK 2). Mythology, immortality, and ancient Greece have been lifelong interests.

A fan of action-adventure movies, she can frequently be found at the local cinema. Although she no longer has any tropical fish, she does follow the San Jose Sharks. She makes her home in Cody, Wyoming.

For more information:
www.lindaraesande.com
Sign up for Linda Rae's newsletter:
Regency Romance with a Twist

9 780989 397391